monsoonbooks

DRAGON

British by birth, Rose Gan first arrived in Kuala Lumpur in 1978 and has been living and working between both UK and South East Asia ever since. Married to a Malaysian, and formerly a teacher of History and Latin in UK and Malaysia, Rose was also Vice Chair for Museums of the Indonesian Heritage Society, a guide and docent in Museum National Indonesia, Jakarta, and Muzium Negara and the Textile Museum in KL. In addition to lecturing to cultural associations, Rose has been actively involved with museum publications in Malaysia and Indonesia, both as a writer and editor.

Dragon is volume one of Penang Chronicles, a series of historical fiction that delves into the backstory of the British settlement of Penang. It is followed by *Pearl* and *Emporium*.

Praise for *Dragon*

'Deeply researched and beautifully written, *Dragon* convincingly evokes the East of the period.'

Nigel Barley, author of *In the Footsteps of Stamford Raffles*

'Enthralling. Gan brings a forgotten hero back to rumbustious life.'

John Keay, author of *The Honourable Company: a History of the English East India Company*

'At last, a novel which engages a crucial and fascinating period of British merchant imperialism and Southeast Asian history. Penang, meeting place of Malays, Bugis and Siamese, here too are freebooting English and a more staid company in Calcutta. Here are mixed marriages, innumerable cross currents with the Dutch in Java and Sumatra, Chinese and Tamil traders, Achenese sultans and a Burma too close for comfort. And in the middle of it all is Francis Light, founder of modern Penang, a man of his times and of history. Britons today are woefully ignorant of the legacy of maritime Southeast Asia in which they played such a key role. This novel is a good start to re-engagement with this region, a meeting place of races, religions and cultures.'

Philip Bowring, author of *Empire of the Winds*

'Having founded the British colony of Penang in 1786, Francis Light is a well-known historical figure found in Malaysia's history books. However, little is known about his early years. Rose Gan, in this fascinating and well-researched novel, skilfully provides the reader with a colourful illustration to the early life and times of Light and those historically connected to him. The author cleverly unveils Light's rise to the rank of captain and his travels to this part of the world while meeting the people who would set the stage for his lustrous future. This serves as a prelude to more important events that destiny has in store for Light.'

Dennis De Witt, author of *History of the Dutch in Malaysia*

'As a veteran journalist who read History at university – and one who has remained fascinated with Captain Francis Light ever since – I find *Dragon* truly enjoyable. Ms Gan has carried out extensive research in creating the world of this novel. It's definitely a first of its kind!'

Wong Chun Wai, Star Media Group, Malaysia

'*Dragon* is a richly imagined yet historically faithful account of the early career of Francis Light, the founder of modern Penang. We follow his journey from his clever revenge on a bully during his schooldays in Suffolk to his heroic service with the Royal Navy, from his apprenticeship as country trader with a Madras agency to his delicate negotiations with the Sultan of Queddah, which will set him on the path leading to the founding of Pulau Penang as the first British settlement in the East Indies. Along the way Light has to weather storm and shipwreck, survive betrayal by company officials, balance palace intrigues and interpret the signals of ambitious royal wives and widows – all the while navigating the cross currents of British, Dutch, Malay, Siamese and Bugis interests in the region, with only his wits, moral compass and ambition to guide him. A marvelous cast of characters populates this well-researched work of historical fiction, with just the right blend of the real and the imaginary.'

John D. Greenwood, author of the Singapore Saga series

'*Dragon* is a rare example of writing about the important country trade that existed alongside of the East India Company and, since 1661, increasingly independent of it. Rose Gan's well-crafted narrative has clearly been written following extensive historical research. Francis Light arrived with high hopes of being accepted into the Company but the circumstances of his birth, past actions and injudicious decisions resulted in him joining the growing community of Englishmen settled in the ports of the East Indies determined to take their opportunities wherever offered. After finally burning the last of his Company bridges, the opportunity Francis is about to grasp was the unspoilt island of Pulau Pinang, Penang ...'

Sue Paul, author of *Jeopardy of Every Wind: the biography of Captain Thomas Bowrey*

In the same series

Dragon
Pearl
Emporium

DRAGON

Penang Chronicles, Vol. I

Rose Gan

monsoon

monsoonbooks

First published in 2021
by Monsoon Books Ltd
www.monsoonbooks.co.uk

No.1 The Lodge, Burrough Court, Burrough on the Hill,
Melton Mowbray LE14 2QS, UK.

First edition.

ISBN (paperback): 9781912049882
ISBN (ebook): 9781912049899

Cover design by Cover Kitchen.

A Cataloguing-in-Publication data record is available from the British Library.

MIX
Paper from responsible sources
FSC www.fsc.org FSC® C018072

Printed and bound in Great Britain by Clays Ltd, Elcograf S.p.A.
23 22 21 1 2 3

For Henry. Always

'To unpath'd waters, undreamed shores'

The Winter's Tale (Act 4 Scene 4)
William Shakespeare

Glossary

(Malay unless stated)

anak	child, son or daughter of
atap	thatched roof of palm fronds
bahasa	language
belacan	paste made from fermented shrimps and salt
bendahara	chief minister of a Malay state
betel	leaf of the piper betel vine used to wrap a betel quid
bunga emas	(lit. golden flower) small ornamental gold or silver tree sent as tribute to Siam
Chulia (Tamil)	Indian Muslim merchant from South East India
congkak	board game widely played in South East Indies (also conglak/ dakon)
encik	mister
farang (Thai)	foreigner, particularly European (from Persian 'farang' – Franks)
gundik	concubine at a Malay court
gunung	mountain, Mt.
janggut	beard
Jawi	Arabic-derived script used to write the Malay language
kapok	silky fibre of the kapok tree
kebaya	traditional blouse worn with sarong by women of the Straits

keris/kris	sinuous dagger of the Malay world
kerongsang	three-part chain linked brooch used to fasten the front of a kebaya
khun (Thai)	mister/madam, polite form of greeting
kuala	river estuary
kuali	Malay wok / frying pan
kueh (Hokkien)	South East Asian cakes and dumplings made of glutinous rice
laksamana	admiral, the minister of a Malay court responsible for security
makan	food, dinner, to eat
medan	square or central ground in town or palace complex
naga (Sanskrit)	ancient serpent spirit worshipped throughout India and S E. Asia
nona (Portuguese)	polite term to address women, similar to miss or madam
nyonya	Same derivation (nonha – Port.) used for non-Muslim / foreign women
orang	man / people
orang Belanda	Dutch
orang laut	sea people
orang Inggeris	English / British
orang putih	white people / man
paan (Hindi)	betel quid
padewakang	large Bugis boat
patola	woven silk fabric of India, usually with a floral motif
perahu	boat, ship, also prau boat, ship, also prau (Eng. prow/proa)
panglima	commander, general
phraya (Siam)	honorific title akin to lord, also phaya
putera	prince

raja muda	crown prince (lit. young king)
réal (Spanish)	coin, an eighth of a Spanish silver dollar
Said / Syed (Arabic)	Arab merchant, from Syed, 'noble' / descendant of Mohammed
selamat pagi / malam	good morning / good evening
songket	silk textile with gold and silver supplementary weave
Tuanku	polite term of address for ruler, similar to Your Highness, Your Majesty
Tunku	Malay noble title, also Tengku
sepoy (Urdu)	Indian infantry soldier
uleebalang (Aceh)	nobles
wai (Thai)	traditional greeting – hands pressed as in prayer, accompanied by bow
Yam Tuan Muda	Young Ruler (Johor), title traditionally held by the leader of Bugis

Place names and Peoples of the Archipelago

Acheen	Aceh, north Sumatra
Achenese	the people of Acheen
Batavia	present day Jakarta, Indonesia
Bencoolen	Bengkulu, south west Sumatra (also known as Fort Marlborough)
Bugis	ethnic group of Sulawesi, settlers in the Malay Peninsula
Celebes	the island of Sulawesi (present day Indonesia) in the Eastern archipelago
Coromandel	coast of SE India, now in Tamil Nadu
Fort St George	Madras
Jangsylan	English corruption of Ujang Salang, the Malay name for Phuket, also Junk Ceylon
Johor	southern kingdom of Malay Peninsula, under Bugis influence
Kutaraja	capital and main port of Acheen, now known as Bandar Aceh
Melaka	Malacca to the Europeans
Mergui Archipelago	island chain off southern Burma
Pulau Pinang	island off the coast of Queddah, also Pooloo Pinang/Penang
Queddah	northern kingdom of Malay Peninsula, now Kedah

Riau	archipelago off east Sumatra under Bugis occupation
Selangor	new Bugis kingdom on the central west coast of the Peninsula
Siak	sultanate of East Sumatra
Thalang	the Siamese name for Phuket island, also Ujang Salang (Malay) and Jangsylan (English)
Trengganu	east coast kingdom of Malay Peninsula
Ujang Salang	Malay name for Phuket island, corrupted in English to Jangsylan and Junk Ceylon

List of Characters

Suffolk

Francis Light	officer of the Royal Navy, later country ship captain in the East Indies
Squire William Negus	guardian of Francis Light
Mary Light	adoptive mother of Francis Light
Margaret Nadauld	married William Negus in later life
James Lynn	school friend of Francis Light
Marianne Lynn	younger sister of James Lynn
George Doughty	school friend of Francis Light
Reverend Thomas Ray	headmaster of Seckford's School
Charles Hythe	senior pupil at Seckford's School

Navy

John Amherst	captain of HMS *Mars, Arrogant*
Thomas McParland	surgeon of the HMS *Mars*
Henry Marshall	surgeon's mate, HMS Mars
Sir John Clevland	First Secretary of the Royal Navy
James Scott	midshipman friend of Light on HMS *Arrogant*
Edward Boscawen	Admiral of the Fleet during the Seven Years' War

East India Company

John Sullivan	Company writer in Madras
Francis Jourdan	head of the Madras Agency and member of Council
Anthony DeSouza	joint partner in the Madras Agency

Andrew Ross	ship's captain, East India Company
Charles Pigou	ship's captain, East India Company
Sir Warren Hastings	Governor-General of India
Edward Monckton	head of the delegation to Queddah

Malay Peninsula

Soliman	orphan boy
Martim Rozells	Eurasian trader
Thong Di Rozells	wife of Martim Rozells, originally from Jangsylan (see also Jangsylan / Lady Thong Di)
Martinha Rozells	daughter of Martim and Thong Di
Felipe Rozells	son of Martim and Thong Di
Sultan Muhammed Jiwa	sultan of Queddah
Sultan Salehuddin	sultan of Selangor
Prince Abdullah	favourite son of Sultan Muhammed Jiwa, his heir
Daeng Merewah Theyan	Bugis leader

Jangsylan

Chom Rang	head of the Ban Takkien clan, former governor
Mahsia	Malay wife of Chom Rang, originally from Queddah
Lady Chan	their eldest daughter
Lady Mook	their second daughter
Lady Thong Di	their youngest daughter (see also Malay Peninsula / Thong Di Rozells)
Phaya Pimon	second husband of Lady Chan
Lord At	husband of Lady Mook
Tak Sin	new king of Siam

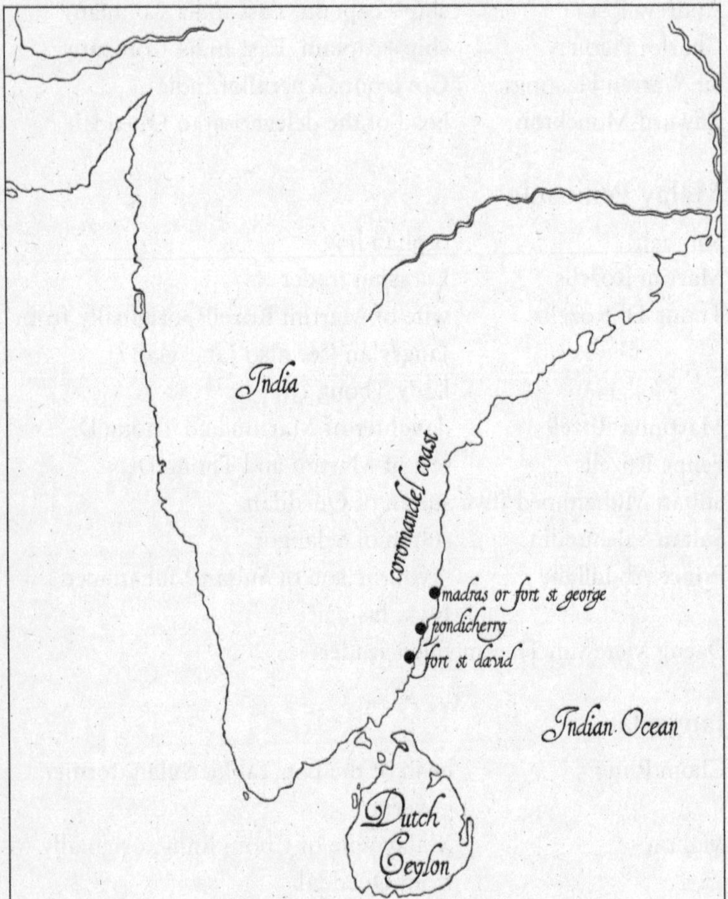

India and the Malay Peninsula

adapted from "A Map of the East-Indies", produced for the East India Company by Herman Moll, Geographer, 1736.

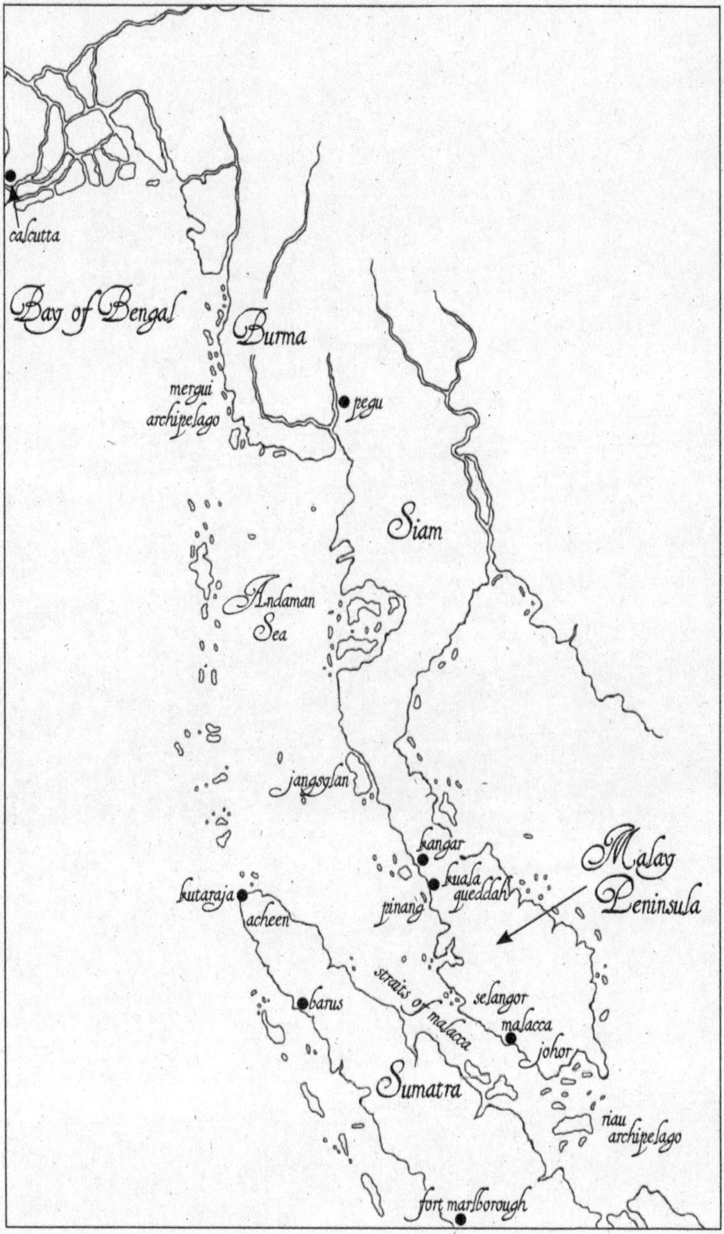
calcutta
Bay of Bengal
Burma
mergui
archipelago
pegu
Siam
Andaman
Sea
jangsylan
kangar
kuala
queddah
Malay
Peninsula
kutaraja
acheen
pinang
straits of malacca
selangor
barus
malacca
johor
Sumatra
riau
archipelago
fort marlborough

Contents

Prologue

Woodbridge, Suffolk. 12th April 1740

He had begun to regret his decision almost as soon as he rode out of Woodbridge with sixty hard miles ahead. Three months since the Great Frost and conditions were still treacherous. The melt had left gaping holes, waterlogged fields, and quagmires for tracks. Here and there, patches of filthy grey snow clung stubbornly to outcrops, resisting the weak spring sunshine. It was still bitterly cold, wind whipping his coattails and a lowering sky threatening more rain – or God forbid, six days past Easter! – another snowfall. Yet the unseasonal weather and the inhospitable conditions were not the cause of William's distress. Indeed, it was liberating to be on horseback again, lungs filled with fresh air and wind on his skin after weeks of enforced confinement. If he had to play another hand of cards, another game of chess, read another book, or spend another evening huddled round the fire glugging brandy and raging at the elements, he would surely have died of the apoplexy. Or the boredom.

And here he was at last, trotting through the imposing gateway crested by armorial lions and the cautionary '*Gens ante omnia*'. William followed the road to the big house along an avenue whose very purpose was to humble. Straight as far as the eye could see, his path was flanked by a precisely laid out poplar walk: beyond that, acres of open, barely undulating countryside, a chequerboard of tidy fields, the vertical line broken only by a perpendicular river. Rectangular ponds were dotted here and there at perfectly spaced intervals. Nothing here proclaimed the wonderful serendipity of nature. This geometric landscape, dreamed by man, shaped by wealth and power, was enough to subdue any intruder of the lesser order to his rightful place in the scheme of things. Our family above all, indeed, thought William.

His ruminations were abruptly interrupted by a brusque cry; his mount shied and a carriage sped past with the confident assurance of its ownership of the road. William grunted, channelling his erstwhile discomfort into righteous indignation. He was an invited guest. He had as much right to be there as anyone. But the wheedling voice of his public awkwardness chased its weaselly tail around his head. Why exactly was his presence required at this grand occasion? He doubted it would serve in his favour.

A corps of footmen and grooms attended as he dismounted some distance from the entrance porch where a queue of polished vehicles disgorged their primped and perfumed passengers. He passed his reins to a young stable lad, brushed down his jacket, fiddled with his stock and adjusted the lay of his hat, allowing the other parties to make their entrance without his encountering them. A senior footman gave him the eye. William mumbled his name and was ushered forward. With a deep breath, he removed his hat and entered.

The Great Hall was a gloomy space, heavily wainscoted in the Jacobean fashion with a proportionately low ceiling that only accentuated the dark interior, despite the plethora of candelabras.

Sounds reverberated off the solid surfaces, a strident cacophony of chatter framed by the measured chords of chamber music. Thirty or forty sumptuously dressed guests milled about, enthusiastic in their greetings but all the while scanning the room for grander fare. William circulated with hapless optimism, trying now one group and then another, but with little success. Where groups parted and drew in one new arrival, they closed ranks and shot him the caustic eye. As he wandered about, he took in snippets of conversation, some of which amused him – but much he heard with puzzled bemusement.

'... don't spread it about, Amelia, but I managed to acquire a copy of Abbé Prévost's little *roman* ... Why, Volume Seven, of course. Manon Lescaut and the Chevalier, no less! I promise to pass it on the moment I have finished with it. It's quite appallingly shocking. Do *not* let your husband find it! Or the chambermaids. I keep mine in my embroidery basket and only read it in the afternoons when I'm supposed to be resting ...'

'... Walpole's finished. Without the queen, who will shore him up now? The old goat's too old to run a country. We need young men with fire in their bellies. Young Pitt and his merry men ... that's the future. Jenkins lost his ear eight years ago. What was Robin waiting for? I know Vernon did a sterling job at Portobello but ...'

'... well, don't just sneak up on a fellow! Introduce yourself instead of listening in like a shag-bag! You must be one of my lord's local men by your garb ...' William startled. He had been unaware that his presence was being observed in the unseemly act of eavesdropping. The speaker, a large elderly gentleman accompanied by his spindly wife, had been pontificating on the recent hostilities with Spain to another gentleman, who gratefully took this opportunity to extricate himself from the old bore and make his getaway. William was to be his next victim. The latter blushed, cleared his throat and garbled a stuttering response. 'No, sir. Suffolk. Not local, I mean … er … with respect … sir …'

The lady wife arched a painted eyebrow, peering myopically, as if at a curiosity in a menagerie. 'A Suffolkman, you say? My son was up at Oxford with one of the Tollemaches. You must know Sir Lionel?'

'By sight, ma'am. I'm from Woodbridge.' He realised as soon as he had spoken that his answer was nonsensical.

'Your name, then, young man?'

'Er … Negus … William … ma'am …'

She cackled, revealing grey teeth and the aroma of minted breath underlain with sour wine. 'Negus? Like the toddy? How *drôle*!'

William grimaced. It was not the first time that his name had gleaned that particular reaction.

But the old gentleman threw up his hands and beamed, his overly curled wig – a remnant of an earlier age, William thought – bouncing in rhythm to the wobbling of his jowls. 'My word! You must be Colonel Negus' boy! As I live and breathe! Haven't thought about the old puff guts for years! You must remember Sir Francis, my dear. He invented the drink, y'know? Named for him, not the other way around, you ninny! A glass o'negus. Just the thing for warming the blood after a winter's hunt! How is the old rogue? Still riding to hounds?'

'Dead, sir. These eight years past.' Their faces reassembled in sanctimonious sympathy.

'God rest his soul, my boy. So, you're the new master-of-hounds, then? Have I seen you at Westminster, perchance? Not that I'm there overly much. I'm right in thinking you took his incumbency at Ipswich, Negus?'

'Er ... No, sir. I find politics not to my taste, I'm afraid ...'

'Not to your taste?' He raised his voice and looked around him with theatrical flourish. 'Politics, not to your taste? What the devil does that mean? Not to your taste? What manner of answer is that?'

Much to William's relief as the discussion rapidly deteriorated, the gentleman and his disapproving wife were waylaid by a new acquaintance. William was dismissed without even a nod, his erstwhile interlocutor – whose name he still did not know – muttering on about 'Young men these days! Are there no gentlemen anymore?' Evading the prying glances of those nearby whose interest in him was suddenly piqued by the whiff of *faux pas* in the air, William accepted a glass of punch and retreated to a quiet corner, right shoulder to the wainscot. He would forego social niceties for the rest of the evening and wait until the true purpose of his presence at the gathering was revealed.

Which did not take long. No sooner had the food table been announced and the frantic, some might say unseemly, dash for a loaded plate ensued, an imperious voice broke into his reveries. 'Negus, I presume? Thank you for joining us tonight.'

The speaker was a lugubrious man of unremarkable features whose elegant silver wig bleached his pale skin almost corpse white. His voice was precise and sombre, complementing his melancholy air. He was neither young nor particularly old. But for the fashionable cut of his attire, one might have taken him for a lawyer or a scholar, a fellow rarely found outside dusty rooms. Yet even William could recognise that this was indeed a man of substance. His coat was leaf green silk lined with cloth of gold richly embossed with floral appliqué. His stock was of the finest Valenciennes held by a nut-sized emerald, his brocade waistcoat buttoned with tiny pearls.

'My Lord!' William gasped, only partly surprised, but nevertheless completely in awe. 'The honour is mine, m'lord!' And bowed in exaggerated fashion.

The marquess accepted his due with an entitled nod, beckoning William to move closer. His eyesight was none too good, although he would never admit it. Despite having met William Negus at some reception or other at Ipswich, he would have walked right past if not for the acuity of his personal secretary. Closer scrutiny revealed only that, even with benefit of an eyepiece, he would never have recognised the ungainly young man standing before him. Which fact played into his hand. Such a tawdry fellow would suit his purpose. Negus was bound to feel at a disadvantage in such august company, rendering the disagreeable interview ahead more favourable to him. This young squire, with thinning hair, pock-marked face and bulbous red nose, dressed in an old fashioned, full-skirted coat straining over his rotundity, was an out-of-towner already uncomfortably out of his depth.

'Whilst they gorge on beef pie and quail's eggs, let's away somewhere more private, eh?'

The marquess led William into a formal drawing room, the din of the party receding as the doors swung shut behind them. A warm glow of candlelight encircled the fireplace; the rest of the room was in darkness. Above the mantelpiece, cast in flickering shadow, was a portrait of a striking woman in rose-pink silk, her auburn hair unbound. Was this his notorious mother, once a royal mistress? If it were, the image was a more visible presence than she herself had ever been in his life. No wonder he seemed such a melancholy soul, William mused.

He followed William's gaze, glancing up at the painting. 'My mother,' he confirmed but elucidated no further. Taking an armchair close to the fire, he indicated for William to occupy the one facing. It was unnervingly informal; William would have much preferred to stand. A servant filled their glasses and then retreated, his velvet slippers silent on silken rugs. Only when the doors closed did the marquess begin to speak.

'I expect you're wondering why I dragged you away from the delights of the evening, sir?'

'A timely intervention, my lord. Social gatherings have never been my milieu of choice.'

He made a sound that might have been agreement. 'One thing we have in common then. I abhor evenings of this nature. But ... one has to do one's duty. We all have to undertake tasks that are not quite to our taste. It is the nature of responsibility and the condition of our class. Don't you think?'

William nodded again, wishing he could think of something profound to add.

'Your father was a larger-than-life character. I knew him vaguely. And your grandfather, quite the political animal, so I believe. Yet you haven't followed your family into politics. Ipswich is a useful borough. I could put in a word.'

William winced, unsure of how he was to decline graciously. Given the earlier comment, he could hardly repeat his assertion of it 'not being to his taste'. Was that not in contravention of the responsibilities of his class, in the eyes of a great lord?

But the nobleman dismissed that line of thought with an impatient wave of his hand. Something more pressing was on his mind. 'We can come back to that, William. Later. As I was saying, a gentleman has to assume many unfortunate responsibilities in life ...' A long pause ensued while the marquess stared morosely into the flames. 'One of those, in my case at least, has been the matrimonial state.' He sighed deeply, the first hint of emotion.

Raising his hand vaguely, indicating the opulent surroundings, he continued. 'This house ... has been the bane of my life, sir. I succeeded to a mountain of debts. The original palace had been crumbling away for centuries. My predecessors *began* the restoration ...' and he paused archly on the word, '... by doing little more than demolishing most of the outer buildings save for this central edifice. It has been left to me to make something of the *débâcle*. But that requires money – a veritable king's ransom – to pay off the mortgages and repair and rebuild, and so on ...'

William was struggling to understand what any of this had to do with him. The maintenance of aging estates was a common enough problem for the great families. He was unable to help out financially. His father had left him the house at Dallinghoo, the estate lands and a decent annual income, but it wasn't in any wise on the same level as the means required to live the life of a peer of the realm. So he continued to listen, picking nervously at a loose thread on his coat, waiting for the sword to fall.

'... And so, to matrimony, y'understand? Find a wife whose father has money and is after a title in the family. I did my duty. Married the lady. And thus, the money to restore the estate was found. But at what cost, I ask you? Sadly, my dear wife and I have never been able to suffer the sight of each other. Not even sufficiently to achieve the other purpose of the wedded state, if you get my meaning?'

William's discomfort was increasing exponentially. He doubted if the marquess felt any more at ease. This confidence was unseemly. It was astonishing that he should venture onto such intimate matters with anyone, let alone a country squire. But somewhere at the back of William's mind, a glimmer of light was flickering. The marquess would not have raised this issue unless he was stumbling towards an even more embarrassing revelation.

The marquess took a thoughtful sip of brandy. 'I hear that you did a favour for an acquaintance of mine last year? Let's not refer to names, Negus. You know to whom I refer. Least said the better. One never knows who is lurking in a dark corner ... But, you helped a gentleman out of a bind. Or rather, you assisted his daughter. Apparently, no one has ever imputed any stain on her reputation. So, you know how to keep your mouth shut.'

At last, William Negus understood. He would not have to sit in Parliament. Or be High Sheriff of Suffolk. Or a Justice of the Peace. Or take on any role to support a political cause or party. It would not cost him money. It was nothing more than his very insignificance that was required. Even so, he maintained his deferential air. It was now to his distinct advantage to grovel and play the fool.

'The child died, my lord. It was a cruel winter. It took the little ones hard.'

'Dead, eh? So much the better then.' His cynical indifference offended William. A palpable silence followed, in which the crackle of a log on the fire seemed deafening. The marquess sensed his reply had been pitiless and nudged out a grudging apology. 'Well, of course, it was damned tragic that the little mite didn't thrive. That's not what I meant, at all. I was referring to the present, not the past. Better in the sense that should another opportunity arise, then there would be little impediment to accommodating it, if you get my meaning?'

For the first time since the unexpected invitation had arrived, William Negus felt in control of events. The pendulum had swung in his favour. This great nobleman had an embarrassing secret and was in desperate need of help. William smiled inwardly while allowing the marquess to twist a little longer on the line.

'I'm sorry, m'lord, but I'm afraid I don't quite understand your intent. What opportunity has arisen? How may I accommodate? It would be a privilege for me to extend my services to you in any way possible but ... what *exactly* might I do for you?'

The marquess narrowed his eyes, his nostrils flaring as if assailed by a noxious smell. 'Let's not beat around the bush, man! You cannot be that much of an addlepate! What I mean is ... I have finally managed to sire a child, but unfortunately not in my wife's belly! Neither I nor the child's mother is free, so to speak. I will say no more on't, as I'm sure you will understand. The repercussions are unthinkable. Surely even you can see that?' There had been a distinct softening in his expression, a certain light in his eyes. He leaned forward, almost as a confidant. 'But we both feel oddly attached to this little mite. We cannot bear to think of it cast out into the world, alone and unloved. I, of all men, know what it is for a child to grow up without parents ... Negus, this woman who took the other child we spoke of. Is she a good woman? Would she be a kindly mother?'

'A fine, God-fearing lady, sir.'

His outburst had moved William. This man, who appeared so superior and cold-hearted, was proving to have a spark of human kindness after all. His solitary childhood and miserable married life had left its mark. The marquess was trying to do the honourable thing.

'With children of her own?' he continued.

'No, sir. She was widowed young. Lost her baby with grief. She is quite alone in the world.'

The nobleman pursed his lips in thought, still worrying the issue. 'What's your interest in her then? You're not married, I believe. Is that it? Have you got your eye on her? Is she trying to worm her way into a gentleman's bed?'

William's gorge rose at the slur on her name. 'Would that she had eyes for me! But no, sir. She was the wife of our young gamekeeper who died in an accident. His father and grandfather before him had given long and loyal service. My Lord, I felt sorry for the girl! We needed the cottage for the new man. She had nowhere to go, a widow at seventeen. That's when Sir … rather, that's when the other baby turned up. She took the little boy in and I found them a house. It had belonged to my grandmother. A small manor over at Melton. She resides there still.'

The marquess swirled the brandy in his glass, deep in thought. 'You'd wed her if you could, though? Even if she is only the widow of gamekeeper. A woman of the lower classes?'

'Yes, sir, I would! But she will not marry me. She told me that as she had married once for love, never would she marry for convenience. She values her liberty. Mary has a good home and a small widow's allowance from the estate. That is more than she expected from life. We are friends, as much as it is possible for a decent man and woman to be amicable without any damage to their reputations. Not that I care a fig for that in my regard. I have my inheritance, my horses and my hounds, and do not give a damn for the rest. But I would not see harm to a hair on Mary's head. If you're asking me, would she make a good mother, sir, then my answer must be yes. Without equivocation. Will she accept another child after the losses she has already borne? In truth I do not know. But I suspect she might. For never was any woman better suited to raising children than Mrs Mary Light.'

His long oration surprised even himself. Given neither to grandiloquence nor public displays of emotion, William could not contain himself when a slight was directed at his beloved Mary. The marquess, however, did not seem offended by the flash of temper. Indeed, William's outrage convinced him that he had indeed found the ideal home for his illegitimate child. His mind was greatly eased and his earlier discomfiture dissipated. It was time for business now that the difficult revelations were done. His supercilious nature reasserted itself once more.

'The child must be brought up a gentleman. Or lady, should it have the misfortune to be female. I will settle a lump sum when it reaches its fifth year, enough to provide a good education and the other niceties children require. Until then, an annual amount should suffice. On reaching maturity, I will ensure a good commission, or living if the church beckons. For a daughter, marriage into a decent house. And you will be its guardian throughout all this, both legal and in daily life. Is that acceptable?'

My Lord Marquess was not prepared to chance his money

on another ailing babe, William thought wryly. Nothing significant until the child was five. But, who could blame him? His proposition was decent and honourable. Beyond that, the difficult matter would have the added benefit of providing William with another reason to approach Mary. Perchance this time, she might be willing to listen to his suit? Regardless of that happy future outcome, their shared responsibility in bringing up a child would inevitably bring them closer. It was the most fortuitous turn of events.

'Most honourable terms, my lord. It will be a privilege to assist in the raising of your child …'

'No! Never use those words. Not my child. Your child. I wash my hands of the matter from this moment on. Any intervention made on the child's behalf will never come from my door. You will hear only from my lawyers in future correspondence. The child is expected past Michaelmas, I believe …'

The great man paused, before continuing as if through gritted teeth. His patience with the matter was wearing thin. He did not enjoy displaying his stained linens so prominently, particularly now that the bargaining had been done. He wanted Negus out of his hair as soon as possible.

'You are, of course, doing me and a dear lady a great service. I will not forget your assistance. Be assured of that. Your good grace will be rewarded in time … and now, perhaps you would like to take yourself off and enjoy the dinner? Good evening to you, sir.'

The curt dismissal was welcomed by both men. The proceedings had been challenging but the outcome judicious for both parties. The noble marquess rang a tiny bell, upon which a footman stepped in to show the guest out. William bowed deeply, perhaps a little more unctuously than good manners required, and withdrew. For the first time that evening he had revealed a little of the fire that lay in his portly belly. Dinner sounded like just the thing. His healthy appetite was suddenly quite renewed.

PART ONE

The Boy from Suffolk

(1740-1755)

1

Dog Days

Woodbridge, Suffolk. June 1754

Few things in life can improve upon high summer in the Suffolk countryside. Little is required to awaken the memories of sunny childhood days: a whiff of newly cut hay, the splash of oar on water, the distant laughter of children, the soporific drone of insects, or the glory of an azure blue sky, deep, intense and cloudless – and one is instantly transported. The senses in wondrous harmony remember what the conscious mind has forgot. It was on such a day, late June, as the fierce heat of noon waned into balmy evening. The very best time of day on the very best day to be alive.

A boy lay on his back on the banks of the river Deben, just outside the inland port of Woodbridge. He chewed on a stalk of grass, observing a tern winging its way, following the river to the estuary and then out to sea. He sighed deeply, utterly dejected, envious of the freedom of the bird. Not for him the joys of this fine day. It was bad enough that the glorious weather had dawned the very same day examinations had begun. Pitiless schoolmasters had no doubt selected the date since time immemorial for that very reason. Yet, despite long, boring hours scratching at a parchment in the airless confines of a classroom, the school day always finally reached its end. Then the boys would dash out of the gates of Seckford's School, a pack of hounds on the scent of summer. The long warm hours of evening would beckon as compensation for the day's trials.

But not today. The school bell had instead found him observing the flight of his schoolmates from the confines of the library, where he had been sent to think upon his transgressions. It had been so singular a day in its calamity that he was sure that whenever the sun shone throughout the rest of his life, this sinking dread in the pit of his stomach would return, depriving him forever of the dog-days of summer. He was finished. His life was over. This time he had done it good and proper.

***

'Please, sir, may I open a window?' The small classroom was stifling, an airless box made up of the combined heat of a dozen or so young bodies and an older youth, their tutor. Heads shot up and around, eyes now on the speaker, Francis Light, and then just as swiftly back towards the tutor, Mr Charles Hythe, one of the leavers who had stayed on to prepare for Cambridge. On attaining his place, he was now wiling away the intervening months until the Michaelmas term as tutor to the younger students, which commission he interpreted as wholesale licence to bully and humiliate.

Charles was a young man with few attractive qualities or features. He was nondescript in appearance, neither remarkably good looking nor noticeably ugly. Nor was he academically gifted or slow in learning. Distinctly average and unmemorable were his distinguishing traits, with the exception of his ability to toady to those above him and to intimidate those below. As luck would have it, they were the very same qualities best suited to rising in society, accompanied, naturally, by the benefits of a decent family name.

On this particular late morning, Charles himself had been equally tormented by the soporific heat. He had even considered pushing up one of the frames for some welcome breeze – but to make life more amenable for this bunch of nick-ninnies was contrary to his current purpose in life. Not only that, but Light's raised voice had jolted him awake from a catnap, a tell-tale trickle of drool running down his chin. The loud grunt of surprise he emitted as he was disturbed had caused a few of the boys to titter at his discomfiture. He could not let this assault on his dignity go unpunished.

Hythe's lip curled unpleasantly, resembling a torn pocket. 'You may not,' he sneered, indicating that the boys should lower their heads to their studies with an imperious wiggle of his fingers. Heads lowered but expectancy now stirred the languid air. They waited for the inevitable response.

'But, it's very hot, sir. I feel like to faint. We can't breathe,' Francis argued. The other boys held their breath, eager for the coming rumpus. Would Light never learn?

Charles Hythe fixed him with a beady eye. 'Then faint, sir. It is nothing to me. A little bit of sunshine and you lily-livered louts come over all girly. Pass me the smelling salts, sir! You think I'm here to nursemaid you? One more word and I'll have you thrashed for insolence.'

Francis opened his mouth to respond. It was exactly what Hythe hoped for. 'Go on, Light, do it! Give me cause!'

James Lynn, a boy in the front row, turned around, his eyes

wide, shaking his head in warning. Hythe shot from his high desk and seized Lynn by his ears. 'Got you, you little weasel. Cheating! Trying to copy from another fellow's answers!'

'But, sir, I only turned around!' Lynn howled as he was dragged from his desk across the room.

'Light ... to the front!' Hythe snarled as he thrust Lynn, face to the wall at one side of the easel, and Light at the other.

'I haven't finished my work, sir!' Light gasped.

'Cheats never prosper. Your marks will be crossed.' There was little distinction between Hythe's snarl and his grin, both marking him out as a man of singular mean spirit.

It occurred to Francis that this turn of events was not about to make much difference to him in the greater scheme of things. He had been quite unable to answer most of the questions, resorting to imaginative fantasy with a smattering of fact dredged up from memory. He did, however, feel for his good friend Jamie Lynn, who assuredly would have polished off his Religious Knowledge questions with little problem. He was a clever boy, eager to follow his father into medical studies. It was unjust for him to be punished merely for trying to aid a friend.

At that juncture, as if steered by a bountiful God, the classroom door opened. The headmaster, Reverend Dr Thomas Ray, entered, his black gown draped over narrow, rounded shoulders, his hands clasped behind him, for all the world like a tall, thin jackdaw, with a long, pointed nose for a beak. 'What have we here, Mr Hythe?

'Cheats, sir. These two rascals were communicating during an imposition.' Hythe had jumped to his feet and was now rocking back and forth obsequiously, the very picture of a dutiful tutor.

Reverend Ray seemed not entirely convinced. 'Indeed? If that is true, it is a most serious accusation. Cheating is a form of theft, boys, the misappropriation of another's toil.' He addressed this to James and Francis, who nodded their heads, wisely deciding not to offer a defence. Meanwhile, the reverend looked about the class, frowning. Turning his attention now directly on Hythe, he said: 'Did you not think to open the windows, sir? Young brains need fresh air, especially on a day like this! Boys near the windows, raise the sashes!'

The windows were lifted. A welcome breeze wafted in, bringing a trace of hay and pollen – and a bumble bee that nosed indolently about the occupants. A few boys sneezed, another squealed and flapped his arms in alarm. The headmaster rolled his eyes. 'Good heavens, boys! Don't be such ninnies. Finish your work and then off to the grounds for a run about. This is not a day for studies! The Good Lord gave us the summer to glory in his bounty!'

Shooting a piercing glance at Hythe, a warning that he was not entirely persuaded of his version of events, Reverend Ray turned his attention to the two accused. 'Boys, to my study forthwith. I will be along anon. Then, we shall talk ...'

Francis and James skittered off to stand outside the dreaded study door. As the minutes slowly ticked by, they waited in growing trepidation for the interview to come.

'You shouldn't be here, James. I shall tell the reverend so. You were merely warning me to hold my damned tongue!'

James placed a finger on his lip. 'Shh! Watch your tongue again, you fool! The reverend has no patience for cursing. You know he has the ears of a hawk!'

Francis grinned. 'The look of one too, methinks!'

James snorted. 'You are a noggin, Frannie! You shouldn't be here either. You did nothing wrong. Even the reverend himself demanded the windows be opened! We were not copying. I shall say so myself and so will all the other chaps. Hythe's a filthy lickspittle. Everyone knows.'

'Even so, it's a wicked shame to be confined in this murky corridor on such a day when all the rest are by now out in the grounds, chomping on their bread and cheese!' Light retorted, anger at the injustice of their position replacing his apprehension. 'Hythe will have it in for us now, you know? The reverend did not exactly take his part. We'll get the blame for that.'

Their conversation was interrupted by steady footfall. Dr Ray appeared, opening his door and indicating for the boys to enter. Seated behind his solid oak desk, he motioned for them to stand before him. Francis noted with wry amusement that his window was wide open; through it he could see his classmates charging out with shouts of glee, clutching kerchiefs wrapped around their lunches.

'Light! Are you paying attention?' The reverend had noticed that Francis was already far away. The boy was such a dreamer. Francis nodded sheepishly in reply. James glanced across, willing his friend to play the game.

'Boys, what is all this nonsense about? I've had a look at both your answers. It's barely credible that either of you could have copied from the other. On the first count, you were placed at a distance and could not have overseen the other's writing. On the second, James' answers show a remarkable grasp of Religious Knowledge. There was not a single error in fact or spelling. I commend you, sir.' James could not contain his pleasure at the unexpected compliment. He was proud of his scholarship.

Reverend Ray nodded his satisfaction and proceeded. 'So, answer me this. Why would a boy turn around to copy from another if he had no need of the answer?'

For some reason, known only to himself, Francis sought to answer this rhetoric question. 'Perchance to help a friend in need?'

James' mouth fell open. What was Light about?

Reverend Ray frowned. Was the boy really a fool, or just painfully honest? 'Mr Light, are you admitting that you were seeking help from Mr Lynn?'

Francis' eyes grew large at the realisation of what his answer suggested. 'Why no, sir! I was just offering an answer to your question. I did not ask Lynn to copy from his answers. I was too far away to do so ...' No sooner were the words out of his mouth than he realised he was now implying that he might have copied had he been nearer. '... not that I would have copied had we been seated closer, of course. That would be most wrong. Cheating is heinous, sir. I did not cheat ... sir ...' His ramblings petered out at the recognition of the irritation on the headmaster's face, reflected in his fingers, drumming on the desk.

'Quite enough prattle, Light. I have also had the misfortune of reading through your answers. Whilst recognising that you do need a great deal of aid in improving your Religious Knowledge, it is impossible that you received benefit of any such assistance today. Your work is arrant nonsense. I have observed you every Sunday at St. Mary's since I came to this living. While you have attended church and your school studies most assiduously, it does not appear that you have "attended" in the least. Per exemplum

... Question: What did Pontius Pilate say at the trial of the Lord Jesus?' Answer, according to Mr Francis Light: "Will no one rid me of this turbulent priest?"'

James Lynn snorted, covering his mouth with his hand to stifle laughter. Light blushed, running a hand nervously through his hair. 'I recall some fellow said that, sir.'

The Reverend paused, taking a deep breath, the faintest twitch of a smile tickling his lip. 'Some fellow did say that, Light. But not Pontius Pilate. Lynn ... who said that famous line?'

'King Henry II, sir.'

'And of whom did he speak?'

'Archbishop Thomas à Becket, sir.'

Francis nodded. 'Of course, sir. I distinctly remember it now, sir.'

'You distinctly remember it? You distinctly forgot it, you mean! All the information ever offered to you in this school is wandering about in your disorganised brain with not the slightest attempt at order or categorisation. You sit at your desk, eyes to the front, but your thoughts are somewhere else! You are not a dullard. You are passably good at arithmetic and geometry. You speak well and make a good argument when debating. You have a decent hand. I have observed you on the sports field and with your classmates. You are well liked. A natural leader. These are all admirable qualities, boy. But when will you put your talents to use? Or do you intend to bury them in the ground like the foolish man in the parable?' The reverend paused for a breath, taking out a kerchief to mop the beads of sweat from his brow.

The boy blinked rapidly, unsure whether or not this was another rhetoric question, ultimately deciding to say nothing.

'Well? What have you to say for yourself?' The reverend went on, his temper fraying.

'We did not cheat, sir ... As you yourself have proved. Mr Lynn is wholly innocent. Nor did I do anything wrong. I merely requested for a window to be opened. It was fearful hot in the classroom.'

The headmaster turned his gaze on James. 'Is this true, Mr Lynn?'

James nodded. 'It is, sir. Upon my word.'

'We will have no swearing in this room, boys. This is not a court of law.' The reverend placed his elbows on the desk, resting his chin on his joined hands, giving his answer deep thought. 'I am inclined to believe what you say. Furthermore, it would no doubt be a small matter to confirm with your classmates. Thus, on the matter of today's incident, I do not intend to proceed further. I shall find a different occupation for Mr Hythe than a monitor.'

Francis and James exchanged glances. Whilst their classes would now be greatly improved, they were by no means sure that their school lives would become easier on account of this decision. Hythe was vindictive; he would hold them to account for his censure. He had friends amongst the older boys, one of whom would now be selected to take his place. What surety did they have that his replacement would not be equally hateful on account of his friend's demotion?

Reverend Ray, however, considered the matter closed. 'Mr Lynn, run along now and take your lunch outside. Give my regards to Dr Lynn and your good mother. I will not be writing to them in this matter.' Francis was expecting a similar dismissal but it did not come. Instead, the reverend instructed: 'Mr Light, remain standing, please.'

Another quizzical glance was exchanged between the boys before James bowed and took his leave, offering his thanks to the reverend for his prudent intervention. There were few schoolmasters as enlightened or fair-minded as the Reverend Dr Ray. Francis straightened his back and waited. What now?

'Francis, you have still not answered my question pertaining to your lack of progress in your studies. Year on year, you have fallen behind yet we have promoted you alongside your peers after you promised faithfully each time to put your shoulder to the wheel. Squire Negus has also intervened on numerous occasions. But, you have not improved, nor do I remark any sign of this state of affairs being remedied. Mr Light, what is your honest opinion?'

Francis heard the word 'honest' and took this opportunity at its word. 'I try, sir, truly I do, but find it fiendish hard to see the point of much of what we learn. I understand arithmetic and geometry – they are necessities. Every educated man must also read well, know the classics, and have a smattering of history and the words and deeds of famous men. But I cannot fathom what use I shall ever make of Latin, Greek or the finer points of Religious Knowledge. I say my prayers and sing out my favourite hymns loudly on Sundays and holy days. But I shall never be a churchman. I leave the Gospels to them. Moreover, I'm an Englishman, not a Roman or a Greek. They're all dead, sir. They have no place in this modern rational world. I would that I could study French or Spanish, so that I might learn more of our enemies. In understanding them and the way they think and live, it seems to me, we might deal more judiciously with them.'

Reverend Ray was astonished at the unexpected eloquence

in equal measure as he was offended by this young rapscallion's words. His eyebrow lifted ominously, usually the sole indicator of his ire. 'You have given the subject of the school curriculum much thought, it seems. I had not expected one so singularly challenged in his studies to have developed such lofty educational principles. Has it not occurred to you that, whilst you may not comprehend the reason, greater minds than yours are fully cognisant why it is deemed the measure of a man that he should know his Latin and Greek? Moreover, I do not intend to defend the necessity of a Religious Education to a mere boy. Why would any Christian gentleman fail to desire a deeper insight into his faith?'

As earlier, Francis heard only what he wanted to hear and ploughed on with his exposition, failing to grasp that he was digging himself a deeper grave. 'How I wish I could learn about the things that matter to me, not to older men who were born in a different age! I long to know more about the natural world and the discoveries of great scientists and engineers! I am curious about how things work. I want to know the world as it is, not as it was hundreds of years ago. I beg pardon if I speak too freely, but that is my honest belief, sir.'

It was at that very moment that the Dr Ray realised that Francis Light was a singular child, a boy of intelligence and courage no doubt, but one wholly unsuited to the strictures of a grammar school education. Once more he tried to reason with him. 'Francis, I admire your interest in the sciences. I am impressed that you wish to understand how machines and other wondrous inventions function. But one cannot proceed further as a scholar without the basic framework upon which our academic world is built. You cannot run before you learn to walk, boy.

May I appeal to your common sense? You are not as other boys here at Seckford's School. When you leave this institution, your future will rest entirely upon what you yourself may make of it. You shall receive no compensation for your lack of academic success from benefit of name or station. Few doors will open to you. No annual sum will be settled on you to ease your way. The only path you have is to study as a boy and work hard as a man. Do you understand what I am saying?' Reverend Ray leaned forward towards Francis, his voice now kindly, unwilling to hurt the boy's feelings, but assured that Francis required instruction in the realities of life.

'You are referring to my birth, sir? I am fully aware of the consequences of illegitimacy,' Francis responded, his demeanour rigid, a defiant tone underlying his answer.

'Are you, indeed?' The reverend's retort was sharper, annoyed by this hint of insolence. 'I am not entirely sure that you have given as much thought to the consequences of your birth as you have to your preferred curriculum. Francis, I am not here to punish you. The incident today is by-the-by. What I am about to say will probably come as a shock. But it is my opinion that Seckford's can no longer offer you anything more by way of learning. You are already almost fourteen. It is time you gave some thought to your career. Tomorrow I will write to your guardian with the purpose of informing him that, at the end of this half, you should withdraw from the school. This is not expulsion; I expect him to request a withdrawal on your behalf. No shame is attached to your leaving. I am fond of you, Francis Light. Understand that this decision has been taken very much for your own good. You must now go out into the world and embark upon your own *cursus honorum*.'

The Reverend Ray stood. The interview was ended. He would brook no further discussion. 'Go to the library for the afternoon and think on all that I have said. Take your repast there in isolation. Browse through the collection of books. Perhaps you will find some measure of enlightenment through contemplation. Then go home to your good mother and be as honest to her as you have been with me. And, Francis, I do thank you for your honesty, although I deem your opinions to be woefully uninformed. Let us part with no bad feelings, eh?'

Throughout this diatribe, Francis had remained stock still. Only the pallor of his skin and the two burning red spots on his cheeks betrayed his emotions. The outcome was wholly unforeseen. He was both humiliated by the reference to his background and bewildered that it should impact so directly on his current situation. Francis bowed his head, unable even to speak, and walked out of the door, arms by his side, back ramrod straight. Reverend Ray watched his retreat, unsure whether his decision would make or break this unusual young man. He had a presentiment that it would be the former ...

***

'Oi, Frannie!' A voice rang out across the water, waking the boy from his reverie with a start. 'We're taking the boat out tonight. Da thinks there'll be good pickings if we catch the breeze on the turn. If'n you run down the harbour, we'll pick y'up ...' Francis, for this was he, bolted upright, shading his eyes against the glare of the sun. The speaker, one Nathaniel Oates, called from a fishing boat rowing downstream towards the sea. Francis momentarily contemplated the welcome offer. Mayhap he should jump aboard with Nattie Oates and his father? Or even better, run away to sea for good and never return?

Good sense quickly prevailed. His mother did not deserve that. Nor Squire William. It was his own arrant stupidity that had brought him to this pretty pass. A fellow must face the consequences of his actions, or be damned. 'Not today, Nattie,' he shouted back.' I must be off home. Mother is waiting. Most kind of you to ask though. Perhaps next time? When school closes for summer?'

Nattie abandoned the oars, cupping his hands to carry his voice. He was a small, skinny lad with a wild thatch of muddy brown hair, a typical river rat. 'Ya mamma's boy, Francis Light! On a day like this an' all! Your loss, Frannie!' His father leaned forward, cuffing him on the head, telling him to mind his manners and get to the oars. Francis smiled and waved back. Nattie was a good sort. Would that he himself might live the uncomplicated life of a fisherman's son with not a care for Latin declensions, Greek augments and all the rest of the nonsensical stuff they tried to beat into his head. No school. No worries. No responsibilities.

Scrambling to his feet, he gathered up his cap and bundle of books. With his jacket over his shoulder, his boots on barefoot, he thrust his stockings into his pockets and fingered his lucky stone. He would need a miracle indeed to turn things around today. Now he must head home. Mamma was waiting with supper no doubt already on the table. He'd better get it over with. Heart sinking at the prospect, he clambered up the embankment towards the Melton road.

Still, it was a wondrous evening for all that. No miserable

curmudgeon of a school master could take that away from him. Whistling as he walked, he kicked out at pebbles and gathered wayside flowers for a posy. His mother loved to set a jug of flowers on the supper table. His natural good spirits restored somewhat as he gave thought how best he might proceed. A problem could be resolved if one approached with imagination. His mother loved him, of that he had no doubts. She would always take his part, assuredly his greatest ally.

But how to smoothen the way with Uncle William? He was a very different prospect from his gentle mother. Francis felt sure a stratagem would come to him in time. Bold action must be employed. Didn't William Shakespeare say something about 'the end justifying the means'? Or was it that Italian fellow who had such a lot to say about decisive tactics? Francis never quite remembered who said what in his studies of the Greats but he invariably grasped the point of their observations, which surely was the only purpose of quoting from the words of old men long dead? He doubted this one came from the Gospels, anyway. They were all about turning the other cheek and loving one's neighbour, approaches he had no intention of employing in this particular instance.

2

Occam's Razor

Melton Manor, near Woodbridge, Suffolk. June 1754

As Francis turned into the gateway, Mary Light waved from her seat by the door where she had been sewing in the sweet light of early evening amongst the fragrant blooms. Much of the quarter acre of ground afforded to the grandly named Melton Manor (in fact a pretty double-storey cottage) was given over to vegetables and fruit, but Mary had always reserved the area around the front porch for flowers. This evening her patch was a riot of colour and perfumes, dominated by her favourite roses garlanded with carnations, hollyhocks and marigolds. She set down her work and advanced to greet her son.

'I wondered where you were! Why so late? Up to no good with the river boys again?' Mary clucked in feigned annoyance, her eyes softening at the sight of her handsome boy, still a gangly youth but already on the cusp of manhood. She mopped her neck with her kerchief, tucking a few frizzy brown curls back under her mob cap. 'It's a hot'un, and no mistake! I had to forgo the kitchen for a bit of breeze.'

Francis pecked her on the cheek and thrust his posy of wildflowers forward. 'Why, daisies and forget-me-nots! My favourites! Let me find a jug to set them on the table ...' Mary rose too suddenly, rubbing her stiff back as she straightened. Francis watched from the doorway while she bustled about inside. His mother was growing old and stout. She worked too hard to make his life better.

'Mamma, please, would you sit again for a moment? I would very much like to talk to you about something of the utmost importance.'

Mary continued to tweak the flowers in the jug. It was unlike Francis to be so serious; something was amiss. Taking a seat by the hearth, she pointed to him to sit by her on the stool. It was where they often sat of an evening, she sewing and he reading or sketching. 'Come, let's sit. It's a cold plate tonight. Supper can wait a while.'

Francis threw down his jacket and squatted at her feet. To her surprise, he took her hands in his, stroking her dry and wrinkled fingers, nails worn down, skin cracked. 'You have Peg to do the washing and cleaning. Why must you insist on working yourself so hard?'

Mary scoffed in amusement. 'Get away with you! I was born with hands made for working, not idling. It's too late now for me to change my ways. What ails you, lad, on this beautiful summer evening? Have you been fighting? Is there trouble at school?'

Francis shook his head. 'Not exactly. Mother, I have to tell you that I shall be asked to leave at the end of this half. Reverend Ray will be writing to Uncle William. He believes it to be the best course for me to begin my trade.' He summarised the gist of his recent interview, with certain details omitted. He did not deem it necessary to apprise her of everything.

His mother merely chuckled, stroking his unruly hair. 'Why, you silly goose, it's not the end of the world! You don't even like school! And you're of an age to enter a trade. Why waste your time on learning if that 'int your inclination? It will not do you any service, Francis. I have always been of that opinion. Whilst it may be a fine thing to walk and talk like a gentleman, what good will it do you? For no one will accept you as such. Better to have a simpler life with a good honest trade under your belt. This other world that good Squire Negus has offered you would be a detriment for a boy like you in the long run. Else you might find that you don't fit anywhere, mind my words!'

Francis was not entirely sure that he followed her full sense, other than that she was neither sad nor angry at his news. 'So, you're not disappointed in me then?'

Mary shook her head, still laughing at his apprehension. 'How could I be disappointed in my fine boy? I dare say the squire will be red in the face and spouting blood and thunder at the news. But he'll get over it. I'll speak with him and put your case. Until then, we must give some thought to what profession would best suit you. You're good with your hands. Maybe furniture making? What do you think of that? We could approach Mr Armstrong and see if he needs another apprentice. His workshop is just down the road! I'm sure that once he calms down the squire would put in a good word ...'

Francis jumped from his stool. 'A carpenter? Mother! I don't want to be a tradesman. I don't want to spend my days in Melton and never see anything of the world! And I would surely never fit alongside those snot-nosed farm boys apprenticed there! I do not wish for such a lowly profession!'

His mother tutted. 'How high and mighty you have become, Francis Light. This is the consequence of being educated with those above your station. Open your eyes, son. What possible careers are there for you? You have no interest in the church. You don't wish to study, so the law and medicine are not open to you. You can't expect an army commission. What then is left? You cannot live on dreams and fresh air!'

Francis strode about the room in frustration. This was the second time today that his lack of social status had been raised. Why had he been raised as a gentleman if he was never to be part of that world? 'There must be something more suitable that I can do! Seven years of schooling at a fine grammar school! For what? And why should my birth count for so much? Everyone knows that the squire is my father. He comes from a well-known family! My grandfather was at court! Allowances can be made for children born on the wrong side of the blanket. Uncle William has always acknowledged me,' he argued with vehemence.

Mary put her hands to her head in exasperation. Her son had come to some conclusions of his own that were far from the truth. It was her own fault for keeping her silence all these years so as not to upset the boy. These sensitive matters had never been discussed as they should have been. 'Francis ... where did you get the notion that Mr Negus is your father?'

'It is obvious,' Francis snapped back truculently.

'Has he ever claimed to be anything other than your guardian?' Mary put to him gently, reaching out to take his hand in hers.

His voice now showed some uncertainty. 'No. But everyone knows ...'

'... knows what?' interrupted Mary. 'I certainly do not know who your real father is – and I am your *adoptive* mother.' She paused on the crucial word, one that had never before been spoken, watching his reaction with some trepidation.

'Adoptive?' Francis gasped. 'But … you are my mother! You have always been my mother!' Even as he insisted otherwise, she saw the realisation in his eyes. 'Then why have you lied to me?' He withdrew his hand forcibly. 'All these years neither you nor the squire ever intimated that I was other than your child, born without benefit of wedlock!' His voice began to crack, betraying his proximity to tears. He swallowed hard, gulping for air and self-control.

Mary stood up and tried to put her arms around him but he shrugged her away. It pained her deeply. 'Francis … neither of us ever said that we were your natural parents. Perchance it is my mistake that I always led you to believe that you were truly mine. I so much wished it to be so that I almost convinced myself of it down the years. It is my fault. I committed the sin of omission. We never meant to mislead you! But the honest truth is, Mr Negus brought you to me when you were a tiny mite, scarce one week old. From that day on I have been your mother. It has been my privilege and joy …'

Her blandishments failed to reach his ears as he staggered back, winded by the blow of her revelation. He gasped, 'And where, pray tell did Uncle William find me? By the wayside? Did I just fall from the skies at his door? Can you not see that he foisted his by-blow son on you? I must be his, even if I am to accept that I was never yours at all! I must be his son even if you are just a mere nursemaid!' Francis spat out harsh words meant to wound, she had no doubt of that, nor could she blame him. His world was collapsing about him. All his certainties shattered in one word.

Mary Light had never known the actual provenance of her

beloved child. It was not in her nature to question the whys and wherefores of her fate. She had lost her husband and baby but had gained a home and a healthy son, because that is what the Good Lord had decreed. It made no matter where he came from once he was here.

'Francis, you are not Mr Negus' son. So much he told me and I have never had cause to doubt his words. But where you came from, I do not know. If you wish to pursue this matter, you must ask Squire Negus for yourself. Please, Francis, let's sit down to supper. It has been a tumultuous day. Such times occur in life, but rest assured the Lord has a plan for us. Nothing is sent to us that we are unable to bear. My life is living proof of that. Had I not been widowed at such a young age – and then to lose my own precious child at birth – none of this life would have been possible. I cannot be thankful for the loss of those I loved but nor can I imagine any other life than this. Great happiness can arise from the greatest sorrow.'

Francis knew something of the sad tale of her girlhood marriage but the intervening period between the loss of her first family and the beginning of her second had always remained a mystery. In his mind, Uncle William, in his brusque but kindly fashion, had helped the unfortunate girl and then lost his heart to her. Unable to marry because of their different circumstances, they had managed the unfortunate consequences in an honest and courageous fashion. The local community had accepted the arrangement, little opprobrium now lingering. His mother was a respected widow of the district and the squire was well regarded by all.

Now, in one fell swoop, his nursery tale was shattered into

tiny fragments. The truth was wholly different. Yet it changed nothing. Whoever had sired him, he was still a bastard. A nobody. It was time for Francis to leave behind the warm cocoon of childhood illusion. He was a man now, about to embark upon the world and all its harsh realities but one thing he knew for sure: it was not his mother's fault. She had risked her good name for his sake, allowing the scandal of immoral behaviour to be spread abroad in order to protect him from the truth.

Francis took her hands again and kissed them gently. He could not hurt her. There would be time enough to think on this matter when he was alone. For now, he would behave like a man and take the blows with fortitude and forbearance.

'I don't reproach you, mother. Everything you have ever done for me has been in my best interests, even at the detriment of your reputation. Furthermore, I'm relieved to know the truth at last. Come, let's eat! Tomorrow we will face the squire's wrath. And together we will ponder my future. But not a carpenter, mother. Not ever! I was not born for that, whoever I am!' Francis managed a rueful grin and Mary playfully ruffled his hair. Her eyes held unshed tears, stored up over years. She had known a day like this would one day come.

***

A flurry of activity met James Lynn at the school gate the following morning. Schoolboys possess an uncanny sense for when something of moment is about to take place. A certain current permeates the air, anticipation stirred by the brisk breezes of supposition and rumour, scurrying like the pox from one to another. Groups whispered in corners, individuals darted feverishly here and there, all stoking up the fires. James made for Thomas Lambert, Stephen Brightwell and Charles Thompson, his classmates, who were loitering inside the gate, eager to see him. 'Is something afoot, gentlemen?' he queried.

In place of an answer, James found himself pulled to the rear of the school building where other members of his class were gathered: George Doughty, Joseph Fielding, Edmund Jenney, Francis Brooke and Thomas' younger brother, James. 'Where the devil have you been, Lynn? You've missed all the fun!' exclaimed Jenney.

'The most fearful to-do!' chortled Joseph.

'Well, don't keep a fellow in suspense!' Lynn said. 'What's the fuss about? Has Light been at his tricks again?'

The other boys exchanged furtive glances, their excitement scarce contained. Edmund Jenney obliged by explaining as much as they so far knew.

'It seems that this morning early, Mr Hythe went into our classroom to gather some of his particulars before the start of the day, probably so that he wouldn't be observed and mocked for his demotion. Apparently Reverend Ray was unconvinced about his story yesterday and raked him over the coals for trying to get you and Light in trouble. He is sacked as monitor. I think he has been put down to keeping the library tidy or some such other menial task ...'

'To the point, Jenners!' James retorted in impatience.

Stephen Brightwell broke in, 'The next moment Hythe was shouting blue murder. Some of the early birds heard him calling out and running for Reverend Ray. The reverend burst out of his rooms with his wife and all the little Rays on his heels. I rather think they thought the place afire, such was the commotion … They say it was such a laugh as they all scurried after Hythe towards the classroom, with Hythe spluttering on about something scratched on a window pane …'

'What was the cause? What was scratched on a window?' James queried.

The boys all shrugged. 'Nobody knows! That's the thing,' Thomas Lambert continued. 'But Hythe has been in the study ever since. The reverend slammed down his window the moment he reached his room. All we know is that something has been scratched on a window in our classroom and the boys have been told to wait outside for the time being. Oh, and Light was bundled inside when he arrived. They are also asking for you, too …'

'… for me? Who is asking for me?' James gasped. 'What can I possibly have to do with it? I've only just arrived,' he protested.

'The other monitors are looking for you. You'd better take yourself along to Reverend Ray or there'll be the devil to pay,' cautioned Joseph Fielding.

James looked around at his friends in disgust. They were eager for shocking developments, even though at his expense. Hythe must be behind all this! Francis had warned yesterday that events would not end there. Bracing himself against the coming storm, he entered the building and climbed the stairs to the study for the second time in two days.

His friends watched him go, both sympathetic and curious in equal measure, but now revealing themselves much more cognisant of the matter than they had heretofore admitted. 'Francis would have been proud of us,' Charles Thompson observed. 'We intercepted Lynn before he learned of it from anyone else!'

James and Thomas Lambert clapped George Doughty on the back. 'Doughboy's the real hero, mind! Never thought you had it in you, man! Stroke of genius to get you involved! Hythe would never suspect you set him up!'

George Doughty beamed at his newfound role of hero, although his pleasure was somewhat tempered by their qualification. He had only been able to accomplish his task because he was such an unlikely candidate for heroics. Yet even so, his adventure had proved something: he was not just a fat boy whose role was as the butt of mockery. He might also be the protagonist in his own story. Francis Light had always been decent to him, defending him when others were unkind. Thus, he had been willing to return the favour, acting completely out of character, particularly as it meant revenge on his chief tormentor, the odious Hythe. 'It was nothing. Let's see if it works out in our favour before we hand out the laurels, chaps,' was his smug reply.

Meanwhile upstairs, James' timid knock was answered with a peremptory 'Enter!' Inside, Reverend Ray was again sitting behind his sturdy desk with Charles Hythe and Francis Light before him. Both boys were solemn-faced. 'You had asked for me, Reverend?' James stuttered.

'I did. Follow us.'

The reverend strode out of his study with the three boys in tow. James tried to catch Francis' eye but his friend resolutely refused to make contact. By the time they reached their classroom, he was in no way the wiser.

'Enter. Take your places by the middle window. Where Light is usually seated,' Reverend Ray commanded. It was impossible to judge his intention other than that something of gravity had occurred.

No sooner had they gathered at the spot indicated than James and Francis gasped in complete astonishment, their hands to their mouths and their eyes as saucers. 'I swear it wasn't us!' James protested. 'We would never do such a thing!'

Francis, too, was stunned to silence, shaking his head in disbelief. Hythe's eyes gave him away, glinting with malevolence. 'Just as I said, Reverend Ray! They have scratched their names upon the window. What wretched boys to deface the glass in such vulgar fashion!'

Reverend Ray peered closely, an eye piece in his hand. There before him, in large script, crudely etched onto a window pane, were the autographs of J. Lynn and F. Light. He straightened and turned back to the three boys. 'There is no mistaking what it says. These are your names, boys. How did they come to be scratched on this window light?'

The younger boys shook their heads in denial, still apparently bewildered by the shocking act. This time, however, Light found his voice. 'I swear on my mother's life, that I have no knowledge of this! Why would we do such a thing? It is unthinkable!'

'I would prefer you did not choose to swear in such crass fashion, sir,' Reverend Ray replied sternly. 'I myself cannot comprehend why you two would do such a thing either. It is not at all what one would expect from Mr Lynn, who is a most respectful and sensible young man. Nor would I expect it of Mr Light, no matter that he can be grossly reckless and thoughtless at times. Neither of you is a fool. To scratch upon glass is one thing but who would sign their offence? It is incomprehensible!'

Hythe began to look uncomfortable, beads of sweat forming on his hairy upper lip. 'Yes, sir. Incomprehensible. But nevertheless …'

'I also observe that the two names appear to be written by the same hand. There is no apparent difference in style. See the capital L in Lynn and Light? Identical. Does that not appear rather odd? That two boys should have the same handwriting?' the headmaster continued.

His observation afforded Hythe an alternative tack. 'Why, I believe it to be Light alone, sir! Such behaviour is in no way typical of Mr Lynn but Light is a low-born scoundrel, sir. He has not only destroyed school property but has incriminated his own friend in his misdeed! An abomination!'

'Enough, Hythe. Empty your pockets, boys.' Francis and James, ashen-faced and shivering, riffled through the usual oddments found in the pockets of boys, laying them out on the nearest desk: the stub of a pencil, a nub of hard biscuit, a whittled piece of wood, a small brass coin. Hythe leapt forward, seizing on the pencil and the coin. 'The evidence, sir!'

The reverend exploded in rage. It was a rarity to hear the carefully spoken headmaster give way to anger. 'I said, enough! Take those implements, you wretched fool, and see if you can scratch upon a pane with them! Glass is extremely hard to mark, no matter with what ease it may break. It would take a substance harder than glass itself to make these scratchings – and neither of these boys has any such tool upon his person.'

Hythe spluttered an unwise response. 'They must have discarded it! Of course, they would not keep such a thing upon their person! They would not wish evidence to remain of their crime!'

The reverend tore at him. 'They signed their *damned* names! What more evidence than that would it require?' The use of a profanity in the mouth of their saintly headmaster shocked the boys almost more than anything else that had occurred that morning. 'Turn out your pockets, Hythe!'

Charles Hythe stared. 'But, sir ...'

'Turn out your pockets, sir. Your persistent eagerness to accuse these boys predisposes me to suspect your motives. It seems to me that if someone wished misfortune on another, what better way than to incriminate them, apparently by their own hand? Turn out your pockets – now!'

The reverend's disposition was glacial despite the heat of the morning. As Hythe gingerly felt into the pocket of his coat, a presentiment registered on his face that moments later turned to abject horror. In the palm of his hand lay an exquisite pebble of mineral, mottled and banded like iridescent snakeskin. The stone was polished to an opalescent shine and sharpened to a unifacial ridge. 'This is not mine, Reverend! I know of no way it could be in my coat pocket!' blustered Hythe in a vain attempt to defend himself.

'It is in your pocket because you used it in this despicable farce to destroy the reputations of these two boys, purely to satisfy your desire for revenge, blaming them for yesterday's humiliation. Which, may I point out, was brought on by your own appalling conduct, not theirs. Take yourself out of my sight, you wretch! I will send for your parents later when I can bear to look upon you again. Until then, do not darken Seckford's halls! Make no mistake, this will go against you in your Cambridge entry. I will make sure on't!'

Hythe slithered to his knees, hands joined, tears running down his cheeks. He begged for another hearing, blubbing like a babe. 'Reverend Ray! I did not do it! I swear I did not do it! It was not me! Do not tell my father, I pray! He will never forgive me … I did not do it!'

Reverend Ray indicated for Francis and James to leave, which they gladly did, dashing from the room, relief evident on their faces. Outside on the corridor as they ran for the stairs, James turned to his friend, only to find Francis punching the air in glee, his face a picture of satisfied elation. 'Did it! Got the bastard good and proper!'

James grabbed his arm. 'What are you talking about? Are you saying Hythe did not do it?'

Francis put a finger to his lip. 'Later. Someone might overhear. After school!'

The school bell was now sounding, so it was hours later before James was let into the secret of the scratchings on the window light. The schoolmates sprawled on the banks of the Deben, in the cooling shade of a willow tree, after school had finally let out for the day. Now at last, free to talk, Francis revealed that he was to leave the school in a few weeks. The others were astonished and wanted to know more, but he waved away their commiserations, pretending that it had been his wish: he wanted to pursue a profession, not an academic career. That was the limit of what he was prepared to admit.

With the others in rapt attention, Francis described how, after making his decision to leave, he had lain awake the previous night, tossing and turning in his bed. Even if he was mightily relieved to be leaving school, his greatest regret was that he must part company with his friends. Thus, he had decided to act on his friends' behalf as a parting gift to them. His target was Charles Hythe, whose malicious bullying lay at the heart of the day's unfortunate events, for he knew that their tormentor would not let matters rest. Francis did not wish for them to suffer persecution at Hythe's hands after he had gone.

Rising from bed, Francis had gone to sit at his window, gazing out onto the June sky, streaks of violet and lavender leaching from a rose-gold horizon, the silver moon adding to the brightness of the summer night. In his hand he fiddled idly with his favourite stone, the lucky one he always carried with him, a flawless agate pebble from the beach near Harwich. He had polished it to a fine lustre, and sharpened it to a razor-like edge.

As he was lost in deep thought, he found himself scraping absent-mindedly at the window pane – and observed the scratchings that his action made. The idea came to him in an instant. It was perfectly adjudged. That Italian fellow (Lynn enquired, with a roll of his eyes, 'Machiavelli, by chance?') said that 'if an injury has to be done to a man, it should be so severe that his vengeance need not be feared'. With that counsel in mind, Light realised that the only course of action was to drive Hythe out of the school entirely.

Climbing from his bedroom window in the dead of night, he had run all the way to school, slipping in through the back door to the boarders' stairs. He had counted on that door being unlocked; at school some boy was always sure to be where he should not be at night. Friends ensured ingress was possible for the late-to-bed. By a stroke of luck, despite the lightness of the sky, Francis was able to pass unobserved, the school now fast asleep, even the most recalcitrant carouser. Tiptoeing along gloomy corridors, he found his way to the classroom, encountering no one. There he scratched their names with his stone and slipped back out, as easily as he had entered.

'But how did the stone get into Hythe's pocket?' James asked in puzzlement.

After returning home and sleeping for a few hours, Francis had forgone his morning hasty pudding, saying he was not hungry – something his mother found hard to believe – and made his way for the Martlesham road to intercept George Doughty on his way to school. There the stone exchanged hands.

George and the other boys were then able to take over the tale, describing how George, with his usual clumsiness, had tripped over as he passed Hythe in the schoolyard, clutching at the older boy to break his fall. With a deftness unexpected in the ungainly Doughty, he had slipped said stone into the older boy's coat pocket, taking a cuff across the ears from the bully for his pains. It had been worth it. From then on, everything had transpired exactly as Light had intended. His low spirits of the day before had lifted in this one act of ingenious conspiracy. He was overjoyed at how it had turned out, as were the other accomplices, who had all played their parts, no matter how small. They had been charged with reaching James first to ensure he went before Reverend Ray with no real knowledge of the discovery.

James Lynn disapproved of the deceit and his unwitting involvement, and was further annoyed that no one had trusted him with foreknowledge. 'It was a great risk – and an unspeakable act of destruction, even if it served our advantage. But it is immoral!

It might ruin a boy's career, even if it is the loathsome Hythe! I deplore my part in it, no matter how unaware. Why use my name, Francis? It might have rebounded on us. Surely, I did not deserve to be implicated? At the very least you might have included me in the secret!'

Francis put his arm around his friend. 'For the very objections that you have put forward. You would never have agreed to it, James. You are too honest and principled to fight bare-knuckled in the dirt, although sometimes that is the only route one can take in life. We would never compromise your nature – and had you known, your face would have revealed it all. You cannot tell a lie. One look at you and the game would have been up. We were never in any danger, Jamie. No one would have charged us with the crime, not least a wise old fellow like Ray. Who writes his own name on a window and incriminates himself? Not even the worst villain would be so foolish!'

Despite his misgivings, James ruefully admitted that school life would be much improved with the departure of Mr Hythe. So, the boys agreed to keep their secret, never to be repeated to a living soul. After swearing on all manner of things sacred to young boys, they stripped down to their nether garments and spent the next hour cooling off in the shallows, chasing after widgeons and warblers on the reedy banks, the heat of the season showing no signs of abating. Later Francis loped home, damp but happy, even if his guardian was still to be faced. Nothing could destroy the sense of satisfaction that his victory had won. He was never going to let a horse control him; he would take the reins and coax it to his will. That also applied to his future, to which he must now give some serious consideration.

But not quite yet. First, he intended to gleefully wallow in today's triumphs: the scratchings on the window and the moment Hythe had realised how soundly he had been trumped. Nor had he lied to James. There had been no chance of failure. It had always been unlikely that anyone would have held them responsible. Only an enemy would have done such a thing to throw blame on innocent boys.

Or someone skilled in the art of the double bluff. For surely it was equally unlikely, on careful reflection, for Charles Hythe so blatantly to have attempted to entrap them? Even he was not such a fool. Francis smiled inwardly, having completely hoodwinked so many people. Not one amongst them all had applied logic to the matter. They had simply seized upon the most obvious conclusion as he had known they would. Therein lies the weakness in Occam's Razor, he thought with a grin. Not every lesson had been wasted on him.

Picking up a pebble, testing it in his palm, Francis skimmed it across the river, its trajectory a series of masterly scoops. He was the lord of all he surveyed. His woes were quite forgotten. A rural village was a paltry kingdom for such as he. It was time to find grander horizons where only his wit and courage would count. It was a pity about his stone, though. It had been his favourite, his special talisman. But it had been well worth its loss. Not only had he won the day, but he had also left an indelible mark on Seckford's School for other boys down the years. Carved on glass. Light. Francis Light. Of Woodbridge, Suffolk.

3

A Wider Horizon

The Gun Wharf, Portsmouth. 29th October 1754

Exposed on the Gun Wharf, buffeted by a fierce blow, the man and boy stood side by side and took in Portsmouth Harbour. The expanse of sea and sky, a wider horizon than Francis had ever dreamed possible, stretched out in every direction, crowded with ships and crafts and men and buildings. Beyond them lay the sea reaching ever onwards to the ends of the earth, a vast distance in time and space to who knew where and who knew what end? For the first time, the prospect of leaving never to return, crossed his mind. He glanced over at his guardian, wondering if perhaps they might never meet again. Equally awestruck by the sight, and feeling similarly apprehensive, William took the boy's hand in his own and gave it a reassuring squeeze, a rare moment of sentiment from bluff Squire Negus. 'Quite a sight, eh, boy?'

After months of waiting and planning, anticipation and regrets, the day had finally dawned when Francis Light was to embark upon his chosen career. He had travelled down to London the week before in the company of his guardian to visit outfitters and be kitted out for sea. Then a mail coach to Portsmouth on Sunday and a night at a decent inn. It would be a long time before Francis next slept in a bed, so a little comfort and a good dinner were in order.

Francis was bewildered by the sheer enormity of the world beyond his quiet little town in Suffolk. After fourteen years in Woodbridge – then London and Portsmouth in the space of a few days – it was almost too much for the boy to assimilate. The swagger and confidence that had seen him bid farewell to his friends and family had disappeared over the past few days. Now at the point of embarkation, he felt very young, and not a little scared.

It was a dull and gloomy spectacle for all its majesty, a seascape dominated by greys: dirty clouds that raced impossibly through a lowering pewter sky; the surge and slap of oily charcoal water against the stone walls of the wharf; the iron grey masts, a skeletal forest, creaking and groaning, for all the world like baleful spirits clothed in pearl-grey shrouds, wailing out a warning. It was a scene of foreboding, not the stuff of seaboard fantasies that the young boy had cherished these past months. To make the morning even more miserable, drizzle was now falling like an ashen mist, casting the dismal scene in an even murkier light.

Even so, the grandeur of this great naval harbour took the breath away. At every angle lay ships at anchor in various stages of fitting, repair or readiness. Further off lay vessels preparing to put out to sea, sails like giant bed sheets billowing in the blow, their hulls rising and falling in the turbid waters, straining against their holding ropes and anchors. Men scurried about dockside hauling bales, dragging carts, hefting sacks, heaving loads. Rowing boats of different sizes and shapes plied back and forth from ship to shore. Everyone had a purpose. It was a complex world of men who knew exactly what they were doing, engaged in feverish activity like ants on a hill, labouring through the rain, oblivious to the elements.

Francis and William wrapped their scarves tighter around their necks and held onto their hats as they made their way to the embarkation dock, where boats were transferring between the ships at anchor and the wharf. It seemed impossible that these small craft would not be swallowed by the angry churning waves, yet still they made creeping headway, even those heavily laden with stores and supplies. Finally, one reached their designated spot. It bore the legend *'Mars'*. Several oarsmen scrambled up the steps to secure the ropes.

'I believe you are sent for us, good man,' William began. A surly seaman wiped a hand across his brow. He was sodden, and in no mood for pandering to gentlemen. 'Depends who y'ar. This boy joining us?'

'Yes, Francis Light. Reporting to Captain Amherst.'

'He ain't aboard,' came the unhelpful reply.

William tried another tack. 'Then may I enquire if the ship's doctor is aboard?'

'Dr McParland, ya mean?'

'Is he the ship's doctor?'

'Only one I know of … *sir*,' the sailor added with a truculent flourish.

'Then we are indeed at the right place. Young Francis is joining the *Mars* as surgeon's assistant. Please convey him over. I also wish to cross to meet Dr McParland, in the absence of Captain Amherst.'

The squire was used to men of the lower orders tugging at their forelocks and jumping to when he spoke. But that wasn't quite how it worked at sea, apparently. 'Can't do that, sir. Only officers and gentlemen on this barge. This lad ain't no officer. He's the new loblolly, I reckon. He can wait for the jolly boat. If it makes it through this swell …' he added sardonically '… and you can't come over to hold his hand, either. What d'you think this is? Mrs Polly's school for bugaboos?' At least that witticism seemed to improve his ill humour for he cackled heartily at his own riposte.

Then all at once he pulled himself to attention and snapped his head right to greet – with more perceptible respect – a few uniformed men and boys who were approaching.

'Welcome back, Lieutenant Allendale, sir, good to see you again. Foul weather you're bringing with you, sir!' And would this be our new midshipman. Mr Jeffreys, is it? Pleased to meet you, young sir! Let me help you there with your belongings … Your nephew, you say, Lieutenant? I'll make sure all the lads look out for the little gentleman. You can be sure of that. As sure as my name is Isaiah Perkins.'

William and Francis stepped back, ignored by both the new arrivals and the men of the barge. Just then another smaller vessel reached the side and, as if from nowhere, a surge of sailors claimed their places. William realised too late, so that all the seats had been taken and the little boat was making ready to return. There was not even time to say farewell. 'In ya get, lad, or you'll be left,' shouted one of the rowers.

Francis' bag was snatched roughly from him and thrown aboard. William patted him on the back, whispering, 'God speed! You will be in our prayers …' and Francis was pushed forward with little ceremony to climb precariously into the bucking jolly boat. He sat atop his bag on the bare boards, clinging to the side as it ploughed laboriously through the heavy seas. Through the now-driving rain, Francis stared fixedly at his guardian standing one arm raised in farewell, grateful at least that his tears were masked by the deluge. He caught the faint 'Write, Francis! Write!' over the wind as the shore was slowly swallowed by the gloom and the boat fell beneath a wave. From then on, his thoughts were on surviving the crossing, such was the ferocious swell tossing the little boat.

William watched heart-in-mouth as the jolly rocked through the fierce water, disappearing one moment to finally emerge just as he thought it had surely perished. Should they even have set out in such weather on so tiny a craft? But, at long last, the little boat pulled aside the barge beneath one of the larger ships lying off in the far ground, no doubt the HMS *Mars*, Francis' home for the next few years.

Trudging back against the driving rain and the blustery squalls, William reflected on how the very elements mirrored his turbulent spirits. He was both wretched to see the lad go, and fearful for his safety, a swirling maelstrom for a man not given to anxiety. The sea might be a useful career for a brave and hearty boy with a decent brain in his head, but it was a most perilous occupation, even in peacetime. The prospect of war was gathering, too; what then for a small boy on a large ship in the midst of a great battle?

William crossed the Mill Pond and passed through the city walls, heading for Lombard Street and the shelter of The Dolphin on the High Street where they had spent the previous night. Inside he threw off his wet cloak and hat and slumped into the window seat, relieved to be out of the inclement weather, but still heartsick. Only last night he and the boy had sat together in these very seats, eating dinner and playing cards. The ghost of that last supper lingered, as if Francis would any moment slip into the opposite bench and they could resume where they had left off. William shook his head to clear the image.

'He get off safely then, sir? Poor little lad on a day like this! He'll be throwing up his innards for the next few days at least, I should say!' It was the innkeeper's daughter, meaning well but only adding to his distress. Francis may have grown up around boats and the river – but he was still a landlubber where the open sea was concerned. A few fishing trips with Nate and his father wouldn't in any wise have prepared him for the greensick to come.

'Ay, lass. He's aboard now. Bring me something to warm me up, if you will. I'm sodden through.'

When a spiced brandy wine arrived, William swirled the glass absently. Had he done the right thing? Should he have insisted that the boy finish his education first, despite Francis' resistance to the notion? Was this in truth the only option open to this boy who had come to mean so much to him?

***

'Asked you to leave the school? How dare he? Your extortionate fees have been paying his damned living these past years! Who is he to tell me to withdraw my boy from school! I shall go and see him tomorrow and read the Riot Act!'

As Mary Light had foreseen, William Negus had not taken the news well. Mother and son sat facing Negus in his study at Dallinghoo with heads lowered, waiting out the expected thunderous response, fully aware that the squire would bluster and threaten before they could begin to cajole. Pacing up and down, banging his hand on the desk or the back of a chair, William ranted and raved about what he would and would not do, until eventually he sank down, exhausted by his own outburst, and the opportunity presented itself.

Just then, the door opened. In came William's new wife, Margaret, who had been waiting outside until William ceased shouting, as accustomed to his propensity for bluster as everyone else. She also knew that her husband was at heart a rational man. It would take time for him to adjust to this unexpected turn of events. Her arrival brought a measure of calm to the scene, for that was Margaret Negus' nature: unruffled and conciliatory, the very opposite of her choleric husband. 'Is something amiss, dear?' she asked, feigning ignorance, although she had been fully apprised of the business by Mary Light herself earlier.

William grunted. 'That old sourpuss Ray has asked our Francis to leave the school, by George!' The boy in question stifled a laugh which turned into a loud snort at hearing his hallowed headmaster referred to in such terms. William shot Francis a cautionary glance, while his mother tugged on his coat in warning.

Mrs Negus continued to appease her husband. 'He is not an old sourpuss, William, as well you know. He is in fact a fine gentleman and scholar. He is also a dear friend of ours. Dr Ray would not have acted thus without good reason. He must have given the matter great thought. How does Francis feel about the suggestion? May we hear his opinion?'

'What the devil does that matter?' William shouted. 'He's no doubt delighted. He's a blasted boy! Of course, he doesn't want to go to school!'

Margaret placed an upright chair at his side and sat down, arranging her dress neatly, then laying her hands together on her lap. 'Nevertheless, William ... shall we ask him to explain?' For all her apparent serene deference, Margaret Negus was implacable when she had her mind set on something.

There was a silence in the room, heavy with anticipation. William stared, first at Francis and then his mother, before shrugging. He never crossed his wife. 'If you must. Francis, what led to this? Have you been a bad lad?'

Francis swallowed hard. It was essential that he chose his words with care – and selectively. There was no reason for the squire to know everything. 'No sir. I haven't been in trouble. Well, not any particular trouble, that is. But I am not progressing in my studies as I ought. It is not a want of brains, sir, to be frank. It is a lack of interest and effort, which is wholly shameful of me, I know. I am fully cognisant of all you have done for me over the years and the great advantages you have made possible for me, yet, as much as I try, I can never manage to keep all the learning in my head. It goes in. It goes out. Unless it is something that seems important to me. Then I can master it perfectly. But most of my schoolwork seems dreadfully without rhyme or reason.'

William nodded in agreement, his earlier spleen softening as he listened. There was evidently no issue with the lad's brains. Francis could turn a decent phrase far better than he would have been able at thirteen. 'To be fair, I was a wooden-head at my studies too, and at most everything I ever did, save hunting. I never saw much point in it all either,' he admitted ruefully. 'But, Francis ... I was heir to this estate. It didn't signify in my case. My future was secured. It is not so for you, my boy. All you have is your wits and your courage – and the benefits of what Seckford's has given you, at no small cost!'

Francis nodded vigorously. 'I understand my situation, sir. Or at least as much as I am aware. I am fully mindful that my future depends solely on me. That is why it has come to me that the reverend is wholly to be commended for his decision. What is the point of my wasting a few years more struggling with Latin and Greek when I am of an age to embark on the only suitable career for a boy in my position?' Francis had been working on this speech all night. He thought it struck the right note, somewhere between humility and independence, praising the adults but at the same time offering a solution to the dilemma, before his guardian came up with one not to his taste. His words made him sound contrite but clear-thinking. It allowed him to stake a claim before any more nonsense about apprenticeships or the like were mooted.

With a deep sigh and a raising of the eyebrows at the boy's mettle, William replied. 'Go on ... you spoke of "a suitable career". What would constitute "a suitable career" in your opinion, my boy?'

Francis inhaled deeply and continued. 'The sea, sir. We Suffolkmen are well acquainted with the sea. It's a promising profession for a stout-hearted boy, which I believe myself to be, and if I work hard I could make my way through the ranks to one day command my own ship. I have more chance of rising in the Royal Navy than on land, sir. It is a well-known fact.'

It was a fair point. All the boy needed was a war and there would be mass promotions for handy young men. And there was always a war, you could stake your life on that. But to send the boy away from home so soon and into danger? William was unsure whether he was ready for such a thing. 'What does your mother think? Mary, surely you don't want him to go to sea?'

Mary Light had been sitting quietly, eyes downcast, wringing her hands on her lap. She looked up at William Negus, her onetime suitor. He could see the distress that this matter had caused her. Sufficient affection lingered, despite his new wife and the fading of Mrs Light's girlhood charms, for him still to struggle at adding to her pain. 'No, Mr Negus. I do not wish Francis to go to sea. Anything but that. It has always been my fear ever since he was a little stripling. You know his fascination for water and boats! But, despite my reluctance and, because I love this boy more than my life itself, I know it is indeed the best profession for him. And it breaks my heart to say so!' She dabbed at her eyes with the hem of her apron, sniffling as words began to fail her.

Margaret Negus stood up, 'Come, Mary, let us go into the garden. I'm sure you'll benefit from some fresh air. You can take a cutting of my gladiolus flower while you're there. It's quite lovely! My brother sent it up from London for my birthday. And a glass of elderflower tonic with a slice of fruit cake, fresh out of the oven ... we can leave the gentlemen to their business ...' She had recognised the turn in the tide. The case was made. William would be better served without the added distraction of a weeping Mary Light to complicate his emotions. Within moments, Mrs Negus had guided Mary from the room with adroit ease. William was composed now and the lad had made a good showing. The women had done their work.

William turned his attention back to Francis. He did not intend to allow Francis to lead him by the horns quite so easily.

'But would you work at it, Francis? Or would you be as lazy and thick-headed aboard as you were at school?'

'Oh no, sir!' Francis replied earnestly. 'I would work like a Trojan, sir. It seems to me that everything taught to me on the ship, about navigation, and mathematics and science and command and leadership would be exactly what would inspire me to learn! I would work like the blazes, Uncle William. I'd be a lieutenant before you know it!'

William smiled sadly. He admired the boy's enthusiasm but the navy was a hard taskmaster. While such a path was possible, it was by no means certain. The most likely alternative was a life at a lowly rank while other men – often of lesser ability but better birth – rose above him. He sighed. 'I am not a navy man and do not have the best of connections in that world. However, I will endeavour to have you enrolled as a midshipman if I am able. But it is by no means a certitude, Francis. Questions may be asked concerning your birth. It is required that midshipmen be gentlemen ...'

'But I am a gentleman, sir!' Francis insisted.

William raised his hand and patted the seat at his side, recently vacated by his wife. 'Sit down by me, boy. I think we need a tête-a-tête ...' Francis took the seat apprehensively. 'If you are of an age to go to sea, you are old enough to understand the limitations of your situation,' William began awkwardly. 'How much do you know of how you came to be my ward?'

Francis shrugged. 'Nothing really. Just what I have surmised and what my mother has recently revealed.'

'Which was?'

'That somehow you found me and settled me with my mother.

That neither of you are my birth parents. That she herself does not know from whence I came.'

William could tell by the boy's tone that he was resentful that he had been left in ignorance. He could not blame the lad. None of this was Francis' fault and yet he would bear the consequences throughout his life. 'I was approached by a great and important man who entrusted me with his secret. He had fathered a child but neither he nor your natural mother were in a position to be parents. Do you understand these things, Francis?' He stared pointedly at Francis who nodded back, a blush of shame colouring his cheeks.

'When you were born, a wet-nurse brought you to Dallinghoo on the day before All Hallows' Eve ...'

'But who were my real father and mother, sir? Do they not care for me? If my father is so grand, why doesn't he intervene to help me now? Just a word in my favour in the right quarters, and I would be set!' Francis must have been storing up these questions. They came out in a torrent, far more direct and heartfelt than his previous well-rehearsed speech.

The boy was too clever for his own good, thought William. 'I am not at liberty to divulge your father's name, Francis. It was a condition of our agreement, one that I will not break. Nor did I ever know your mother's identity. Your father did not want any hint of scandal against her name. But they did care for you, boy. That is why your father approached me when he could simply have sent you to the Foundling Hospital ...' The very name made Francis shudder. Had he been so close to abandonment? 'He insisted that you be raised a gentleman and that money be provided for your education and care and that, when the time arose, a suitable commission or living be found for you, depending on your inclination ...'

'Then surely he can now make good on his promise!' Francis shouted gleefully.

William shook his head sadly. 'Your father passed away before you reached the age of five, at which time he had intended to commit instructions to his lawyer for the provision of your future situation. As he had no legal heirs, his estate and title went to a distant relative, who knows nothing of your existence and, undoubtedly, would care even less. I'm very sorry, Francis, but no such help will ever be forthcoming. Perhaps if I knew who your mother was, I could somehow appeal to her, for I am sure she is a great lady herself and would want to see you well set up in life. But I do not know how to find her.'

Francis' eyes blinked rapidly as the enormity of the misfortune dawned on him. He had been promised the life of a gentleman but cruel fate had torn it from him. It seemed so unjust. 'So ... what did my father offer you in return for this service?' Francis asked. His question was accusatory but his tone was not.

'I received nothing, Francis. Had his untimely death not taken him away at not yet forty, then he might have offered me support later in life in return. But that day never came.'

'But still you raised me and sent me to a good school and gave me everything I needed!' the boy broke in. 'Why did you do that? You were under no obligation!' Francis gasped.

William smiled and put his arm about the boy. 'Oh, I was under an obligation, boy. I did it because you are my son, in all but name. Francis, I have no children of my own. I never thought to marry until I met my sweet Margaret Nadauld and she did me the great honour of accepting my suit. By then we were both too old for children. But I had you, my handsome, clever, dear boy who could charm the birds from the trees. Your mother loves you, even if she did not bear you. And, so do I, Francis. You are the son I never had! I even named you for my father. Is that not proof enough of my sincerity?'

William Negus was not a man given to intimate confidences, which made these heartfelt words all the sweeter. He had once thought Squire William and Mary Light his unwed parents and had been heartbroken when his fantasy was shattered. The truth, however, was much more poignant. Two people who had no reason to care for him had loved him better than most real parents. Given his situation, he had been exceptionally fortunate. It was an opportunity that fate had given him, not a disadvantage.

The boy flung both arms around his guardian and hugged him tight, as he had not done since he had been a small boy. William's florid face grew even redder at this sudden show of affection, and tears pricked at his eyes. 'I am the most fortunate of boys, sir! I do not deserve the love I have been given all these years! To think, I have been such an ungrateful and devilish nuisance to you both when all along I should have been labouring hard to prove that I deserved such charity!' Francis exclaimed.

William chuckled. 'It is not charity, Francis! Nor shall I hear any nonsense about debts to be repaid. We are a singular little family make no mistake, you, your mother and I. But we are a family for all that. And this is what families do for each other.'

Francis did not venture to ask then why William had never adopted him to make him his legal heir. Perhaps the question had never occurred to him, although William thought it unlikely that the shrewd boy hadn't given it some consideration. He deserved to know the full story. He owed him that much honesty. William did not want him to think that his generosity went only so far.

'As you know, I have a sister ...' he began.

'Aunt Bess?'

'Yes, my sister Elizabeth. She has a son, your cousin William Castle, born before you. The estate is entailed on him. If I had tried to adopt you, it would change very little. His claim takes precedence and no judge would allow otherwise. It would also be awkward socially for my wife and your mother if I did so, as it would appear that I was publicly acknowledging that we had fathered you out of wedlock. Nor would it have changed your position in society. You would still be regarded as illegitimate. But, know this, Francis, I have remembered you in my will, although I wouldn't put it past the Castles to challenge that in the courts when I'm gone ...' he muttered bitterly.

Francis smiled. 'I don't want the estate, sir. It isn't mine and you have done well by me already. I wish to go to sea and make my fortune by virtue of my own talents. I want to show you that I can be a man to be proud of. Please, sir, may I have your permission?'

William ruffled up his hair. 'I am already as proud of you as ever I would have been of a son of my own body, lad! Let's see what we can do for you, Midshipman Light! It does have a certain ring to it, don't you think?'

Francis could not resist adding: 'Captain Light sounds even better, sir!'

***

'Can I get you a bit o' lunch, sir?' The serving girl was back. William was abruptly woken from his reverie, embarrassed at having been observed far away and moist-eyed.

'That would be very kind of you,' was William's gruff reply. Food was always a balm to him. Wine even more so. 'A nice bit of game pie if you have it, with a decent claret, my dear ...' It was no use worrying over the past now. Francis was at sea and that was that. The boy's luck had lasted thus far. Perhaps fate had more in store for him ahead.

4
The Orlop

HMS Mars. *28th October 1754*

Meanwhile, aboard the *Mars*, the arrival of young Francis Light had passed unnoticed. After he had scrambled aboard and claimed his bag, no one had showed the least interest in his presence. All the other men knew the lie of the ship and immediately scurried off purposefully to report to who knew where. The gentlemen officers were greeted by the first lieutenant, and escorted to the wardroom. Francis found himself abandoned, although far from alone – for the deck was a fever of activity. He endeavoured to ask for assistance, but his polite 'Excuse me, sirs' were ignored, until he wondered had he been rendered invisible. But no, that could not be the case, for whenever he spoke, he found himself pushed out of the way or cursed for his very existence.

Unsure what was his best course of action, Francis sat on a box beneath an overhanging spar for shelter from the rain, his bag on his knee, while he gave the matter some thought. It did not seem entirely wise to wander around the ship. He would most assuredly lose himself on so vast a vessel. Furthermore, the heavy roll of the ship was beginning to affect him. He had no wish to throw his breakfast up by means of announcing his presence. Breathing deeply of the bracing air, he hoped his nausea would pass.

The smell of the sea hit him squarely. It was not the muddy, estuarine stench of Woodbridge, a low-tide blend of sewage and dead fish, but a wilder scent of salt and seaweed, of damp clothing and rotting wood overlaid with the acrid reek of smouldering tar. Strange noises assailed his ears: creaks and groans, slapping and thumping, loud enough to imagine that the sea was smashing this hulk to bits and swallowing the pieces. Around the towering masts, seagulls shrieked and dived, suspended in the savage gusts, battered but undeterred.

'Who the devil might you be?' shouted an older man, with impressive mutton chop whiskers and not a strand of hair on his entire pate, save for a band of grey frizz at ear level. He had appeared from nowhere. Francis shot up.

'Francis Light, sir, reporting for duty!'

The older man pulled a woollen cap on his head, glancing up at the skies with a seasoned eye. 'November gales come early. It's as well we're staying put for a few days ... so, Mr Francis Light ...' He stared at the boy fiercely, but his bright blue eyes suggested amusement rather than anger. '... exactly what duty are you reporting for?'

'I'm the new surgeon's assistant, sir. I'm to report to the ship's doctor,' Francis answered.

'Then why pray are you sitting here idling and catching your death in raw wind and rain?' His voice was a deep bass, his tone rich and melodic.

'I don't know where to find him, sir.'

'Well, there is evidently a tongue in your head, so perhaps you might have thought to use it and ask one of the sailors?'

'I tried, but they wouldn't listen, sir.' It was a feeble excuse.

The man rolled his eyes heavenward.

'Looks like we've got another one with wool for brains here. Do you know who I am, lad?'

Francis shook his head forlornly. He was making such a muddle of it all, when he had hoped for a good first impression.

'I'm the master of this ship, which means I sail it, boy. A ship of this size has both a captain and a master. Mr Bryn Morgan to you. Not many boys have the pleasure of meeting me on their first morning aboard. I take it you are new to the Royal Navy?'

Francis nodded.

'It's customary to answer a question, boy, not stand there like a dumb animal nodding your head.'

'Sorry, sir. Beg pardon, sir. Yes, sir. I've never been aboard a ship this size before, sir.'

Mr Morgan chuckled. 'We were all new once, lad. You'll get used to it. Dobbs!' he called to a sailor ducking past. 'Take this boy down to the doctor in the orlop. On your way, get him a berth on the gun deck.' And before Francis could even thank him, Mr Morgan had sauntered off, his rolling gait perfectly attuned to the buffeting of the ship.

The young sailor, Linus Dobbs, seemed friendly enough. He disappeared through what looked like a cubby hole but turned out to be a ladder, sliding down with practised ease. Francis lowered himself tentatively, still clutching his bag. This was a companionway, Linus informed him, as they made their way down three levels, the air growing noticeably mustier as they descended, the motion of the ship still heaving side-to-side.

Neither smell nor movement affected Linus who danced nimbly ahead, avoiding the oncoming traffic, all the while keeping up a nonstop chatter about the ship, its crew and other random matters. He was a gangly lad of sixteen or so, all lines and edges with a hollow face and pointed nose framed by greasy hair so straight and jagged at the ends that it might have been hacked by a knife. It turned out, unsurprisingly, that he was a topman who climbed the rigging and saw to the sails. Linus, for his part, wanted to know everything about Francis, questions gushing out, most of which Francis attempted to sidestep. Linus promised to become his very best friend, undertook to watch out for him against the older lads, and insinuated that without a special shipmate, life could become very difficult on board.

Francis might have been inclined to trust Linus had he not also observed the sideways glances that the older boy kept making towards his well-stuffed kit bag, and up and down at his clothing. 'Nice bit of cloth you're wearing there, Francis. Looks like your ma and pa got you all you needed in that bag an' all. You wouldn't have a twist of baccy or a bottle of rum to spare for a mate, would you? Us sailors share everything, you know.'

By the time they reached the lower gun deck, and Francis was shown to a hammock strung between gun carriages, close to Linus' own berth, he felt the first stirrings of suspicion. Caution might be preferable to mistaking Linus' offer of companionship for true friendship.

'Throw your bag down there and I'll take you to the doctor.'

'Will my belongings be safe?' Francis inquired, assessing his surroundings. Although there were personal effects on other hammocks, there didn't seem to be anything of value.

Linus put his hand flamboyantly to his heart. 'Safe as houses, Francis. Why Captain Amherst would string up any sailor who thieved from a fellow crewman. As I live and breathe, you can leave anything here. If you're worried, I'll keep an eye on it while you see the doctor ...'

Francis gave Linus a knowing smile. 'Much obliged, Mr Dobbs, but I reckon I'll keep it on my person for now.' After that, there was a conspicuous cooling in their budding relationship as they made their way down one more deck to the orlop. Linus was not so voluble in his camaraderie, sensing that this new lad was not as green as he had first thought. Francis felt his initial vigilance had been justified. If he wouldn't trust any stray boy he met in Woodbridge without taking proper stock, why should he suddenly think the world was any different at sea? Probably much worse, he supposed.

Linus knocked sharply at the door and ran off with a cursory: 'That's me then ...' Francis waited; there was no response. He tried again, a more forceful rap, and waited some more.

The orlop deck was at the very bowels of the ship, on a platform lying directly above the great hold. It was an area mostly used for storage but also home to the surgeon's cabin and the dispensary, along with the medical apparatus and stores required for the care of so many men on a long sea voyage. It was gloomy and dank at this deep level, with little natural light, save what filtered through tiny windows high above the open area near the cabin door. An unnatural stillness after the din of the other decks amplified ambient sounds: an ominous creaking, the steady drip of water, and the occasional heavy thud from the hold below. Francis felt completely alone. Even the pitch and roll of the sea had diminished to no more than a gentle rocking.

Behind him, the door was wrenched open. 'What do you

want?' a hoarse voice demanded.

Francis spun round to find a man of senior years, supporting himself against the doorframe with his elbow. His skin was the tell-tale veiny purple of the seasoned drunk; his eyes were rheumy and yellow-rimmed; his grey hair was scraped back carelessly in a mousy tail. He was rumpled, as if he had been disturbed from rest, shirt hanging open and breech-flaps only partially buttoned.

'Francis Light, sir. Reporting for duty. I'm the new surgeon's assistant ...'

The man grunted, whether in annoyance or recognition Francis could not say. 'Get in then,' was his surly reply, staggering back to allow the boy entrance, almost losing his footing in the process. Francis closed the door and waited until the man had stumbled back to his desk, slumping down into the chair with a heavy sigh.

'Pass me that jug,' he mumbled. Francis followed his pointed finger and saw a flagon on a nearby shelf. It was beer, long since drawn, well stale. He carried it over while the man fumbled around in the detritus on his desk, riffling under books and papers and partially consumed plates of food, to where a tankard lay on its side. Righting it, he indicated that Francis should pour. Then he drank long and deep, dragging his hand across his face after he had taken his fill, ignoring the drops that had spattered his chest and shirt front, joining the other various stains that spotted the once-white fabric.

'John told me about you. I forgot,' was his only remark.

'John?' Francis enquired.

'Amherst. Captain Amherst to you. He told me about you but ...' he puffed, throwing his hands up. 'I expect you don't know who I am, do you?'

'Are you Dr McParland, sir?'

The man sank back in his seat and laughed wryly. 'At your service, boy. I am indeed the surgeon aboard this vessel, so help me God.'

There was a silence that neither seemed inclined to break for a while until …

'Tell me about yourself. Start with your name. I can't remember it.'

Francis embarked on a hesitant re-introduction while the doctor slurped more beer. It seemed to have a beneficial effect, however, because his bearing became distinctly more upright and his attention improved.

'You seem a bright lad. Can you read and write?'

'Yes, sir. I went to Seckford's School in Woodbridge …'

'Indeed? You sound like a gentleman. Then why are you not enrolling as a midshipman?'

Francis dropped his head, still bitterly disappointed that Squire William had failed to secure him entry at that rank. 'There was no availability, sir. So many ships are on quarters …'

McParland snorted. 'We need a war, eh? Well, that will give you and me plenty to do, you can be assured of that. Let me review … you're an orphan. The ward of a gentleman. But no one knows your father so your chances of gaining a commission depend wholly on your ability to survive the next few years and hope plenty of others don't. Is that the long and short of it?'

It was brutally put, but it was nothing that Francis had not already understood. He nodded. The doctor was evidently not one for the niceties of conversation.

'I'm a doctor, Francis, and a damned fine surgeon. I am also a hopeless drunkard. I need an assistant to make sure I don't inadvertently poison the sick when I misread the label on a bottle. I need someone who can read, write my logs in a legible hand, keep this cabin neat and trim, learn how to clean a wound and wrap a bandage. I need, furthermore, someone to hold a man down when he's about to lose a limb. To hold a man's guts while I try to sew him back together. To stitch a dead body into its hammock ready for throwing overboard. As you can see, I need more than a loblolly. I would prefer a surgeon's mate but when we're on quarters, there's no call for two doctors aboard. When we're at full crew, there are few young physicians willing to work with me. So, you're neither mate nor helper. Have you the stomach to be my assistant?'

Francis had no idea if he had the stomach for the gruesome task ahead, but it was his intention to grasp this chance once offered and make something of it. Despite the nature of the bloody work, one consolation was that he would at least be working directly for a man who called the captain 'John'. At some point that might bring him to the attention of those far above him upon whose beneficence any chance of promotion would rest. He would also, if he won the doctor's trust, have his intercession if any of the other men saw him as an easy target.

'Yes, sir. Most honoured, sir,' Francis replied humbly, revealing none of the inner workings of his mind.

The doctor lurched out of his seat, shook the boy's hand, and then staggered off to a cot in an alcove. 'Get this place ship-shape. I'm for my bed ...' And no sooner had he hit the little cot with a worrying thud than he was snoring loudly. Francis put down his bag, took off his hat and coat, and rubbed his hands together. Now to make his mark on this ship. He decided to begin with the noisome chamber pot.

***

In many ways, Francis was fortunate to have joined the ship when he did. The *Mars*, a 64-gunner captured from the French, had been recommissioned at Plymouth with quarter crew as a guardship under the command of Captain John Amherst, an up-and-coming naval officer. Its visit to Portsmouth had been as part of a convoy accompanying Admiral Edward Boscawen, during which time it stocked up on both new recruits and Portsmouth beer, said to be far superior to the local Plymouth fare. The men had even emptied the Plymouth ale into Portsmouth harbour to make room for more barrels of the good stuff. This had naturally not been the sole purpose of their trip. The more pressing matter was the planning of a new campaign against the French in North America, a war that everyone on board was eagerly awaiting, despite the fact that the forthcoming action was a closely guarded secret. The senior captains, commodores and admirals had taken themselves off to the Admiralty in London for confidential planning talks.

While Francis began his medical apprenticeship under the spasmodic tutelage of the mercurial Doctor McParland, the *Mars* prepared for its imminent orders. More men and officers were joining the ship daily; consequently, the demands on the sick bay increased. Back now in Plymouth, the major ailments treated were the effects of drunkenness, whoring and fighting, along with the usual assortment of injuries and ailments expected from a body of soon to be five hundred men. But Francis' duties were still relatively light and he had plenty of free time to explore the ship, make acquaintances and wander the streets of Plymouth town. Indeed, he had not in truth been the green boy for long since the arrival of so many new crew members, both experienced hands and first timers. Thus, he had avoided many of the rites-of-passage that were doled out on the lower decks to unsuspecting new recruits. He had suffered some sea sickness at first, treated by the doctor with peppermint infusions, but as they were either in port or skirting coastlines for most of the next few months, Francis had time to acquire his sea legs without too much discomfort.

He learnt quickly. Within a few weeks, he could abrade an infected wound and stitch up cuts neatly, his initial squeamishness soon overcome by his curiosity about disease and cure. He was eager to learn about different medicines, ointments and preparations, about herbs and roots and the other mysterious botanicals locked up in the dispensary. He bombarded the doctor with questions until he was chased off, then read up medical tomes himself at night, trying to make sense of the details and recommendations. McParland was an old-fashioned doctor, not much given to research and reading new treatises, but he had the knowledge of experience – and an unexpectedly steady hand when performing surgery. Considering he was rarely completely sober, Francis thought this quite an achievement, although he regularly hid the doctor's wine jugs and brandy bottles, doling his measures out carefully to restrict his over-indulgence. He worried that the doctor would find out and rage at him, but after a while, he realised that this was exactly what the doctor had hoped of him: someone to protect him from himself.

He berthed with the men but his days were mostly spent in the sick bay or the doctor's quarters in the orlop. Francis was surprised to find that, although there were some very nasty characters aboard, and the intimidation of the young or weak did occur, a close camaraderie existed amongst the seasoned tars. As the weeks advanced, a protective atmosphere developed that at time was almost maternal. The older men taught the younger how to do their jobs, cope with the restrictions of life in a crowded ship without a moment of privacy, entertain themselves in the long boring hours that were part and parcel of sea voyages, and gave them advice and support when trouble was brewing. Compared to the dog-eating-dog world of Seckford's school, the hierarchy of this world of humble men could teach those on land a thing or two about teamwork.

Evenings were noisy down in the hammocks. Men lay cheek-by-jowl between the guns, sharing the foetid air and the inevitable bodily emissions – and even hammocks when shifts changed. Some played cards for *abel ackets*, a heavy whack on the hand for the loser, which caused much merriment and helped to relieve the inevitable tensions. Others blew on their tin whistles or sang shanties. Older men entertained the younger, wide-eyed boys with lurid tales of adventures at sea, guaranteed to be mostly lies and give the little lads nightmares. Some darned holes in socks or jackets, others knitted ganseys, while those who had managed to stow a bit of extra grog got steadily drunk. Francis grew to enjoy these evening sessions, despite the discomfort of the stifling heat and the sweat of so many none-too-clean bodies. It was a comfortable familiar time, full of teasing and knockabout, that eased the loneliness of life at sea.

One old sailmaker, Billy Goggins, with very few teeth and more hair up his nostrils than on his head, was one night regaling them with a terrifying story about a shipwreck off the coast of Cornwall in a storm, where every man had drowned, even though they were not far from land. That very night the seas were rough and the wind was howling a gale; the ship was lurching about fiercely, the first real taste of storms they had so far encountered. The little lads had already been nervous but were now very frightened.

'I'm a good swimmer,' said Francis. 'I'll bet I could have swum to shore from that ship. Maybe I could teach some of you when we get back to Plymouth? Then you wouldn't be worried about drowning!'

The other men laughed loudly. Billy cackled, his tobacco pipe, anchored precariously to his few remaining teeth, waggling up and down. 'Swim ashore? Sailors don't swim, me lad. You go into the sea, then you better wish you can't swim. Best to go straight down to the bottom than flap about for hours until you die of exhaustion. It's a blessing if you can't swim. Sailors don't swim. We know the sea. If the sea wants you, it'll have you. You can't swim a ship's length in wild seas. Every stroke will throw you back ...' The others nodded. Francis felt foolish. Swimming in the Deben at low tide was hardly to compare with the roiling seas they were now encountering off the south coast. He blushed bright crimson and slumped back down on his hammock, listening to the tittering of the men who were still amused at his show of ignorance. But the moment passed soon enough. Old Billy had already moved on to another topic. That of the fate of the *Mars* itself. He believed the ship to be cursed.

'Shut your mouth, Billy,' shouted Mattie Tibbett, a gunner. 'Stop frightening the young 'uns. If'n you knew it was cursed, what you sign up for, y' old bastard!'

'When your time's up, it's up, matey,' was the old man's morose reply. 'Don't mock. The *Mars* was a Frenchie, captured off the coast of Ireland. Our lads had chased it all the way from Americay. Most of the men were already dead. Plague. Bad luck to be on a plague ship ...'

Linus Dobbs broke in with a grin. 'You were there then, Billy?'

Goggins cleared his throat to spit out at a rat scuffling past. 'I heard about it from a mate. Dead they were. Not enough men left to clear the bodies even ...'

'Well, there's no plague now, Billy. The ship was near rebuilt the past few years. Shut your gob and let a man sleep,' Tibbett rolled over and wrapped himself in his thin blanket.

'Still cursed ...' mumbled Billy. 'Mark my words, you'll see. Fifty years at sea and Billy Goggins knows a thing or two!'

It was an odd sort of family. There was kindness and unexpected sentiment alongside bad language, ribald humour and fisticuffs. The men teased and scared the young ones but took care of them all the same. But then, when it came to the battles ahead, or the task of handling a ship through the rages of a terrible storm in the middle of an open ocean, they had to feel a solidarity that could not be shaken. The sailors had to trust their fellow men. Their lives might one day depend upon each other.

Francis was to discover that the conduct of the upper ranks was somewhat different. Bullying was much more prevalent, on the assumption that harsh and unfair treatment made an officer tougher and less given to mercy when dealing with men beneath him. Fear was probably the one thing that might keep the crew from mutiny in extreme situations when the officers were so outnumbered. An incident one late December night just after Christmas brought this home to Francis. As he was leaving the doctor's cabin, he stumbled upon little Midshipman George Jeffreys curled up in a corner of the orlop by the companionway, snivelling and clutching a locket to his chest.

'Sir, are you well?' Francis asked kindly.

The boy dabbed at his face and made to scramble away upwards, but Francis stayed him. 'Don't run off. Is that your mother, sir?' He referred to the pretty lady on the locket. George nodded, his strangled sob threatening to start the tears rolling again. 'No matter. Everyone has low spirits from time to time. Especially at Christmastide. Why, even some of the grown men cry out for their mothers or their girls in the night! I've heard them in the berths.'

George was heartened by that information. He sat up, his back against the side and opened up. 'It's not just that I miss Mamma, although I do, most dreadfully. But the other gentlemen are so damned unkind to me! They make fun of me. They mock my curls! They call me Georgiana, and a mummy's boy and other dreadful names that I dare not repeat. Y'see, I make such a fearful mess of everything. I cannot work out my calculations and my readings. I make so many mistakes. They will not let me rest!'

Boys could be most unkind if they sensed weakness in another, especially when they themselves were eager to deflect from their own inadequacies and fears. School had taught Francis that already, never mind shipboard life. He considered young George's rosebud mouth, his chubby, pink, tear-stained cheeks and his cap of golden curls. There was no doubt that such a little prince was born to be the butt of other boys.

'You'll learn the ropes in time, Mr Jeffreys. Why not ask Lieutenant Allendale to assist you in your studies? You are fortunate indeed to have an uncle aboard!'

At that George's face fell even further. 'But he's the very worst! He thinks me such a nick-ninny. My father, too! They say Mamma has ruined me and I must go to sea to learn how to be a man! If I complain to him, he would torment me endlessly and write to my father. Then there would be hell to pay when I go on leave. I hate the navy. I never even wanted to go to sea at all. It's so unfair! It's so unfair!'

George thumped his fists against the floor and kicked his heels, for all the world like the spoiled child they accused him of being. Francis' sympathy was wearing thin. What he himself would give for the opportunities George Jeffreys took for granted! But he listened to the boy's grievances and even shared with him some of his own misfortunes. When George dried his eyes, Francis showed him around the dispensary to take his mind off his worries, allowing him to handle the macabre implements of the surgeon's chest, an experience that cheered the young boy up no end.

A few weeks later, on his way to attend a patient in sick bay, Francis had to pass by a group of midshipmen descending from the poop deck. They had been receiving navigational instruction from First Lieutenant Brydges. Francis noticed that young George Jeffreys was among the group, acknowledging him with a smile and a nod. To his astonishment, George leapt forward, his face thrust belligerently into his.

'Who do you think you are, boy! You ought to stand to attention and salute when you see me, never mind grinning over like a loon! Look at this insolent lout, lads, acting above his station. Let's give him a midshipman lesson, eh?' George drew mocking laughter from his fellow midshipmen, who all surged forward, eager for a rumpus.

Francis prepared for a sound beating. He didn't dare defend himself. Whatever they did to him, it would be far lighter than the punishment that he would receive for assaulting an officer. But he glared back at George, a look that showed the younger boy he was in no way fooled by this aggressive behaviour. George had discovered that the coward's way to combat bullying was by becoming one himself, it seemed. The sneer on Francis' lip, unwise perhaps in the circumstances, made plain to George his low opinion of him.

'He needs a sound thrashing,' shouted one older boy whose cap was set at a jaunty angle, a new fashion amongst the young gentlemen.

Approbation from his erstwhile tormentors drove on George's enthusiasm for a scrap. 'He thinks he's a gentleman because he went to a grammar school! But he's a nobody in truth. An orphan boy. Nothing but the leavings of a gentleman!' George had taken Francis' own confidences and thrown them pitilessly back. The other boys tittered and called out 'bastard' and 'by-blow'. Francis' blood boiled. He reared up with a roar, his fists clenched, struggling against the overwhelming desire to give George Jeffreys a bloody nose.

'What's going on, men?' A pair of long legs, followed by the blue jacket and epaulettes of a first lieutenant, appeared down the companionway.

The belligerence subsided instantaneously. The four midshipmen stood to attention, lowering their heads respectfully at the approach of one of the most senior officers on board, upon whose recommendation their very careers depended. Brawling outside the wardroom would be considered evidence of very poor conduct indeed. James Brydges surveyed them coolly for some time, during which they all squirmed with discomfort. He roughly adjusted the jaunty cap to regulation style. The other boys hurriedly righted theirs. The lieutenant did not, however, reprimand them.

'On your way, lads.' Lieutenant Brydges eventually dismissed them, waiting until they had scampered off down the corridor before turning back to Francis. 'Did they mishandle you, boy?'

'No, sir.' Francis' reply was succinct. He would not be a tittle-tale.

Brydges nodded, hardly expecting honesty in the circumstances. 'I heard it from above. It was most uncalled for. But, remember your place in future. Do not presume to mix with your betters. Now, off you go along to sick bay and get on with your duties.'

Later, as he fed slops into the mouth of a sailor raving with a fever, Francis pondered the incident. He couldn't actually blame George Jeffreys. Had those boys ever found out that he had been blubbing to one of the crewmen, his miserable life would be even less worth living. George's fear of discovery as a cry-baby had prompted him to strike out cruelly merely to defend himself from worse. He had learned this strategy out of necessity.

Was that then the rough material that made a man a gentleman? The capacity to brutalise those beneath you? If Jeffreys one day rose through the ranks, what kind of senior officer would he make? Brydges had been kindly enough but he hadn't intervened until he had deemed it entirely prudent – and then had lain the blame firmly at Francis' door. The upper classes looked after their own. Whilst Brydges might mark the boys down for bullying, he might also view their actions favourably, as gentlemen insisting on their due in respect of the improper behaviour of the lower orders. That was simply how it was. It was another important lesson learned.

Nor was he entirely despondent. He had learnt a few things about the Honourable George Jeffreys as well. Who knew when that information might be of advantage? Knowledge was always the ultimate seat of power. After all, he would not always be a loblolly boy.

5

All at Sea

HMS Mars, *Bay of Biscay. April 1755*

By spring, the *Mars* was ready for the off, buffed up like a bridegroom: boards tarred, scrubbed, polished, painted; sails hauled up and down until handling like a well-oiled clock; guns polished and greased, the gunners running them in and out daily until three volleys every five minutes were possible. Even the men looked impressive, the crew in their new issue clothes and neatly braided hair; the officers in their dapper blue and gold. The captain discouraged facial hair, excepting certain older men, like Master Morgan, who wore the fashions of an earlier age. Captain Amherst was a stickler for cleanliness and order. He believed in firm discipline, competence and neat appearance, his definition of 'ship-shape'.

The medical staff aboard had been substantially increased: a few more attendants – true loblollies whose main function was to clean and feed the patients – and a surgeon's mate. Young doctor Henry Marshall had come aboard just before the fleet was due to sail. Despite earlier bemoaning his lack of assistant on numerous occasions, McParland treated Marshall with cool reserve, highly critical of his diagnoses, ever ready to find fault – even when the young man was obviously correct.

Francis observed the interplay of the two men with interest.

While McParland was certainly in need of an assistant physician, this talented young doctor inadvertently exposed too many of the elder doctor's failings. It did not help that the Doctor Marshall, whose cheeks were always a high colour from his regular constitutionals on deck, was highly abstemious and devoutly religious with the fervour of a missionary in wishing to combat the evils of drink and licentious behaviour aboard. It was not an ideal meeting of minds. But Marshall was not ingenuous. He showed deference to his superior and refrained from comments on McParland's heavy drinking and his frequent fruity cursing. To his credit, he bore the disapproval and fault-finding with humility, whilst ploughing his own course regardless. Thus, an uneasy truce was forged between the two doctors, with Francis somewhere in the midst.

Francis spent much of his spare time in the young doctor's company for Marshall was endlessly patient with the boy, recognising that he had a good brain and had already mastered medical skills beyond what was required of him. In the quieter hours, while the surgeon was sleeping off his liquid lunch, Dr Marshall spent his time reading from the chest of books and pamphlets he had brought aboard, from which he encouraged Francis to borrow freely.

'Have you ever thought of medicine as a career, Francis? You have the learning and the interest. You could make a ship's doctor, if you applied yourself.'

Francis grinned back. 'Not me, sir. It's an interesting profession, to be sure, but I don't want to be down here with the sick all my life. I want to have my own ship one day.'

Marshall raised his eyes from his reading, amused by the

boy's guileless honesty. 'I approve of a boy with ambition and vision. It's a hard road ahead you've chosen, but not impossible. You don't seem wet behind the ears, either. If there's anything I can do to help you, I would be happy to assist.'

Francis smiled, genuinely touched by the offer. 'Thank you, sir. You're most kind.' The doctor returned to his book but Francis was not finished. He had something on his mind and this seemed to him an ideal time to broach it. 'If I may interrupt, Doctor? Might I ask you something of a personal nature?' Francis had been hoping for a chance to wheedle some information out of the genial Doctor Marshall, whose open nature seemed ripe for a little gentle manipulation. He hoped he hadn't misread the moment or pushed too far, too quickly.

The doctor gave him a considered look. 'What is troubling you, my boy?' Perhaps young Francis was being bullied – or even molested in unnatural fashion by one of the men. He was aware such things happened in a society where there were no women.

But Francis did not seem unduly distressed, although leaning closer and lowering his voice confidentially. 'Not troubling, exactly, sir. It's just that it seems to me that Dr McParland has been very harsh on you, yet you never seem to be discommoded. Why do you not stand your ground when he opposes your decisions? You are a qualified doctor, too!'

Marshall smiled, relieved that it was merely curiosity not disturbing revelation that had prompted him. 'For many reasons, lad. First, I am not too long out of my own medical studies. I can assure you my professors were much more merciless than the good doctor. Just as the captain is rigid in his expectations of his officers, so I must accept the criticism meted out by my senior officer. Or how else will I learn?'

'But he isn't always right. You know many new things he has never heard of!'

The doctor shrugged. 'That is not significant, Francis. Dr McParland has more experience. Until this voyage I have never been a ship's doctor nor have I ever taken part in action at sea. There will come a time when I will rely completely on his judgement and expertise. My own wounded pride is of little consequence set aside what I can learn from the doctor. And secondly, he is my commanding officer. Naval regulations apply equally to doctors, too.'

'I think he worries that you know more than he does about modern discoveries,' Francis insisted, still worrying the question of fairness.

Dr Marshall looked around to make sure that Dr McParland was still sleeping in the adjoining cabin. Rhythmic snores confirmed it. 'He has suffered greatly in life and deserves our compassion. Captain Amherst knows the doctor's true worth despite his ... shall we say personal idiosyncrasies? McParland is a fellow of great heart who has seen the worst of what war can do to men. And for his charity and forbearance, it seems to him that he has been abandoned by God. He lost his wife and daughter to typhoid whilst he was away on a voyage some years back. He blames himself for saving the lives of others but not being on hand to save theirs.'

Francis felt a sudden sense of shame for his blithe assumptions. He should have known the doctor was carrying heavy burdens. 'Men are driven by such complexities,' Francis observed, almost to himself. 'Nothing is as simple as the sermons tell us.'

'Indeed,' Marshall agreed with a nod. 'You have perception beyond your years, Francis. Many men live their whole lives without considering the sorrows of their fellow men. Whatever your own beliefs, do not condemn people by judging them to your standards. We cannot know what has happened in the lives of others, so we should hesitate to make rash suppositions. Let he who is without sin, cast the first stone, eh? Remember John, Chapter 7, verse 8 ...'

Francis smiled weakly. It sounded vaguely familiar. But whether it was John, Matthew, Mark or Luke, he would not have known. Yet, it had been an informative discussion nevertheless, shedding light on both the surgeon and his mate. Encouraged by a positive response, Francis decided to move on to less weighty matters. The doctor was enjoying the conversation and was evidently eager to take Francis under his wing. It seemed a propitious time to develop their friendship. 'How long until we make the coast of America, Doctor? Is it a fearful long distance?'

Marshall leapt from his seat and indicated the chart on the wall of the cabin. 'See here, Francis? Let's instruct you in a little basic navigation. Can you point to Plymouth?'

Francis surveyed the map with deep concentration. He had little cartographic knowledge, merely a vague idea of the shape of Britain. But he did know that Plymouth lay on the extreme south western end of the island. He tentatively pointed a finger in the general direction until he found the legend 'Plymouth'. 'There! I have found it!'

'Good man,' said the doctor taking Francis' index finger in his own hand and outlining the route the *Mars* was heading. 'It is a fearful distance but a very direct route. First due south ...' and he traced a line downwards. 'We sailed past the coast of Brittany until we entered the wild Bay of Biscay, which is where we now lie. You may have experienced the stronger motion as we left the lee of the coast for open water. We head due west and maintain almost a straight line across the expanse of the Atlantic Ocean. We are crossing in the month of May, so we should expect a comparatively easy journey, although one never can predict this body of water, so I'm told. We shall see a lot of what sailors refer to as "weather" on the way, no doubt. After perhaps four weeks or so ploughing this straight arrow, we arrive at Nova Scotia, please God ...'

'Is that America?' Francis asked.

The doctor nodded. 'We call it Nova Scotia. Do you know your Latin, Light?'

'New Scotland, sir?' It came as a surprise to Francis that for the first time his Latin studies had proved useful to him.

'Correct. It is our territory, named for part of the British Isles, but the French have settled many people there and refer to it as Acadia. They now wish to stake their claim on Nova Scotia, the larger island of Newfoundland, and the territory of Labrador to the north. They have even built forts, attempting to drive us from our own colonies. Thus, we are sent to restore rightful ownership. The fleet assembles off Halifax, then we set out for the Gulf of St. Lawrence. See up here?'

The doctor pointed to the great inlet that separated the continental mainland from the island of Newfoundland and also indicated Labrador and beyond. The names alone thrilled Francis, as did the prospect of this vast icy wilderness. 'Our orders are to prevent reinforcements reaching Québec, the French settlement at the neck of the St. Lawrence river, and to prohibit them rendering aid to other significant forts. We are not strictly at war, Francis. This is mostly a defensive engagement. But we will fight if attacked or threatened. That is our right. We are here to stop the French – and take their ships if necessary. Do the men not speak of our orders amongst themselves?'

Francis nodded. 'They do, but they don't concern themselves with particulars, sir. All the talk is of taking prizes off the French. They are sure of British victories,' he replied.

'Then pray God they are right. But the French also have a great navy which they have been fortifying, just as we. And they are in greater numbers, although we've got the jump on them and should reach our destination well in advance. Our mission is to prevent them reinforcing their settlements with goods and men. We have intelligence that they are carrying thousands of infantrymen aboard their warships, which would give them significant advantage on the ground. They must be stopped! It could mean lengthy blockades or a few short, sharp engagements. We shall see,' Marshall added thoughtfully.

Another question came to Francis as he contemplated the vast expanse of land that encompassed the new territory of America. 'Are there not aboriginals living in Nova Scotia and Newfoundland? I have heard tell of native peoples with savage ways. Where do they live? Do they accept the occupation of their lands by foreign nations?'

Francis' question seemed to confuse the doctor, who frowned as if the very idea caused offence. 'Of course, there are native peoples in America, primitives who have no understanding of God and civilisation. It is our duty to lead them to the light, to save their souls and offer them an honest way of living. That is the purpose of our colonies. To enlighten the darkness of the poor, uncivilised wretches.'

'I expect they don't much like strange people occupying their land though, any more than we would,' Francis observed wryly. 'And I thought we desired the colonies so that we might become more powerful in the world and for Britain to grow rich with the wondrous products of other continents.'

The doctor tutted his disapproval. 'Where do you get these odd notions, Francis? You are a very peculiar boy at times. We are doing a great service to mankind when we deign to cross oceans and save savages from themselves. It is God's work. If wealth should flow from our efforts, then it is because God wills it, thus to aid us in our endeavour …' and he broke into fervent song in a reedy, tuneless voice:

'Rule, Britannia! rule the waves:
Britons never will be slaves!'

The enthusiastic singing caught Francis by surprise, as much as the passionate defence. He had thought Dr Marshall more of a Nonconformist, but it seemed that he was equally convinced of the Divine Right of the English gentleman as were all the other officers.

It also woke up Dr McParland, who stormed from his cabin, 'What the devil is that infernal racket? It sounds like the rats have formed themselves a choir …'

Dr Marshall's embarrassed blush flared from the top of his stock to the roots of his thinning brown hair. 'Excuse me, sir … a patient …' and he dashed out before the surgeon could say more.

McParland stood in the doorway, one arm on the lintel and winked over at Francis. 'That shut him up. I liked your question, boy. I didn't much care for his answer. You were correct. Our country is driven by one thing and one thing only – the pursuit of trade and money. To this end, the lives of ordinary men and women are sacrificed on an altar of greed, without a single care for their humanity. In return, we have to listen to endless religious sermonising to justify our actions, all dressed up in a tubthumping frippery that would make the Good Lord Jesus turn in his own tomb …'

Francis was not sure he understood wholly what the doctor was saying – it was often the case that McParland spluttered out statements that befuddled him. But he felt that something of the doctor's grievances aligned with his own. If a well-educated boy such as he, brought up by a good family, was regarded as a nobody because of his lack of birth, what chance for those who lay at the very bottom of the social order, never mind the rights of poor savages at the ends of the earth? Who would have imagined Dr McParland was the Dissenter after all?

***

The weeks crawled past, every day much the same, as they floundered across the rough Atlantic, the view unchanging, enclosed by the vastness of the sky and the infinite horizon of sea betwixt it and their insignificant wooden world. Below surged the deep troughs of the waves and the foaming white peaks of the breakers, smashing against the hull and then trailing behind, plough lines on an endless field of water. At a distance from time to time, they spotted the occasional whaler. They also glimpsed the other ships of the Boscawen fleet. Acknowledging shots were exchanged, signals were raised, but other than that there was little to break up the endless tedium.

Time was measured in bells and tasks, the men kept busy to distract from the temptations of boredom. Rituals were held: services on Sunday, the daily distribution of the grog ration, the nightly lighting of the smoking lamp in the forecastle for men to enjoy a pipe. Day and night were divided into watches, meals, duties and rest periods. The minutiae of the shipboard activities each had their unique place in maintaining at least the impression of a civilised life aboard a world of men.

One morning, as Francis was on deck posting the binnacle list, he came upon little Jemmie O'Reilly, the youngest boy at scarcely eight years old. He was a powder monkey, a job reserved for the tiniest lads who were able to dodge between the guns, supplying powder for the gunners. It was highly dangerous: the volatility of the combustible powder and the proximity to the fight left these children exposed to great danger. But Jemmie was a cheery soul, one of eleven children born to a poor Irish family. His life aboard the *Mars*, with clean clothes, three meals a day and a tot of rum at night, seemed like Paradise. He was incapable of worrying beyond the current moment; the future held no fear for him, for it was improbable that he would ever reach it.

'Morning, Mr Light. Whatcha doin'?' Jemmie asked, squinting up at the list Francis was pinning.

'It's today's sick list, Jemmie.'

'What's that?' Jemmie replied. Like all young children 'what and why' were his favourite words, until one of the older men chased him off for bothering them.

'It tells those in command which men cannot report for duty on that day on account they are in the sick bay or confined to berth,' Francis replied.

'How do they know what it says?' Jemmie asked.

Francis knitted his brows trying to work out what the little boy meant. 'They read it, of course, Jemmie!'

'What's reading, sir?'

Francis knew that most of the men were unable to read or write; it was hardly necessary for them to do more than recognise their name and make a crude signature. But he could not imagine that there might be those who didn't even know what reading was.

'Have you never seen a book, lad?'

Jemmie shook his head. 'I seen them put our names in a big ledger when we came aboard. Is that a book?'

'Yes, but there are many kinds of books. There are books full of information and also story books. If you learn to read, you can discover many things from books ...'

'Stories like what Billy Goggins tells?' The idea of a story caught Jemmie's interest.

'Yes, but other stories, too. Not always tales that frighten the breeches off you!' Francis laughed. It gave him an idea, something to while away the hours of boredom. 'How would you like me to read to you one night? Then I can show you how reading works. Every mark on the page is a letter. The letters join together to make the sound of the words we speak ... that's reading,' Francis explained, pointing at the letters of the names on the sick list.

'Oi, Jemmie, you idling again and annoying people with your daft questions?' Mattie Tibbett shouted. 'Get below and fetch oil and rags. And when you've finished bring us some biscuits and cheese ...'

That evening Francis gathered some of the younger boys and showed them a book he had borrowed from Dr Marshall, who fully approved of the idea that Francis should read to them, suggesting various religious tracts to improve their minds. Instead Francis helped himself to a copy of *Gulliver's Travels*, settling down in the corner of the gun deck, the boys huddled around him. They were entranced from the first lines. Nor were they the only ones. Nearby sailors listened in, then little-by-little moved closer, the better to hear. They sat down cross-legged and hung on every word, equally caught up in the adventures of Lilliput, Brobdingnag and the brutal Yahoos. From then on, Francis' readings became a popular nightly ritual, attracting a larger and larger audience, until they had to move on deck for more space. It wasn't long before this unusual activity came to the attention of the captain.

At dinner one evening, Captain Amherst raised the subject of the reading of *Gulliver's Travels*. His questions elicited a mixed response from his officers.

'Is literature such as this novel suitable for the common man? The story is allegorical, I believe. Some say that Swift criticises his betters in devious clever fashion. Do we not fear the men might get ideas?' Lieutenant Brydges asked.

Captain Amherst passed the port around as he gave this observation some thought. 'You think the men will understand the deeper significance? Good God, man, I enjoyed it as a tale. I didn't give a thought to its social criticism!' he guffawed. Most of the other officers agreed. They had not construed any hidden subversion beneath the adventures either.

Dr McParland spoke up, a rare occurrence on such occasions when he usually slumped in his chair, taking advantage of the better-quality ports and brandies on offer. 'Light's a good lad. A clever boy. Natural leader, if you ask me, Captain. I cannae think it will do any harm. Much the opposite. The men are being entertained in wholesome fashion, instead of gambling and quarrelling their rest hours away. It's good for discipline and it's good for the soul. I would not like to see it ended,' and with that he accepted the bottle as it circled, and poured himself a large measure.

'I'm inclined to agree with you,' said the captain. 'Let's keep an eye on it for now.' He turned to Dr McParland at the end of the table. 'I'd like to know more about this lad, Thomas, could you give me a few minutes after dinner?'

Unbeknownst to young Light, he had finally achieved his ambition – that of reaching the captain's notice – in a manner he would surely never have anticipated. Later when the other officers had withdrawn to their bunks or watches, McParland remained behind, bleary-eyed but still awake.

'Go easy on the brandy, Tom. You've had enough to sink this ship already,' John Amherst observed with an admonitory grin.

McParland snorted but set down his glass all the same. 'There isn't enough brandy in all the world to sink me, John,' he replied morosely.

'Perhaps. But I want to speak with you while you can still talk some sense. This lad, the one who does the reading ... what's his name again?'

'Francis Light.'

'Hmmm … Francis Light. I recall a letter from his guardian. Isn't he a grammar school boy?'

'Yes, Seckford's in Woodbridge. It's a good school. I know a few colleagues who studied there.'

'How's he shaping?'

'He's done everything asked and more. Reliable and intelligent. He has initiative. Doesn't moan or make excuses. Thinks for himself, a little too much, perhaps …'

'Meaning?' Captain Amherst queried.

'Don't misunderstand me, John. He's respectful and polite. But I can see he has his own ideas. I'm not always certain what goes on in his head. Nonetheless, he has been a boon to me. And he has impressed Marshall greatly. He thinks Light has the makings of a doctor.'

'But you don't?' Amherst asked intuitively.

'Oh, we could make a doctor of him if he had a mind. But that's the thing. He's learning everything but it isn't where his heart lies. He wants to rise, John. For now, he's taking advantage of the sick bay to make a mark. But what he wants is a commission. And by God, he deserves one compared to some of the snot-nosed middies we've been landed with. When will the navy learn to choose the best men for the job and not the ones with the best connections?' McParland slammed down his glass and reached again for the bottle.

Amherst shook his head wryly. He himself was merely the son of a Kent lawyer. It hadn't been easy to reach his current position, fourteen years' service until he was made post, while others jumped ahead through benefit of influence. 'It's the way it is, Tom. It will do no good railing against it, like Canute against the waves. I'll keep an eye on this Light. If an opportunity presents itself, I'll see what I can do.'

They talked on awhile about their mission. In a few days' they would reach the coast of Nova Scotia, to rendezvous with the convoy in Halifax Bay. After that, the realities of engagement would begin. Amherst hoped that a reinforcement fleet of British ships was on its way already or they would be outnumbered. His feelings were mixed. Blockading the forts was one thing but he believed at some point, if they were to make any real progress in this stand-off, open battle would be necessary. They were inching closer and closer to war.

McParland, with his bitter cynicism, had no doubt that hostilities would occur and that lives would be lost on both sides. He knew that an appetite for war was strong amongst both officers and men. Everyone wanted prizes. Nobody considered the human cost. Although Amherst shared some of his concerns on needless glory-hunting, he was a navy captain after all and he too relished the thrill of combat when the moment came. The two men respected each other's stance and agreed to differ.

Finally, they bade good night. Amherst indicated to his manservant that he should help the doctor back to his cabin safely. As they turned to leave, the captain called him back. He rummaged on his shelf and selected a tome, which he handed over to McParland. 'For Light. To read when he's finished Gulliver. The men will enjoy this one. It's a favourite of mine ...'

The book was *Robinson Crusoe.* Dr McParland bowed unsteadily, leaning heavily on the servant's arm. 'You're a good man, John Amherst. With just the right of amount of sentimentality.'

6

The Little Admiral

The Cabot Strait. 6th June 1755

Fog. Dense, drifting banks of fog, deadening sound, dulling vision and confusing senses. For ten long days, the *Mars* had wandered through this vapourish hell, scarce any difference between night and day. If tedium had marked their crossing westwards, the weeks after their rendezvous with Boscawen's fleet had worsened into a sightless nightmare. As they sailed on blind, without point of reference from stars or land, any moment might hurtle them to destruction. The monotony of the past weeks seemed like halcyon days now. The 'weather' was upon them.

Watches had been doubled, then trebled, the duties falling on every able-bodied man, for eyes were their main resource in these hazardous conditions. Night and day, men lined the rails and stared out into the thick brume, often rain-lashed for hours on end, grateful that the deluge at least kept them from sleeping at their posts. One instance of inattention could mean the death of all. In silence, sailors and officers together gazed off out into the gloom, searching for the unexpected light, the tell-tale shadow of rocks, or their greatest fear: icebergs, calved in the far north as pack ice thawed in the warmer currents of the spring and early summer. Everyone was exhausted from both lack of sleep and the cold grip of fear, not to mention two months at sea with scant fresh food left, their diet mainly aged salt beef and hard tack. Even ale and rum were closely rationed.

Their arrival off Nova Scotia had initially augured well; the fleet had met up and found themselves well ahead of the French, the ideal advantage in the cat-and-mouse to come. There was further good news: Admiral Holbourne was by now only a few weeks behind, bringing a second fleet of seven more warships. Their numbers would be equal to the French, who would run straight into this mighty gauntlet.

The seas were full but the weather was brisk and sunny. Spring in these waters came with abundant marine and bird life and long, bright days. Plenty of traffic passed them in the strait, usually keeping at a safe distance. Fishing fleets and whalers were loath to risk contact with warships; many of these smaller vessels were French or Spanish, both natural enemies of the British forces.

Boscawen, the famous Cornish vice-admiral, himself boarded the *Mars* in the days following their rendezvous, the other captains already assembled to greet him. Six ships were to accompany his on patrol through the southern waters of the Gulf of St. Lawrence, whilst the balance of the fleet would remain to blockade Québec and await the arrival of the rest.

Francis was on deck to witness the arrival of the dignitaries, particularly eager to catch a glimpse of the famous Admiral Boscawen, the great hero of Portobello and Cartagena. He took his place at the end of the line of ordinary seamen, ducking under the arms of older men to secure a better vantage. The crew were arrayed in their best, all spruced and combed, equally keen to spot 'Old Dreadnought', as Boscawen was fondly known.

The boarding was conducted in full ceremonial, as befitted

the assemblage of seven captains of the Royal Navy and a Vice-Admiral of the Blue. The boatswain piped the signals. Several seamen, designated as 'sideboys', ran forward to assist, anticipating a weighty load of well-fed Cornishman, typical of a senior officer of lofty reputation and station. The entire roll call snapped to attention, every hat or cap or woollen bonnet tucked beneath the arm. A smart salute in unison was given by the captains, the officers in their resplendent gold and blue dress uniforms, and all the lower ranks of sailors, right down to little Jemmie, who had even taken the trouble to slick back his hair with who knew what substance.

A stifled ripple of amusement spread through the congregation when the admiral jumped sprightly over the side, apparently in no need of assistance. Edward Boscawen was not as they expected. Where they had envisaged an aging admiral of imposing stature with the prosperous belly of a man of the highest rank, there stood a nimble forty-year-old, who might have passed for younger. He was a diminutive figure, astonishing considering the magnitude of his name, for all the world more like a child dressed up in the uniform of an admiral. Edward Boscawen resembled a lively bird, constantly twitching and turning, his eyes black and beady, missing nothing. His head was small, his nose beak-like curved, his hair sleek and brown. The admiral's physique was remarkably lithe and slender; even his hands were soft and white, and his feet were narrow and pointed, as comely as a girl's. Everything about him was smart and spotless, from his immaculate uniform to his carefully coiffured hair, as if he had just stepped out from a gentlemen's outfitters in the Strand. It was near impossible to imagine such a fop about town, such an effete and tiny man, commanding sailors in the sweaty cauldron of a naval bombardment, yet he had the decorations to prove it.

The captains and their officers completed their pageantry of welcome. The 15-gun salute boomed out, volley after volley, assaulting the virgin environment with a foretaste of things to come. The officer party was then swept off below, where the cooks had somehow managed (with a great deal of trips between vessels to supplement their waning supplies) to produce an excellent lunch, followed by several hours of talks, dry throats moistened with copious amounts of wine and brandy. It was rumoured that the admiral ate like a bird and drank like a maiden. The men were sorely disappointed that their hero had such feet of clay, or rather of dainty buckled shoes.

'Here's to Our Beloved Majesty, King George!' Boscawen raised the loyal toast and the entire company stood to lift their glasses to the king far away in whose name this action was to be conducted. They sat back down. The niceties and chit chat were accomplished and the business of the day was about to begin.

Boscawen outlined his intention. 'We are not at war. But soon will be. One side will break this stalemate and hostilities will be declared. I, for one, do not intend for us to be caught napping. If we are to fight – then we shall lead the attack. If we take the fight to them, we shall win. I say we bite them hard and push the advantage. We want ships and prizes, which will require seamanship of the first order, close contact, and stout hearts for boarding. Hand-to hand combat if required. Don't fire, my lads, until you see the whites of the Frenchman's eyes! Some of their ships are carrying infantry. Sink those. Every dead French soldier is a living Redcoat. Remember that!'

The captains nodded solemnly, although not all appeared in agreement with the bellicosity of the war talk. John Amherst's face was set, his lips pressed tight together as if attempting to control his urge to disagree. The captain of the *Anson*, Robert Man, looked around the table, seeking support for a more cautioned approach. His eyes met Amherst's; they exchanged a meaningful glance.

'Let's raise a toast to the admiral!' cried Lord Richard Howe of the *Dunkirk*, the youngest captain by far, the age of most lieutenants. 'We are indeed fortunate to be led by such a noble sailor who has brought us countless times through the trials of battle to the glorious skies of victory!' His sycophantic ardour made objection to the admiral even more difficult.

'The men are tired, sir ...' Captain Alexander Colville interjected in firm but measured tones. 'It has been a long crossing. I have scurvy, diarrhoea, vomiting and infections galore on the *Northumberland*. No man has had a decent sleep in days. We're low on food and our water is stale. Ale and rum are in short supply. We need to put ashore to take advantage of this lull to recuperate so that we may be fit and healthy when the enemy arrives worn out by the crossing.' He spoke equally for Amherst and Man, aware that their position as officers of humbler origin put them at a disadvantage amongst the mostly aristocratic warmongers, or at least ambitious careerists hanging on the shirttails of their betters. Colville was Viscount of Culross, a Scottish lord of ancient family. He had no need to pander to the others.

The admiral scoffed at the suggestion, waving his elegant hand dismissively. 'Fie, man! We could find ourselves blockaded by the Frenchies while the men whore and drink themselves into worse conditions than a touch of scurvy and a bout of the shits!'

'Sir? If I may?' Thomas Andrews, captain of the *Defiance* broke in, deferring to his commanding officer. 'I concur that while the journey has taken its toll on the men, conditions are in no wise different for the French. This is the navy. We endure and we win. It would be dereliction, in my humble opinion, to have this opportunity and let it slip by mollycoddling the men. They would not thank us for it, either. These men want prizes! That will perk them up. Just see if it don't!'

There was general agreement around the table, accompanied by the thumping of fists and the clinking of glasses. The admiral surveyed the table in satisfaction, smugly pleased that most seemed to share his opinion. But he was not satisfied until all had shown themselves ready to accede to his will. 'Amherst? You haven't spoken ...'

The captain of the *Mars* was in a quandary. His career might depend on his answer for Boscawen did not like to be gainsaid. He cleared his throat, took a swig of port, and spoke: 'I see both sides of the argument, sir. No doubt the men would benefit from respite on land. We may face months at sea ahead. Yet, if we control these waters in advance, the moment lies with us.' He paused, aware that he had not answered the real question asked.

'That is not an opinion, Amherst. It is an equivocation. Are you for or against immediate deployment?' The cards were on the table. He could not escape.

Captain Amherst pursed his lips, then made up his mind. 'On balance, against, sir. I think we are not ready for wholesale war. It would be preferable to strengthen the men and wait for the second fleet. My doctors also report serious issues with the men's health. It may affect our performance in an engagement.'

The table fell silent. Robert Man took the moment to add his own weak contribution. 'I would tend to agree with Captains Amherst and Colville.' It fell on the gathering like the craven attempt to hide behind others that it was.

Admiral Boscawen gave a curt nod, accompanied by a mirthless smile. 'Thank you, gentlemen. For the record, Captains Spry and Colby? Would you favour a more "courageous" approach?' He turned his gaze on the two remaining men, Sir Richard Spry of the *Fougueux*, a fellow Cornishman, and the elderly Captain Colby, the commander of Boscawen's own flagship, the *Torbay*. Neither man would be inclined to contradict the admiral.

They both nodded eagerly, gushing forth their agreement.

'Then, the vote is cast in my favour. Five against three. We are for sea, men. I will make note of the objections of Captains Colville, Amherst and Man. It will be reported in my log ...' Admiral Boscawen's menacing tone was clear. He would not forget this opposition.

The upshot of the most interesting day for several months on the *Mars,* was that they were not to put in for a few days ashore to revictual and rest, as everyone sorely needed. Instead, the admiral intended to seize the advantage and keep the fleet at sea, so that they might intercept the French as they arrived in dribs and drabs. That way lay easy pickings. The British ships would soon be pocketing rich spoils in prize money. The men were heartily cheered at the prospect, even if they had been looking forward to sampling the many delights of Halifax town. Money in the pocket was a significant motivator of tired men.

The two doctors, however, were mightily displeased at the

news. Sickbay had seen men with scurvy already; a few of the boys had bad cases of rickets. Fresh food and water were essential. The fleet needed to recuperate before engaging on a battle footing. For what good would it be if they were all too sick to fight? And it seemed that fight they would. Boscawen, for all his elegant refinery and finicky appetite certainly had the stomach for engagement. His personal interpretation of his admiralty orders was to fire on and capture – or at the very least destroy – as many French ships as possible. He was not interested in long blockades and months of inactivity.

'He's a glory-seeker,' McParland told Marshall one day as they were reviewing patients in his cabin but had inevitably returned to the subject of the intransigent Admiral. 'It's well known but tolerated as long as he gets the required results. I suspect that's why they put him in charge of the fleet. If anyone will provoke hostilities, it's Edward Boscawen.' McParland evidently disapproved of the commander.

Marshall was outraged. 'I thought war was only to be countenanced as a last resort! Surely we are here primarily to keep the peace between the two nations!'

McParland laughed heartily, 'If you believe that, sir, you have a lot to learn about the Royal Navy and the politics of Westminster. It's a bear pit. War is the meat that feeds the beast. Oh, they make pretty enough speeches about peace and harmony between nations but anyone who promotes compromise or negotiation is seen as an appeaser. Nothing wins power so much as a good war and a few famous victories.'

'But the waste of human life!' the idealistic Marshall exclaimed.

'Casualties of war, my boy. It's enough to drive a man to the bottle, eh?' he quipped as he poured himself a glass. Marshall shook his head sadly. 'Now, to the matter in hand. How many with scurvy?'

'Forty-nine in the early stages, twenty-odd manifesting bleeding gums and fatigue, and eight in a serious condition with fungous flesh, putridity and wounds that will not heal. I suspect more cases imminent. There'll be a lot of men who haven't yet reported sick.'

'Many had weakened constitutions even before we sailed. We could soon have a quarter of the men afflicted,' McParland groaned. 'And that's before we take account of the fevers and the rickets, the venereal disease, the chronic ailments and the day-to-day injuries. We'll be lucky if we aren't tossing bodies overboard in their dozens before we see Halifax.'

Marshall sighed, then began shuffling through his papers looking for something. 'I have just read a very interesting treatise by a Dr James Lind. He's from Edinburgh, sir. Are you acquainted?'

McParland rolled his eyes. 'I'm from Aberdeen, man! I am not familiar with every damn Scotsman ...'

Marshall blushed and cleared his throat to hide his embarrassment. 'I thought perhaps you had read his work on the subject of scurvy. It's causing quite a stir already, even though it was only published these two years' past. During his time as ship's surgeon with the Mediterranean fleet on the *Salisbury,* he conducted a clinical experiment on twelve sailors with the disease. He tried six well-known treatments on the men in groups of two: cider, elixir of vitriol, vinegar, sea water, a paste of various botanicals, a drink of two oranges and one lemon daily. The two men who drank the citrus water recovered so quickly that they were soon nursing the others! If only we had some oranges …'

McParland exhaled impatiently. 'Yes, let's just ask the captain to make a detour down to Jamaica for some limes. How the blazes will that help our current predicament, Marshall?'

'I was just remarking that it is something we should consider in future …'

McParland gave him the full benefit of his intimidating stare. 'Is it possible you could stay here in the present with us and not in the realm of fantasy, doctor? Perhaps, as Dr Lind believes, some quality of the citrus is the key. But until such time we venture into Spain for its oranges or Italy for its lemons, then my suggestion is to ask the little boys to catch as many rats as they can. Give them a farthing each, that'll get them going …'

'Rats?' Marshall queried. 'To what end?'

The doctor rested back in his chair and tapped his nose. 'Old sailors' remedy for scurvy. Skin a few rats and add the flesh to the gruel in sick bay. It won't cure them but it slows the progression of the disease. It will give us some time. We may not have oranges, sir, but of rats we have plenty. It has the added benefit of keeping down their number.'

Marshall tried to make the doctor see reason, citing the possibility of disease from the rats spreading to the men, but McParland was obdurate.

A few of the youngest boys were offered a monetary reward for rats, under the pretence of reducing their numbers in the dwindling stores. Little Jemmie proved the champion rat-catcher, his pockets permanently stuffed with bodies, amassing quite a sum in coin. 'I used to catch 'em for me Ma,' he observed when complimented for his skills. 'We had 'undreds of 'em in our place.' Marshall did not dare inquire as to his mother's purpose, suspecting that the rodents may have been a food source for the starving family. The loblollies were instructed in the preparations of the porridge – and sworn to secrecy. No man would eat or even report sick if he suspected what was being fed in sickbay, should the story come out.

Thus, the unorthodox treatment was ladled out meal after meal, and to Marshall's astonishment, the results were remarkably promising. Just as McParland had said, the men were not cured but their condition did improve, sufficiently in many cases for light duties to be resumed. The worst of the outbreak was kept at bay for the time being. An unexpected consequence of the treatment was that many of the patients, formerly exhibiting the dejection of spirits that always accompanied scurvy, now began to show more interest in life, particularly at meal times. 'I never ate gruel so tasty,' one said. 'Just like my mother used to make,' said another. 'The good doctor even put some meat in it!' Marshall recorded his findings with incredulity. Medical school had surely never prepared him for the likes of this.

***

The flotilla of seven ships had sailed out in a convoy, scattered across a wide area for maximum coverage, but in sight of each other. They headed for the Gulf of St. Lawrence to pick off French ships on course for the southern coast of Newfoundland. But either the French ships were delayed or providence was against them: time and time again, the enemy eluded them, until it seemed that they were sailing in an empty sea.

And then came the fog. The weather had been changeable throughout, very wet but not overly cold. It was late May when they had set out, and mild summers were to be expected in these seas. But the further north they sailed, the more unpredictable the weather became.

Older hands shook their heads. 'S'always like this in these waters. If'n you don't like the weather one minute, no mind. It'll change before the next bell ...'

They entered the first fog banks on the 25th of May, passing within minutes from blustery but fair, a blue sky spattered with spots of white cloud, to a swirling miasma, conjured up by some malicious spirit to confound them. At first it was more mist than fog, but day by day visibility decreased until lookouts spotted a small iceberg some distance off to the northwest, but a worrying development, no less. How many more were drifting in this channel?

Then, finally, a different sighting on the eastern horizon when the worst of the fog began to dissipate. Through swirls of vapour, they made out distant objects. This was no frozen rock. Five, six, no – seven far-off ships, full-sailed and on course for their position! Warning shots were fired. It was either Holbourne's fleet or French vessels detached from their armada in the fog. No answering cannonade replied, no friendly flag was raised. It was indeed the enemy, which immediately made to scatter. Feverish activity erupted on all sides as the *Mars* tacked and raised sail: seven British warships on the chase of seven French. The odds were even. How could the British navy lose? Anticipation billowed through the ranks.

And then the fog descended again, appearing from nowhere to pitch them back into a blind and soundless world, where even the wind and waves were silenced by the all-encompassing blanket of grey. It seemed that God might be a Frenchman. No thoughts of prizes now; self-preservation was their one consideration. For nigh on a week they lay stranded in this state, sails furled, on constant watch and in constant fear, grappling poles and hooks to the ready in the event an ice floe should rear up, the ship was dragged by currents onto unseen rocks, or another disoriented vessel should loom up on collision course.

During the morning of June 7th, the fog began to burn off; first thinning to a thick mist, then a swirling vapour, and at last, by early afternoon, jagged patches of blue emerged from the wispy grey remnants. Then came the cheers, gaunt faces flushing in expectation as they saw what lay ahead. God was an Englishmen after all! Three French ships in reaching distance – and fair weather ahead. Seven ships bore down on the enemy. There could be no escape.

The *Torbay* raised a signal for the *Mars*, the *Nottingham* and the *Anson* to stand off, while the other four ships surrounded the French vessels. Amherst waited impatiently on deck for his orders to arrive, his gaze firmly fixed on the impending negotiation. It made sense that some of their ships should be held in reserve in the event that a French vessel might slip through the cordon, but it came as no surprise to Amherst which three captains had been left in the rear. A launch came by and an oilskin bag was raised over the side. The captain ripped it open, fumbling the parchment in his hurry to read the contents.

'By God!' he gasped, his face paling, his body tense with anger, controlling his urge to vent his feelings openly. His men looked in askance at each other.

'Our orders, sir?' asked Lieutenant Brydges tentatively. Master Morgan's face was grim, expecting the worst and already turning towards the helm.

With remarkable self-discipline, Captain Amherst composed himself and addressed the gathered officers. 'We are to withdraw, along with the *Nottingham* and the *Anson*. It is the opinion of Admiral Boscawen that our men are not battle-ready, due to sickness and general poor health.' He spoke through gritted teeth, his voice gruff with bitter resentment. 'We are to return forthwith to Halifax – and mend.'

The announcement rippled through the ranks, astonishment followed by the murmurings of dissent and even anger. The crew to a man was furious. They were not only denied action but were being sent away even before the fight was joined. It was a grave injustice that meant, after all they had endured, they were to be forbidden a share of the prize money.

'Didn't I tell you we was accursed,' crowed Goggins. 'This ship will never take a prize. We're lucky that it's still afloat.' His ramblings suddenly took on the ring of prophesy.

In defiant silence, the men followed the commands to raise sail, but their glowering truculence simmered all the while. They had no understanding of the whys and wherefores but suspected that these unexpected orders were some form of punishment. The three captains must have disagreed with the admiral. Now all the men were paying the price for their officers' bad judgment. They had suffered the deprivations of the journey for nothing.

Captain Amherst remained on the poop deck for a time, staring stern-faced back at the action as they sailed away from it. He spoke to no one. No one dared address him. Finally, he lunged for the mizzen, climbing up with an ease that belied his thirty-seven years. From the lookout, he glowered at the disappearing ships. From that vantage he witnessed the opening shots of the engagement. The British fired first, to devastating effect.

The first hostile shots of what would be seven long years of war had been discharged. The French responded with gusto, the subsequent battle raging for five hours, but the victory, as to be expected in the circumstances, went to the British. The *Alcide* and the *Lys* were captured; the third ship, the *Dauphin Royale*, however, managed to slip away late in the day under a sinking fog. Had the three other ships still been present, it would have been apprehended, although no mention of this possibility was included in the dispatches. It was generally regarded as a fine victory and a worthy prelude to the forthcoming campaign, justifying the declaration of war.

Meanwhile the disregarded ships were on their way back to Halifax, unaware as yet of the outcome of the battle. That night on board the *Nottingham*, the three captains reviewed their predicament in the light of Boscawen's mean-spirited retribution. Their unanimous decision was to make for Halifax as ordered – but in sluggish fashion. The excuse of fog banks could be utilised should they need to explain any delay. They aimed to apprehend some French ships for themselves on the way back. For who could condemn them if they brought back spoils?

Several weeks they lingered fruitlessly in the channels, making vain chase a few times but failing to secure a prize, until it was decided that they dare not stay out longer for fear the others should reach port before them. Their luck was evidently in short supply. It was also likely some consequences would be faced by the captains in the near future, particularly if Boscawen returned covered in laurels. Old Billy Goggin's fateful words began to carry the weight of premonition.

7

Scylla and Charybdis

Halifax Bay. 24th June 1755

Shrouded in a deep dark spattered with isolated lights, the coast of Nova Scotia loomed; the *Mars* had finally reached the shelter of Halifax Bay. At last they were in sight of land after near three months at sea. As they made their approach, a summer storm was rising, driving them to the west of the entry channel, visibility limited further by a heavy mist and even heavier swell. Their world took on the entire spectrum of night from blue-black to coal: land, sea and sky merging as one. The *Nottingham* and the *Anson* lay off in the rear on a similar course.

The men were less sullen now, resentment replaced by merry expectation after the weeks of intensity in fog and enemy seas. On deck, one man started up a shanty and others joined in. No reprimand demanded silence of them while they carried out their tasks this time. Even the watch officer grinned and sang along. The atmosphere was almost festive, the nearer they came to the port and its many delights.

'When I was a little boy, so me mother told me,
Way haul away, we'll haul away, Joe!
That if I did not kiss the girls, me lips they would grow mouldy.
Way haul away, we'll haul away, Joe!'

Up on the quarterdeck, Master Morgan alone appeared unsettled, regularly ordering soundings and muttering to himself. He knew these waters well; anyone paying close attention would have observed uncharacteristic discomfort in the usually unflappable master. 'I'm not liking the feel of these currents. We're too westerly. Hold to the middle channel,' he ordered his mate, 'and pray ask the captain to join us. I need his eye ...'

His mind momentarily distracted – itself an indicator of the level of his concern – Morgan failed to avoid an overhanging spar and took a blow directly to his forehead. He reeled back on impact, blood gushing into his eyes. Sailors ran forward to assist but he shrugged them off, pulling at his neckerchief, mopping vainly. It was of little use. The gaping scalp wound would need attention. Slamming his hand down on the rail, he called Parry, his mate. 'Take the helm, sir. I need a stitch from the doctor. I'll not be long. You're in command until the captain relieves you. Keep away from the west channel and your eyes peeled!'

Francis was down in the orlop, packing a bag for Doctor McParland who planned to visit a friend in Halifax when they put ashore. Marshall was attending to a patient on the surgery table in the open space outside the cabins, manipulating a dislocated shoulder into place. Urgent pounding of feet and raised voices alerted them to the arrival of a new patient. Then down the companionway stumbled the master, heavily supported by a seaman, both bloodstained.

'Get this sewn up ... I'm needed on deck!' the master gasped.

Francis dashed forth to lend assistance. They hauled the patient off the table with little ceremony, leaving a loblolly to complete the binding of his arm. Morgan was lowered down and

Marshall examined his wound.

'I can give it a stitch but you must stay down here under observation, sir. You took a bad knock. I fear concussion,' he observed.

'Bind me up, man! I need to be on deck!' Morgan was already struggling up, fighting off the medical staff. 'Let me go!'

Then he froze, sensing an unnatural motion, his attention now fixed on the movement of the vessel. A shuddering convulsion caused the entire ship to lurch at an obscene angle, immediately followed by a hideous, juddering groan, the splintering of weathered timber and the thunderous grating of hull against rock. 'Dear God!' Morgan exclaimed, his face sepulchral white beneath the blood spatter. 'We've run aground!'

The ship continued to heave and roll, lamenting like a great beast felled. Beneath them they could both feel and hear the displacement of the cargo, as the load was tossed about like trinkets, metal crashing against wood. From their position on the open platform of the orlop, they had to brace themselves against the danger of sliding over into the deep chasm of the hold or being dashed against the wooden hull. Peering over into the bowels below, a scene of disaster lay before their eyes. Seawater seeped through shattered beams, here and there already spurting strong. Alarm bells sounded far above them but strident enough to be faintly heard even where they were. Guns rolled about the deck above, having broken free of their moorings. It was the very Apocalypse.

'Above!' Men dashed for the stairs, dragging the master and the other injured sailor, pushing each other upwards. Temporarily paralysed with fear, Francis remained rooted to the spot.

'Francis! Get a hold of yourself! To the deck!' Dr McParland grabbed his shoulder, thrusting him onto the steps roughly. It was enough to spur him into action. He shinned up, waiting at the top to give a hand to the doctor. Then they made their way, accompanied by the stampede of men, dragging injured along with them. It was an organised chaos. The men were panicked but knew that any chance of survival lay in orderly behaviour. Such was the benefit of the endless hours of drills and the experience of the older hands.

'Will we sink, sir?' Francis gasped to the doctor as they emerged on the deck.

'The ship's gone but not all is lost,' the doctor answered, indicating the two other companion ships standing off a distance. Lanterns were flashing signals and boats were already being launched. 'We can abandon into the boats, lad. See, the shore is only a short way off! Fishing boats are setting out to help us, too. Their lights are bobbing over the wave!' It was true. From both land and sea, rescue was at hand. They had been fortunate indeed, if providence could be cited in such circumstances.

'But what if the ship breaks up before they reach us?' Francis cried, staring in horror at the sight that met their eyes.

McParland shook his head. 'It'll take the best part of a day, God willing. We are holed but the rock will hold us for a time. Pray it will be long enough!'

Francis accompanied the doctor towards the quarterdeck astern, staggering and grabbing at any stable object against the pitching of the helpless vessel, tossed at the mercy of the wild waves. Captain Amherst called them forward. He was without his coat or hat, his shirt unbuttoned at the neck, caught as he had been relaxing in his cabin and looking forward to the imminent landing. There was no sign of panic in his face; he was calm and focussed on the task in hand now that the dread moment of shipwreck had arrived. 'Come up, doctor. Have we casualties?'

McParland dragged himself up, the full force of the wind almost knocking him back down. Francis sidled up next to him, out of both curiosity and the need to shelter against a protective figure. He was only a boy when all was said and done. No one objected; it was unlikely he was even noticed amidst the general alarm. 'Master Morgan is concussed, sir. There are minor injuries. But as yet no reports of anything more serious. However, I would recommend a search. Bodies may have been overlooked.'

The captain nodded, directing Lieutenant Allendale to assemble a party to ensure all the decks had been fully evacuated. The doctor joined him as they surveyed their predicament. 'Our chances, sir?'

Amherst shrugged. 'Good to fair if the boats can reach us. The men can be offloaded. We shall pray for no loss of life. The old *Mars* is done but she will take her time a-dying. We're safe for the time being. But I want the guns, Tom. I will not lose them!' He intended to haul all the guns onto barges and lighters, an ambitious plan. 'It can be done. But it will delay the evacuation. We'll first take off the young and old, the injured and infirm, but any able-bodied men will be needed to haul the cannon.'

'Brydges!' he broke off, and called the first lieutenant over. 'Assemble the first group for the boats. The little lads, the old men and the infirm.'

'Yes, sir!'

'They cannot get aside, Captain!' called Morgan, wearing a

crude bandage oozing blood; he had insisted on being in the thick of the deliberations. 'The seas are too powerful. The lighters and the little boats would be driven onto the rocks. We need to rig a pulley.'

The captain leaned over to assess their situation. The ship had reared up on the hidden rock and was now too high above the water for access. The shoals and the ship together created a deadly vortex, which threatened to suck in and smash any boat that ventured near. Seconds ticked by in silence, broken only by a wavering voice from amidst those assembling for evacuation. 'I knowed this ship was accursed! Didn't I say so, lads?' Billy Goggins was crowing, obscenely proud to have been the portent of disaster all along.

'Shut that damned man up!' commanded Amherst. 'Or I'll throw him overboard myself, irrespective of his age! Damn bloody fool!' Goggins raised his arm as if to fend off a blow as Brydges pushed him roughly towards the rear of the line. Little Jemmie meanwhile whimpered and hid his face in his hands.

'We need a man who can swim,' Captain Amherst said pensively. 'A volunteer. He will be roped and ballasted. If he can reach the nearest lighter then we can rig up a seat to get the men off, and a pulley to move the guns ...'

The men on the quarterdeck looked around at each other. 'Jump into that maelstrom and swim across! It's certain death, John!' McParland forgot himself in his astonishment at the suggestion, addressing the captain by name, a serious misdemeanour on the quarterdeck, but it passed unremarked.

'Goddamit, man! It's certain death if we don't!' the captain bellowed back.

At first there was silence. Then the master sent the mate to ask around the men, while the officers spoke amongst themselves. There was no movement from either group to suggest that anyone was stepping forward.

Suddenly a small voice spoke up. 'I'll do it, sir.' Francis was noticed for the first time.

The captain's head swivelled round, astonished as he saw the source of the offer. 'Who in God's name are you, boy? And what are you doing on the quarterdeck?' he exclaimed in disbelief at the boy's brave proposition.

'Francis Light, sir. I can swim. Quite well. I can try to take the line across, sir.'

'No, Francis!' yelled Dr McParland. 'You're just a boy! The waves will swallow you whole! Have you seen the seas?'

Francis looked over the side, momentarily baulking at the ferocity of the crashing waves. The sea was a vast bottomless cauldron with mighty surges and gigantic eruptions of spray, churning and boiling like a monstrous living entity of destruction. It was a scene from ancient legends, the terror of Scylla and the deadly whirlpool of Charybdis. He swallowed hard, petrified with fear. 'I shall try. I will do my best, sir.'

There was no shaking him. Nor were there any other volunteers to call upon. Three times the captain challenged the older men to come forward, beseeching them not to let a mere boy risk his life on their behalf. But no man stepped out. Few could swim; the rest would never admit it.

The boy was their only chance. In no time at all, they stripped him down to shirt and breeches, secured a stout line around his waist, and found a sturdy timber spar for flotation. The captain gave his directions and exhortations. Francis was to make for the nearest launch, already brightly lit with lanterns, a beacon amidst the hellish waters. 'Make for the light, Light!' the captain encouraged him, squeezing his arm fondly. 'You are the bravest lad I've ever seen. When you reach that boat, you will be a hero. Make for the light, I say, Mr Light. It is no more than half a furlong!'

Half a furlong. He could run that in a few minutes. He had swum twenty times that in the river Deben. Francis was helped up on to the lower rail, supported by the men who knew him best. All fell silent, in respect of his sacrifice. Linus Dobbs, no longer the cocky lad now that he was in the face of impending drowning, whispered, 'Go, Frannie, lad! You can do it, mate!'

Francis looked down at the abyss. Captain Amherst continued his encouragement: 'Jump well away from the ship, Francis. As far as you can jump. Then dive and rise, dive and rise until you see the lights!' He barely heard. Now, at the moment of decision, his courage almost failed him. What man could throw himself willingly to certain death? His whole body shook, from fear and cold; he was already soaked to the skin in the hammering rain and the fierce spray.

The image of his mother, Uncle William and Aunt Margaret, his school friends, Reverend Ray … so many people he had known and loved all his life appeared before his eyes. What would they think if they saw him now? He knew not what they would say, but he knew for sure what comfort they would gain if they heard of this deed in the years to come. If he died tonight, he would die a hero; someone would remember him, he felt sure. But if he was lost when the ship went down with the rest of the men, he would be nothing but another dead sailor. At least his family and friends would have the comfort of knowing what he had attempted for the sake of others. He would no more be a worthless bastard, but a man of courage who had risked all to save his friends.

With one mighty heave, he tossed the wooden spar from him as far as he could – it would only hinder him – and then dived headlong in its wake. He did not hear the shout raised by his heroic action nor the screams and exhortations that followed. Down, down, he went into the cold, black water, into a vortex so strong that he was sucked far, far below – and then by some miracle spewed out until he surfaced in a violent burst that all but stunned him. Gulping and spluttering, temporarily blinded by the deep trenches of the waves and the stinging salt, he treaded water to steady himself until his vision cleared sufficiently to search for the lights. The starry sky had never looked so brilliant. Then he was thrown up on a crest and saw, away to his left, the flickering gleam of safety.

No thought from then on but survival. He plunged, kicked, kicked again and rose, plunged, kicked, kicked again and rose. Over and over he went, heading for the lights until his movements became merely mechanical, his own strength long depleted, only determination and the will to live propelling him forward. He expected to die. He thought that perhaps he was drowning but his brain did not yet understand. Shadowy figures lurked at the edge of his vision, ghosts of sailors long drowned dragging him to the bottomless deep, like one of old Goggins' tales? Or perhaps his true parents come to take him home at last? But he would not go with any of them. They would not have him. Again, he dived, and again he rose and on and on and on ...

When the launch of the *Nottingham* pulled young Francis Light from the water, scooping him out on a grappling pole like a huge fish, they thought the boy had drowned. For tense moments water was pumped from his lungs as they pummelled on his back. There was no sign of life. The boy lay wan and ice cold, already a corpse.

Whilst this frantic attempt at resuscitation took place on the floor of the boat, other men were hauling on the rope Francis had carried round his waist. It towed over the mighty cables, a huge sea serpent slithering through the dark, churning surge. A pulley was rigged and then more ropes were conveyed to other vessels to set up similar. The evacuation had begun.

And just when they had given up all hope on the poor lad, Francis opened his eyes, staring wide as if he had seen a ghost, then vomiting the detritus of the sea upon the boards. He drew a lungful of air, gaping about. 'I am not dead?' he gasped. The sailors laughed as they wrapped him in blankets. 'Not yet, lad,' said one, 'but you came fuckin' close, to be sure. You saved your men, boy. Every last one of them. Officers and tars. Even the bloody guns are being shifted. I'm damned if I've ever seen the like ...'

PART TWO

The English Captain

(1763-1769)

8

The Navy List

The Admiralty Office, Whitehall, London. 14th May 1763

It had not been easy to extricate himself from the tender mercies of Aunt Louisa at whose unexpectedly fine rooms in Conduit Street he had been staying during his London sojourn. After years at sea, the fussing and fretting of women was alien to Francis. Aunt Margaret's sister-in-law, Miss Louisa Stoker, a spinster fortunate enough to have inherited from both her father and elder brother, still regarded Francis as a boy, despite the fact that he was now two and twenty and a battle-seasoned naval officer. She rarely had visitors, so a handsome young lieutenant was more excitement than she had known in years. Francis descended the steps at a pretty pace, concerned that she might follow up on her original suggestion to accompany him to the Admiralty itself.

It was a mild morning with more than a touch of summer in the air, but the scudding clouds hinted at rain to come. He rounded the corner onto Bond Street with the intention of hiring a hackney, preferring not to arrive sweaty and dusty for an appointment of this magnitude. Approaching a jarvey lounging by the side of his carriage, he inquired as to the price of a ride to Admiralty House.

'Shilling,' barked the laconic jarvey.

Francis baulked. 'For such a petty distance! I could walk it in half an hour, man!'

'Then walk, sir. All the same to me,' came the offhand reply. There were plenty of people around with coin to spare. This was London, not the provinces.

'Then I will, sir!' Francis snapped back, grateful that the rain had so far held off.

Francis was as jittery as a sack full of kittens. Perhaps a brisk walk would be beneficial to calm his racing heart and steel his nerve. Up at dawn, he had been pacing about his room since then, answering imagined questions and assaying every possible attitude, from humble deference to blustering self-confidence. It all depended on what Sir John Clevland looked for in a naval officer. He would only be able to ascertain the measure of the man when he met him. Might it be advisable not to think at all and leave it to his instincts? Or was that too great a risk to take? Navigating the crowded streets would give his mind something else to settle upon. Perchance a suitable stratagem would come to him by and by.

Francis had a general idea of the direction of Whitehall, having wandered about the day before, but London was a confusing place; it was easy to lose one's path in the warren of streets and alleys. He never ceased to be amazed at the enormity of his own capital city. Despite his travels, he had never visited anywhere its equal.

Aunt Louisa's maid had starched and pressed his best uniform rigid, requiring him to flex his neck to stretch the collar, which was near choking him. But at least he looked the part. Appearance mattered. First impressions were vital. Francis wished to exude the air of a gentleman and officer: young, handsome, intelligent and earnest – with a touch of arrogance as befitted his station. With little else in his favour, he would have to rely on these externals, along with the testimonial of Captain Amherst. Beyond that depended on the preference of the First Secretary himself. So much rested on this day. Yet he could not complain. To have been afforded the opportunity to meet the Lord Secretary of the Admiralty himself was indicative of the support and reputation of Amherst, and attested to Clevland's personal curiosity in him.

With his best foot forward, Francis strode out onto Piccadilly, already thronging with people even at this time of the morning. As fascinated as he was by the shops, tradesmen, molls, guttersnipes and passers-by of every class and uniform, he found the constant presence of milling, unwashed bodies unsettling. He ducked and dived around the elaborate costumes of ladies and gentlemen, shrugged off the beggars and potential pickpockets, waved away the hawkers, and side-stepped the bawds. All the while, he scanned the footpath for potholes, open drains, and the foul detritus of thousands of bodies. A part of him wanted to run for the wide, open space of the parks to distance himself from the crowds. In a few weeks he would be chomping at the bit with boredom in Woodbridge, but right now he wished for nothing more than his sleepy country home.

The bells of St-Martin-in-the-Fields chimed the half hour as he rounded Charing Cross to Whitehall. He had time to spare. Forcing himself to slow his pace, he took a few deep breaths and surveyed the vista of this grand thoroughfare. In a mere few strides he had left behind the masses of Piccadilly and entered a different world. That men could design and build such edifices where once was virgin soil! To his left, the remains of the former palace of

Whitehall attested the ancient heritage of the English monarchy and to his right, the imposing Admiralty buildings proclaimed the supremacy of Britain in the modern age. This small island nation held the world in its grasp. Francis smiled ruefully to himself. How many naval men had walked this way, only to be reminded – just as he – of his own insignificance in the greater scheme of things? He was a mere brick in the wall. Furthermore, he stood the chance of no longer even being that now that the war was over.

The crowds thinned and the quality of people distinctly improved the nearer he came to the high wall flanking the Admiralty Office. Groups of gentlemen stood about here and there engaged in conversations; naval officers strode past with papers tucked beneath their arms; ladies sauntered by on their morning constitutionals. It was busy, but with a better class of person, one who either had business in such a place or who had the means to live close by in this most fashionable of districts.

At the gateway, Francis paused to allow a gilded coach to turn into the yard then followed it inside. It was quieter within, a haven of calm after the streets outside, with a handful of people crossing the forecourt. At the porticoed entrance, a coachman in black and gold livery helped his passenger down. It was Captain John Amherst, dusting off his ceremonial uniform and placing his braided cocked hat firmly on his head.

'Captain!' Francis exclaimed, mightily relieved that he would not have to linger alone in such a place.

The captain spun round, equally delighted to see his young protégé. 'Why, Francis! Good to see you, boy! You look well!'

They shook hands firmly. 'As do you, sir!' John Amherst

patted his belly ruefully; he was not quite as trim as when Francis first knew him. 'Mrs Amherst has been fattening me up already. I need to get back to ship board rations or I'll soon need hauling aboard,' he laughed. Turning, he dismissed the coachman; he would not be needing a ride home.

Francis eyed up the carriage. 'You certainly arrived in style, sir, while I was forced to take Shanks' nag!'

The captain shook his head. 'It is not mine, Francis. A captain on half-pay can hardly afford a public hackney, let alone a vehicle of such grandeur. I'm staying at my brother's apartments at St James's Place. You are familiar with Sir Jeffrey?'

The younger man's eyes widened. 'General Sir Jeffrey Amherst, the hero of Louisbourg and Governor of North America! I should say so, sir. I had heard he was your brother.'

'There were many heroes at Louisbourg, most of whom were in range of the guns. My brother is still over there causing trouble, you know?' There was little love lost between the siblings, it would seem. 'Despite the peace, Jeffrey has managed to find himself another war – this time with the indigenous folk, poor buggers. They don't stand a chance. The very odds Jeffrey most likes.'

The captain's sunburned skin reddened an even deeper colour, aware that he had spoken too freely about a man considered a national treasure. 'Ignore me, Light. I should not involve you in family discord. Jeffrey and I are not close but Jane, his wife, insists that I should stay here when in town. And the carriage has its conveniences ...' he added with a sardonic grin.

They entered the lobby and made their way to one of the clerks located at a desk in the foyer. Amherst gave their names and the fellow scratched them off a list. 'This way, sirs, if you will ...' They followed him towards the imposing staircase that branched off into galleries on each floor to the right and left.

'Well, are you ready for this? Remember, Clevland wouldn't see you if there wasn't a chance he'll find you a commission. But the war's over and most of the navy's confined to shore. So, don't expect too much. Keep your head and show your best side. After all, you're the boy who jumped off the *Mars* and saved us all. This cannot be as intimidating as that!'

Francis shrugged. 'I'm not so sure, sir. The Admiralty is not a place where I feel at ease.'

'Nor I. We're ordinary fellows, you and I, and this is where the high and mighty roam. But we have a right to be here. Don't forget that. Without men like us, there would be no navy, Francis. Come, let's get it over with, eh?'

They were led upstairs to the first-floor offices of the first secretary to the Admiralty, their footsteps echoing on cold marble. It was impossible not to raise one's eyes to the overblown decoration of the ceiling adorned with cherubs, goddesses and naval victories, the typical fusion of mythology, Christianity and national braggadocio. Portraits of former sea lords stared at them from the walls as they climbed. Amherst winked over and Francis grinned back. It broke the tension. 'It's worse than a trip to the headmaster's study at Seckford's!' Francis whispered.

'Imagine passing your life in these gloomy halls,' replied the Captain. 'I'd rather be dead at the bottom of the sea than spend a lifetime stuck behind a desk in here.'

Francis agreed. 'Well said, sir.' It helped his mood to think on that. The privilege of the corridors of power held no attraction for him. Each man to his own.

Their escort left them waiting in an anteroom whose lofty windows overlooked the parade ground at the rear, and then beyond to the leafy expanse of St James's Park. 'After this, do you have any other appointments? If not, let's take a stroll through the park to Pall Mall and have a spot of lunch?' Captain Amherst suggested. 'We'll need a strong drink after this interlude, no doubt!'

Francis agreed. 'I have no engagements today. It would be an honour, sir. You have been too kind already.'

Amherst gave him a wry look. 'We're not at sea now, lad. Let's take the opportunity to meet as friends and comrades. After all, you may be a fellow officer soon, eh?'

On that positive note, the door within opened and they were summoned into the spacious office of Sir John Clevland, First Secretary to the Admiralty. Amongst his very many administrative tasks, was that of overseeing the Navy List. He could make or break a career with a stroke of his pen.

Clevland sat behind a large desk stacked with documents neatly arranged in piles. He was reading, holding the sheet close to an eyeglass and frowning, despite the light from the window behind that cast him in an oddly saintly glow against the otherwise sombre room. The scene resembled an oil painting commemorating the life of a great man recently deceased. The two naval officers stood to attention, hats beneath the left arm, and saluted. The First Secretary carried on perusing the paper as if they were not present.

Sir John Clevland was of an indeterminate age, dry and shrivelled, hunched like an ancient. His skin was sallow and pasty.

His clothes hung off his body. Even his wig seemed a weight on his scrawny neck. From time to time he coughed, a harsh, raspy sound, hawking sputum into a handkerchief that he bundled in his left hand.

'You're late.' The First Secretary snapped, still without raising his head. The ormolu clock on the mantelpiece chimed the hour.

'It's nine o'clock, sir,' Captain Amherst replied. It was not an auspicious opening.

'One would expect your attendance well before the hour for an engagement of this import. I regard that as late, sir. It shows a lack of courtesy.' All this without looking up. The atmosphere in the room was icy, despite the fire burning in the grate and the sun shining through the window.

'I have been reading your testimonial, Amherst,' Clevland set down the eyeglass with precision and then peered at the two men before him. 'You hold this young man in high regard, it seems, despite the fact he has dubious origins and began his naval career as a mere loblolly boy.'

There were to be no niceties of introduction or welcome. 'A surgeon's assistant. Not loblolly, sir,' Captain Amherst corrected brusquely. 'In which capacity, he was very well thought of by the doctors with whom he served. Subsequently Mr Light was promoted to midshipman in '56 on account of his outstanding bravery and leadership ...'

'Hmm ... the wreck of the *Mars*. Your command, Amherst. For which you were later court martialled, I believe?' Clevland countered, pinning Amherst in his watery gaze. His eyes were expressionless, rheumy and grey-ringed. His face full on appeared jaundiced. Clevland did not look a well man. Perhaps that explained his irascibility.

'I was exonerated and reinstated, sir. Nor did the responsibility for the wreck fall on young Light's shoulders in any way, my Lord. Very much the opposite. Without his courageous action, we should have lost most of the men – and the guns. Because of him the crew to a man was saved – and we salvaged the entire arsenal.'

Amherst's vigorous defence was greeted with a curt nod. 'He was well-rewarded by promotion to midshipman. He cannot continue to dine out on that one act, sir, however much fortitude it demonstrated. There is more to command than raw courage. Since then he has served on the HMS *Captain* at Minorca. I am sure I do not need to remind you of that débacle, which resulted in the deaths of Captain Catford and the ship's doctor, Marshall, not to mention the execution of the late-lamented Admiral Byng. It would seem Mr Light has the misfortune to be associated with failure, sir.'

Something about Clevland's tone made Francis think that he was purposely provoking Amherst. Was he playing devil's advocate – or had he genuinely invited them here merely to humiliate? Clevland's assessment of the battle of Minorca was brutal. There was no adequate response should the First Secretary choose to blame all the men aboard for the loss of one battle, an engagement that should never have happened in the first place. But the Admiralty refused to recognise their culpability in that failure, which is why Byng had so unjustly been the sacrificial scapegoat.

'His subsequent service has been exceptional, sir. Mr Light has mastered the arts of seamanship, navigation and armaments to a high level, and he has become a great example to the younger men. Furthermore, it is two years' since he passed his lieutenant's exam after which I made him third lieutenant aboard my ship *Arrogant*, which office he has carried out with the utmost rigour. I believe he has earned a place on the List.' Amherst was measured in his tone but there was an underlying note that he could not keep from his voice. He was not used to being on the other end of naval discipline.

Cleveland raised an eyebrow. 'Oh, you do, do you? Captain Amherst, the disposition of commissions is not unfortunately in your remit unless you are at sea and without sufficient officers. May I remind you that Mr Light served as *acting* third lieutenant during his two years on the *Arrogant*, a role he was allowed due to the paucity of officers of that rank in the midst of a war. We are now at peace. The navy's requirements are wholly different. Have you any idea how much seven years of war in several theatres across the globe has cost this nation? Have you any notion of the number of British officers on half-pay who would bite my hand off for a position as even fourth lieutenant on a sixth-rate sloop? The figures before me indicate that there are now two hundred and fifty lieutenants of all classes who have been paid off – and were all already on the List. Pray tell me why Mr Light is deserving of preference over them?' Another extended bout of coughing and expectoration prevented Cleveland from continuing, and made it impossible for Amherst to reply without appearing ill-mannered.

Thus, he chewed on his lip and ground his fingers into his hat, all the while struggling to tamp down his anger. Had they been summoned just for this? Surely a curt note would have sufficed if Clevland had no intention of making an exception for a young lieutenant recommended by his commanding officer? And what of Francis, who had not so far uttered a word to show his mettle? It was the utmost cruelty to have given hope to a brave young seaman and then to crush it beneath the heel for sport.

The silence in the room was profound, only broken by the hacking. Amherst stole a look over at Francis. He was surprised by the steel in the younger man's upright stance, and his steady, composed gaze. You never knew quite what was going on in Francis' head. Poor McParland had told him that years before. And the old doctor had always been an accurate judge of character, able to see beneath the masks that most men wear, despite rarely being entirely sober. The lad certainly possessed an affable charm, but it concealed hidden depths.

'If I may, sir?' Francis spoke as Mr Clevland pocketed the kerchief and took a sip of brandy.

'Medicinal,' he muttered, but nodded for Francis to continue.

'I would like to thank you for receiving us today. You have far weightier and more important matters than my career to preoccupy you. Captain Amherst and I are both cognisant of the long and loyal service that you have given to this country – and to the navy in particular. The service has been good to me, a boy from humble origins, and I am most grateful for every opportunity it has extended. I have been proud to serve my country and would not seek to deprive any other serving officer of his rightful commission. It is enough that you have given me this chance to present my case and to have read through my record with such close scrutiny. If I were to receive a commission, I assure you that you would never regret the decision for I intend to go far in my chosen career. And I shall persevere, should it take many years. May I wish you well, sir, and again, my deepest gratitude ...'

There was a distinct relaxing in the secretary's demeanour as Francis made his gracious speech. It appeared to have pierced a chink in the old curmudgeon's armour. Or had this been his intent? Had the purpose of this tetchy exchange been to discover if Francis had sufficient presence of mind to take control of a difficult situation? Something had to single him out from the rest for Clevland to intercede.

'Fine words indeed, sir. You are a decent fellow and I have no doubt you make a fine lieutenant. I will think on't. But I am not hopeful in the next few months. Frankly, since the men came home, it's been a damned mess. I feel deeply for the officers who have been paid off after their years of service in such egregious conditions. And most have the benefit of influence and wealth behind them unlike yourself, Light. But I promise I will keep your name in mind. Captain Amherst may be stepping down from the *Arrogant* but we will not keep him portside for long. He is too valuable for that. Amherst, when you receive your next ship, contact this office. I will then see what I can do. It is evident that you work well together, a factor that should not be overlooked aboard ship. That is all I can offer you at the moment, lad.' Clevland wiped a desiccated hand over his brow to mop up the beads of sweat that threatened to trickle down his face. This interview had severely taxed him. But he gave a slight smile of reassurance as he nodded his head, indicating that the interview was at an end.

They were dismissed. The future was not bright but hopeful. It was as much as Francis could rightfully expect. As soon as the doors were closed, Amherst swung round and grasped his hand. 'I was so proud of you in there! I could have strangled the wrinkled old toad when he spoke to me as he did! These landlubbers in charge of appointments know nothing of the sea! That's what's wrong with the navy, By God!'

Francis put a warning finger to his lips. 'Captain Amherst, please! Not here! But thank you mightily for your support, sir. I could ask for no more.'

As they made their way down the stairs and across the hall, Amherst ruminated on Light's prospects. 'If this leads anywhere, Francis, it will be because of what you said, not my pathetic ramblings. He listened to you and he liked what he heard. We must pray he honours his promise, although it may not entirely be in his hands. Clevland's a sick man. That's a churchyard cough, if ever I heard one. You'd better pray he lasts a few more years yet, lad.'

Francis sighed. For the second time, his fortunes depended on someone living long enough to make good on a promise. To cheer him up, the captain clapped him on the back and steered him to the rear entrance. '... Let's take a stroll across the park and shed this place from our clothes. I know a decent place on Pall Mall which serves a fine new Hollander beer.'

Over a jug of Princesse Royal and a platter of roast ham, cheese and pickles, the two men mulled over the uncomfortable interlude. The more they thought about it, the more they were sure Clevland had purposely unsettled them, probably to gain the measure of them both in the shortest possible time. 'He may not be a well man, but he has to be a shrewd old goat to have held that position for so long. Imagine how many men enter that room prepared to grovel and fawn to get a commission! He must be heartily sick of the whole charade,' Amherst observed.

That had also been Francis' impression. 'Now, sir, we merely need for your new appointment and, with any luck, Clevland will give us the nod.'

The captain paused, observing Francis with a gleam in his eye. 'Damn it, lad, I can't sit on this news! But you must keep it to yourself. Tell no one until it is formally announced. It has been indicated that I will make Admiral of the Blue once the aftermath of war has settled. I am confined to shore for the while, much to Mrs Amherst's delight, but soon I will have a flotilla at my disposal. Make no mistake there'll be a post for you, I'll make sure of it!'

Francis' face lit up. 'I'll drink to that, sir! And to your appointment, too. Long overdue! Many congratulations!' He called a server to bring another jug and a bottle of brandy besides. 'It's early yet but this calls for a celebration!'

Oiled by a few more glasses and strong liquor to boot, any reserve that both men felt in each other's company was soon discarded. They began to talk as men, free from the hierarchy of their profession. 'What happened to Dr McParland, sir? I had heard he passed on.'

The captain took a snort of brandy, holding up the empty glass, either in tribute to his fallen comrade or in bitter irony at the cause of his death. 'The drink caught up with him, boy, a salutary lesson to all sailors. His body gave out eventually. Old Tom died at sea in '57, off the Leewards. He lies at the bottom of those waters, finally at peace, much as he would have wanted. If ever a man consciously drank himself to death, it was he, poor bastard.' Amherst sniffed and wiped away a tear. 'The drink is making me maudlin, Francis, but he was a good man and a dear friend who went too soon, as many of my comrades have. Still, he lasted longer than young Henry Marshall, eh?'

Francis nodded. 'I was at Gibraltar when he died. The hospital there was a fearsome place. If you weren't dead when they took you in, you were sure to be dead before they carried you out,' he muttered, still angry when he recalled the foul conditions and the dreadful plight of the many injured seaman. 'Captain Catford was in a nearby bed. He lingered a few weeks longer but … sir, it was the dirt and the disease that killed them! Their injuries were bad, but they were not deadly. Dr Marshall knew! But what could he do, lying there helpless?'

The two men sat awhile, contemplating the pointless loss of their companions. 'Byng was right. We should not have been there. We didn't have enough ships, men nor armaments and what we did have was outdated. The French fleet was vastly superior. They merely toyed with us.'

'Byng was the very opposite of Boscawen,' Francis mused. 'Boscawen held back our ships to punish you for defending your men – and was decorated as the hero, even though he provoked a war that led to the deaths of thousands and the waste of so much money. Byng, on the other hand, held back as many ships as he could from a battle we could not win, thus saving countless lives and most of the fleet … But he was shot by firing squad on his own ship in front of the entire fleet …'

'Dangerous opinions, Francis. Take care to whom you voice them. I was a witness at his trial, you know? My testimony played a part in his death sentence.' Amherst looked shrewdly at Francis, wondering what reaction his admission would elicit.

'The lawyers twisted and turned your words, sir. They did not allow you the chance to speak your true mind,' Francis defended his captain.

Amherst gave a bitter laugh. 'Not entirely, sir. I knew their game. As did Byng for that matter. The outcome was inevitable. Either way, my words could not have saved him. Thus, it served no purpose throwing away my own career. Life in the navy is ever a sail through unpredictable seas. A man has to know when to sail against the wind and when to let it carry him where it will. You must measure your chances of success against the cost of failure. If all is equal, you must decide whether to take a risk. If you cannot win, then don't venture anything. But if there is no alternative, if you cannot change your fate, then take the leap, as you once did off the *Mars*. That's my advice to you, boy. Never be reckless for recklessness' sake. Throwing your life away for nothing is pointless. But having the courage to take the step into the unknown when you believe the dice could fall your way ... now that's an entirely different matter.'

9
Self-Preservation

Covent Garden. 16th April, 1763

Later that week Francis made a visit to the Navy Pay Office on Broad Street to discuss his financial settlement. He was overdue the matter of his prize money from the *Arrogant* (a substantial amount) and the transfer of his half-pay (a measly sum) to his banker in Woodbridge. To his surprise and pleasure, he ran into a former shipmate, one James Scott. They had first met as midshipmen on the *Arrogant,* had passed their lieutenant's exams together, and had both served as acting lieutenants during the latter years of the war. It seemed London was the place to find out-of-work navy men this season.

'Well met, Frannie! Good to see you, man! I was planning to write with my news, but now we can celebrate in style and savour the delights of this most wicked of cities!' James slapped him on the back as they shook hands vigorously.

They were an unlikely pair, the kind of mismatched odd fellows who often form close bonds. James was ruddy and lanky where Francis was lean and dark. Scott's face was boyish and freckled, his hair wispy and ginger. He had an endlessly sanguine nature yet his cheerfulness belied a shrewd and calculating grasp of the world. Francis was somewhat in awe of the self-belief that had advanced his friend to the rank of lieutenant at the tender age of sixteen.

'Good Lord, James! How fortuitous! What's this about good news? Don't tell me you've made the List? How did you manage that, you damned lucky bastard!'

The two young men laughed loudly, to the disapproval of the sour-faced officials and senior officers who tutted loudly and cleared their throats in warning at the exuberant pair. Throwing an arm around Light's shoulders, Scott steered him outside, where they took the steps two at a time, relieved to be free of authority and out in the open air.

'Where shall we go then with all this newfound wealth?' Scott asked, striking the pose of a thinker. 'I know just the thing. Somewhere with good liquor and bad women!' James was well known as a womaniser, even more so than the rest of the young officers. He always knew where to hunt and invariably caught his prey.

'Good God, man, it's too early in the day for both, surely!' Light replied, knowing full well that once Scott had an idea in his head, there would be little shaking him.

'Too early? It is never too early for wine and women, Francis! Remember, we are naval officers who have sailed the Seven Seas. It must be the right time in some port somewhere, methinks!'

This time, with two passengers and a long distance across the city, Francis thought nothing of hailing a carriage. While the hackney struggled through the crowded streets at barely a walking pace, the two young men sat back and had the opportunity for conversation, before they went on to drink too much and lost their wits. James was excited, bursting with his new opportunity.

'Out with it then, or will you dangle it before my eyes all day?

I'm beginning to think you are merely spinning a yarn,' Francis grinned.

James folded his arms smugly. 'I have an exciting new prospect.'

'A ship?' Francis gasped.

'Of sorts,' was his oblique reply.

'What the devil does that mean, you rogue?'

'Patience, my good fellow. I have been offered ...' He beat a tattoo on the side of the carriage, confusing the jarvey who stopped the hackney, and had to be instructed to continue. '... I have been offered a position with the Honourable Company. I'm working my passage as purser on the Indiaman *Anson*, departing forthwith. Now what do you say to that?'

'You've left the navy?' Francis was astonished. 'But ... but you've burnt your boats, James. They will never put you on the List now!'

James burst into laughter. 'They will never put me on the List anyway! I'm the son of a humble Scottish lawyer. My uncle Robbie is a merchant captain with the Company. He put in a good word for me and they offered me a post. I can't waste this chance. By the time another war comes and they find themselves in want of officers, I'll be too old to be considered anyway!'

'You're only eighteen, man. I have near five years on you!'

'And every year more gentlemen of quality join the ranks, whilst our names sink lower and lower down the ladder. I can't afford to wait. What would I do meantime? Clerk in my father's office? That would never do me. I'm young and restless and want to make my fortune, a challenge in the navy at the best of times. The East is where there's money to be made, Frannie, my lad.

You can forget eking out a living on a paltry half-pay and endless begging letters to the naval board. Wake up, Francis! Neither of us stands a chance, no matter how well we distinguished ourselves in the war. We'll never make the cut.'

Francis could not say he was surprised at Scott's decision. James was a fine officer but not an instinctive one. If he showed leadership, intelligence, imagination or courage, it was because it served him best to do so. By the same token, if he were not to gain anything by an action, he would never embark upon it. Everything he did was driven by self-interest. In many ways Francis admired him for his single-minded pursuit of ambition, untrammelled by the constraints of duty, sacrifice and honour. Of the two, James seemed to be the elder; Francis had learned much from him already. Yet, James could be an unmitigated fool, arrogant enough to believe that he was always right and that others could not see through him. It was his main weakness.

'Well, that's where you're wrong, my friend. John Amherst and I recently met with Sir John Clevland himself who all but promised me a posting with the good captain when he receives his next commission!'

It was Scott's turn to be impressed. 'Hobnobbing with the gentry, no less! What a toady, Light. You were always John Amherst's pet.' Francis swatted him playfully. 'But well done, sir, however you achieved it. I hope no unnatural favours were involved.'

At this Francis and he began to wrestle playfully, until the driver shouted: 'Everything all right, back there, young sirs?' with a note of warning in his voice.

Straightening down their clothes and assuring him that there was no problem within, they settled back on the seats. 'Good for you, Light. But a word of caution ... it may be awhile until Amherst is reappointed. Have you given any thought how you keep yourself in the meantime?'

On that sour note, the driver announced their destination. 'Half Moon Street, sir.'

'I thought we were headed for Covent Garden,' Light observed as they jumped down and settled the fare. He surveyed the narrow alley with interest.

'The Great Square of Venus is but a few streets away, sir, do not concern yourself. I know this area well. I've rented a room nearby. Firstly, however, I want to visit a certain emporium in order to make some essential purchases for my journey East.' James gave a knowing wink, rubbing his hands in glee. He sauntered along with Light in tow until he spotted the establishment in question. 'Ah! There she is! The Green Canister – after you, Francis.'

From the exterior, there was little to single out this shop from the others on the street, save the signboard which gave no clue as to the goods within. Nor did the name itself suggest any particular product. The twin bow windows that flanked the entrance were paned in bull's eye glass, obscuring the interior except for a row of porcelain statues on the sill that on closer inspection proved to be an array of naked Greek goddesses.

The tinkle of a doorbell heralded their arrival. Francis looked around with interest. Shelves containing books, jars, potions and powders lined the walls; in the centre of the room a large oak table artfully displayed a curious selection of goods and implements. A board, propped up on a gilded stand, contained an announcement decorated with chubby naked *putti*, and lettered in embellished script:

To guard yourself from shame and fear
Votaries to Venus, hasten here.
None of our wares e'er found a flaw
Self-preservation's Nature's law!

'You rogue, James Scott! This is an emporium for machines!' Francis exclaimed. 'Trust you to know where to go!'

At that moment, a woman bustled in from a room beyond. She was a sight to behold. Primped, powdered and perfumed to a degree that bounded on the farcical, the comely but extremely abundant lady stopped the two young men in their tracks. Draped in rose pink silk, her décolletage was so disturbingly low that her ample bosoms struggled against the delicate fabric, and were nigh escaping. Her face was whitened, her cheeks and lips red-blushed, her white wig piled high with tumbling ringlets. Francis estimated she was of distinctly mature years, yet her outfit and deportment were girlish and coy, if somewhat in the fashion of a harlot.

This was none other than Mrs Teresa Constantia Phillips, the famous courtesan, who in her time had made and lost a number of fortunes, predominately on her back. Her name had been associated with several distinguished members of the peerage, although there had never been any sign of a Mr Phillips, despite her married title. Ten years or so ago, as her looks faded and her waist widened, Mrs Phillips had set up shop in Half Moon Street with money provided by her most recent lover, in return for complete discretion as to the nature of their former entanglement. The doughty lady was never short of investors; she knew the secrets of half the aristocracy. Her business had subsequently boomed, bringing visitors from all over England and beyond to buy her so-called 'Venusian' wares. The resourceful Mrs Phillips had even set up a mail order service for gentlemen in the American colonies and the East India Company. Her entrepreneurial genius was legendary, as was her flamboyant personality. She was one of the toasts of London.

'My goodness, what handsome gentlemen we have here! Welcome to my humble establishment. Please browse at will. If any item requires explanation – or you do not see your particular fancy – please do not hesitate to ask. I have much more within ...' With that, she fluttered her eyelashes and gave them her cow eye. Unsure exactly what she was offering 'within', Francis took an instinctive step backwards.

James, however, was more than game for whatever was on show. He dashed to the shelves, exclaiming with ribald amusement at the goods on offer. 'Preservatives galore! Every size, shape and fabric!'

'We call them "cundums", sir. Sheep intestines, very sturdy, secured with finest lace ribbons in whatever colour takes your fancy!' Mrs Phillips regaled. 'Checked for leaks then softened to make them more comfortable ... for the larger gentleman ...' she gave another bashful smile, the effects somewhat contradicted by the accompanied playful wink. 'Mrs Perkins, my assistant, will be delighted to show you round.' Another buxom lady, a smaller, less gaudy version, was ushered forward with a tray of drinks, while Mrs Phillips gratefully lowered her bulk into a seat at the rear, rearranging her garments to her satisfaction, and helping herself from a plate of bonbons.

'A glass of sherry while you browse, good sirs?' Mrs Perkins asked, her voice high-pitched and squeaky, like a little child.

Thus fortified, the two young men wandered about, unable to contain their prurient interest. Aside from the array of cundums, were a host of other remarkable implements, all of carnal purpose. Widows' comforters of leather, ivory and wood in a selection of sizes from average to disconcertingly thick and long were lined up on a bed of cushioned velvet. Whips and other instruments of flagellation were on display, with a sign discreetly offering 'flagellation machines available to order'. Boxes adorned with images of shy maidens, containing sponges with attached ribbons, and pots labelled vinegar and lemon juice for 'intimate douching', were placed next to powders and glass phials proclaiming themselves 'prophylactic' potions against conception, or remedies for 'sustained' potency. On the other side of the room were toys, garments and masks: 'aids for play and amusement in the boudoir'. The shop was a cornucopia of delights for both priapic men and fleshly ladies.

'What is your particular delight, sirs?' squeaked Mrs Perkins. 'I'm sure you would be most interested in what I prefer to call "a box of C". It seems to me a little indelicate if one is overly descriptive in language, wouldn't you say? These preservatives are highly recommended for the adventurous gentleman. Most efficacious for preventing unwanted accidents and also for the health of both participants,' she continued with the matter-of-fact delivery of an apothecary selling cough linctus.

'I always say, don't leave anything behind, and don't bring anything back with you!' guffawed Mrs Phillips from her perch, pouring another tot of sherry for herself. Mrs Perkins shot a look of disapproval that only amused the older lady further. There was obviously a difference of opinion between the two in regards to appropriate retail conduct.

James purchased a number of items to be delivered to his lodgings, preservatives in the main, but also pills for enhancing male potency and powders for 'relaxing tension' in young ladies. Francis disapproved of the latter as tantamount to unbecoming behaviour, but James scoffed at his unease. 'Come on, Frannie! Don't hang back. You like the ladies just as much as I do! They love it but sometimes need a little "loosening" up. Nor do I think you wish to be encumbered with the unwanted consequences of a passing romp between the sheets!'

Light frowned but reluctantly made his own small purchase so as not to appear a prude. He would, in fact, have liked to buy more, but was inhibited by his natural reserve in the company of his ebullient friend. He intended to return alone on a future occasion to indulge more freely.

Taking their leave of the two obsequious shopkeepers, the two naval officers made their way to Covent Garden for a day of carousing and, fortified by their purchases, a night of erotic delights. But first, a leg of mutton washed down with claret at the Cooper's Arms on Rose Street, followed by The Shakespeare's Tavern in Covent Garden proper.

Their earlier high spirits were soon replaced by the contemplation of the sobering realities of their lives. It had been a woeful hardship to return from the intensity and danger of war at sea to the boredom and uncertainty of life back home. The dawning realisation of their lack of prospects had only reinforced the extent to which the sacrifices made by so many sailors and soldiers on behalf of the nation had been rewarded with blatant abandonment.

'We have been treated ill, Francis,' James pronounced, as he poured a healthy measure of whisky for both of them. 'There is no care for the ordinary seaman, even officers. I'll wager though that all the upper classes will be settled first while we, those with no other means of support, must beg and scrape to make ends meet for goodness knows how long. By God, we won North America for them!'

'It is shameful but I expected little else,' Francis opined. 'This is the world we live in where some dine off plates of gold and the rest fight for scraps from the table. I well understand the hierarchy aboard ship but I had forgotten the cold hard truth of life ashore.'

'Then come to India with me!' Scott cried out. 'There's nothing here for men like us, as you rightly observe. We will always be nobodies, passed over in favour of lesser men with greater names. But over there, amongst the natives, every British man is a gentleman. We would both make our fortunes. Come on, man, see sense! We work well together. Imagine: "Scott and Light Esquires, Merchant Trading Company"' He waved his hands in the air dramatically, framing the imaginary signboard above their future offices. Scott's whisky-fuelled exuberance caught the attention of other drinkers. He was told to 'Keep it down!' and 'Mind your talk!'

Francis sighed deeply, swirling his glass around thoughtfully. 'I'm not sure I'm ready to leave the navy just yet. It's a life I've come to love, James. And it's all I damn well know! What do I know of commerce and trade? No, I can't go yet. I want to see this to its end. Maybe next year. If things don't work out ...'

'You're a romantic fool, Francis Light. I'm warning you, you'll be in the same place a year from now, only poorer and more disillusioned than ever, mark my words.'

At that, Scott's attention was caught by someone across the room. In his usual mercurial fashion, he leapt up mid-sentence, the thread of his conversation forgotten. 'One minute, Francis. I need a word with the good Mr Harris.'

He scurried over to the head waiter who was leaning on the bar handing out notices to any fellow who came up. James exchanged a few words, passed over a coin, received a pamphlet, and patted the waiter on the back in thanks. Moments later he was back, gleeful as a schoolboy who had found a sixpence. 'Lookee here, Frannie ... a copy of this week's Harris' List. Take your pick, man. Ladies of every age, type and size. Specialities described in detail. Prices kindly recorded. Jack Harris is doing a wondrous service for mankind! And it makes life easier for the better class of girls since they no longer have to hang about on corners alongside the threepenny uprights.'

Francis scoured the pamphlet, shaking his head and rolling his eyes at some of the contents. 'Two pounds for Miss Lolly Labelle!' he exclaimed.

'She's top drawer, Francis. A bit beyond the likes of us. But a guinea should get you a fine little mare in one of the more salubrious establishments. And we have our machines. No time like the present to test them out, eh?'

Despite his feigned discomfiture, Francis was as eager for sport as his friend. He gathered up his hat and pulled out a few coins. 'The night is yet young, and so are we, Jamie. The ladies of London await ... Let's go hunting. Forget our worries for a night, old friend?'

***

James Scott's admonition proved to be prescient. When he sailed out to the East the following month, Francis returned to Suffolk to await the navy's pleasure. It was to be a thankless period. Despite discharge in the spring of '63, the crew of the *Arrogant* received no news about their half-pay until the end of the summer, at which time they were finally officially paid off. Six months without pay already, other than their initial prizes. No money was even then forthcoming. The Admiralty claimed forbearance, citing the magnitude of the task of settling such a vast number of men ashore at one time.

Francis was luckier than many. Sir William employed him as estate manager for a decent wage, far above that usually paid, but it was a lowly position for a naval officer. His new command comprised woodsmen, huntsmen, farmworkers, pig and cowmen, hardly comparable to the crew of a 74-gun warship of the line. The worst challenge they faced all summer was a persistent fox in the henhouse. Moreover, he was embarrassed in the company of old friends, all now settled in decent professions, even though he was grateful for employment. But it seemed churlish to be bitter. Many of his former comrades were infinitely worse off than he.

The first major blow to his hopes came on a sultry evening in late July as he settled back after dinner with a tot of Scotch whisky (a vice acquired from his old friend Scott) and his copy of the weekly *Ipswich Journal*. He waded through the usual hotchpotch of articles until, turning over a page, Francis cast a cursory eye over the obituaries. At the age of not yet twenty-three, they held little interest for him. Yet one notice caught his attention. It was set within an ornate black frame adorned at four corners with a hare salient, the arms of the unfortunate deceased. His heart plummeted.

THE HONOURABLE SIR JOHN CLEVLAND

On the 18th of June 1763, at Home in Tapley in the County of Devon, John Clevland, Esq, lately Secretary of the Admiralty, of a complication of Disorders brought on by his constant approach to the discharge of his Duties which occasioned his Death. For the space of forty years he served his King and Country with the greatest Honour and Fidelity, the last seventeen years of which he was Joint and Sole Secretary of the Admiralty. He leaves behind three sons and three daughters ...

Sir John had died weeks ago. The news was only just reaching the counties. Where did that now leave his chances? It was discourteous that self-interest should be his first thought but he could not help his bitter disappointment.

Hot on the heels of the report, came a missive from Captain Amherst delivered the next morning. He had also only recently been informed of the death of the first secretary, news of which had similarly taken its time to reach him at Sevenoaks in Kent. The letter was blunt and to the point, in typical John Amherst style:

My Dear Francis,

Bad news, I'm afraid. Old Clevland didn't last long, as I'd feared. The new Secretary is Philip Stevens, formerly

Cleveland's Deputy. He's a 'by-the-book' sort of fellow, by all accounts, a Stickler for the rules. Damned bad luck for both of us. Sir Philip has delayed all Appointments so that he can 'scrutinise' them carefully. Can you imagine how long until any of us are recalled with a fol-de-rol like that? The man's a damned idiot. I'll wager he was in Clevland's shadow for too long and now wants to make a name for himself by painting the Former Secretary as a careless incompetent or a man too easily swayed. It's the typical meanspirited behaviour of the little Man who wishes to cast a larger Shadow. They love nothing better than to wield their Power over worthier fellows. Francis, we must both be patient. My Promotion will come in time and then I will endeavour to find you a suitable Appointment.

Until then, my regards to Sir William and your mother,

John Amherst, Capt. R.N.

Be patient. Wait. Amherst would endeavour to do his best. It was now even less certain that Amherst would have the freedom to offer him a rank, even should he become an Admiral. Secretary Stephens did not appear to be of a mind to accept any infringement of naval regulation.

'I have to get back to sea. The navy has ruined me for the quiet village life!' he muttered, splashing out a larger measure of spirit and throwing it down. How long could he fritter away his life in Suffolk, wasting his best and most productive years down on a country farm? One year. That was all he would allow. If he had not secured a position by this time next year, it was his intention to apply to the East India Company and follow Scott out. If not the navy, it would have to be the Honourable Company. The sea was all he knew.

10

East Indiaman

Johanna Roads, Comoros Islands. September 1765

The lively port town of Mutsamudu receded little by little as the *Clive* gained the channel and the stronger currents of the deep. Brilliant sunlight reflected off the distant whitewashed stone houses clustering the shore, and dazzled off the crystal waters. Dhows and schooners, sloops and merchantmen, canoes and rafts, all manner of oared and sailed vessels, busied around the wide bay as far as one could see. From the vantage of the poop deck, the island, a mere dot on any chart, appeared little more than a pyramid of rock spewed out from some ancient volcano, its vertiginous cliffs falling away to narrow strips of palm-fringed beaches. From afar it was much like countless other tiny islands they had passed in the archipelagos they had traversed these many months at sea. But on landing – the first time since Madeira sixteen weeks before – Francis Light and his fellow travellers had discovered paradise.

For centuries, the natural deep-water harbour of Mutsamudu had been the centre of the Zanzibar–Africa trade, as well as a way station for traders from every corner of the globe. Set in a bay shaped like two wide arms of welcome and sheltered from the deeper ocean waters, it was a vibrant commercial centre, a wondrous place, all the more so after the deprivation of their long voyage. Pale-skinned travellers from cold, grey lands faraway who believed themselves God's chosen found it difficult to comprehend that there could be such a place where poverty and want did not exist and peoples of different languages and religions worked together in harmony. This tiny piece of land, set in the midst of nowhere, thronged with men and women from lands of which they barely knew, speaking a polyglot of strange languages, was a veritable eye-opener. Francis himself felt like a counterpart Gulliver in an alternate world where everything bright and good lay just beyond the horizon.

In this Utopian dream everyone ate well and dressed in style, like Turkish pashas. Gaudy costumes and elaborate rainbow headdresses, bright-dyed cottons and shimmering silks cast their sober English wool and linen into dowdy shade. Even common folk visited the many public bathhouses and carried beautiful daggers wrought of silver. Francis might have been a sailor accustomed to foreign parts, but North America and the Mediterranean had not prepared him for this Arcadia.

The *Clive* had rested up at Johanna for a week to repair and to revictual their stale and dreary food supplies. For weeks they had existed on hard tack, dried meat and mouldy cheese; scurvy had flared up amongst both the passengers and crew. On Johanna island, they had made the most of the fresh fare: fish, chicken, cassava and as much fruit as they could eat. Francis had stuffed himself with bananas and coconuts, and tasted mango and soursop for the first time. But there was also business to be done. Johanna was more than just a stop off in the Mozambique Channel on the India route. It was famed in its own right for coconut, vanilla and perfume plants, as well as precious tortoiseshell.

It was also an exchange post for mail; passing ships deposited letters in bottles by a great tree near the harbour. The officers of the *Clive* had collected those bound for Fort St George, replacing them with their homeward correspondence. This extraordinary postal service, based on mutual support and cooperation, worked, even if despatches might take years to reach their desired destination.

A fresh sea breeze with the salt-sharp tang of open ocean wafted away the lingering fragrance of the land. Francis leaned against the deck rail, pensive, the black sand shores disappearing into memory. He had never seen a more idyllic place in all his days. If this was the promise of the East, he had the taste for more.

It had been early April when the *Clive* sailed from the Downs, heading for Fort St George on the Coromandel Coast, a journey of at least six months in a plodding East Indiaman, if they met no misfortunes on the way. And there were many dangers. The deep oceans were unpredictable: storms could rise from nowhere and they were often too far from land to hope for shelter. The ship, weighed down with goods and people, might run aground on reef or shoals, which meant certain death for all. Greater by far, though, was the threat from pirates and raiders. Many an East Indiamen had fallen prey to that evil scourge. Even 26 guns and sailing in convoy offered little protection; Indiamen might look like warships but they were nothing of the sort. They were heavy and slow as turtles, even more so at night when they doused their lights for fear of attack. Thus, sailing blind, they did not dare move faster than a snail's pace.

Six months on an outward passage was an age, even for a seasoned naval officer like Lieutenant Light. For much of the past four months, they had been without any real sight of landfall, or even the other accompanying vessels in their convoy. They felt alone en route to the ends of the earth, so lonely and isolated had they been. The course south had traced the remote perimeter of the African continent, turned eastwards at the Cape of Good Hope into the Indian Ocean, then north by Madagascar, for the most part enjoying fair conditions since they had been becalmed in English waters for a few weeks at the outset. April was the month for eastern crossings; Francis had lost six months at home merely waiting for a suitable departure. One whole year of his life frittered away even before he made a start towards his future. Two years lost since he had been discharged from the navy. And what was there to show for it? Very little, if truth be told.

As the wind picked up and with the late morning sun full on his face, Francis pondered, as he often did, how little he was leaving behind. That brutal reality saddened him greatly, for he was saying farewell – perhaps for ever – to the people whom he loved most in the world. Nor was he in any wise insensible to the potential dangers ahead. The East was a dangerous place, no matter its exotic allures. Even if he survived the ravages of the tropical diseases that had claimed so many of his countrymen, there were hostile natives, wild beasts imagined and unimagined and, even before he arrived, the unpredictable perils of half a year at sea in some of the world's most notorious currents. But still he deemed it was his only course. He was even eager for the challenge.

Before he had left, all the necessary had been arranged. He had written his will, leaving his estate (such as it was) to William Negus, who in turn had taken upon himself to provide for Mary

Light until Francis was established enough to take responsibility for her. He had taken leave of his close friends with promises to write often and keep them appraised of his adventures, although God knew how long it would take their letters to travel back and forth. He had visited John Amherst, still waiting on his own appointment, thanking him for all his support, and wishing him well. Without the good captain's aid, he would not even have secured this temporary post on the *Clive*; his former commander had vouched for him to Captain Allen with assurances that he could not find a better officer in the land for free. For those were the terms under which he was employed. Free passage to Madras as second mate on an East Indiaman. He was grateful even for that.

After abandoning all hope of a naval appointment, Francis had followed his friend Scott's advice and applied to the East India Company. To his intense disappointment, his illegitimacy had precluded him even from consideration. He was neither gentleman nor commoner, thus no suitable posts were open to him, not even the lowliest office job, regardless of his naval experience. Amherst had suggested an alternative, if unorthodox, course of action. Whilst it was illegal to travel to India without a Company appointment in order to safeguard their monopoly, it was perfectly acceptable for a sailor to take service on India-bound ships, conveying goods and passengers on Company business. Once he reached Fort St George, however, Francis would be on his own, with nothing but a recommendation from James Scott to visit a certain agency in Madras town. Alongside Amherst's testimonial, it would have to be sufficient.

Yet, despite the uncertain future that lay ahead in that

unknown land, the further Light travelled from England, the surer he became of the rightness of his decision. Once aboard ship, he knew in an instant that he was indeed home. He no longer had the legs for land; the wind in the sails and a distant shore ahead were his environs. No matter how many concerns weighed upon his soul, a bracing stroll on deck, the deep roll of the waves beneath him, and the unbroken ocean about, were enough to set his spirits right. Whatever life threw at him, it was bound to be better than what awaited him on land. In this *terra incognita*, he would be his own man and accept his fate with the determination to succeed against the odds.

One sadness lingered. He might never again meet the people he held most dear. Sir William was aging, as was his mother. Who knew how long they might be for this world? All the same, his love for his family could hold him back. One day soon they would be gone, along with any chance he might have in life to make his name. His one lasting regret, however, was for another, whose memory still haunted him, despite the miles between them. Plunging his hand into his pocket, Francis crushed the petals of a yellow blossom plucked that morning. Pressing them to his face, he inhaled the heady fragrance, rich in the exotic notes of tropical fruit and jasmine. This flower grew wild everywhere on Johanna island. He had bought a small vial of its oil as a gift should he ever return home.

***

Not even the unseasonal rain could dampen the high spirits and warmth that radiated from George Doughty. His ruddy face was one enormous smile, transforming him from diffident boy to genial man of substance, an unexpected metamorphosis that was wholly the result of his devotion to his bride. The new Mrs Doughty, a slender girl, all the more so next to her solid husband, had brown doe-like eyes and a pert little mouth. A tender and amiable young lady, more modest than beautiful, she had brought young George out of his self-effacing shell. Their mutual fondness was evident. With her light brown hair laced through with pearls, swept off her shapely neck, and decked out in white silk and lace, Anne Doughty had likewise come into her own that day.

The congregation huddled in the vestibule for shelter to share their congratulations and good wishes. The inclement weather didn't allow them outside to admire the floral bowers that Anne had erected over the porch and lychgate. She smiled when people commiserated. Nothing could spoil the occasion. Furthermore, the couple took no offense that many of their friends chose to gather round one of their guests, relegating the bride and groom to near-bystanders. Indeed, it gave them an opportunity to openly hold hands, touch and whisper to each other, relishing in their new freedom.

It had been nine years since the old school friends had last been together. George was now a married man, James Lynn a qualified doctor practising in Woodbridge, Francis Brooke an up-and-coming lawyer, and Reverend James Lambert, now of Cambridge, an academic already making his name as a literary scholar. Captain Charles Thompson, of the 12th Suffolks, wore his uniform and a patch to cover the eye he had lost at Minden. Edmund Jenney, the son of a prominent landowner, carried himself with the lustre that was born of an Oxford education on top of a large annual income.

In the midst of this melée, Francis accepted the handshakes and welcome with more pleasure than he had anticipated. He had felt misgivings about meeting the old crowd. His life had taken a radical turn and, for the most part, theirs had continued on a prescribed path, that of country gentlemen. But the intervening years had fallen instantly away. Despite the façade of responsible adulthood, these were the self-same boys who had once shared his childhood at Seckford's.

At the splendid wedding breakfast in Martlesham Hall, Francis and his family were seated on a table with his good friend James Lynn, his parents and younger sisters, Marianne and Sarah. The elder Lynns struck up a warm conversation with the Neguses, whilst the girls amused themselves at the abundance of fine young men on show. Francis and James meanwhile renewed their old friendship.

There was much to talk about. James had only recently returned from service as a military surgeon in North America. After the horrors and deprivations of campaign, he now hoped for a quiet life as a country doctor. Francis briefly catalogued his own adventures at sea: his shipwreck at Halifax, the ill-fated battle of Minorca, the siege of Louisburg and the capture of Belle-Île. James was impressed, Francis was dismissive.

'What next, Light? Are you planning to settle down at last?'

'I'm a navy man, James. There isn't much else I can do. But it's a lean season for sailors. Half the navy's been paid off. There's no need for us in peacetime, I'm afraid. Let's hope for a war soon, eh?' he grinned.

James shuddered. 'Heaven forfend! I would never wish that

on anyone, not even in jest.'

Francis looked about them, indicating the other guests. 'Is this enough for you, James? You have seen something of the world. Can you bear to spend the rest of your days in this little corner of England amongst the self-same families you have known all your lives? Do you not feel the slightest constricted by the smallness of it all?' He had only been at home a few weeks but was already champing at the bit.

'Of course, it was a struggle to adjust at first,' James admitted. 'Not the least, sharing a surgery with my father, who still treats me as a green boy. Yet as the months pass, I begin to enjoy the routine of the seasons and the humdrum country life. If this is all until I die, then it will be enough. I count myself blessed to have survived that terrible slaughter. In the light of all that and in respect of the many who did not return, a modicum of the mundane seems like a worthy way to pass one's days.'

He could not argue with James' convictions. War was not much to his taste either. But what else did he have? Unlike his school friends, Francis had no alternatives: there was no great estate, family business or comfortable profession waiting for him in Woodbridge. He had taken a chance on the one world that had been open to a boy such as he, and now even that opportunity had been denied. Searching for a change of subject to something less disheartening, Francis enquired about Anne Goodwin and her family. She seemed to be a lady of some means. Martlesham was a fine property.

'Old Doughboy's done well for himself,' James replied. 'His father was already a prosperous businessman, as you know, but this marriage propels him into quite another society all together.

They are an old family with huge estates. John Goodwin died of a fever in '58; his son had passed away as a boy, so young Anne inherited everything at only eighteen years of age. You can imagine the number of young fellows that came calling on her, but she has a level head on her shoulders and would have none of them. George and she had been friends since childhood, and so it goes. Good for them both, I say,' James added, raising a glass and smiling over at his friend. Francis did the same.

He could not resist enquiring if James also had his eye on any of the comely ladies of the district. Surely marriage would be the next significant step for him if he were to settle down in Suffolk? His friend blushed, a tendency since boyhood. 'As a matter of fact, I do. I have already approached her father; he has agreed to allow us to walk out. She is Miss Eliza Wall of Aldeburgh. Her father is a merchant trader. She is rather lovely,' James mooned, his cheeks growing even redder.

'That's a fair walk, James,' Francis grinned. 'Aldeburgh must be twenty miles from here at least!'

'A metaphorical walk. I ride over twice a week,' James added wryly, as his two sisters giggled over his discomfiture. 'You must come to lunch next Sunday after church. Father and Mother would be delighted. Eliza will be present with her parents ... it will be a most congenial gathering!' James insisted.

'Oh, do come, Mr Light,' interjected Miss Marianne Lynn, the elder of the two sisters. The annoying little girl of Francis' memory had blossomed into a charming young lady of not yet twenty. Her blonde hair fell in soft curls from an elaborate topknot. Marianne was lively of manner, much more so than her serious brother, with a gleam in her eye and an upturn to her nose that was most appealing. 'It will be a fearful boring lunch with James blushing and stuttering and Miss Eliza giving him sheep eyes across the table. Please say you'll come! Else Sarah and I shall die of boredom!'

***

Miss Marianne Lynn. The heady perfume of the bruised petals brought her vividly back, evoking the floral scent that she always wore. Deep in the night in his lonely bunk as the ship lumbered through the dark, Francis imagined his future self, a rich nabob with a great fortune. He would return home to claim Marianne's hand and they would live together with no impediments to their happiness. But in his more lucid moments, and because he was not given to self-delusion, Francis knew that Marianne would not wait for him. How could she? He might never return, or not for so many years that she would by then be an old maid, past child-bearing, her best days lost in hopeless anticipation. They might hardly recognise each other.

Although they had parted as lovers, it had been in the full knowledge that this was the end for both of them. Francis even suspected that Marianne had always known the inevitable outcome. For all her tender years, she possessed a matter-of-fact astuteness that surprised him. He had expected gently brought-up women to be naïve and given to girlish fantasy. Marianne had shown him otherwise. Perhaps he had merely been the plaything? A taste of the unattainable before she settled for the rural life with a more suitable partner? Or was his conscience now rearranging the details of their relationship to a more palatable truth, since he had chosen to leave her anyway? There would be many earthly temptations in the East, nor was he a man to resist them. Francis crushed the petals in his palm and tossed them into the foaming wake. It was time to take leave of the past and its encumbrances.

'So, this is where you're hiding, is it?' His reverie was disturbed by the gravel voice of the captain. Francis spun round, tensing his brow instinctively. John Allen was a hard taskmaster for whom little was ever good enough. He sensed a particular resentment towards him due probably to his naval background; there was ever a sense of inferiority amongst merchant seamen towards their peers in the service. Throughout the whole voyage, Allen had niggled and scrutinised his every move, hasty to criticise, but without a single word of praise for things well done. Francis had been singled out amongst all the other officers for this unwarranted treatment but had resisted any provocation to retaliate, for he suspected that was exactly what Allen desired. Francis was a naval officer. There could be no harder regime to train a man to obedience than that.

'Sir?' He did not apologise; he had done nothing wrong.

'I wanted to sound you out on a matter of mutual interest. Let us walk the deck?' It was not the response that Francis expected.

'As you wish, Captain.' The two men strolled a while, nodding, chivvying and, on occasion, addressing, crew men as they passed. The ship had a good wind and, as the sails filled, the hectic activity of their departure was slackening. The atmosphere was merry and full of expectancy, typical at the onset of a voyage, before inevitable boredom sets in. Perhaps Captain Allen, too, was in better humour after his sojourn on the balmy island.

'You've been aboard four months now, Light. Time enough

to learn the ropes.' Captain Allen walked stiffly, hands behind his back. Francis sensed awkwardness. The captain was not finding it easy to broach whatever subject he had in mind.

Allen was not a natural leader, lacking the qualities of humanity, courage and good humour that Francis had observed in the best men under whom he had served. As a navigator, however, he was second to none, his seamanship impressive. But he was no commander. That was quite another skill. Allen's mean and disparaging manner was the shield he wore to mask his discomfiture.

'I believe I have acquitted myself well enough so far, sir,' Francis answered warily.

The captain harrumphed, his swarthy hatchet face giving little away. Silence lay between them as they ascended to the main deck, one behind the other, stepping over a young sailor swabbing at their feet. 'Just so,' Allen finally replied. 'Just so.'

'If that is all, sir, perhaps I might attend to some of my other duties?' Francis asked, more than ready to end the uncomfortable interlude.

Allen stopped dead, placing a hand on his shoulder. 'Not yet, Mr Light. I haven't finished.' He paused, then blurted out. 'I understand that when you reach Fort St George, you intend to hawk yourself around the country agents in Madras town?'

Francis gave him a cool stare before answering. 'Yes, sir. I have hopes for a ship of my own.'

The captain scoffed, taking out a kerchief to mop his brow despite the amiable breeze. 'It strikes me, my lad, you are green behind the ears. Have you any idea what awaits you out there?'

Francis bridled at the use of the word 'lad'. He was twenty-four and a lieutenant in the Royal Navy. With luck he might have been a captain of a warship by now. Lad, indeed. 'I can sail anything, sir. I have the experience,' he replied tersely.

'No, you don't, boy. The Royal Navy is no training for a country ship in Andaman waters. You've no bloody idea. If you're lucky, all you'll have to worry about is pirates or going down in one of their hellish storms. Most like, your own crew will throw you overboard and sail off with your cargo. You won't be commanding British tars, you know? Your crew will be a raggle-taggle of lascars, blackamoors and the odd slit-eyed yellow-skin. Any white men aboard will only be there because they've got a fuckin' price on their heads. They'll eat a jack-a-dandy like you for dinner and spit out your fancy buttons.'

The foul-mouthed tirade left Francis speechless. All he could manage was a weak: 'I beg your pardon, sir?'

Captain Allen wiped a hand across his mouth, still spattered with spittle from his vehemence. 'I mean no disrespect, sir. I'm a plain-talking Yorkshireman, not a fancy grammar school boy such as yourself. I know country ships, because I manned them for many a day. It's a damned hard life. Few men do more than scratch a living. I can offer you something better. What say you sign on permanently with the *Clive*? I'll make you first mate next turnabout. Decent wage. Your own cabin. There's real pickings to be had on these Indiamen. We can charge the passengers whatever we like and there's ample opportunity for a pretty penny of business on the side. Are you up for it, Light?'

Francis' initial rage now evolved into utter astonishment. From insult to partnership in a few sentences? Allen was the oddest fellow. 'I ... er ...' Francis blew out air slowly as he searched for an adequate response. 'May I think on it, sir? This is not at all what I anticipated. Your offer is most unexpected. Most generous too, of course, but such a matter would require a measure of consideration.'

'Good man, good man,' Allen clapped him on the back, evidently expecting Francis to accept, insensible to his hesitation. 'Over dinner tonight then. We'll open a few bottles and thrash it out, eh? I've had my eye on you since we left Kent. Captain Amherst had the right of it. You're a fine seaman. Intelligent. Deep-thinking. You could go far, lad, with a bit of right guidance from me.'

And with that, the good captain gave a rigid nod and took an abrupt leave. Francis smiled to himself. He had thought he was on trial for being a navy man when all along the captain had been taking his measure! This was only Allen's second journey out as master. Advancement had been a weight on him until along came Lieutenant Light, the perfect second-in-command, someone to take over the onerous duties of leading the men, while Allen settled back as sailing master to make his own private fortune on the side. Francis was under no illusion that this proposal was entirely to serve Allen himself. If he agreed, Allen would no doubt do all in his power to retain him as first mate for as long as possible. He might never make captain at all, although he would probably make a tidy penny, enough perhaps to return to Woodbridge and marry Miss Marianne Lynn.

But plough the oceans at snail's pace back and forth for the rest of his career? The boredom and the deprivations would age him prematurely. Even should he eventually secure his own ship, it was no life for a man of passion. And if he did secure Marianne's hand, what kind of marriage would it be for both of them? He would never see his children from one year to the next. She would be alone in society without her husband by her side. He could not be expected to stay celibate. Marianne Lynn would not accept such terms, for she was too gay and lively to live such a sedate and lonely existence.

This was not the time, however, to reject the captain's offer with two months' hard sailing ahead. Allen would be sour and even more vindictive if he thought his plans for an easier life had been thwarted. Francis must keep him dangling until they reached Madras. Once in port, he would humbly beg pardon and reveal his change of heart. His mind was set; no temptation could sway him now.

He would have his own country ship, no matter how humble, even if Allen was right when he described it as a poisoned chalice. Allen's description of the dangers aboard a local trading ship were probably exaggeration, adopted to scare him into accepting his proposition. Or was it? Perhaps he was about to take the single most injudicious decision of his life. No matter. It was his firm belief that once one's route is fixed then there must be no deviation as long as there is a chance of success. In the meantime, he must be forearmed against every eventuality, including disaster. Know your enemy. Learn his ways. Francis had two months of endless ocean to ready himself for the task.

11

Fort St George

Madras town, The Coromandel Coast. 25th November 1765

The offices of the shipping agent languished in a narrow alley on the edge of the European settlement on the upper storey of a building that would hardly strike much confidence in a prospective employee. Francis Light stepped over a bag of sleeping bones stretched across the doorway and climbed up dusty, cobwebbed stairs. There was a ripe odour of decay, plaster peeling from the walls and patches of mould creeping down. At the upper landing, he came upon a solid wooden door bearing a brass plate with the company legend: '*Jourdan and DeSouza*'. At least it was the right place.

Knocking briskly, Light waited but there was no response. He rapped again more forcefully this time, but still no answer. Trying the door, he found it unlocked, stepping inside with a tentative 'Halloo?' The antechamber was empty of people, but stuffed full with clutter: a wooden desk scattered with administrative paraphernalia; wooden boxes half full of assorted books; and journals piled haphazardly. The office was in the process of either being emptied or unpacked. On one wall stood a cabinet, still half-full of ledgers, its door hanging open. A side table contained a jug of water and a few terracotta cups. Against the facing wall stood a bench decently upholstered in a sturdy cloth of a colourful weave. Light took a seat and waited.

It was hot in the tiny room whose only source of air or light came from a row of meander-like apertures high up along the length of the outside wall. The sticky heat of Madras was already a torment, not the least because he was dressed most inappropriately for the clime. His wardrobe was limited, purchased for the English summer, thus not in the least suitable for India. Apparently, he had arrived during the cooler time of year, at the onset of the north-east monsoon, but found it hard to credit. Surely any hotter would roast them all alive? The rains had indeed recently set in, but the humidity was high. As were the mosquitoes that hung round him in droves, relishing his virgin European blood. The infernal biters gathered thickest in dark corners, such as beneath the bench he was sitting on. He found himself constantly shaking his legs, like an old man with the tremors.

Light loosened his neck tie, stood up and propped the door open, then picked up a piece of discarded paper to make an impromptu fan. Sweat trickled down his face and back, pooling unpleasantly in his neck, armpits and groin. He helped himself to a glass of tepid water, praying that it had been well boiled. The last thing he wished was an illness of the bowels; the spicy food alone was already causing him a fearful loosening.

Just at that same moment, Francis heard a tread on the stairs below. He hurriedly closed the door, replaced his cup, attempted to smarten his attire, and took a seat back on the bench, just in time for the new arrival to burst in. It was a young man, not much more than a boy, carrying a voluminous leather bag stuffed with documents. His fine features still bore the fresh bloom of boyhood, although he was sweaty in the late morning heat, his black glossy waves scarce restrained by an untidy ribbon. He took in Francis with a cool appraisal. 'Good day to you, sir. May I be of assistance?'

The young man's voice had the mellifluous lilt of the cultured Irishman and something of their typical ease of manner. Yet there was a note of reproof, politely reminding Francis that it was not quite acceptable to enter the premises of another without invitation.

'My apologies for entering unbidden. The door was open and, as it is an office, I supposed there would be persons within. My name is Lieutenant Francis Light, formerly of the Royal Navy. I bring letters of introduction ...' Francis reached into his pocket and withdrew two envelopes.

The young man set down his bag and waved the letters away. 'I have no authority here, sir. I am merely present today as an advisor to the partners ... Mr John Sullivan, at your service.' This time he extended one hand in formal greeting with more warmth than his initial reception. 'We expect Messrs Jourdan and DeSouza after luncheon. May I ask, do you have an appointment?'

Francis shook his head. 'I arrived in Madras but a few days ago. This is my first opportunity to call. Your employers come highly recommended.'

Sullivan's smile carried a touch of the unctuous. 'You have chosen well, sir. This company is one of Madras' most respected private traders. As you can see, we are in the process of moving to offices in a much more favourable district. All due to the excellent endeavours of the owners ...' Francis had an odd notion that the lad was courting him. Sullivan spoke elegantly, evidently an educated young man, at ease in society. For an Irishman to display such qualities would suggest great wealth. John Sullivan was not the usual bog hopper Francis had come across in his naval days.

'May I ask your position here, Mr Sullivan? Are you a member of the agency?' Francis wished to ascertain whether Sullivan was a significant employee or merely a meddlesome junior.

'Call me John, sir. Madras is a small place and one soon knows everyone by their first name. No, I am not in official employ here. But I do assist the office with their accounting procedures a few days out of the month. For the most part, I am a writer with the Company but, of course, everyone in Fort St George has other irons in the fire. Or why indeed would we even be here? Welcome to Madras, sir. May I ask who introduced you to Jourdan and DeSouza?'

There was already something of a cat and mouse game in their interchange. For a junior accounts clerk, Sullivan was most presumptuous, but then, so was his own presence in the offices without leave. 'Captain John Amherst of the British navy, and one James Scott ...'

'James Scott? You are an acquaintance of Jamie Scott? Well, well, well ... it is indeed a small world, sir.'

'You know Lieutenant Scott? From Makerstoun in the Borders? Previously of the HMS *Arrogant*?' Francis ventured. It was a common enough name. Perhaps he knew a different James Scott?

'One and the same, Mr Light. Yes, you might say we are acquainted.' And with that non-committal answer, John Sullivan patted Francis on the back, a friendly grin forming on his fine-boned face. It was as yet unclear in what light he regarded Scott. 'A bite to eat and a cool ale? I know a decent place not too far. Mr

Jourdan will take his time after the council meeting. The directors are famed for their long Monday luncheons. Thus, I shall have plenty of time to answer your question and the many others I am sure you have. What do you say, man?'

They took their meal in a tavern not far from the Sea Gate, in an upper room with large windows giving out over the wall of White Town. Within it was shady and cool, in contrast to the fierce heat and brilliant light outside. The view of the sea and the wide, open sands of the Coromandel were pleasing to the eye, the first time Francis had objectively appreciated them since his arrival. He took a deep breath, grateful for the lively sea breeze that stirred the muslin curtains. White-crested waves boomed on the shore; the tide was on the turn. On the horizon, distant clouds were roiling grey, promising rain.

'A welcome gust,' Francis observed, leaving the ordering to Sullivan with the request that the food be 'gentle on the spices', patting his guts with a pained look.

'You'll adjust, Mr Light. Give time,' Sullivan smiled back. 'Looks like a storm's coming. A pleasant wind now, to be sure, but I doubt you shall be saying that in an hour or so. I have never seen the like of the tempests in these parts. You would think the end of the world was nigh.'

Lunch arrived, a plate of rice and meat called 'biryanee', with a jug of surprisingly cool ale. 'They keep it in earthenware jars, stored in underground chambers. The Lord knows why we use wooden barrels, eh?'

Sullivan was an easy companion. The younger man had himself not been long in Madras, having arrived only the year before, in which time he appeared to have quickly assimilated.

John Sullivan originated from Cork, where his father was a judge. He had been educated at Greenwich School in London, with the support of his uncle Laurence, a director of the Company. Greenwich was a naval school meant for the sons of deceased officers. Strings would have been pulled for John Sullivan to attend without a navy background in his family. Francis listened to Sullivan's casual reference to his progression from schoolboy to civil servant, and wondered at how easy life was for some. John was not yet seventeen, with no experience other than his prodigious talent for mathematics, information he had volunteered with no sense of embarrassment or boast. It was simply a fact. Sullivan was not a man for pretence.

Shrugging off his personal sense of injustice, Francis decided to dwell on his luck at having already made such a fortuitous acquaintance. Turn disadvantage into advantage, he reminded himself. He was also eager to deflect the subject away from that of personal histories at this early stage in their relationship. He did not want to prejudice Sullivan's opinion before he had time to prove himself. 'But you have not yet told me how you know James Scott!'

'Ah, the indomitable Captain Scott!' Sullivan replied.

'Captain?' Francis gasped. 'I thought he was a Company clerk?' Sullivan polished off the last spoonful of his lunch, wiped his mouth on a napkin and settled back with another glass of ale in his hand before continuing. He was enjoying the novelty of his position as local authority on Madras and its affairs.

'James was a writer at first. For a very short time, I believe,' Sullivan confided. 'This would be a year or so before I arrived. Apparently, the rigours of office work and the restrictions of

Madras society proved not to his taste, if I may be so bold as to say. The Honourable Company and Mr Scott parted company. Honourably. For, in truth, had they not done so, they would soon have parted dishonourably. Or so I have been told!' Sullivan's eyes, gunmetal in the office, now glinted pale blue, savouring the wit of his own turn of phrase.

Francis recognised the impetuous Scott between the lines of the story. 'I, too, cannot quite see James Scott constricted behind the confines of a desk. So, what then? I had a letter from him but it was written many months ago and did not elaborate on specifics, other than a description of the town and a glowing account of the many opportunities here. I presume he joined Jourdan and DeSouza? Is that how you met?'

Sullivan shook his head. 'No, he did not join Jourdan. We met socially through acquaintances. But you are right, of course. James was wasted as a Company servant. His talents lie in an entirely more "entrepreneurial" direction. Through the benefit of mutual friends, Scott was introduced to Mr John Call, the chief engineer of Fort St George, who had just acquired a ship and was looking for a captain. It seemed that Scott was his man, so in one swoop, Scott was off the Company's hands, but still making goodly profit for himself and a few of his erstwhile colleagues. *Omnia bene.* We expect him back in April or May when the winds change. You've only just missed him, I'm afraid.'

It was to be expected that Scott had gone back to sea. In truth, Francis knew that had been his friend's intent all along. 'How does he know Mr Jourdan then? And why did he not recommend me to Mr Call?' Francis wondered aloud.

A sudden fierce blow sent the curtains flying and knocked

over a glass on the table. The wooden shutters slapped back and forth; a waiter hurried to secure them. 'Come, let's leave before the onslaught. We don't want to be caught in this storm ...' They headed down to the street where the rain was already falling: fat, heavy drops, each as large as hail. Light was still no wiser about the relationship between Scott and Sullivan.

It was decided that Francis should attend on the morrow at seven before the heat became too intense and everyone retired to rest. The owners of the office would not return today in such weather. Sullivan promised to make an appointment on his behalf and assured Lieutenant Light that he would vouch for him himself. They exchanged thanks and addresses with promises to meet again soon, before Sullivan ducked off in the direction of the offices and Francis to his lodgings. It was only after they had parted company that Sullivan realised he had learned very little about Francis Light other than a bare outline of his career, whilst Francis recognised that his introduction to the agency now depended solely on Sullivan's recommendation.

***

Madras had not so far lived up to Francis' initial taste of the East. In truth, it appeared a settlement at odds with itself. Centred round Fort St George, the walled White Town was little England, if one removed the heat and the native workers. At its heart lay the military fort, dominated by the edifice of Government House, surrounded by a large square and adjunct buildings: the armoury, the arsenal, and of course, the offices of the ubiquitous East India Company. Not far from the fort itself was the Church of St.

Mary's, the first Anglican church east of Suez. It occupied its own little square, flanked by the quarters of the Company servants. The residential streets comprised tightly packed tenements with wooden verandas on the upper floors. The roofs were flat, topped with crenelated parapets where men often slept under the stars when the heat inside was too unbearable. The exterior walls were plastered in a polished white stucco, known locally as *chunam,* that gleamed marble in the sunlight. If one discarded the dirt and noxious smells, the rats and the blocked drains, there was a charm to these dwellings. It was certainly more appealing than many port towns he had visited in the past.

The senior members of the trading, military and administrative community preferred to live outside White Town, in the new neighbourhoods that had sprung up to the north-west on a slightly higher elevation. This area was separated from Black Town by a man-made channel dug in the early days of the settlement in order to alleviate flooding, inevitably channelling more distress to the poorer seaboard streets of the indigenous quarter. The wide tree-lined avenues bordered handsome mansions with spacious gardens, most of which had been rebuilt in the past decade or so after the devastation of the French attack. It was a world apart from the higgledy-piggledy squalor of Black Town and the crowded commercial areas of the fort.

The all-essential well was also situated within the fortified site. Water was always at a premium. Although the city was looped round by two rivers that fed into the bay, when the rains came they regularly broke their banks to form a seawater lagoon. The meagre sandy fields between that struggled to supply food at the best of times then became a salty flood plain.

Madras was not an ideal situation for a settlement. There was no natural harbour. Ships moored far out, with passengers and crew taking their chances through the pounding surf on tiny local canoes. Transporting cargo was commensurately even more difficult. But there were those who heartily approved of its position. The long stretches of the Coromandel Coast made for relatively safe sailing, the balmy sea breezes considered conducive to health, far preferable to the swampy, disease-ridden river forts of Bengal. There were also plenty of local commercial opportunities for a community of merchant traders: the diamond mines of Golconda were only a week away inland, and the villages of the coast were famed for their textiles.

Francis had taken a room within White Town where the dingy alleyways were filled with lodgings, punch houses and brothels to cater for the lower class of employee and soldier. It was no worse than a similar area of London. One thing in its favour was, that in living cheek-by-jowl with the British community, companions were never in short supply. Fellow countrymen were more inclined to socialise together when far away from home, irrespective of their social standing, one of the great levellers that allowed Company men to rise beyond their capability at home.

The rain had now stopped and the night air was cool and fresh, although the streets were still underwater, meagre drains gushing forth in fountains. Light's lodging was nothing but plastered walls, a packed dirt floor and one small window with shutters. It was sparsely furnished with a *charpoy* and wooden stool; his sea chest serving both as storage and a shelf for his few books and candle. The austerity of his room bothered him not at all; even an officer expected but a tiny personal space aboard ship, and in his early days he had shared a gun deck with dozens of men. This was luxury by comparison. But, tonight it was stifling inside, compared to the rain-cooled balmy evening. He was drawn to the fragrant night air now that the stench of humanity had been washed from the streets and the sweet flowers of night time wafted in on the land breeze.

Outside, he wandered awhile, enjoying the welcome freshness, while taking in the rowdy sights and sounds. Sailors in port were accustomed to riotous behaviour; they were almost encouraged to behave so before returning to their closely disciplined shipboard world. It was considered a necessary letting of the frustrations of months under the strictest of regimes. But from what Francis could tell, most of these men were locally based civil servants and soldiers. They appeared to behave to excess every night of the week. Surely it was not conducive to public order if such conduct was condoned? Something of the laxity of social constraints struck him as unhealthy. These men were bored. It led to every manner of problem – from disorder to corruption. It offended his naval sense of order.

Francis entered The Albion, a popular punch house packed to the rafters with revellers. Food was served and every manner of drinks was available, contingent on the purse, especially the eponymous punch, a beverage of alcohol, lime juice, sugar, tea and spices, a popular thirst quencher in these parts. Punch was not the only speciality on the menu. Upstairs were dark-eyed local girls, wrapped in brilliant jewel fabrics, meant for the enjoyment of the guests; a stream of men went up and down at an alarming rate. Francis secured a seat on a bench at the end of one long table, ordering food and a mug of said punch. He listened with amusement to the drunken conversations, watched a few hands of cards, and generally kept to himself.

His table was mostly occupied by a group of gentlemen, well in their cups, whose conversation was boisterously crude, on the edge of becoming disagreeable. One man in particular had already accused a companion of cheating at cards. They might even have come to blows if the accuser had not slid off his seat in the midst of their argument, having to be carried outside to recover from his over-indulgence, thus settling the matter.

It was at that point that a seemingly harmless incident set off an unexpectedly unpleasant chain of events. A portly young man seated next to Light accidentally knocked over his mug. Francis jumped up, but fortunately the liquid had mostly spilled over the table top, barely catching his clothes.

'No harm done,' Light remarked easily, brushing down his breeches.

'Lemmee buy you another mug o' punch ...' garbled the drunken neighbour.

'Why, thank you, sir,' was Francis' reply. The young man stood up and called over a server, demanding another jug.

'Y'ever wonder why it's called punch?' the drunk queried, almost as if thinking aloud. 'Maybe for the fistfights it causes?' he cackled.

Francis laughed. 'I believe, sir, that it owes its name to a Hindi word *pancha*, meaning five, for the five essential ingredients used in the making of it,' he answered.

Suddenly a voice boomed down the table. It was the obnoxious gentleman from earlier, the possible cheat, who was obviously still spoiling for a fight. 'Nonsense, sir! None of this Hindoo garble, if you please. Punch is a good old English word. Puncheon, as any sailor knows, is a large barrel used in the transport of alcohol. Hence punch – beverage.' He delivered his final comment with a hectoring roar, guaranteed to arouse his sycophantic companions, who bellowed their approval.

Francis nodded, sensitive to the sudden hostility and at pains to restore calm. 'Indeed, sir. There are always many different folk tales about such matters. As it happens I'm a sailor myself, so am familiar with the puncheon. But I was told by a Hindu lascar aboard my ship on the journey out, that the word for five was punch.'

'And you take a black fellow's word above mine, y'dog? What sort of gentleman cavorts with natives? Are you a bugger, man? Got a taste for brown buttocks, have you now? Come here, y' unnatural dog, and I'll ram something up you that'll cure you of that!'

Francis staggered back, completely stunned at the gratuitous accusation. If he had expected anything at all in response, he presumed that the other men would settle the inebriated fellow down, perhaps even taking him home at this juncture. But the men were drunk themselves and just as keen on fisticuffs. They were incapable of sound judgment. Everyone rose to their feet, banging their fists on the table and roaring: 'Fight! Fight! Fight!' Onlookers, unaware of the cause, picked up the refrain, shoving each other to view the imminent brawl. Rough hands grabbed Light, who found himself jostled forward. His accuser had now produced a knife, which he was waving around for maximum effect, his eyes glaring and his tongue salivating like a mad dog.

'Good God, desist! Are you all quite mad?' Francis protested vainly, wrestling against the surge of the crowd, warding off the blows that were now raining down on him. The room was out-of-control, bordering on frenzy. Sanity had vanished, replaced by utter madness. Was he about to be beaten to death by a drunken mob in a punch house? Was this how he would reach his end, his promise unfulfilled?

Suddenly a gunshot rang out, so loud that it shattered even the uproar, immediately restoring a modicum of sense to the baying horde. 'Sit back down and take breath, you foul drunken bastards!' shouted an imposing Scottish voice from somewhere in the rear. The sheer authority of the tone brooked no resistance. Everyone sank back, muttering darkly to themselves, the hysteria of moments before seeping away. Light found himself freed as those holding him stepped down, distancing themselves from involvement.

'Are you hurt, sir?' His saviour approached, tucking his pistol back into the sash around his waist. He was a tall, fine-figured man in the dress of a sea captain but with the air of the buccaneer about him, despite the formal attire.

'Only my self-esteem, thank God. I am in your debt, sir. Lieutenant Francis Light, late of the Royal Navy.' Francis was unsteady on his feet, the shock of being the target of a dangerous mob only now sinking in.

'Captain Andrew Ross, at your service.' Ross gave a slight bow of his head. He had a broody quality to his face, accentuated by thick black eyebrows and an angular chin weathered by nature itself. His skin was nut brown from years in the sun and wind. His dark eyes glowered, coal black chips ringed with white. Yet, despite his intimidating presence, Ross' manner was reassuring.

He indicated that Light should join him and his companions in their private room.

The others were jovial men, all captains or senior officers of East Indiamen on the China route; it was a stroke of good fortune that they had been within earshot. They commiserated with Francis, whilst throwing out warning glances to his attackers, who by now had settled back as if nothing had happened, laughing and sniggering, evidently unwilling to take on armed opponents. They preferred more favourable odds, such as an unarmed man alone.

One of Ross's companions, a Captain Charles Pigou, steered Francis to a chair and poured him a glass of brandy. 'Take this. For shock,' he added kindly. 'An unpleasant moment, sir. That spineless excuse for a gentleman is the Honourable Frederick Tavernor, accompanied by his usual toadeaters. You would not be the first innocent man those prodigals have targeted. They're a pack of baying hounds and you were the chosen fox. You're lucky Ross was carrying sidearms. I'm not sure we would have stopped them else.' Pigou was the direct opposite of the morose Ross, a short, stocky man, bald of pate with the face of a pug dog. He was voluble and affable where Ross was saturnine and reserved. Light took to him immediately.

It seemed the Honourable Frederick Tavernor, the younger son of a peer of the realm, was a notorious figure in Fort St George, a noted drunkard, brawler and gambler. No one was surprised at the night's behaviour. Only his noble connections had kept him out of gaol on numerous occasions.

'I cannot thank you enough, gentlemen,' Francis remarked when the shot of decent brandy had brought the colour back to his cheeks. 'For a moment there I thought my time had come. But will there be repercussions, Captain Ross? Discharging a firearm in a public place surely cannot be acceptable to the powers-that-be. I would hate for you to be censured in any way.'

Ross grimaced a tight smile. 'No one will have heard or seen a thing by tomorrow, you can be assured of that, sir.' Ross was a Scot. Francis wondered if he was from the Highlands; there was an enigmatic quality about him, a latter-day Rob Roy. 'Tavernor might be a bastard but he's not one you have to worry about. He's shipping out to Bencoolen this week. They've had enough of him here ...'

The remark caused general hilarity amongst the other men. Light did not understand. 'Bencoolen? Isn't that our base in Sumatra? Why does it amuse you so?'

Pigou took over the explanation. 'It amuses us to see that wretched rantipole receive his just deserts at long last. Tavernor was sent out here because he was an embarrassment to his family in London. He left gambling debts all over the place, has a reputation for violating even well-born women, and killed a man in a duel a few years back. So, to offset the scandal back home, they rewarded him with a senior post in the Company, and despatched him to Fort St George, where he has continued to be a menace to all good people. The Council here has tolerated his excesses long enough. Now, in its wisdom, it has decided to "promote" him further. Perhaps I should explain that a posting to Bencoolen, no matter the seniority, is either a death sentence or a move that ends your career for good. Fort Marlborough is nothing but a swamp of disease and corruption. But there'll be plenty of brandy and dice to keep the Honourable Freddie happy.'

His rescuers were men of the same ilk as those he had served with in the war. Captain Ross, indeed, had been a lieutenant in the navy but had forsaken the service some years before for the more lucrative India trade. He had little patience for English self-importance and the closing of ranks around money and birth. Ross believed that men who would succeed were the ones who forged their own path, despite the obstacles that society threw in their way. 'Hardship makes men of us, Light. The rest are mere inward-looking sycophants who make their fortunes from the toil of better men.'

'Excuse my gloomy friend Ross,' laughed Charles Pigou. 'He's a miserable long-shanks, at the best of times. Not that I do not find his argument convincing, sir, but I prefer to use the blinkered narrow-mindedness of the majority to my own advantage. There is nothing wrong with the making of fortunes, *per se*. We are all in pursuit of wealth and the ease which it may bring. But it does not follow that a fellow has to be a bully just because he can.' He poured another round of brandy and raised a toast to the King. They all held up their glasses, excepting Ross, who sneered into his glass. Francis was sure he was a Jacobite.

'You say, you're looking for work as a country trader?' Pigou went on. 'It's a dangerous existence, young man, but you're correct in your assumption that it is the way to make your fortune. If you have the stomach for adventure and a few brains in your head, the Andaman route is where the future lies. India's finished for trade. It's all about territory and taxation now that the government's moved in. The Company wants China but they can't get it on their terms. The Straits holds the key, mark my words ... That is where they shall go next.'

Francis gave Pigou's advice some consideration. 'I was warned that my naval background might not serve me on a country ship with a native crew. I've been trying to learn Hindoo so that at least I can converse with the men. What other lessons might I learn?'

Pigou and the others nodded their agreement. 'Hindoo is useful, of course. We all have a smattering. Learn as many of the heathen languages as you can. Tamil is spoken by the local traders here and most of the lascars know it well. But if I were you, it's the Malay tongue you'll need the most. Everyone in the waters east of here speaks Malay. Doesn't signify if they are Javanese, Sumatrans, Balinese, Bugis, Siamese, Illanuns, Arabs, Chulias or what have you ... Malay is the lingo of the southern seas. Learn that and you'll have a head start, man.'

There was general consensus to Pigou's suggestion. Even Ross spoke up. 'The Malays are amongst the best navigators you'll ever meet, Light. The Bugis, too. It's in their blood. Some call them pirates, but don't be fooled. These men are traders and sailors going back down the ages who can turn a ship on a pin head and find their way blind just by smelling on the wind. They don't need maps and charts. Get a lascar crew and win their trust. I'm telling you now, you'll not be sorry.'

Francis' head was crammed with information, gleaned by chance on that one very eventful day after six months of endless nothing at sea. He was inordinately grateful to these sailors and their camaraderie. But then, it was the naval code. Sailors were never long in port; they did not waste a moment when they could make acquaintances with their peers. Plying these waters, he felt sure he would rub up against these men in the years to come.

Strolling back to his lodgings, a little unsteady on his feet himself by then, Francis stumbled at the entrance to his lodgings over another collection of starving bones. This poor unfortunate appeared to be a small child. Whether due to his maudlin state of inebriation or some sense that he ought to return the kindness of strangers that he had received that night, Francis crouched down to the level of the child. Black eyes stared back at him, rigid with fear, out of a face so dirty that he could make out no features. A tangled mop of mud-stiffened hair framed the tiny face. He couldn't tell if it was male or female.

'Don't be scared, I mean no harm ... Francis murmured kindly but his words only increased the child's alarm. It backed against the wall, eyes now darting this way and that, searching for an escape route.

Thrusting into his pocket, Francis searched for something to offer by way of food and found a tiny nub of sugar, which he extended slowly, rather as one might feed a skittish horse. The eyes fixed on the morsel and then, in a move so quick it barely registered, the sugar was gone. Francis heard a grinding sound and then saw white teeth smiling up at him. A hand extended, asking for more.

Would he have acted as he then did if he had been entirely sober? In later years Francis pondered on his next action. Without hesitation, he picked up the tiny body and carried the child to his room, where he washed him down and gave him bread and water. The child was a little boy, perhaps six years old; it was hard to tell since he had been reduced to nothing but a skeleton with swollen belly. The little boy ate slowly, as if each movement was a great effort, and then curled up on the floor and fell asleep, much as a puppy might.

Francis lay on his cot and marvelled on the strangeness of the day. Some purpose had guided his hand through each of his encounters. Luck or madness? Time alone would tell.

12
The Foundling

The Kokkilai Lagoon, Dutch Ceylon. April 1766

They waded ashore like ghostly shadows, dragging their shallow-bottomed canoes onto the sand bar in a blue-black dark so deep that only the gleam from the inky water shed any ambient light. The hour was perfectly judged, when rolling clouds of perse obscured the luminous firmament of night. Only an imperceptible paling above the distant horizon marked the border between sea and sky, foretelling of the forthcoming dawn. It was the time of deepest slumber and darkest deeds.

The rain had been relentless but the worst of the storm had now abated. The sea was choppy but manageable for the narrow crafts that skimmed to shore, cutting through the swell with the grace of sea creatures. The native crew paddled as one, impervious to the constant drizzle, although wet to the bone. It would be near impossible for any passing vessel to observe them. Only a few nights in a sailing season were so well-suited for their mission.

Waves slopped lazily onto the sand, as if turning over in their sheets to sink back into dreams. An occasional plop or splash from the lagoon beyond heralded nothing more than fish in the shallows or a wading bird disturbed from its upright rest. The men listened, breath-held, straining the silence for unnatural activity or movement. Alone in a world of water, it seemed unthinkable that firm ground was but a short distance away.

Then, as if an apparition had crossed the portal from another existence, human figures materialised from the denser dark on either side. Escape in any direction but the sea was impossible. They were surrounded both by mangroves and by strangers. The sailors drew their weapons. Had they walked into a trap? Were the Dutch waiting for them after all?

A muttered exchange in a language Light did not recognise reassured his men. Blades were returned to sheaths and cursory greetings shared. With the speed of the seasoned smuggler, the two cargoes were checked and exchanged: the finest cinnamon, coffee and pepper for which Dutch Ceylon was renowned, in return for the guns and powder to assist the men of Kandy in their struggle against their hated European occupiers. The locals were also grateful for fresh *bonita*, caught the day before in the rich waters of the Maldives, fish for the market that would fetch much-needed cash. Not to mention the opium, a commodity valued everywhere, both for use and barter.

As quickly as they had appeared, the traders melted back into the darkness. The rain was slackening off, a faint dusky smudge of purple tinged with sandy gold announcing that day was but an hour or so away. Shimmering at the prospect, the watery surface of the sea replicated the blurry moon and cloudy sky. The land vanished; they were suspended in space with nothing but the heavens above and below. It was an ethereal effect, but lost on the men whose only thought was to make their getaway before the dawn.

The lagoon beyond the sand bar was already stirring into life at the promise of morning. Where before it had seemed an empty mudflat, now the waters revealed egrets and pelicans, wild ducks bobbing asleep in the reeds, cormorants swooping for an early morsel – and impossibly strange, long-legged waders, creatures from an absurd nursery tale.

'What the devil are they?' Light muttered at the sight of a large bird picking its elegant way through brackish water, shaking sleep and rain from its feathers with the poise of a slender beauty arranging her delicate pastel cloak.

'Flamencos. Portuguese name,' replied one of his crew. 'Taste good. Feathers can sell. Good price.' Light shook his head. '*Bukan sekarang. Lain hari*,' Not now, another day. They waded further out, pushing the canoes back into the surf, eager now to reach their ship and deeper water or they risked an unwanted encounter with a Dutch warship cruising for interlopers.

By midday they were in open ocean catching the south-west winds with home a mere three days away. Light's gamble had paid off. This had been his maiden voyage, Madras to the Maldives, with a cargo of rice, tin and cotton thread in exchange for coir fibre and cowrie shells. For Jourdan and DeSouza, it was a practice run to gauge the fitness of their new employee. Much rested on the results, a chance to move beyond the tedious apprenticeship of the past few months, ferrying supplies and mail along the coast from Madras to Fort St David and Pondicherry. But other competences were under scrutiny; the new captain had demonstrated to his crew his understanding of the 'business' of country trade. They were well pleased with the opportunity to deal in contraband, from which they all would benefit.

It had been a relatively easy haul but not without potential pitfalls all the same. To his satisfaction, the run had been smooth, his task accomplished as instructed. His employers might now consider trusting him with the more lucrative Andaman routes. But in the meantime, no earthly reason prevented making a little profit for himself and his men. The detour to Dutch Ceylon on the return passage had been suggested by a crewman, a man of Kandy himself, and had been set in play during their enforced halt in the Maldives. Yet it had been Francis Light's inspiration to solicit from his crew the prospects for a foray into smuggling, which might breach the Dutch embargo and bring some welcome trade to the locals, establishing a valuable future sideline. Not to mention accrue some vital coin for his own personal reserves. As Sullivan had said: 'After all, isn't this what we are here for?'

***

Francis had sent several letters home already: from Madeira, Johanna, and on his arrival to Madras, with no assurance they would arrive or, if they did, in what order they might reach Suffolk. The perceived wisdom was to dispatch the letter and trust in God, then take comfort from imagining the family reading it. It was now time to take up his pen once more to send positive news of his current turn of fortune, written, of course, in judiciously selected words. The people at home need not know everything.

Dear Uncle William,
May this Letter find you well and enjoying the last of autumn (for it will be at least October before this reaches you 'though only April here). Today marks one year since I sailed East on the Clive. My mind dwells heavily

on the Home I have left and the People who wait there for me. So much has transpired in a twelvemonth! First there was naught but the tedium of an endless sea, each day dragging after the other with little variety. Then we reached Madras and the time has flown, every moment full of new sights and novel experiences, almost too many to recount. But I will endeavour to present a flavour of my Adventures in order to allay any fears you may have, and to bring you some amusement.

It is always Summer in the Tropics, where the Sun burns hot and the air is heavy with moisture, quite unlike a sunny day in Woodbridge. The Land is lush with vegetation; flowers and plants grow to extraordinary sizes, and display an inconceivable array of hues. Everything is imbued with light and colour, from the Natural World to the bustling Town and its people, who deck themselves in gay colours and flamboyant cloths. Then there are the coastal waters beside whose wide beach the Settlement flourishes. The Sea is an ever-changing palette of blue: from turquoise to deep purple and indigo depending on the time of day and the depth of the Water, which is so clear that one can see down to the sandy seabed and observe the play of colourful shoals of fish. Rolling surf breaks on white sand beaches that are everywhere fringed with palms. Rivers meander to the sea flanked by steamy mangrove Swamps, alive with every species of plant and animal life, many you could scarce imagine. A veritable Garden of Eden. But still, I long for a cool fresh shower of rain and the bracing morning of a fresh autumnal day.

No Countryside in all the world compares to matchless Suffolk!

At the moment we are entering the time of year known as the South West Monsoon, so there is much rain, and storms of terrifying force. This is the time for Homeward Crossings so perhaps this dispatch will not be too tardy in reaching you, should the Ship on which it is conveyed find a favourable blow.

My introduction to the company of Jourdan and DeSouza was successful, I am heartily pleased to report, thanks to my excellent references and the support of a Company clerk by the name of Sullivan who spoke most kindly on my behalf. He is a refined Fellow who has proved to be an invaluable acquaintance. Thus, I was immediately offered not only Employment but – I can hardly believe it even now! – a Ship of my own. So, dear Uncle William, it is now Captain Francis Light at your service, if you please. Remember my dreams as a Boy setting out to sea? Now they have come to pass. My new Ship, a handy little snow, the Speedwell, is well-named for she is a lively boat, fast and alert, gliding along as neatly as a swan, even in these unpredictable waters.

Of my employers Francis Jourdan, is an English Gentleman and member of the Madras Council, while Anthony DeSouza, is a Portuguese Señor with family tentacles in the maritime trade of every significant port of India and beyond – even as far as South America! They are both thus well connected. The Agency is the most respected in Fort St George and well known even in Bengal. I am most fortunate to be in their employ. At last, a stroke of luck!

Since I assumed my Commission, I have been familiarising myself with the Coromandel Coast, running back and forth on local trading missions, whilst waiting for the Sailing Season to commence. For six months of the year, November to March, the winds blow from the North East only: travel is only permissible in one direction, excepting short coastal runs by way of tidal currents. Then, wondrously, at the onset of April, the winds change entirely and for the rest of the year they blow solely from the South-West, thus stranded travellers may embark on their journeys homeward. The change of season is accompanied by Storms and Rains and is cooler than the accustomed fierce heat. But, despite the relief from burning sun, the rains inevitably bring other disadvantages, namely floods and outbreaks of disease and calentures.

Finally, in March, taking advantage of the last weeks of the North East sailing, I received my first real orders to deliver a much-needed Cargo of rice, tin and cotton thread to a distant island chain, the Maldives, that lie far to the south-west of the Indian mainland. It is a wondrous place, an Archipelago of coral reefs set in an aquamarine ocean of incomparable beauty. The locals call these islands 'Atollohu', rendered in English as Atolls. One would not imagine that these tiny rocks might sustain life, but they are a busy little trading centre. What could they export, you may well wonder? The Ingenuity of

Man is assuredly his greatest attribute. The people of these reefs trade in a shell known as Cowrie, a medium of exchange throughout the East Indies. Nothing much of value grows but the people have ingeniously found many usages for the ubiquitous Coconut Palms. They waste nothing of this tree: its fruit gives food, water and fermented liquor, whilst its unwanted parts make roofing, shelters and woven goods. The Fibre of the coconut, namely Coir, is sturdy and impervious to saltwater. It has become a boon to Mariners for whom high quality rope is essential. Mirabile dictu! Deserted islands at the edge of the earth discover their own particular means to enter the Mercantile World!

By the time we had achieved our goal, we were forced to linger awhile to await the change of Season so that we might make our return journey with our new Cargo. It was a pleasant Sojourn on these balmy atolls. On the way back, we made a landing to deal in fresh fish and local spices on the Dutch island of Ceylon, until we found the wind and headed for home, my first voyage as a Captain realised! Now I eagerly anticipate the challenge of the Eastern route across the Andaman Sea, to trade in the calmer waters of the Straits of Malacca. How the very names roll off the tongue and bring to mind Adventure on the High Seas!

My crew are sterling men, competent seamen who know these waters as no other, for they are mostly Sea People, born and raised aboard. I have struck up an amicable understanding with them, aided by my growing

Proficiency in their language. Dr Ray would not credit how successfully my former dullard brain has taken to the tongues of the East. I have been assisted in my learning by a cabin boy whose serendipitous appearance near my lodgings some months ago has proved of enormous benefit, I believe, to both our Fortunes. The lad knew not one word of English when I met him; already he has gained a fluency hardly creditable. He has also proved to be the most assiduous of teachers. Not only has he imparted his language to me, but he also has instructed me in the Customs and Traditions of the native crewmen. Thus, I have been able to negotiate the murky currents of Mutual Understanding with far more skill than many of my Peers. He is a very intelligent boy, already reading fluently and able to write in two languages. His aptitude has confirmed my suspicions that Intellect lies not in the upper classes alone; it is a Human Trait randomly assigned by God. It is a wicked thing that we deem the Poor not deserving of Education!

The young Boy goes by the name of Soliman. He is an Orphan who knows not even his place of origin. He can neither tell me his Age nor does he seem even to understand the concept. At first, I thought he was but five or six, but now I realise that he is older, probably more akin to ten years old. His small size, typical of his Race, and the state of Malnutrition in which he presented, gave the impression of a much younger child. The poor boy knows nothing of his Mother, other than that she died long ago, after which his sailor Father raised him largely on the seas, before he himself passed away from a Cruel Fever. It is a melancholy tale, to be sure, that touched my heart. I am determined to do what I can for this exceptional boy. I believe there is a debt that I must pay in return for the great Love and Protection that I have received in life. A different Fate might have made of me an unwanted orphan, like Soliman cast out alone on the Four Winds.

So, sir, please be comforted that your Prodigal boy is well and thriving, on the road to bringing back his Fortune! Please God it will not be long before I am Home and we can share a toast to adventure and to life. Give my fondest regards to Aunt Margaret and wish her well. I would also be most grateful if you could narrate these words to my Mother. As you know she struggles with her letters and her eyes are poor these days; it would be a great comfort to know that she might hear my idle Musings read aloud in your deep and hearty voice.

Ever in my thoughts and prayers,
Your loving son,
Francis Light (Capt.!)

While the ink dried, Francis scanned the letter, the euphemistic tone a cause for wry amusement. The past few months had not been quite the idyllic existence he wished his family to believe. Letters home required only as much genuine detail that loved ones needed as reassurance. Whether in the navy, the military or in the Company, service men far from home learned that from the start. Good news relayed in hearty tone was recommended. He had often heard of chatty letters arriving home long after families were notified of the author's death. Such dispatches would at least offer consolation of happier times to temper bitter grief.

The core of his account was honest enough, if embellished in such a way as to relieve their concerns. There was no need for them to know that he had near been killed in a tavern brawl; that he had initially found little favour with Francis Jourdan (who seemed disinclined to regard James Scott's opinion as character reference); or that Anthony DeSouza preferred new employees to work their way up the junior ranks aboard ship for a few years until they were well-versed in the local environment. Only then were they allowed command.

It had come down to the timely intervention of John Sullivan that the two men finally made an exception and offered Francis Light a vessel of his own. It was fortunate that the agency had recently acquired new ships and partnerships and were in dire need of competent masters. Light owed his friend for that intercession, although he was unsure what had stirred his new acquaintance to express such confidence in his abilities, when they hardly knew each other.

His first boat had been little more than a glorified lugger, with a tiny crew and few comforts. His employers kept him close to home for many weeks, on postal duties, fetching and carrying missives, orders and reports south to Cuddalore and Pondicherry, and to the small fort at Masulipatnam, further north, rarely out of port for more than a day or two. They hadn't even trusted him to sail to Calicut or Bengal. But there was wisdom in their decision and, instead of railing against it, he had used this time to prepare as best he could. This trial period was not to demonstrate his seamanship; any lieutenant in the Royal Navy had that competence. No, his future with the agency predicated on whether he had the qualities to command his motley crew, and to negotiate the complexities of an alien trading environment.

Light was no longer in a world where the normal rules and regulations of naval life applied. This period of tedious coastal runs allowed him to acclimate himself to more than just the weather– and he used the opportunity well. His prime aim had been to learn the languages of the East Indies, or at least a smattering to make passable communication possible. In this he was ably assisted by the young foundling boy. His description to Uncle William of the importance of Soliman had, if anything, been vastly understated.

For the first few days after he had taken in the boy, Soliman had been his shadow. With huge black eyes in an elfin face, the boy remained otherwise impassive, showing little expression, and making no effort to speak. Light had even wondered if the child was deaf until he had reacted to a loud noise in the street. The boy had seemed stunned into a state of limbo by whatever misery had befallen him, caught somewhere between death and life, capable only of the most fundamental of responses.

And then a week or so after his arrival, a flea-ridden kitten in the street had caught the child's attention – and the little boy had smiled broadly, crouching down to fondle it. Francis rescued the cat, dunked it in water to remove the worst of the infestation, and then indicated that he should feed it milk. From that day on, Soliman's recovery commenced. The child now had a creature on whom he might pour his starved affections, something even more fragile than himself. Through nurture, Soliman found his way out of the darkness into the world of light.

Francis often observed the boy whispering to the kitten, repeatedly using the word '*susu*' and something else that sounded to his ears like 'Harry'.

'Do you call him Susu? Or perhaps Harry? Francis asked him gently, although the latter was an unlikely name for a foreign child to use. The boy paused, obviously understanding something of what Francis had tried to repeat.

He shook his head, saying: 'Susu ...' and indicating the sound of a kitten lapping milk.

Francis gasped aloud, 'Susu is milk?' He pointed to the dish of milk and repeated the word. The boy smiled, nodding his head in agreement.

'So ... what then means "Harry"?' Francis asked.

The boy breathed deeply as if trying to find a way to explain. Finally: '*Nama anak kucing ini ... Hari ... harimau ...*'

Francis seized on the word *nama*. 'Nama? That means "name"?' He tried it out, pointing to himself. 'Nama Francis.'

Understanding flickered in the boy's eyes. '*Nama saya Soliman.*'

'Your name is Soliman! Is that so? Am I right?' He made another guess to test his hypothesis. '*Nama saya Francis.*'

'Fran-sees?' the boy repeated uncertainly.

'Francis, yes, that's it exactly! Francis! Good lad!' Pointing first to himself and then to the child, he said in English: 'I am Francis. You are Soliman!' repeating it three times, to give the boy the chance to understand.

The boy listened carefully, mouthing the unfamiliar words then laughing out loud with pleasure. First touching his own chest and then extending his hand towards Francis he tried it out:

'I-am-Soliman. You-are-Fransees. Ya?' He picked up the kitten and held it out. 'Hari! *Nama kucing ini* Hari!'

'The cat is called Harry! My word, we understand each other! Well, I never!' Francis grinned, delight illuminating both faces.

Now that he had found his voice, Soliman was as eager to talk as before he had been silent. 'Hari ... *harimau*!' He set down the kitten and went on all fours himself, mimicking the prowling gait of a cat. Then splaying out his fingers, he curled them in a clawing motion before pausing and roaring loudly, displaying his teeth fiercely, as though they were fangs. It was immediately obvious to Francis that the child was enacting the behaviour, not of a kitten, but of a large wild cat. This was India. It had to mean tiger.

'A tiger! The word for tiger is ... hari-mo?'

Soliman shook his head. '*Ha-ri-mau.*'

'Harimau. A tiger is harimau and you have called your little kitten Hari because he is striped like a tiger. My God! We are talking at last! Soliman ... are these words Hindi? Tamil?'

'Hindi?' The boy repeated the word. '*Bahasa Hindi, na*?' He shook his head. '*Ini Melayu ... Bahasa Melayu. Saya anak Melayu, Fransees.*'

'Melayu? That means Malay, doesn't it?' Francis retorted. What a piece of good fortune. The boy was a Malay speaker!

'Ya. Malay. Fransees ... *Inggeris*?'

'*Inggeris*? English? You are asking if I am English? Why indeed I am, lad. I am Francis. I am English!'

Soliman chortled, striking a brave stance, and banging both hands on his chest in pride. 'I am Soliman. I am Melayu!'

From that simple beginning, progress proceeded at a rapid

rate, at least on Soliman's part. The boy inhaled the English language, with an aptitude that was astonishing, daily introducing new words into his vocabulary that he seemed to pick up from the aether. All this time when he had spoken not a word, Soliman had been listening, and like every child from babyhood, his agile brain had been making sense of the foreign tongue. Then one day a key had been turned – and the words spilled out. Soon he became able to express himself clearly enough to translate for Francis, which revealed another unexpected surprise. Soliman could speak not only Malay but Tamil also, with a smattering of Hindi too. It was not unusual, he was to discover. Every man jack aboard was multilingual.

Francis' advancement in Malay was more laboured but Soliman proved to be a patient teacher. By the time Light was allocated his lugger, bringing Soliman aboard as a cabin boy and Hari as a useful ratter, he had sufficient proficiency to hold a simple conversation with the crewmen who, just as Captain Pigou had indicated, understood the language wherever they had originated. It was a polyglot company of men. There were local men of the Coromandel, but also a surprising number of others from the length and breadth of the Indies. By the time Francis took command of the *Speedwell* three months later, his crew comprised Indians, Malays, Javanese, Sumatrans, Siamese and even a few Chinese. Yet Captain Light could ply his trade in a language that all of them fully understood.

One feature was shared by every man in common. Where Light expected sullenness or the feigned obedience of an English tar towards an untried officer, these lascars were entirely impassive, much as Soliman had been at first. They stared openly at him, with no apparent expression on their faces, to such a marked extent that at first Francis wondered if they could not understand his clumsy Malay. He confided his confusion to Soliman, who tossed his question over for a while before answering.

'The men not know you. They listen. They do what you say. But not know you yet. Later. You will see. You must wait. They not know you yet.'

Francis recalled his early years at sea as a lowly surgeon's assistant and the front a seaman must present to his superiors. If an officer was senior, they gave due deference, even if behind his back they cursed his very name. If he were lower down the chain of command, he received mostly sullen compliance, the least demanded without causing offence until, of course, the officer in question proved his mettle. Men always had their particular ways of showing respect – or the lack of it – despite the strictures of discipline on board. These lascars might present differently with their aloof reserve, but much the same process was at work. As Soliman had said 'Wait. They not know you yet.' They were wisely reserving judgement until he had won their acceptance.

Folding up the letter to Squire Negus, Light tucked it carefully in a leather pouch ready for when he could place it in the hands of a trustworthy officer on his return journey to England. Indeed, he thought to himself, his men must surely know him now. The trip to the Maldives and the unscheduled stop at Kokkilai had shown them everything they needed to know. Their captain had demonstrated his seamanship, his trading acumen, and his ability to command. But even more importantly, he had shown that he was not averse to a little smuggling on the side. Each man had received his personal cut, however small, apportioned fairly according to his status aboard.

These men were proud; reputation and loyalty stood for much amongst them. Their emotionless faces hid a maelstrom of passions: of dignity and honour, of justice and respect. Soliman told him that Europeans '*orang putih*' – as he called them, were generally mistrusted and regarded as arrogant, faithless and entirely stupid; they were dirty and without respect for God. They drank until they fell over, acted behind men's back like cowards, and did not 'give face' to other men. This meant they were '*kasar*' in their eyes, of low character. Francis pondered this assessment, fascinated by the different way of viewing his countrymen. These sailors misunderstood many things which they weighed according to their own cultural taboos. Notwithstanding, it was the face the English were displaying to the peoples of the East, with no apparent regard for whether their behaviour might offend or not. And it was an unpleasant face to say the least, one Light himself quite recognised. For he had been on the receiving end of the cold cruelty and disdain of English society many times himself.

Nor was he naïve. His crew were rogues: sailors who lived on their wits. They were as light-fingered a mob as he had ever encountered, which is saying much to a man who has slept in a hammock on a crowded gun deck. Not only was theft deemed normal amongst these lascars but it was regarded an insult to call a fellow out for it in public. His men lied with abandon, seemingly incapable of giving a straight answer to a question, even when the truth was not injurious to them. They were also born killers. Every one of them carried a fearsome *keris* or a keenly honed dagger, which they used without compunction. Taking life meant little. There were some, so Soliman warned, that would even take a head for a keepsake, if they so wished. Vigilance and attention to their fragile egos was a constant caution.

Light still had much to learn but at least he had survived the first hurdle. Night was drawing on; they would reach Madras by daybreak. He rested back his head, suddenly bone weary. It was the first time that he had felt at ease in several weeks. Soliman handed him a tot of rum; he ruffled the boy's glossy straight hair in fondness. 'We did good, Soliman. We did damned good. Life's looking up, just you wait and see. Everything will be better in the days to come.'

The young lad settled himself at his feet, Hari curling up on his lap, purring in comfort. They made an oddly happy family. 'Everything already better, Mr Fransees … very better.'

13
Patola Cloth

Tharua, Jangsylan, Siam. Late April 1768

The house stood in a clearing a lengthy walk out of Tharua port, down a long straight road following a sluggish stream choked with lotus plants. Shady trees either side of the path framed the fields beyond, dotted with rice smallholdings where farmers toiled in the hot sun, unbending to stare curiously at the *farang* stranger. Water buffalo waded through the paddy at plodding pace; it was the ploughing season. Egrets picked their delicate way between the rows, searching out juicy frogs and insects. Plumps of ducks waddled officiously along the banks, their ducklings trailing obediently behind.

For months Light had been entirely at sea, sailing nonstop to-and-fro between the teeming harbours of the four-way country trade route: from Madras to the Bay of Bengal, across the Andaman Sea to Acheen in Sumatra, then on to Queddah on the Malay Peninsula. His final stop this circuit before returning back to India was Jangsylan, a prosperous trading island off the coast of Siam, which had as many names as races. The Siamese knew it as Thalang, the Malays as Ujung Salang. It was even sometimes further corrupted to Junk Ceylon, although it was nowhere near the island of Ceylon. One day it would be named for its new settlement of Phuket Town in the south. To find his feet planted at last on *terra firma* on a glorious tropical morning in such a bucolic setting – with nothing at all to do – was a balm to his wandering soul.

This deceptive tranquillity, this hive of languorous industry, uplifted his spirits. It was near impossible to imagine that life here would ever change, despite the turbulent upheavals of the world outside. Momentarily, Francis was back in Suffolk, infused in the sleepy ambience of a rural English village. Was the pastoral life there really so much different, when all was said and done? The further he ventured from home, and the more alien the world he inhabited, the more conjunctions between this life and that did he encounter. People everywhere shared much the same needs and desires, aims and ambitions, loves and hates. It was only in the manner of their resolution that communities found their own singular solutions.

His directions, given by an old Siamese fruit seller in thickly accented Malay had been: *'walk long, long to elephant place then down alley to little spirit table. After that, you see house.'* Francis could find no fault in them. There was indeed a large stockade, walled in thick columns of bamboo and bars of iron, enclosing a large herd of unexpectedly docile elephants, sounding only the occasional melancholy trumpet. There he turned down a path dense in foliage, passing from blinding light into cool, green shade. It was eerily quiet, other than the ubiquitous sounds of nature: bird song, monkey chatter, and the worrisome rustling of undergrowth. But, just as promised, after turning a bend, he spied the little wooden wayside altar festooned with flowers and fruit, dedicated to some local spirit. And beyond that, a clearing in which he found a cluster of teak buildings and the clutter of family life.

Light stopped awhile to mop his brow with his headcloth and brush back his hair with his fingers, in a vain effort to restore respectability. After his arduous walk in the heat of day, he was drenched in sweat, despite the baggy cotton breeches and his loose white linen shirt. Swinging his canvas bag back over his shoulder, he advanced towards the main dwelling, a simple but handsome stilted house in the traditional style, with lofty upswept roof and ornately carved wooden steps leading to a shady veranda.

'Anybody home?'

A loud thud from inside and the pounding of footsteps preceded the appearance of a somewhat startled, but very familiar face: 'Good God, Francis Light! My heart near stopped! I fell right out of my chair! What the devil brings you to the middle of nowhere?'

James Scott tumbled down the steps to swing his visitor off the ground. 'You are a sight for sore eyes, indeed! Francis Light, my old shipmate!' It was an unexpectedly effusive welcome. Scott appeared genuinely moved by Light's arrival.

The two men took each other in. Five years since London and the passage of time had not been kind to Scott. His red golden curls were receding from his forehead and his fine, pale skin was now reddened and wrinkled, like the last apple left in the barrel come springtime. The narrow waist of his navy days was gone, replaced by a prosperous paunch. Scott already looked older than his twenty-three years. In comparison, Francis was lean and fit, his skin golden brown and his hair thick and wavy, tied in a neat bow.

'You're a hard man to find and no mistake!' Francis replied.

'I've been chasing you these past three years but everywhere I went you had just passed through, until I began to suspect you were avoiding me! It's damn good to see you at last, Jamie, you old rogue, but what has happened to your hair, man? Those burnished curls that so won the hearts of the ladies?'

Scott chuckled, running a hand over his thinning forehead. 'As to my hair, my lad, I couldna say, but my pinky skin was never meant for climes such as these. Fortunately, the ladies here are not so choosy. Come, meet the family …'

'Family? You have a wife?' Scott had never struck Light as an uxorious man.

'In every port, Francis, in every port!' He winked, placing a finger to his lips. 'She thinks she's the only one …' The glint in his eyes revealed the roguish boy he had once been.

James had taken a local Malay wife and now had two small children, both with dark gold hair and dusky skin. William and Barbara were their unlikely names, after Scott's mother and father, the only contact they were ever likely to have with their grandparents. Ina, his wife, spoke no English, which suited Scott very well; he counselled Francis to find a local woman if he wished to improve his command of the language. Scott was fluent in both Siamese and Malay, and when in Jangsylan lived much as the locals did, particularly noticeable in his dress – a sarong and flowing shirt – where he had once been known for sartorial elegance.

'James, if it were not for your red nose and ginger mop, I would have taken you for a Malay. You've gone quite native, sir! But wait! I have something for you that will soon bring back the Scotsman …' Francis dug deep into his canvas bag and pulled out a jar of whisky, carefully wrapped in calico. 'From Madras. I've carried this damn bottle back and forth across the Andaman countless times for such an occasion as this!'

Scott was delighted. 'Ya fine wee barra! Let's find a shady spot and drink ourselves to oblivion!'

The bottle was quite empty – and another near finished – before the two men eventually fell asleep, sprawled on rattan chairs until nudged inside by servants as dusk descended and the mosquitoes came out to feed. The next morning, with sore heads and thirsts raging, the two men sat back down again, this time drinking tea and settling their roiling stomachs with bowls of hot, soupy noodles. Now that the bravado of the drunken night was past, they settled in to reminiscing on the past years.

Scott was hazy on the details of his departure from Madras, but Francis knew enough already to piece it together. James had been most fortunate in convincing John Call, an engineer making his first foray into private trading, that he was the man to take charge of his newly purchased ship. The venture had attracted the ire of Francis Jourdan, who had expected, as a friend of Call's, that the business would be conducted through his agency. James had escaped Madras, just in time. It did, however explain Jourdan's initial reluctance to employ Scott's friend, Francis Light. They had both walked a fine line between luck and disaster in their initial dealings with Company personnel.

The first year or so Scott had spent almost entirely at sea, endlessly back and forth across the Andaman and up and down the Straits, working night and day to establish his contacts and to buy his own ship, much as Light was currently doing. Now Scott owned more than one vessel and, more importantly to him, was entirely free of agency or partner. Despite his tainted reputation in Madras, there proved no shortage of merchants there willing to buy from him. After all, business was business. He was an established trader who could source any commodity at the best of prices. It was not essential to like the man you dealt with.

For his part, Francis described his progress with the Madras agency, now known as Jourdan, Sullivan and DeSouza since young John Sullivan had become a partner. Scott interrupted at that point, banging his hand down on the table in amusement.

'John Sullivan! So, the little Irish weasel wormed his way into partnership, did he? I knew it! That lad was scheming the moment he stepped foot on Fort St George. He never took to me, you know? Ruined my chances with Jourdan and DeSouza into the bargain. Saw me as some sort of rival, God knows why. As if I would be interested in that goddamned agency and all those smug-faced Company scavengers! The politics of that town turn my stomach. I want nothing of it. But that young cockalorum wouldn't know the first thing about straight-dealing and honest broking ...'

'But you would?' Francis interjected wryly.

James had the decency to concede that neither were his strongest suits, but claimed that, unlike Sullivan, he rarely went behind a fellow's back or spread false rumours about him. Francis wondered just how false the rumours might have been, but let it pass. For his part, he was fond of both men, but knew that neither one would put conscience before personal gain. It did explain, however, why Sullivan had championed his cause back then. Francis' arrival had provided Sullivan with a tasty morsel to prove his value to the agency at a time when it was on the brink of expanding. Now he was partner in the established trading company at the tender age of nineteen. It was an impressive rise by any measure.

Scott, on the other hand, had always been a lone wolf. His years as a country trader in these waters had only increased his isolation. Where Francis was the epitome of a Company man, Scott had remained aloof, now even more so, running his private one-man business, surrounded only by locals. Yet, Francis sensed that Scott was melancholy. His appearance had rejuvenated his friend's despondent spirits. No matter how enterprising a man was, he was not an island. Out here, far from home, men needed their fellow countrymen. For who else might understand what passions and ambitions were driving a fellow?

'Come on, Francis! Break with Jourdan's! Let's form a company together, based right here in Jangsylan, far away from Company interference. This place is the ideal spot. They have no truck with the Dutch but welcome other private merchants, especially European, for they have enough troubles of their own from the local rulers, and value our presence. I've a few ships and you could purchase your own with a bit of funding from here and there. '*Scott and Light, Private Traders*', how does that sound? Or '*Light and Scott*', if you want to put your own bloody name first. We'd make our damned fortunes, you know we would! And return home as two wealthy nabobs to buy our own country estates. Who then would dare to turn their noses up, eh? I have the trust of those who count in these waters. They prefer to trade with private masters. And we can still deal with the Company. Nor will the Dutch see us as a problem. Thus, we play all sides. Just think of it! Come on, man! You know it's the next step. And we can work together. We already have the trust.'

Francis was unsure. Undoubtedly, there were benefits in being one's own man and working with a tried and tested partner, but these were dangerous and uncertain times in the Straits. Siam was rising again in the north under new king, Tak Sin, who wished to unify all Siam under his control. What might lie ahead for Jangsylan? The Dutch and the Bugis were in a constant struggle to control the southern Straits, and neither were tolerant of competitors. Raiding and piracy were rife amongst the Straits people. He and Scott could find themselves abandoned in the midst of chaos, with no nominal support. His preferred strategy was to work within the system, exploiting its weaknesses and taking advantage of the conflicts, rather than become the victim. But most of all, he intended to make a name for himself amongst the great and the good. Money was one thing, but reputation meant a great deal more. One day he would have them all sit up and respect him.

'I was recently in Sumatra with Gowan Harrop on a scouting mission. Jourdan's sending out another embassy to the sultan of Acheen next year, this time a larger delegation. I want to be part of that. Sultan Alaudin is desperate. His local chiefs are growing ever more powerful as his own authority diminishes. He needs our support to keep control. Imagine if we held the Acheen monopoly? We could bypass the Dutch and own the Arab trade! Our own route to China would be secured now Bencoolen is falling in line!'

James scoffed at the idea. 'You think they'll give you some official post? Governor of Acheen, or the like? It's an impossibility for the likes of us! Some overbearing Company man will step all over your hard work, and you will be the jobbing ship master doing their bidding. Nor does Acheen have a future. The Bugis are the men of the moment. If they can hold the southern Straits, they've got us by the balls! Once they've seen off the Dutch, who are fast fading into the realms of history on account of their venality, they'll turn on the Company. But the Bugismen will always trade with private men. They know the advantages. We can do the business the Company cannot, and we don't come burdened with demands and treaties, armies and warships. See sense, man! You've no more chance of advancement out here than you did back home!'

But Light was not inclined to be dissuaded. Scott, however, did not relent. He spent the next few days waging a war of attrition, introducing Francis to his contacts in Jangsylan, and showing him around the opportunities that were available if they struck out alone. It was an interesting experience, tempting even, opening Light's eyes to the future potential of Siam, Jangsylan and the archipelago that stretched from Burmese Mergui down to the island of Langkawi.

Firstly, they visited the nearby elephant traders. The mainland of Phang Na and the island itself were lucrative sources of elephants for export to India. Francis had so far shied away from carrying these unpredictable animals despite their undoubted value. James was persuasive. 'Local price, fifty Spanish dollars per animal. They pay 400-800 for one on the Coromandel, dependent on size. Ya canna turn your nose up at that profit!'

'Pray tell how you sail a herd of elephants to India? Even one or two would take too much space, not to mention the vast amounts of feed that would be required. And the potential damage if they startled and broke free. I fear that one rogue buck alone could sink a ship, never mind a troop of those leviathans!' Francis demurred.

'Ganja,' Scott replied smartly. 'You starve them into submission for a few weeks then feed them local ganja before they embark from the jetty at Pak Pra. Use a tame one to lead them aboard into specially separated stalls on deck. Feed them sparingly. Just enough to keep them alive. They're as docile as little lambs as long as you keep topping up with ganja on the crossing.' It was an intriguing solution – and the profits were undeniable. It certainly explained the passive behaviour of the elephants that Francis had witnessed at the local stockade.

'Not to mention tin,' Scott continued. 'The Bugis and the Dutch are cornering the market in the Peninsula, but the mines here are turning out to be as rich as Croesus. It's a whole new independent source, virtually untapped. Chinese coolies are coming over in their droves, snapping up the claims and tax farms, virtually running the smelting operations. And they're treated like dogs by locals, Dutch and pirates alike. We could oversee the entire island's tin exports with the contacts I have, and the Chinamen would be thanking us for it! Then there's the pearls. I know the fellow who has the entire monopoly in the Mergui Isles, where you'll find the best pearl divers. They've got lungs like whales, and reach depths few divers ever can. Pearls as big as hen's eggs! This good friend is a Portuguese Eurasian chap married into the best family on Jangsylan. We could be sole traders of all the Indies pearls sold in Europe. What do you say to a trip up to the islands to see for yourself?'

Which explained why, a few days later, Light and Scott

travelled inland to the village of Ban Takkien in the interior of the island, where the most influential Siamese family on the island had its estates. The recently deceased paterfamilias, one Phraya Chom Rang, had previously been governor of the island until Malays from Queddah had taken over Jangsylan the year before. The clan had withdrawn inland to their ancestral lands, ostensibly to lick their wounds, but their teeth were still sharp, and their authority remained as wide-ranging as ever. Even the new Malay rulers relied on them to coordinate and advise on the island's trade.

Scott explained the family's tentacles in the region. 'Some believe the Ban Takkien were actually behind the Queddah invasion and that this 'mourning period' is mere show. I'm inclined to agree. Governor Chom Rang feared King Tak Sin and the Burmese more than the sultan of Queddah. The two were old pals, hand-in-glove for years. The current climate perfectly suits the family's interests.'

'But I thought you said the former governor had died during the invasion?' It's unlikely a family would sacrifice the head merely to give the pretence of opposition to takeover by a foreign invader.

'I said he died *around* the time of the invasion and it has suited the family that the Malays be held responsible. But everyone knows it was a rival Siamese clan that sent an assassin to steal into his house at dead of night. No Malay could have found his way inside the mansion by stealth. It was a local conspiracy by enemies who took the opportunity of the invasion to take revenge over some old grievance. Perhaps even a servant on the inside was paid to do the deed. It's how they work here. It's why they're so easy to control. They're at each other's throats all the time. There's always one family willing to betray another.'

In the light of that confidence, Jangsylan did not seem to Light to be the ideal environment for outsiders, but he kept his reservations to himself. By then, they had reached their destination, a thriving self-sufficient community, more like a small town, spread around the outskirts of the Ban Takkien walled compound. Every person seemed in some way attached to the powerful ruling clan: feudal peasants, slaves, bondsmen, retainers, distant relatives – and every degree of social status in between. It would indeed be difficult for enemies to approach this stronghold undiscovered.

Passing through an intricately carved teak gateway guarded by dragon-like serpents, they found themselves in lush gardens, transported into a world of privilege and wealth that seemed unimaginable on the hot and teeming streets outside. An abundance of carefully pruned trees and skilfully cultivated flowers were artfully arranged around ponds and man-made streams crossed by ornamental bridges. In alcoves and groves, peering out from amongst the foliage, like guardians lining the path, were scores of stone statues depicting warriors, hideous demons, dancing girls and mythical beasts. The sun was beginning to set; servants ran about with tapers, lighting concealed torches and lanterns set amongst the greenery. It was cool and shady, the air heady with fragrance.

'My God, it's like the Garden of Eden!' Francis gasped, eyes wide in surprise.

'Then may you beware the serpent' was James' oblique reply. Male attendants, dressed in silk jackets and sarongs, appeared on bare feet, as silently as if they had materialised from thin air. There was little conversation but a good deal of bowing and *wai*-ing as they carried their bags to their accommodation. They were important guests.

Bathed and refreshed, the two men followed a silent young servant, Dong, who had stood sentinel outside during their ablutions. He had been detailed as their guide. In his wake, they traversed wooden walkways that linked the separate pavilions of the grand complex. Up steps and down they went, over exquisite pools of golden fish; past vibrant arrangements of orchids; across open-sided terraces furnished with plump silk cushions, priceless ceramics and bronze lamps, ideal for wiling away hot afternoons.

Finally, they were led through a peristyle garden to the main building, a grand Siamese structure with a soaring roof of brightly painted terracotta tiles, trimmed in gilded serpentine finials. A carved stairway led to a sumptuous loggia dominated by a vast central low table edged by a sunken bench. The other guests were already assembled, seated cross-legged on flat hassocks, staring with undisguised curiosity at the new arrivals.

'Welcome, welcome!' A big, bluff, friendly man jumped to his feet with a traditional wai of greeting. He was sharp-featured and swarthy, with wiry black hair and impressive mustachios, like an Ottoman worthy. This apparently was the Portuguese Eurasian merchant Scott had mentioned. His name was Martim Rozells. 'Thank you for honouring our humble home with your presence ...' He spoke Malay, which everyone appeared to understand. His appearance was greatly at odds with the rest of the party, all slender, elegantly impassive Siamese. The British visitors settled down by Rozells, somehow comforted by his presence, as if he were the closest to a westerner that they had seen for some time.

The evening was an eye-opener for Light, although Scott seemed to take it in his stride, a familiar guest, it would seem. The food was exquisite, steaming fragrant dishes served in silver bowls, accompanied by perfumed rice and scarce-cooked vegetables that retained the bite of the raw. Light had not known food so succulent and lavish existed in Siam. In the port he lived on fried fish and coarse rice with a few stringy vegetables. Another surprise was that alcohol was served: glasses of red wine, with brandy to conclude the meal. Neither the local brew, a strong fermented coconut wine, nor the rough arrack found all over Asia, had a place at this refined table.

Yet the greatest surprise of all came with the entrance of the new head of the clan, arriving fashionably late after all the other guests were assembled, as etiquette dictated. Following the tragic demise of Phraya Chom Rang, his successor was not one of his sons, who were also present, but his eldest daughter, Lady Chan. The deference with which her entry was greeted told Francis all he needed to know about the esteem in which she was viewed by the other family members. Or perhaps they cowered in fear of this formidable matriarch.

Lady Chan was beautiful, although the word was trite to describe such favours as she displayed. Francis could not begin to guess her age: her skin was flawless and unlined, her hair ebony black without a hint of grey. Yet, as the elder member of the family, and with the elevated status she enjoyed, she must have been mature in years. Her body, clad in a traditional silk gown that fell lithe and sinuous about her narrow frame, covered everything, but revealed all even if the only skin displayed was that of her ankles and feet, both tiny and perfectly formed. Lady Chan's countenance was regally passive but her clear brown eyes revealed a guarded intelligence. It was impossible to conjecture her thoughts.

On introduction, Lady Chan merely nodded her serene head, the ghost of a smile of welcome vanishing as quickly as it arose. Throughout the meal, she remained silent, other than muttered commands to servants or whispered observations to her sister, Lady Mook, who sat on her right side, or to her brother-in-law Lord At on her left. Martim initiated much of the conversation, to which other guests politely commented or bowed their heads in agreement. Scott talked – and drank – too much, at ease in the company. Light endeavoured to limit both conversation and alcohol so that he might keep his head, but found himself, by virtue of embarrassment, babbling on insensibly then retreating to his glass to silence himself. By the end of the evening, plans had been made to visit the Mergui archipelago, accompanying Martim on his forthcoming voyage. Thus, despite the awkwardness of the occasion, the visit had been a general success sufficient enough to give Light the courage, before she retired for the night, to step forward and personally thank Lady Chan for her hospitality.

'My deepest gratitude, dear lady ...' he began in English, before repeating himself in Malay.

In the most unexpected moment of the entire evening Lady Chan replied in heavily accented, but entirely correct, English. 'My pleasure, Kapitan Lit. Please, come again.' And then she smiled, revealing perfect ivory teeth. Her direct gaze was oddly disconcerting; Light recalled Scott's earlier reference to 'beware the Serpent' and wondered if Lady Chan was whom he had meant. For a moment Light could neither look nor move away, caught like an animal in the gaze of a predator. He swallowed hard to find his voice again.

'Please do me the honour of accepting this small gift from my travels on the Coromandel.' At least Light had had the foresight to bring an appropriate souvenir for his host, unfolding a sumptuous *patola* cloth, much prized throughout the East Indies. He had been long enough in these waters to understand the honour a guest bestowed by the gift of textile. Lady Chan bowed once more, directing her maidservant to accept it; it was deemed unseemly for a man to touch the hand of a noble lady. Then she took her leave with the dignified progress that one might expect of a queen.

It was only when the two men had reached their own rooms that they dared discuss the evening. Francis threw himself down on the low divan that served as his bed. 'Who is this woman? She is like the goddess Aphrodite reborn!'

Scott laughed long and hard. 'Step carefully, young Francis. That is Lady Chan. She is the power on this island, no matter there is now a Malay governor. You would do well to keep on good terms with her. For she is ruthless beyond words, if crossed.'

Francis sat up, deep in contemplation, while James uncorked a flagon. He swigged deeply before passing it over to his friend. Francis sipped, still distracted by the lady. 'Tell me more about her.'

James settled down opposite on a cushioned teakwood stool, stretching out his long thin legs. 'I will tell you what I know and what I have heard, but make no mistake, she is an enigmatic woman. I doubt anyone knows all there is to know about her complex affairs. But let me warn you first, she is a married lady, although her husband is conveniently rarely on the island, being the governor of a nearby mainland province.'

Sometime later, after both men had finally settled down to sleep, and Light had sunk into a feverish dream in which Lady Chan played a sensuous part, he was suddenly startled awake by a gentle tapping on his arm. The young manservant, Dong, seemingly unembarrassed to have entered a gentleman's room unbidden, gestured for Light to follow him.

'What? Follow you? It's the middle of the night! Where are we going anyway?' he demanded, but there was no reply, simply another dainty gesticulation bidding him forward. Light considered calling out to Scott in the adjoining room but intuition told him he was not in any danger. Nor did he wish to be accompanied in truth. This was a mystery he wished to experience alone.

Dong led him on a winding route to the other side of the compound, far from his own chamber and set some distance apart from the main dwellings. He was directed to a small but well-appointed pavilion, simply but tastefully decorated, less gaudy than the rest of the apartments. At an ornate teak doorway, Dong placed a finger on his lips and indicated that Light should enter. The servant disappeared on silent feet.

It was dark inside. Francis waited for the diffused glow from the gardens outside to adjust his eyes to the gloom within. He could discern the outlines of furniture but there seemed no sign of life. Suddenly an infinitesimal tremor in the still night air and the scent of jasmine assailed his senses; he felt, rather than saw, a silk hanging fall aside. Someone had entered the room. Light's heart raced in fear and anticipation. His eyes struggled to make out the form that slowly advanced towards him.

A goddess shrouded in patola cloth. The fabric slithered to the floor.

14

The Pearl Tank

The Mergui Archipelago, Burma. May 1768

Without benefit of a seasoned guide, it would have taken days to find the ideal pearl grounds in the thousand-island chain, like looking for needles in a haystack. But Martim Rozells had been trading in these waters for years and knew exactly where the best moorings lay. The impromptu three-ship convoy followed a long, narrow strait that neatly bisected the scattered archipelago, a comparatively safe and speedy passage, taking only three days to reach their destination. The outlying islands formed a bulwark against the worst of the south-westerlies; if a bad storm threatened, they could retreat towards the coast and shelter in one of the many bays, protected from the worst.

The weather was typical for the season. Fine, calm mornings that darkened over mid-afternoon, when a sudden surge in the prevailing wind, a clouding of the sky, and the tell-tale swell of wind-whipped waves presaged the first droplets of rain. Within minutes this pitter-patter gathered pace and became a hammering storm. The southwest monsoon was a fierce and unpredictable element, but it speeded their journey northwards towards the landmass of southern Burma.

With little else to do but hoist sails to the wind, Light made hasty maps for future reference, noting deep harbours, natural anchorages, and distinctive landmarks for orientation. The channel might be straight but it was not without its dangers; these waters abounded in coral reefs, some lying treacherously just below the surface, invisible at night. A ship might founder, its keel ripped clean out. This was still largely uncharted territory for European merchants. A detailed knowledge was as valuable as any cargo of pearls he might acquire.

When the sun shone, the archipelago was a beautiful sight to behold. Thickly forested islands, some little more than towering rocks, speckled the deep blue waters abundant in sea life. Marine mammals of every species idled by: schools of whales, sharks, dolphins and porpoises, curiously investigating the intruders into their deserted waters. Dugongs lay basking on outcrops, for all the world the voluptuous, preening mermaids of the ancient tales.

This archipelago was a scarce-tapped resource of rich commodity: ambergris, *bêche-de-mers*, turtle shell, not to mention the ubiquitous harvesting of pearls. So plentiful were the oyster grounds, Scott had told him, that most locals merely gathered them in the mangroves at low tide. Small shells were ground for lime paste, while the better quality were collected for mother-of-pearl. The meat of these oysters was plump and juicy. Nothing went to waste, everything held value to traders. But the best grounds were in the further waters off Lanbi Island, according to Rozells, where the deeper seabeds were reputed to be entirely covered in shells, in some places several layers deep.

Their first stop was a tiny outcrop where a small community of natives dealt in birds' nests, farmed in the caves of the largely barren islet. Any forest that had once existed there had been burned down long ago to facilitate access to the caves, and to destroy wildlife that might interfere with business. The lovely beach, pristine white sands trimmed with shady casuarina, hinted at the original beauty of the now-carbonised wilderness.

The island dwellers were a tribe of the indigenous Moken people, who lived their whole lives entirely aboard boats moored in the shallows. This custom was both by choice but also by necessity, for these gentle people were constantly preyed upon by the pirates and raiders who infested the more remote islands. The shy, but canny, traders would scatter if they sensed danger, abandoning their settlements, taking only what they could carry, to return later and rebuild. It took great resilience to survive in these islands. The three merchants, however, were more than welcome, for Europeans meant rich barter: the essential staples of rice and cloth in return for birds' nests and sea cucumber that they smoked and dried on the shore. Both delicacies would be snapped up by Chinese traders in the Straits.

Soliman was fascinated by the Moken youths who spent their free time diving and larking in the deep waters. He could swim, like all the children of the *orang laut*, but not with the adroitness of the Moken, for whom the sea was natural habitat. Nor was it entirely playing; this was their schooling, for their livelihoods depended on the sea. One of the many marine skills that they mastered was deep-diving, building up their lung capacity to swim down to the great depths required in the retrieval of the best oysters.

Soliman befriended these local boys when they came by with their wares, handling their skiffs like extensions of their own bodies. With business done, they would dive into the water and playtime began. Light observed them from the deck, entertained by their antics and tomfoolery. They were like any boys the world over. He was gladdened to see Soliman spending time with children of his own age. The boy lived entirely in a world of men.

Not that the men did not join in. His sailors loved nothing better than to swim themselves, as inclined to splashing and playing as any child; it was a popular recreation for them. Every lascar was an accomplished swimmer; to them it would have been nonsensical to set foot on a boat without that capability. Stories of incredible feats of survival were told of Malay sailors who had been shipwrecked or washed overboard in storms, then floated for hours, sometimes days, clinging to driftwood, until they were rescued or made it independently to shore. It was the very opposite of British tars who believed a quick drowning was the best fate for any sailor unlucky enough to fall into the sea. But then, these were not the dark grey, churning waters of the North Sea, or the wild, boiling troughs of the oceans. In the sparkling crystal-clear Andaman, leaping into several fathoms was not a daunting prospect. It was exactly what any sane person would do on a hot afternoon. Light stripped to his linens and followed them.

The next day, the little fleet made anchor in the deep harbour of Zadet Kyi to stock up on perfumed aloes wood, ambergris and turtle shell. This time they visited the shore to conduct their barter, but were eaten alive by vicious sand flies, much to the amusement of the natives, who did not seem in the least troubled by the nuisance. But the juicy purple fruits that Soliman called *manggis,* plentiful on the island, were well worth the landing. Light and Soliman even wandered up the headland, climbing the black granite cliffs whose jagged edges gave vicious slices to unwary arms and legs. He told the boy how as a child he had once gathered quartz on English beaches far away, then polished them to a shine. They were his lucky stones. Soliman was captivated, insistent on finding his own talisman to ward off evil. Together they searched for broken chips, attractive pieces shot through with shiny purple veins, glinting like jewels in the reflected sunlight. The boy gathered up a number of them. On a whim, Light slipped one into his own pocket, in a moment of nostalgia.

The final destination of this expedition was a short trip further north to an area known locally as Pouleygaw, or the Pearl Tank. The waters here were very deep, in some places up to 12 fathoms. Only the most experienced divers were able to survive the terrifying plunge to the bottom. But their rewards were great. Surfacing with baskets full of large oysters, they deposited their booty into shallower netted areas, where younger boys retrieved and opened them for traders, once a price was settled. The transaction was something of a lottery; the majority of shells contained nothing but a thick morsel of meat.

Yet, the nacreous shells, much prized for inlay work, fetched a good price in themselves, so the risk was minimal. Furthermore, sufficient oysters nurtured ivory-pink pearls that more than warranted the transaction. To purchase at origin rendered them astonishingly cheap, a merchant's dream. A bag of these gems tucked into a corner of a sea chest might fetch as much as the rest of the cargo. The Madras agency need know nothing about Light's little business venture on the side. These pearls could be the route to his own ship at last.

Another unexpected bonus at this same anchorage was rare black coral that grew to heights of between six to nine feet, harvested by the same pearl divers. It seemed that everything on land and sea in this region was a priceless treasure elsewhere, but for the locals it was virtually unwanted, something merely to barter away for basic necessities, the very essentials of life that they lacked. Anything you could not eat, wear or use as tool or weapon was useless to them.

On the last night of their trip, and to celebrate both the successful endeavour and their new friendship, Light, Scott and Rozells dined aboard the *Speedwell.* They feasted on grilled fish and oysters, accompanied by a hearty turtle stew, washed down with a potent coconut toddy supplied by the natives. On the morrow they would take their leave of each other, sailing to different destinations: Scott to Jangsylan, Rozells to his family home in Queddah, while Light was heading down the coast of the Peninsula to Malacca with his rich haul.

'Call in to Queddah on your way back!' Martim suggested. 'I will introduce you to Sultan Muhammed!'

Light grinned sheepishly. 'I have already met the sultan. Last year I spent some time along the west coast and frequently stopped off at Kuala Queddah. Finally, I was summoned to an audience. Sultan Muhammed was curious as to this new young Englishman who was regularly in port.'

'The old bird never misses anything,' Scott laughed. 'Mind you, he has his spies everywhere. No doubt he was sounding you out as another potential informant. Foreign sea captains are his ideal recruits for they visit everywhere, hear everything, and yet have no particular stake in the intrigues, other than a desire to make coin from it!'

Rozells agreed. 'Information is as much a business venture

to him as trading. Our family has benefitted greatly from these mutual exchanges for years. Everyone does it. Thus, everyone knows everyone else's business. Secrets are as rare as giant pearls in the Straits,' he added with guileless innocence, virtually admitting the family involvement in the Queddah invasion. Light imagined that the sultan loved to chat with Martim Rozells.

'I'm not sure how impressed he was with me. I made a fool of myself in front of the court, much to the general merriment.' Light took a swig of the rough toddy and grimaced, as much at the embarrassing memory as the taste. 'I was ushered into the hall where the sultan holds court, already the subject of much amusement, like a prize pig at a fair ...'

'An unfortunate simile at a Mohammedan court, Francis,' Scott interjected.

Light rolled his eyes at the interruption. 'The sultan gestured for me to come forward, then looked me over with much curiosity, indicated with a turning motion of his fingers that I should circle around so he could see me from all angles. There were titters of laughter from those gathered as I performed like a dancing girl ...'

'Prize pig or dancing girl, Francis? Make your mind up, man!' Scott teased.

Francis glared in mock anger. 'Do you wish me to tell this story or not, sir?'

'You may continue,' was Scott's unctuous reply. Rozells smiled beatifically, well-oiled by toddy and delighting in the jovial company. He spent too much of his time amongst inscrutable Siamese and conniving Queddah courtiers; it was pleasant indeed simply to pass the time in idle camaraderie.

'Then the sultan calls me to his side and asks his manservant for a dish. The silver platter is held out and, calm as you please, the old fellow spits out the quid he is chewing and offers it to me. "*Silakan*," he says with an oily grin. The sultan says "Please?" Now what was I to do? I had no choice but to pick up the salivated parcel and pop it in my own mouth, chewing on the betel while trying not to vomit it forth.'

Both Martim and James roared in amusement, slapping their palms on thigh and table in glee. 'He always does that! He's such a grand old rogue!' Scott exclaimed. 'It's his favourite joke. Every time a white man comes to court, he acts the uncivilised native chief that most Englishmen expect him to be. Although I doubt it is entirely for his entertainment. He was also testing your mettle. Many pompous asses would disdain the proffered gift and refuse to take the quid, which in itself is an insult when given in welcome by a potentate. They would bluster and bumble about it not being their custom ... with the greatest of respect ... and so on ... and so forth ... And thus, they reveal their true colours to the sultan.'

'Scott speaks the truth,' Martim added. 'Of course, no one wants to take something from the mouth of another, but if you wish to make money from trading in the sultan's state, then he believes it is a small price to pay to show him respect. He wants to see how hungry you are. After all, to give his own *paan* shows the highest regard for a guest, even if it is something few would desire to chew on! But it is an important token and an astute man understands that. If you refuse to take it, he refuses to trade. One must be prepared to sacrifice for his patronage.'

Light shook his head in bemusement. 'So, perhaps he didn't think I was a fool after all? Everyone laughed so much as I stood there grinning like a village idiot along with them.'

'But did he invite you back to Queddah?'

'As a matter of fact, he did. The sultan also went on to compliment me on my knowledge of his language, saying that I was always welcome in his kingdom. Then, he asked how many guns and how much opium I could supply him.'

'To which you obliged, of course?' Scott inquired, one eyebrow raised archly.

'I most assuredly did oblige. I also sold the venerable sultan as much powder as his heart desired. Since then, I must admit, we have done much business together.'

'The sultan has many enemies,' Rozells observed. 'At court and throughout his kingdom, never mind from outside. The weaponry is necessary if he is to hold his throne. Siam is growing strong again. King Tak Sin has demanded the *bunga emas* tribute again this year.'

'And he paid it?' Scott inquired.

'He did indeed. He does not wish for a Siamese invasion, despite his own occupation of Jangsylan. However, rumour has it that he also sent a golden tree to the king of Burma – just in case. You have to be impressed by his guile. Muhammed Jiwa's no fool or how else has he held his throne for fifty years or more? Just like the betel quid, Francis. What does it cost to bend the knee a little? False pride is fool's pride, he would say.'

Francis smiled. 'Then it seems I grovelled with sufficient obsequiousness to win him over. How fortuitous!'

It had been a fruitful time for all three men. Scott had benefitted from the good company, Rozells had met a future trading partner while Light had made valuable connections. Of those, perhaps the most delicate was with the mistress of Jangsylan, Lady Chan.

While he still bathed in his lover's favour, Light had the island trade in the palm of his hand, but love was a fragile basis for partnership at the best of times. Scott had warned him but Francis had merely laughed off his concerns. He could handle himself. She was a married lady. She knew the boundaries, as did he. It was an affair where only the baser emotions were involved.

'I know Lady Chan as well as most for, as you know, she is my wife's elder sister,' Martim observed when the subject came up on that last evening. 'She is a very clever and resourceful woman, and undoubtedly a great beauty. Francis is right. She takes lovers easily enough and once she has tired of you – and she will, Francis – she will happily keep you on her list of men to work with. In fact, she knows that her lovers will harbour fond feelings that will be to her benefit long after the flame has died. But, as James says, never cross her. Never cheat her. Her revenge will be thorough, I can assure you. In this she takes after her father.' Time would tell if this liaison would be a benefit or a disaster. Light was still young and reckless enough not to care.

The drink had loosened Martim's tongue. He lacked the tolerance for alcohol of the two seasoned navy veterans. 'Of course, Lady Chan is not as beautiful as my wife. No woman is lovelier than Lady Thong Di. She is the perfect wife! My flawless jewel. Mother of my two children ... My son Felipe, and my daughter, Martinha ... oh, my little Muti! My pearl ... the loveliest child that ever was born ...' he continued in increasingly maudlin fashion.

That seemed the appropriate juncture to put Rozells to bed for the night. After copious farewells and embraces, Martim was hauled down the ladder and ferried by barge back to his own vessel. His head would be sore come morning.

'Have you ever met Martim's wife?' Francis asked as they finally waved him off. 'Is she anything at all like his sister?'

Scott scoffed at the very idea. 'The three sisters are chalk and cheese! You have already met Chan and Mook so will have observed the difference there. Chan took her father's acumen, Mook her father's looks, I'm afraid. No, Lady Thong Di is nothing like either. She is as beautiful as her elder sister, but where Chan is fiery and spirited, she is stately and serene. They are the sun and moon. Lady Thong Di is also the epitome of a dutiful wife, rarely seen in public other than to church with the family. You would never see her taking lovers behind her husband's back. Nor have I ever known Martim to be tempted for all that he spends half the year at sea. I suspect, however, that she has more influence than the outside world credits. I'll wager she's the real power in that household! Poor Martim does seem a rather simple fellow, for all his mercantile knowhow. I suspect she may be his guiding hand. Rozells evidently adores her and the two little ones. The daughter's going to be another beauty, mark my words. She's a surprisingly fair-skinned young thing, all considering. But then who knows what comes out of the pot with these half-breeds? He'll have to watch out in a few years though. There'll be flies around that little pearl's honeypot before long. By the way, do you know Chan's mother is Queddah royalty? That family has tentacles everywhere.'

It was a fascinating and powerful family with which to be associated, perhaps his most significant alliance yet, one to be maintained at all costs. A relationship of the utmost pleasure, too. What a fortunate happenstance!

The morning of their departure dawned fair, so much so, that while the other two ships took the early tide, Francis lingered to allow Soliman one more day in the pleasant waters before they set sail south. It proved to be the worst of choices. By late afternoon, the weather had deteriorated, a full-blown tropical storm breaking. It was impossible to make headway against the prevailing winds; to do so might prove ruinous. They must wait out the tempest in a safe coastal harbour, protected from the worst of the battering that was to come. After a treacherous few hours in raging seas, they reached shelter in the pitch dark, and dropped anchor in the lee of a small islet off the main landmass, out of the storm's eye. Each man aboard thanked his own particular god for seeing them to safe harbour.

Sometime in the night the storm abated and the howling winds subsided. The sailors rolled over in their bedding, anxiety relieved, the prospect of a calm sail ahead the next day. Light intended to make no further mistakes; he would set off on the first tide.

Early sunlight crept across the boards, flooding every corner below, gentle fingers of morning caressing them awake. The ship was bobbing lightly in a moderate breeze, perfect conditions for their journey. Sleepy men sat up, scratched and broke wind, dragging themselves from pallets to douse their heads in the barrel of water. Light himself was the first up the ladder, if one discounted Soliman, always one step ahead, his cat bounding behind. The horizon was empty, the sea a millpond, a glorious dawn just broken. Then a cry of distress from Soliman alerted Francis that something was amiss. He spun round landward. His heart stopped.

What they had missed in the middle of the storm was that this little offshore island had been very far from deserted. Now they could plainly see a bay swarming with boats, most of them outriggers, perahus and *padewakangs,* with numerous small skiffs and canoes. Taking centre stage – and now alongside the *Speedwell* – were two large boats with a number of smaller vessels lined up in between. Men stood in serried ranks along their decks, bearing a fearsome collection of weapons: guns, pistols, keris, swords, spears, bows and arrows, even a few cannons. It seemed that they had taken refuge in a pirate hideout.

Why had he not left yesterday with the others? Travelling alone in these waters was notoriously dangerous. He had been lulled by the intoxicating lure of the place and the excellence of the trading opportunities. Even the most basic precautions had not been taken – they had not even posted watch, presuming nothing was about in such a storm. It was the rank incompetence of a novice! How could he have made such an error? Everything was now lost. His cargo. His fortune. His crew. Soliman. Perhaps even his life. It could not end like this. This is not why he had travelled so far and worked so hard. It could not be!

But panic served no purpose. Drawing on all his reserves, Light thrust fear and dread down deep inside. What he should have done was a path he had not taken. This was where his journey had led him. He must now mitigate disaster as best he could. At least, for his men. It was unlikely he would be allowed to live. Light breathed deep and long, then squared his shoulders, taking in every detail of the scene.

Despite the shock afforded him by the terrible realisation that they had sailed into a pirate's lair, one salient fact leaped out.

Something was out of kilter. Why had these raiders waited for them to wake, when they might have raided as soon as the storm abated? They could have slaughtered the entire crew in their cots, their bodies tossed overboard, and their ship and cargo seized, with no one ever the wiser. Perhaps the intention was to seize them for the slave trade? That at least might give them a fighting chance. Or was he deluding himself?

'*Selamat pagi*! Good morning!' Light called out brightly, his voice affecting an insouciance he certainly did not feel. But he knew that this greeting would be the last thing the enemy expected. It would delay the inevitable and supply some thinking time 'May we be of any help?'

His ludicrous civility in the face of a pirate attack was greeted by total silence from the host of sullen faces. Light took hold of Soliman, nudging him behind his back, although the boy insisted on peering round him, eyes wide with terror, clinging to his cat for dear life. 'Orang Bugis, Kapitan Fransees!' he whispered.

'I know, boy, I know. Don't worry. They won't hurt you.' He consoled the child with little hope in his own assurances. His men were blank-faced, staring out with the same intensity as the Bugismen were viewing them. Light knew they were ready to fight should he ask it of them, but what would be the purpose? He had allowed them to be caught blindsided. They would lose any test of strength. If they reached for weapons, in moments these fierce warriors would swarm aboard and they would be finished. He could not demand his crew to sacrifice their lives for his mistake.

One man pushed his way forward to the prow of the largest vessel; he was youngish, dressed in finer textile than the others, sporting an elaborate headcloth, obviously the leader of the band.

His keris rested in a gilded scabbard, encrusted with jewels. If he was a pirate, he must surely be a successful one. Planting his feet akimbo, the young man placed his hands on his hips in bravado, and shouted across: '*Orang Belanda*?'

Light shook his head. '*Inggeris*.'

'*Dari mana*?'

'Madras.'

'Why you here?'

'*Mutiara*.' Light decided to tell the truth. Should he lose his cargo of pearls, then it was a lesson learned. Better that than their lives.

'I can take your ship. I have many men.'

'I know. This is your victory. We do not want to fight. My men are good sailors. Do not hurt them.'

'I no hurt men. Men worth money. But I kill Dutch men.'

Light smiled. 'Then I am safe, for I am an Englishman. And I also kill Dutch men. So, we can be friends then? Can or not?'

Silence reigned over the hostile tableau of men, the slapping of waves against hulls the only sign of life. And then the young man smiled broadly. 'You are funny! And you speak Malay good. Better than me!' He looked around at his men and they also began to laugh. There was a tangible easing of tension on all sides, weapon hands dropping and shoulders relaxed.

'What is your name, Englishman?'

'Captain Light.'

'Kapitan Let?'

Light nodded. 'And your name? After all, I should know my new friend's name ...'

Again, the young man laughed. 'New friend? I like you

Kapitan Let. My name is Daeng Raja Merewah Theyan. You call me Theyan. I come on your ship.'

With an impressive mobility, Theyan jumped nimbly down onto a small skiff that conveyed him to the *Speedwell*. A rope ladder was lowered; he skimmed up the side. As he leapt down from rail to deck, young Soliman stepped forward, placing himself (and his cat) between the marauder and his beloved Francis. The boy upbraided the pirate, shouting angrily in a babble unknown to Light, although it was evident that the Bugis leader understood. It must be Bugis talk. How in God's name did the child know that? Soliman had constantly confounded him over the years, but never as much as at that moment.

Whatever he was saying, Theyan received the verbal onslaught with amusement, grinning at the little boy and holding up his hands as if in surrender. Turning to Light: 'He say you his father. How you his father? He not white boy.'

'His father died. I take care of him. He's a good boy. A clever boy.' Light did not say too much. If this pirate knew how he really felt about the boy, he might be more inclined to harm him.

'The boy speak good *Ugi*.'

'*Ugi*?'

'*Bahasa Ugi*. My language. How you know it, boy?'

Soliman stood tall, although his iron-like grip on Hari the cat suggested he was frightened half to death. 'My father sail Bugis ship. I live on Bugis ship long time.'

'You slave boy?'

'No! My father sailor. Good sailor.'

Theyan nodded. 'It is sad your father die. This man look after you good? He beat you? Touch you in bad way?'

'No! He my friend. He save my life. He my father now,' Soliman insisted.

Theyan appeared to give the matter some thought, switching his gaze from man to boy and back again. Finally: 'Then Kapitan Let, this good day for you. Today, you not die. Tomorrow? Maybe. I don't know. What is your cargo?'

Light sighed inwardly. This would be a substantial loss. He was heavily committed for the agency and had invested much of his private funds in the trade in the Mergui isles. If he got away from this, he would be left with nothing – and quite possibly penalised by Jourdan for being in these waters without authority, carrying agency goods and funds. 'Rice, opium and sea products.'

'Guns? Powder?'

Light nodded tersely.

Theyan beamed again. 'Then, my friend, we can do business. I take your opium, rice, guns and powder – and you can go. The rest I don't need.'

Light considered the demand for barely a moment. In the circumstances this was a fortunate escape. His losses would not be devastating. He would keep his ship, his men and half of the valuables. Moments before he had been facing ruin and death. Light nodded his assent.

Theyan continued to smile broadly, now chatting to Light's crewmen who, realising that slavery or death were not to be their fates, seemed considerably well-disposed to their erstwhile assailant. Why would they not be? The men themselves had no issues with Bugis warriors.

'May I ask you something?' Light ventured. It was a stab in the dark, but his instincts told him that this was a gamble worth taking. Theyan turned back to Light, curiosity and suspicion replacing the pleasantries. He might have shown his jovial side so far, but this young man had darker qualities, Light was sure. He must step carefully. 'Are you a pirate? Is raiding how you make your livelihood?'

Theyan reared up. He did not like the accusation. No Bugis ever did. They did not consider themselves brigands. 'I am not a pirate! I am a warrior from a noble family. My great grandfather was Daeng Merewah. We are traders and fighters, not pirates. You are the pirates. You and the Dutch and all the rest of you *orang putih* who come to steal our wealth.'

Light had touched a nerve, exactly as he had hoped. 'So, if you are traders and I offer you a good trading opportunity, you would take it?'

Theyan eyed him warily, his eyes narrowing. 'What trading opportunity?'

It was Light's turn to smile. 'Daeng Theyan, it seems you hate the Dutch as much as I do. What say you, that instead of taking half my cargo, you escort me down to Melaka where, as a country trader, I will be allowed to do business. I sell my goods to the Dutch – and any of yours you wish to entrust to me. Then I will give you twenty percent of my cargo, to compensate for your good will in letting us go. And you will give me ten percent of your goods on behalf of my services to you.'

The young man burst into disbelieving laughter. 'You madman? Why should I give you anything? You are my prisoner! Why give what I can take?'

'Because this way, Theyan, we can both make money. More money than if you seize my cargo. We can make money not just now, but in the future. You are Bugis. You cannot enter Dutch waters or they will fire upon your ships. But I can. The Dutch need tin and rice, cloth and spices. They pay well. You can supply them in abundance. They also want luxury goods. I trade in everything. I can supply you with weaponry and opium. Each of us is better off. Think well on it, Daeng Theyan. How many other Bugis traders have access to Melaka? Through me, you could open up a new conduit for the Riau and Selangor trade.'

A less astute man might have laughed in Light's face at such an audacious proposition from a potential captive with so little obvious bargaining power. But Theyan was an enterprising fellow. Commerce ran through his veins as it did with all his people. Conflict and raiding were one thing, but Bugismen were first and foremost traders since time immemorial. They would not deny themselves an opportunity merely for a casual raid on a passing fool who had wandered into their waters.

'Kapitan Let, you a lucky, lucky man. You also very clever man. I think maybe we can work together. We must talk more about this business as we journey down the Straits. I travel on your ship. To make sure you not trick me. If anything happens to me, you know what will happen to you, na? And to your son. And to his little cat.' Theyan drew his keris, brandishing it with menace, again bursting into manic laughter. 'So ... where I sleep?'

Light's pulsing heart finally began to slow, leaving him lightheaded and weak-kneed. Like Daniel, he had faced down the lion in his den, and had somehow emerged alive. Or was it Androcles? Even now as a grown man, he could never separate his Bible from his myths. How absurd the random thoughts of a man on the brink of dying. They say a man's life flashes before his eyes in such a moment. It surely had today.

Once again, he had taken the leap when his only other option lay in death or ruin. He felt in his pocket, and there it was, the shard of quartz picked up the day before. Maybe Soliman was right about the lucky stone? Light was of the opinion that it was not the charm that had saved them, but the boy's brave defence that had turned the tide. On this day, Soliman had certainly repaid any favour owed to him. Who knows which arbitrary decision, made on the spur of the moment, might one day become the act of grace that saves one's very life?

15

A Seat at the Table

Bintan Island, Riau Archipelago. December 1769

With a surge of pleasure not felt since boyhood Christmastides, Light took heart at the excess of bounty provided by the mail of many months piled on his desk. A Company ship from Madras had delivered a bag of official post, amongst which were several letters from home that had been lingering in various stations for months. A Chinese junk heading for Batavia had dropped off another collection from Jangsylan; by merry chance they had arrived the self-same day. Riffling through the stack, Light set aside personal notes and attended first to official correspondence, not as the consequence of exceptional devotion to duty, but rather to prolong the pleasure that news from friends and family would inevitably bring.

Late afternoon, with the fiercest of the heat abating, Light took a jug of wine and strolled out of the dilapidated fort, his current lodgings, to make his way along the beach towards the edge of a rocky promontory. Soliman tagged along, chomping on chunks of guava that he deftly pared with his little knife. The sea was calm, dazzled with reflected light as the sun began its journey to the horizon in a blue sky streaked with flame.

With a large flat stone as his bench and the boy at his feet teasing a few large ants, Light laid out the letters in order of preference, each held in place by a small pebble. The most precious he would keep until last.

The first, from Jangsylan, written in an elegant Siamese hand required Soliman's assistance. Whilst they both struggled with this difficult language, Soliman was already more advanced, both in speech and the written word. Between the two of them they might be able to construe the contents well enough.

Honourable Captain Light,

A long time has passed since your last visit during which our family has much felt your absence. Circumstances continue much as before although there has been one recent alarm. King Musika of Ligor, my cousin, attempted to remove the Malays from Thalang in a feeble assault, more noise than vigour, much like my relative himself. His forces were driven off with ease and without excessive loss of life. Except, sadly, for the Vice – Governor Lord At, my sister's husband. He was executed by the Malay governor who believed him complicit in the invasion. My family is now in mourning, retired from public life. Resistance to the Malays, however, has not disappeared. There are many on the island, both local and foreign, who are tired of Queddah's authority. Meanwhile King Tak Sin moves south. Few people wish to fall under his yoke, for he demands total subservience to his will. Thalang would lose its traditional independence. Even the Malays would prefer King Musika to Siam. On the other hand, I have not seen my beloved eldest son, Lord Thian, for many years since he joined the royal armies. The return of the king would bring him back to me at last.

On the subject of family, my husband and I have been blessed. In three months, we expect the birth of a child. Phaya Pimon, my husband, will return from his province for the happy event. On your next voyage you will have the great honour of finally meeting the head of my humble household. He is most eager to make your acquaintance for he knows the support and commercial acumen you have brought to our affairs.

Rumours of your recent travels have also reached us. It seems you spend much time in Queddah, Acheen, and Riau. Beware! Between the Bugis and the Dutch, you have chosen perilous waters in which to trade. Perhaps it would be wiser to return to Thalang where commerce thrives and you have many friends upon whom you can rely? These Malays are inconstant. They lie with relish. Do not trust them! And always carry your knife close at hand.

Your friend Chan

By now, the sun was setting, amaranthine daubed with burnished gold. Nothing in the world compare to the palette of the evening skies in these waters. Light sat back, admiring the view, apparently sunk in his own thoughts. The child watched him, amusement writ clear upon his face. Very little escaped Soliman's perceptive grasp.

'What do you think, Sol? Is she warning me off or asking me back?' Light grinned. Soliman smirked, a hint of disapproval on his face. He did not like Lady Chan, whom he found sinister and cunning. Light suspected the child was simply jealous.

'She let you know her husband coming back. Maybe he already know? Or maybe he no care? Who knows? Siam women always itchy. Everybody know. Even husband. He gone long time. What to do? Maybe baby have white skin?' Soliman giggled at the thought.

Light cuffed him lightly. 'Watch your tongue, you little rascal! I haven't seen Lady Chan for almost a year. In her own devious way, she's informing me that I am not the provenance of her little blessing. While I haven't the least surety that this baby is her husband's or no, it damn well isn't mine.' He had taken every precaution to ensure no accidents occurred, fully cognisant that a fair-skinned child would have been difficult to pass off in the circumstances. His regular supply of machines waited for him in Madras, supplied by his good friend Captain Pigou who carried them back from England, one of his many alternative sources of income.

'So, Lord At was executed, was he? I wonder if the Ban Takkien really were behind King Musika's invasion? I wouldn't put it past Chan to connive both with and against Queddah. And she speaks of not trusting Malays!' Light shook his head in amusement. You had to admire the woman.

Soliman grunted. 'I no trust nobody. Friend or enemy. Except you, Kapitan Francees. Soliman always trust you.'

For that his hair was ruffled fondly. This was the one person in the world who would never let him down, his eyes and ears everywhere they went, particularly here in this Bugis stronghold. 'I wouldn't disagree with you, boy. Keep your wits about you always, whoever you are dealing with. And that goes for friends as well ... particularly this one!'

He had fished out the second letter and prised it open with a smile. 'This one's in English, Sol. You can run and play awhile. I can manage myself, unless I've forgotten my own language these past months. Not that James Scott is known for being intelligible.'

Tharua, November 3rd

My dear old friend Francis,

Are you still alive and breathing or have your Bugis friends finally seen sense and thrown you overboard, tied up like an offering for the spirits of the deep? In the unlikely event that you are still in this world, I must keep you abreast of recent developments. I have had the dubious fortune of experiencing the recent hostilities from both sides, having been back and forth from Queddah to Jangsylan several times. The Sultan is furious at the attempted rebellion, convinced Lady Chan was the primary malefactor, for what byzantine purposes only the good lady herself might know. Either she wants the Malays out or she wishes to warn them that, without her, Queddah's position is precarious. Most likely, she has had enough of power-sharing and would prefer her cousin as her overlord, knowing full well King Musika will be as good as invisible. But that would bring Tak Sin on our heads, for he will not countenance his subjects trying to make hay while he fights the Burmese. What a to-do, eh? All this with a bairn aboard, so rumour has it. By God, she is a formidable woman! It's a blessing that you're not a blue-eyed, red-haired Adonis like me, Francis, or the little mite's parentage might be questioned. Perchance it would be wise to keep your distance until after the happy event, when the matter will be resolved.

I am eager for news of your adventures. A wee bird has told me that Jourdan plans a factory in Acheen and that one Captain Francis Light is favoured to administer it. Give me some intelligence that I can chew upon. I sail to Sumatra after Hogmanay, which I still vainly attempt to celebrate as best I can in these heathen parts. Let's see what we can do together then? Anything to inconvenience the damned Dutch gives me the greatest pleasure and fills my coffers in the most satisfying manner. I am also reliably informed that Riau is becoming a first-rate landing place. Perhaps your Bugis pirate friend will prove himself useful after all?

Sad news, I'm afraid. Our mutual friend, the affable Martim Rozells, has shuffled off this mortal coil. His heart gave out. Most tragic. He was surely only fifty years or thereabouts, with such a hale and hearty look about him. One never knows. His poor wife remains in Queddah with her mother and children. I visited to pay my respects last month. She is a fine lady. The other sister, Lady Mook, has also lost her pompous husband, Lord At, in the invasion. He was blamed for it. I suppose someone had to fall? It might as well have been him. He was as ineffective as a fish in a desert. Lady Chan must look to her own dear husband now. There has been at surfeit of ill fortune amongst the men of that family, wouldn't you say?

Until New Year then. Do nothing foolish. For that is my role in this partnership,

James

Poor Martim! He surely did not deserve that. In the year or so since their trip to Mergui, Light had regularly met with him, most recently in Queddah, and had come to value his friendship. Such news gave one pause. A man's entire endeavour snatched from him in moments, with so much left unfulfilled! He almost feared to touch the letters from his family. Was heartbreak awaiting between those yearned-for pages?

Death was everywhere in these parts, by violence, disease and misadventure, yet Martim had died of what appeared to be natural causes. Light thought it hardly worth a jot to give such morbid matters a moment's concern. Foreknowledge would never change one's fate. A man must live his life until he died from it, whether that be in bed, at the bottom of the sea, or with his lifeblood ebbing away on some foreign soil. He raised his eyes to the glorious setting of the sun against the darkening horizon. This was his moment. All else was dust.

'Run back and fetch a candle, Sol. The light is fading. I cannot read by it.' The boy set off at a lively pace, returning shortly, bobbing along with a lantern on a stick.

'Ali say *makan* ready soon. We must eat.'

'Just one more then I'll save the rest for after dinner.'

Soliman nodded, placing the lantern on the rock to sink down cross-legged and wait for his master. Or his father. Light lay somewhere between the two in this boy's heart.

Light held the third letter up to the flickering light. It was from England, crumpled and faded from both its journey and the many hands through which it had passed. The author's name, however, brought a delighted smile to his face. Old Doughboy George, now lord of the manor! How curious to be sitting here on a clifftop in a remote native trading post at the other side of the world, a location quite unimaginable to his old friends back in Woodbridge, reading sheets of paper that had first seen the light of day in the study of a gracious manor house in Suffolk.

The letter was dated almost seventeen months ago. Where had he himself been on that very day when George had penned it? Light counted back the months. He had been heading for Acheen on his first expedition for his agency, the most junior captain amongst a group of experienced officers charged with opening negotiations for a British presence there. So much water had passed under the bridge for him since then, while life had ticked by for George, unchanging season after season. Light had lived ten lifetimes in that short space of years. He eagerly scanned the pages, written in George's florid style, affectionate but long-winded. His voice rang out clear in every sentence.

Martlesham Hall, this twenty second day of July,
in the Year of our Lord 1768

To Francis, my very dear companion of boyhood days,
More than three long years has passed since you departed Britannia's shores, during which time little has been heard of your Fortunes. Good Squire Negus informed us of your arrival to Madras and your initial impressions of the East, but since then it has been a Barren Season.

I pray that you are well and prospering in those far off Waters, where Fortunes may be made but many Dangers lurk. Know that you are always in our Prayers.

We are well and thriving, blessed with good fortune, God be praised! Our little household is now three with the addition of a healthy Son born this spring past, little Georgie. My dear Wife Anne has a goodly Constitution, for which I thank the Lord daily. She is quite back to her own self after her Labours. The child will be baptised at St. Mary's at Lammastide. We expect a grand occasion with old Friends galore, many of whom are now wed themselves and Parents to the next generation of little Rascals heading for Seckford's. Reverend Ray is still Headmaster, don't you know?

Belated sad tidings to impart, I'm afraid. Marianne, the younger Sister of dear James Lynn, passed away in '66, in the dark of Winter. The Season was plagued with La Grippe, that wicked sickness that is no respecter of tender Age, Sex or Class. Even with two Doctors in the household, she could not be saved, poor Lass. We attended the funeral, a most sad occasion. James was heartbroken. They were always such a close and loving Family. Some news of happier times for the Lynns: James married a Miss Eliza Wall of Aldeburgh this Eastertide, the Celebration having had been delayed out of respect to allow a decent period of Mourning. Pray forgive me as the Harbinger of this sad news but I felt sure that you would wish to know. You were once very close with the Lynns yourself ...

Light could read no further. Marianne! That charming, lively, most beautiful of girls, whom he had once hoped to marry. All these years, whilst he had presumed her breaking the hearts of every eligible buck in the county, poor Marianne Lynn had been mouldering in her grave. The horror of decay where once there had been vitality caused him to shudder. In vain he tried to replace the ghastly spectre with the image of her lovely face, once so dear to him, but she had already faded from his recollection. All that was left was an impression, a vague and distant memory from long ago. In truth, in the intervening years, he had rarely given more than a passing thought to his former love. Guilt gnawed at him for his callow disregard. She had deserved at least a letter, never mind the occasional reminiscence.

'Francees? You sad? Bad things happen in your home?' The child had recognised his altered demeanour.

Shaking his legs and blustering to hide his discomfiture, Light replied brusquely: 'The mosquitoes are biting. Come, let's not tarry. We'll go back for dinner now. The rest can wait until this evening.' He could not share this story with the boy. For how could the death several years before of a young girl he had never known mean anything to a little child who had seen and experienced such tragedies as Soliman? Life was inconstant and death ever-present for all, but nowhere was as unpredictable as the East. Straits people lived largely in the moment. The future was rarely contemplated; the past set aside. Locking dear, departed Marianne deep down, Light trudged back to the fort. Untimely deaths and unexpected births in each letter he had opened thus far, life whittled down to nothing but the beginning and the end. He whispered a prayer that his final missive, from Squire William, would not follow in this woeful pattern.

His prayers were answered, or so he discovered after he had sent Soliman off to bed and was left in peace to savour his final letter. His guardian's correspondence was as ever a joy to read, full of hilarious digressions about village life with much nonsensical tittle-tattle of the estate and the adjoining farms. As he aged, Squire William grew more and more curmudgeonly, engaging in never-resolved campaigns against his neighbours, largely over insignificant or imagined insults. This time he ranted effusively about dogs from nearby farms venturing on to his lands bringing distemper to his precious hounds and cattle. Light chuckled at the choleric diatribe much as he would have done had they been ensconced on a winter's night in Uncle William's study at Dallinghoo, with a bottle of brandy by a roaring fire. That a mere letter could bring his home back to him so vividly!

Francis' mother was well and busy as ever, always pining for news of her son, Uncle William chided. Aunt Margaret thrived, Squire Negus assured him, still the only person who could calm him down, although she tested his patience daily. What a gloriously compatible partnership they were for all that they were complete opposites! Light made a mental note to reply in the morning. If he was sharpish about it, his letters could accompany his official correspondence to Madras on the evening tide by way of the ship that had delivered them, perhaps enabling them to catch the homeward sailing season. That night, he retired a happier man than he had expected a few hours earlier, his dreams peopled with Woodbridge and the hunt, his mother in her garden and Aunt Margaret bustling around her home. The ghost of Marianne Lynn did not return to haunt him.

The next morning was entirely given over to composing affectionate and newsy letters, begging forgiveness for his long silence, blaming the length of time to travel far distances and his busy schedule. He regaled about his travels in a light and breezy style, peopling his balmy tropical seas with imperious native sultans, hard-bargaining but charming Arab traders, and a willing polyglot crew of sturdy lascars from every corner of the East Indies. It was the stuff of romances with scant resemblance to his reality, for the truth – a far more rousing tale – would have brought sheer terror to their hearts.

Finally, he turned to the hardest task of sending his much belated condolences to James and the Lynn family on the loss of their beloved Marianne. Dr and Mrs Lynn had not approved of their friendship, which did not make the correspondence any easier. Not that it had been personal, for they had known and respected Francis almost all his life, but they had high expectations of a marriage of more distinction for their eldest daughter. Francis Light had not been in a financial position to offer their daughter the standard of living to which she had been raised. No doubt his departure for India had brought a sigh of relief; the matter had been resolved without any need for unpleasantness. James himself had also disapproved, which had driven a wedge between their friendship in those final months. He adjudged that Francis had toyed with his sister giving her false hope. How little it mattered now. At least Marianne had known some passion in her short life. He hoped they were thankful for that small consolation.

His familial duties done, Light returned to his official correspondence. First, a letter to his agency to apprise them of the situation in the Riau islands. His brief had been simple: to continue with his habitual activities between the triangular stations of Acheen, Queddah and Jangsylan whilst conducting clandestine operations with the Bugis through his personal connections.

His relationship with Theyan, as tenuous as it was, had been instrumental in bringing him to the notice of his uncle, Daeng Kemboja, the King of Riau, a gambit which allowed him access to the intricate political gameplay of the region. But he was mightily exposed for all that, with no guarantees from either party. The Bugis only dealt with him because he was an independent trader; Madras had not granted him official sanction. The challenge remained to keep both sides engaged while insinuating himself into an unassailable position. For that he needed some measure of Company authority. His report to Jourdan, Sullivan and DeSouza must give the illusion of a regular update, whilst disguising the implied commitment that his superiors would never openly accept. They might, however, give assent after the fact, should commercial benefits be proven.

Riau Islands 8th day December

Dear Sirs

The Vicissitudes of Distance and contrary Winds and Currents have delayed the arrival of your communications, having only taken receipt of the mail bag yesterday. In the next few weeks, I will begin my mission to Acheen, carrying a Cornucopia from my recent sojourn in these islands. I intend first to spend a few weeks in Queddah, to procure the required Tin and Rice for Fort St George to complement the Goods already obtained. Aside from the usual China trade of Ceramics and Silk, Riau has proved an invaluable source for the commodities usually monopolised by the Dutch. Here is an abundance of Pepper, Gold, Spices, Betel, Dammer and Sticklac. Furthermore, traders from all parts have begun to flock to Riau in preference to Dutch-held ports, bringing with them all the Variety of their own trade items. The harbour today is alive with vessels from every part of the East: Arabia, India, Java, Pegu, Cochin, Siam, Sulu, Cathay, Japan.

My present anchorage is Bintan, the largest Island of the group and the central emporium of the Buginese rulers. These Bugis originate from the island of Celebes in the Eastern Archipelago. They are a totally free and independent People, making their living through Commerce and Privateering, being wholly known throughout the East Indies for their warrior prowess as much as their navigation. Their boats are 15-25 tons and carry upward of 40-50 men, the greater part of whom are fighters. Each year over seventy Sails visit the Straits of Malacca. Many more now inhabit the offshore Islands and the coastal area known as Selangor on the west of the Peninsula.

The self-styled King of Riau is one Daeng Kemboja, Daeng being some honorific amongst their tribe. He also holds the ambiguous but grandiose title of Yam Tuan Muda of the Johor-Riau Sultanate, a rank which implies a Cadet position, yet is the real Power behind the Throne. The actual Sultan is a mere Puppet of his choosing. Kemboja's influence stretches even further up the Peninsula as far as Pahang in the east and in the west Selangor, a newly settled Kingdom reputed to be rich in Tin, ruled by another member of his family, his younger cousin.

As a consequence of this unprecedented shift in the Balance of Power, Riau is fast establishing a clandestine control of the Straits' trade, to the discomfiture of the Dutch, who fear their stranglehold is waning. Bintan, 'star' in the local tongue, is aptly named, for it is indeed a most promising Location, as yet untrammelled by any Christian nation. It lies at the very entrance of the Straits; whosoever controls this Archipelago is master of the Straits and thus master of the entire trade of the Indies. I urge that the Council recognises Bintan's vast potential, and humbly beseech your Good Sirs to advise Bengal of the same.

The king of Riau is particularly wary of National Powers and is unlikely to look favourably on an official embassy. Yet, they are eager for the benefits of external Commerce, with preference for country ships which they regard as unencumbered. To such vessels, they offer protection from the local Pirates who infest the seas, as well as fair prices and reasonable harbour duties. Their violent antipathy to the Dutch is well known, for they were driven from their home waters by VOC incursion. Thus, they look to English captains as their natural allies, aware that we have no love either for Holland. Raja Kemboja has proposed that the deserted Fort in which

I am currently dwelling could be made permanently available as a Base from which to trade and establish a Garrison. Without the authority to commit to such an undertaking despite its promise, I have informed the King that it is beholden upon me to await leave from Madras, some eight months' hence. I do not think he is satisfied with the delay but grudgingly tolerates the situation for the present. Should the Dutch decide to move against him in the meantime, however, I fear he may look elsewhere for Friends. I took the liberty of refraining from discussing our imminent rendezvous in Acheen lest this knowledge should encourage the King to force our hand. Until then, I hand the matter over to you, trusting that a successful outcome, channelled through the Agency, would be most lucrative for all parties.

A peaceful Christmastide and the very best of the Season to you all and your Good Families! I look forward to joining Harrop and Gibson in Acheen in March. May our endeavours bring this long-awaited Enterprise to fruition at last,

Your humble servant,
Francis Light, Capt.

It would have to do, thought Light, although the limitations of his epistolary skill frustrated him. He was a man for face-to-face negotiations where his ability to read character and response favoured him, not a clever wordsmith. His employers would see through his obscurities; they were too shrewd for that. He expected them to refuse outright any alliance with Bugis rulers that might embroil them in local hostilities. Conflict with the Dutch and involvement in the labyrinthine politics of the Straits would be rejected out of hand. But the leeway of eight months before he would be commanded to withdraw, would benefit his own profits exponentially. He had already acquired his own vessel, to add to the agency ship he now owned outright, which would continue in his absence to conduct his private business from Bintan. Jourdan, Sullivan and DeSouza's loss would be his gain.

There was, of course, another stratagem to employ, that of appealing to the network of Company captains he now regarded as friends. If it should be private trade alone in Riau, Light intended to be at its very heart, the conduit through which all introductions must pass. A long overdue letter to his friend and erstwhile saviour in Madras, Captain Andrew Ross, was required. He would ensure the information was disseminated throughout the brotherhood of country captains.

Bintan, Riau, December

My dear Ross
In the vain hope that this Letter finds you passing the Winter in Madras, may I wish the tidings of the Season to You and Yours, and the same to Pigou and his Brood. It is my sincere hope that all is well with you and that your Finances prosper. For my part, I am thriving.

I reside at present somewhere South of the Straits in an Island chain until recently desolate other than of Sea Turtles and Pirates. Indeed, some might avow that little has changed, notwithstanding the roaring trade now conducted in these Waters, for the occupants are somewhat still inclined to the Buccaneer Life, and the Turtles still lay their eggs.

Herein I have stumbled upon a rich vein of unexploited Opportunity likely to be ignored by the Hon. Com. and its Worthy Masters. In consequence, it seems incumbent upon me to share the Bounty with sailors who know how to value my Intelligence. But I ramble on. Let me go back somewhat. A while past, I had the misfortune to be taken by a group of Bugis privateers, led by a devious but amiable Anak Raja by the name of Daeng Theyan. With little but my silver tongue, I evaded Death and Ruination whilst securing for myself a Partner of this unruly fellow, having talked myself into doing business with him. Since that time, I have managed to win the trust of his people, most particularly his Uncle, the King of Riau. The Raja has granted me unprecedented access to his Bintan Emporium and in return I have been assisting him as an Intermediary, conducting covert trade with Malacca. The Bugis and the Dutch are mortal enemies. Malacca waters are forbidden to them.

It has proved a most lucrative Affiliation, despite potential hazards, for Riau has recently become a Thriving Centre for those who wish to avoid the brutal Taxes and Levies of the Dutch ports. Merchants of every nation are bypassing Malacca and Batavia to transact with the Bugis, especially in the Commodities the Dutch control most assiduously: Tin, Opium, Weaponry, Spices, and most of all Pepper, so abundant that Bintan is also known as 'The Beautiful Land of Pepper'. The Islands also serve as hideouts for raiders and their booty, for the Bugis are as much inclined to Privateering as to Commerce. All is the same to them.

They welcome Private Traders as middlemen in dispersing of these Stolen Goods, most particularly Slaves, which are valuable barter throughout the region. They also pay good premium for the loan of bigger Vessels to facilitate their raids on larger ports. These opportunities for Risk-free Ventures should not be the sole preserve of Merchants from China, India and Arabia. I urge you to broadcast this around the Captains in Madras. It is not in any wise considered Illegal Practice in these waters, for the local Rulers of the Straits themselves readily avail themselves of this Conduct and its Fruits. Raiding is regarded not so much as Piracy but 'Legal Privateering'. A subtle but vital difference, I am assured! A further Advantage of engaging with the King of Riau: ships in his employ need have no fear of falling prey to marauders. His Protection stretches throughout the region, such is his Influence. That alone makes Alliance with him of inestimable value.

It is my strong belief that the English should enter into a more formal relationship with the king, who is interested in allowing the Building of a Garrison on Bintan. The Company might baulk at the notion of Military Commitment, but I believe the time is ripe for such Incursions. The VOC is on the Decline and the Bugis on the rise. I shall continue to make my case, howsoever it may fall on stony ground. But I am damned if we should fail to make some Profit out of it in the meantime. Give the matter consideration, my Friend. I await your thoughts.

I shall be in Acheen in the spring. Perchance we may yet win a Factory there, in which case it might become my Home for the near future. Who knows where the wind blows?

The Compliments of the Season,

Francis

Light slumped back in his chair, scanning through the letter, more satisfied with this note. Should the Company eschew a golden opportunity, he doubted sea captains such as Ross would not wish to make a Riau visit. And he would be the intermediary between them and the wary Bugis leaders. It was a significant moment, progressing from apprentice to master in the convoluted politics of advancement, where a single misstep forward could thrust one off the ladder forever. Yet, what did he have to lose? If the worst happened and the Company or his agency cut him adrift, opportunities now abounded for him: Jangsylan, Queddah, Riau, Johor and Selangor were already in his pocket. But fortune alone was not enough to satisfy him. Not until the men in power with their titles and their landed estates stood up when he entered a room and ushered him to a seat at the head of the table, would he be done.

PART THREE

The Nyonya Lady

(1770-72)

16

Burning One's Boats

Factory of the Madras Association, Kutaraja, Acheen. June 1770

REPORT TO THE MADRAS COUNCIL

On the morning of March 3rd, under cover of heavy rain, we rounded Aceh Head, a convoy of Achenese vessels under the command of Admiral Panglima Hassim Ali, accompanied by the Speedwell at the rear. Visibility poor. The Surat Passage is known for dangerous tidal waters with eddies and whirlpools fatal to mariners unfamiliar with these waters. At this time of year, however, with the wind behind and led by navigators accustomed to the strait, a safe passage was achieved, staying close to the mainland and evading the worst of the seas. From then on, an uneventful sailing: blustery conditions, grey fast-moving clouds and a deep swell indicating more rain ahead, ideal conditions for the venture. An estimated four days until rendezvous at Singkil, the final landing point before entering the disputed coastal territories of Tapanuli district. No hostile vessels encountered. Local fishing craft observed at a distance.

At Singkil, we laid at anchor until sunset, hidden from the mainland in the lee of an offshore rock. As light fell, we entered Barus Bay by stealth, aboard numerous landing craft, a motley selection of skiffs, canoes and bumboats. My force of thirty armed sepoys was deployed with strict instructions to hold fire unless fired upon. Their purpose was twofold: to create a distraction by bringing terror to the occupants of the fort, and subsequently to protect our ship during its trading mission in Barus. On no account were we to partake in any unsanctioned military aggression, but only what self-defence demanded. The men were told to wave their guns and create an atmosphere of fear, nothing more. A troop of bearded sepoys descending on the enemy is a fearsome sight indeed.

The inhabitants of the fishing village fled the swampy beach into the mangroves at the sight of the Achenese force. There were no innocent casualties, no alarm was raised. Nor did it appear that the natives held the occupiers in any regard. It is my belief that they took the Achenese troops for a liberating force, the district being part of the sultanate until the recent Dutch incursion.

The fort lay on the opposite headland from our landing, which we gained by skirting the mangrove forest. We found the gate fortified with a scant complement of four guards. A few Achenese advanced in pretence of being fisherman with a catch to sell, calling out in the local dialect. The ruse succeeded. Panglima Hassan then led his men inside, accompanied by the howling sepoys brandishing their loaded rifles. It was sufficient to convince the occupiers that surrender was their only option. Barus was thus taken with the loss of only four lives – three Bugis mercenaries and one Dutch corporal.

Our business kept the Speedwell at Barus for two weeks, during which time a cargo of camphor and sappanwood was obtained, commodities which have been in short supply of late. The Speedwell then took its leave and returned to Kutaraja ...

'Had you completely lost your wits, man?' Francis Jourdan bellowed across the table, flinging down the report in temper, his face an overripe plum. He was a portly fellow whose unusually smooth and unmarked skin gave him the peculiar appearance of an adult baby. 'Your action contravenes every condition of your employ! What possible justification could be offered for such errant infringements of the explicit instructions laid down in your contract – and repeated at regular intervals each time you have attempted to wheedle concessions from us? Speak up, man! What have you to say in your defence?'

Light kept his gaze lowered and his face devoid of emotion, in the vain hope that his expression would portray contrition. Jourdan's tirade, however, indicated that he had failed to convince. He was hard pressed to put forward any vindication of his behaviour. The foremost principle of the East India Company had been broken, of that there was no doubt. He had taken part in a local military expedition with Company sepoys making up part of the attacking force.

To be fair, Light had taken great pains not to advertise his participation in the Achenese attack, expecting to escape scot-free, his agency none the wiser. But word of his involvement had soon been broadcast. It had been naïve in the extreme to imagine that someone would not relish tittle-tattling to Madras. Loyalty is a fluctuating currency based wholly on personal advantage. Every man in these ports was on the make. Information was gold.

His chief suspect was Captain John Gibson, the commanding officer on the initial expedition to Acheen, a man who had never forgiven Light for his appointment to the factory, which he had believed was his by right of seniority. Or perhaps the faithless sultan himself had been the source of the revelation, whispering the nugget to Gibson, knowing it would find its way back to the Council. It was typical of that fickle ruler to bite the very hand that had extended him support. No doubt Sultan Alaudin had hoped to coerce the British by means of this incontrovertible deed that they would have to own. It would never have worked. The Honourable Company and its agencies would never be manipulated.

When the facts had become public knowledge, Light had still not been unduly concerned, merely expecting a censure from the agency, or perhaps a monetary penalty. Never had he seriously envisaged a personal visit from Jourdan himself, now the celebrated Director of the Madras Association. This recent amalgamation of Jourdan, Sullivan and DeSouza with a number of smaller houses had created a formidable alliance, the main mercantile arm of the East Indies trade. For a Council member such as Jourdan to travel to an insignificant spot like Acheen was testimony to how seriously the Company viewed Light's malfeasance. It only remained to be seen if his dexterity with the spoken word and his ability to think on his feet could in any way serve to mitigate his predicament.

The arrival of his director the previous evening on the *Indian Trader*, his personal vessel commanded by the formidable Gowan Harrop himself no less, had given Light little time to prepare a defence. He had immediately hastily penned the predated report, weakly blaming its lateness on the time of year now that the monsoon winds had turned, but he had in no way readied himself for the vitriol of Jourdan's attack. Light had no need of a contrite face. The knowledge of how far his behaviour had overstepped the mark in the Company's estimation had tinged his usually bronzed face with a ghastly grey pallor. His discomfiture was also visible in the nervous tic that troubled his right eye. Would he be able to talk himself back from the brink this time, or was ignominious dismissal beckoning?

'I have no defence, sir. My behaviour was unconscionable. I made the gravest error in judgement. Thus, it is with profound regret that I must tender my resignation forthwith ...' Light would fall upon his sword. If Jourdan's mind was made up, at least he could truthfully claim to have resigned rather than face dishonourable discharge. By this means he might retain some measure of the higher ground. On the other hand, there was a chance, slim but still worth playing for, that Jourdan would not wish to bring an untried man into Acheen after Light had spent nigh on two years making significant progress in the kingdom.

Jourdan grunted, whether in acceptance or approval it was impossible to tell. A ponderous silence hung over the table, broken only by the irritating beat of Harrop's knee against the underside of the table top. The supercargo was a gaunt, lanky Yorkshireman with hawkish nose and hooded eyes, who never wasted a word where a silent stare might do. Known to be devious, with fingers in every pie in Asia, Harrop knew the game inside out. Who could guess where his real sympathies lay? Light's performance was as much to win him over as to pacify his irate employer; the young captain might have needs of a new patron before long. All the while, Harrop had been observing the dialogue with the eyes of a basilisk, rarely seeming even to blink. It was most disconcerting.

'Well?' Jourdan broke in. 'I'm still waiting for an explanation, man! Don't imagine you can hide behind a pretence of penitence and the melodrama of your resignation. Whether you go or stay depends entirely on me, not on your flimflammery. You signed a damned contract!' Jourdan's tone was still aggressive but the force of his wind was dying down. A volte-face might be imminent. The other two men sensed the moment, with the instinct of sailors reading a sudden change in the weather. Light saw his chance; Harrop turned to stare direct at him, giving him the full force of his piercing scrutiny.

A deep breath and: 'As unconvincing as it might now sound, sir, my original motives were wholly opposite from what came to pass. I beg your indulgence if I might review the circumstances that led to this ill-advised adventure, which predicated on the complex and treacherous politics of Acheen. These men are not gentlemen as we understand the term, Mr Jourdan. Their word is not their bond ...' Jourdan growled again in response, but indicated impatiently for Light to continue.

'Sultan Alaudin sits upon a precarious throne. Only six years ago, a violent rebellion temporarily unseated him, installing his chief minister as the new sultan. It seems this former *Bendahara* had won the support of the real powers in the territory, the men of rank who are mere local chiefs, known in the Acheen dialect as "*uleebalang*". In the past fifty years they have eaten away at the sultan's authority, rendering him little more than a puppet king, albeit one who lives in extremes of luxury and comfort. These changes have been brought about as a consequence of the exceptional demand for pepper, the major output of the region, which is now wholly under uleebalang control.

'The sultan is capricious, even more so since his reinstatement to the throne. He now demands a greater share in the pepper profits but finds himself increasingly isolated and without authority to make his nobles obey him. Thus, he has invited representatives of several Christian nations by means of the inducement of trading contracts. His real aim, nonetheless, is to secure the support of a foreign army to force the uleebalang to heel and also to keep the Dutch at bay.'

Jourdan was losing patience. 'I do not require a history lesson, Light! Keep to the point. Are you saying that the past two years have been for naught? Must we be dangled on a string until we throw our own men into some disastrous conflict, all for the sake of a heathen potentate? If that is the measure of it, you should have recommended our withdrawal months ago!' But Jourdan was still listening.

'It is more convoluted than that, sir. We have done an extraordinary amount of business since we opened the factory. Our profits have been most promising, as you well know. Acheen is an excellent location for the Arab and India trade, not known as The Porch of Mecca for nothing. But in that very fact lies its disadvantage. The Achenese are devout Mohammedans; they mistrust all who do not share their faith. The sultan's court is dominated by Arab Saids and Indian Chulias who do their best to prejudice him against us. This sultan's ears are very light; he shares the opinion of whomsoever spoke to him most recently. Furthermore, he vacillates between the Danish, the French and the English so much so that whenever one is on the brink of drawing up a contract, one finds oneself suddenly out of favour, merely because a Danish captain has arrived with gunpowder or a French vessel loaded with cannon. The only certainties are that the sultan hates the Dutch and is eager to curb his own nobles.'

'So, you gave him precisely what he wanted, despite implicit instructions to the contrary? I would rather lose every ounce of pepper in Sumatra than bring our country into needless war with Holland or with a gaggle of natives on the warpath.' Jourdan's temper was gaining steam again. Light wondered if he had overplayed his hand.

'Let him carry on, Mr Jourdan. Mayhap his venture was more carefully adjudged than first it seems ...' Harrop's intervention was unexpected. Francis shot him a grateful look. The other man returned it with an almost imperceptible nod.

'My advantage lay in the fact that the sultan admires me whereas he generally has little regard for Europeans. I have his ear more than the other captains, so I intended to make use of that position. We have already benefitted in ways that no other external power can match, in that ours is the only factory with a complement of soldiers to defend it. That concession has been given to no one else, not even the Muslim merchants. The sultan claimed he was now prepared to offer us sole licence to trade, with the result that all other merchants must go through our agency to buy and sell in Acheen, tantamount to turning over the entire port to British control. In return, he asked that our soldiers be available to subdue the uleebalang and other restless elements. He had no intention of further aggravating the Dutch, beyond that of restoring his own rightful territories, which would be to our advantage if the pepper trade was entirely channelled through English agents.'

'But ... but, we do not sanction military involvement!' Jourdan spluttered.

'Exactly,' Light replied. 'So, I decided that the mere "pretence" of military aid would suffice, while in actuality extending no such thing. I merely accompanied an armed convoy for protection whilst on a trading mission, which is an accustomed practice in dangerous waters, with sepoys to guard *my* crew and property. There was strict instruction not to join the fight. Should a British ship with guns happen to alarm the natives sufficient to encourage their surrender, then it could not be helped. But it was never my intention to engage ...'

'... but should you have been attacked? What then?' Harrop interrupted, his eyes glinting darkly. He had already seen the ploy, knew Light's answer, and was offering him his cue.

Light shrugged. 'If a Company ship is fired upon, then it is incumbent upon the captain to defend himself and his men. That is accepted policy.'

Jourdan closed his mouth, pursed his lips, and made a huffing sound. 'You're a clever devil, Light, and no mistake. I'm not sure I believe a word you're saying but it will dot the "i"s and cross the "t"s at Council. They haven't the first idea what's really happening here anyway. I'm still not sure about you, Light. I think you're a reckless adventurer, no better than your scurrilous friend Scott, who by all accounts is living as a perfect Malay up in Jangsylan.

But you make money for us, even if you sail as close to the wind as any man could without drowning. However, you have come a cropper this time and no mistake. The Dutch seem to have a wholly other perspective on the sultan's claim to Tapanuli. By the skin of your teeth, Light, you are avoiding the most shameful of dismissals, by the skin of your teeth ... for that's how near I am to accepting your resignation and kicking your skinny bastard arse out of the Indies entire.'

While Light swallowed down a strong desire to punch the smug Mr Jourdan about his dapper head, he managed to restrain his baser instinct. The taste in his mouth was bitter, but if grovelling was required, he would acquit himself perfectly. 'Thank you, sir. I fully understand that I have acted most recklessly. I assure you that such circumstances will never happen again. I am most humbly grateful for your clemency and understanding.'

'Clemency? Understanding? I am not sure you have either, you reprobate. Nor am I convinced by your unctuous grovelling. It's not part of your arrogant nature. And as for such outrage happening again, I suspect it will. Over and over, whether or not I am informed of the matter. This time you have been found out. I doubt you will be able to pull the wool over the eyes of your betters so easily from now on though. You've burnt your boats on both sides, I should imagine. To the immediate point, what next for Acheen? Did your feeble plan gain us any advantage?'

Light shook his head. 'As soon as they were forced to retreat from Barus by the Dutch, the sultan withdrew his favour. Since then I have been *persona non grata* at court. In truth, sir, despite all we have achieved, I do not believe he will ever grant us what we desire. He intends to keep us hanging, giving nothing but false promises in return. It is now almost four years since our first foray into Acheen and what have we really gained?'

'Then you think we should withdraw?' Harrop snapped, a dark crease forming across his brow. The Acheen station had been his original command; he did not like the implication that it had failed.

'No. I do not think we should withdraw. We have a remarkable advantage in this factory and should continue with brisk and steady trade. But we should look elsewhere to establish a British port. To a location that isn't already mired in politics and corruption.'

'Are you about to suggest for the umpteenth time that we throw caution to the winds and ally with those Buggee pirates in bloody Riau?' Jourdan exclaimed. 'Goddammit, Light, surely we have had enough of that nonsense! They are robbers and murderers. In any other part of the globe we'd be hanging them from yardarms for their crimes! We cannot truck with buccaneers and brigands!'

'It is a matter of perspective, sir. One man's pirate is another man defending his way of life. Good Queen Bess once sanctioned Sir Francis Drake to be little more than a pirate and we regard him a national hero!' Light replied, somewhat unwisely in the circumstance.

'Do not compare the behaviour of Christian gentlemen to native savages,' Jourdan answered. 'God give me strength, Light!'

Light raised his hands in apology. 'I know what the Bugis are. They are raiders; I myself was taken by a Bugis pirate. But I have also lived amongst them. I have done business with them and traded for them. They may be dangerous and warlike but the pirate legend is misleading. First and foremost, they are skilled navigators, formidable warriors and merchants of exceptional business sense. They, too, are Mohammedans but unlike the Acheens, they will deal with any man who offers them a fair transaction. They may be crafty but they never bite the hand that feeds. Nor do they have need for troops for they have warriors aplenty. Furthermore, Riau controls the very entrance to the Straits while Acheen looks over nothing but an empty sea and the Nicobars, full of cannibals ...'

Harrop stopped him with a hand raised. 'Riau will never be sanctioned, Light. War is brewing between the Bugis territories and Holland. The Company will never stand in the midst of that. Do not hold false hopes for your Riau adventure. It will not happen. You have Acheen. Be grateful for that.'

***

Six frustrating months had passed since that uncomfortable interview, months in which Light found himself the unwitting butt of both sides, much as Jourdan had warned. The Association sought to grind him down as punishment for acting without sanction; the sultan blamed him for failing to defend Barus from the marauding Dutch. For the first time he felt close to giving up. Scott had been right. These people would never offer a man like him the opportunities he deserved. Perhaps he should write his resignation after all, take his two ships and return to Riau? Or establish the trading house in Jangsylan with James Scott?

It had been a time of dashed hopes, loss of face, and a sense that he might now be permanently relegated to the backwaters of the Indies, to whittle away his remaining years as a lowly cargo-shifter, his experience and knowledge spurned, watching younger and lesser men rise above him in the politics of the Company. Harrop had remained to take the reins in the negotiations. As a result, Light had been evicted from his relatively comfortable official residence and was now quartered in a ramshackle stilted house, amidst the noisome and pestilent lanes portside. There were many men like him who had ruined their health in disease-ridden postings in the vain hope of an advancement that would never come. His earlier disillusionment with the navy was being ominously replicated in the downward slide of his East Indies career.

To lower his spirits even further, when the rains came and the incessant downpours saturated the muddy coastal plain of Kutaraja, Light had fallen sick with a debilitating ague. It was a common ailment in the tropics where mephitic odours and foul miasmas rise from flooded swamps. Pale-skinned foreigners seemed the favoured target of this terrible illness. Until this time, Light had counted himself fortunate not to have fallen victim to its insidious creep. But it had found him when his spirits were at their lowest – and he had barely recovered. Those who survived carried the noxious poison within their bodies evermore, to suffer further bouts at regular intervals until their weakened constitutions finally succumbed. Even a return to England and its cool fresh climate was no protection; sufferers were accustomed to periodically falling ill with the relentless remitting fever.

Soliman had nursed his benefactor with fierce application, rarely leaving Light's bedside in the dangerous days when his fever had raged one moment, sheets drenched in sweat, to the descent into shivering chill the next, where even a mound of blankets failed to warm his blood. Light's memory of that time was vague and monstrous, his nightmares peopled with horrific, distorted visions. Throughout this precarious time, Soliman had trickled watery rice gruel into his mouth and pressed cool cloths upon his skin day after day, until the fever had broken and Light had been restored into the conscious world, weak and frail, but still alive.

Since then, Light had made a full recovery but it took many weeks during which he had made no trading missions, relying on his own masters to carry on with business, aware that they would no doubt be cheating him of rightful profits, as well as seeking to undermine him with Madras. Where once he had been accumulating a fortune, his income was drastically reduced, to the extent that he might have to sell off one of his ships. Yet for once he could not summon up the energy even to care. He was close to giving up the ghost. Memories of Suffolk autumn days beckoned. Mayhap it was time to go home, admit his adventure had failed, and settle for a humbler life?

Until one morning in December, his office door was thrown open and a round-eyed Soliman ducked in, hopping from one leg to another, so eager to make an announcement that he could barely contain himself.

'What is it, then? Have you red ants in your sarong?' Light snapped. His temper was short these days, even towards Soliman.

'No, sir. No ants. Just auntie. She come see you.'

'Auntie? What the devil are you on about, boy? I thought you could speak English?'

Soliman was rarely cowed by Light's bad humour. The boy was always unfailingly happy, more especially now that the captain had recovered. Such insults rolled right off his back. 'I speak very good English, sir. A lady is here. A Nyonya lady. Very beautiful. She ask for Kapitan Light. She say she come from Queddah to talk to you.'

Light scoffed at the very idea. 'What? A Nyonya lady? On her own? Chase her away, Sol. She's probably some Chinese whore trying a new gambit.'

'No, sir. This very nice lady. Honourable lady. With guards and servants. Very fine Nyonya lady. Come, you must meet with her.'

17

The Cynosure of the Indies

Light's residence, Kutaraja, Acheen. January 1771

The dilapidated *atap* house was set in a shabby compound within walking distance of the muddy dockside, from where the foetid stench of rot, decaying fish and human waste wafted on the sea breeze. It was a forlorn place, a few chickens pecking the dusty earth, a stray dog foraging in kitchen refuse. Lady Thong Di suspected it was a place of men; she could see no evidence of a woman's hand. Even a slut would keep more order in a home than this.

The residence surprised her. Her knowledge of European ways was scant, mostly gleaned from gossip and stray observation, but she carried a notion that white people lived grander lives. After all, they strode around as if they owned the world by some god-appointed right, disdaining the very cultures that they sought to plunder, treating the people of the East like primitive children. They regarded themselves as the bringers of the light. She had observed this even in her own adopted religion where the faithful were exhorted that Jesus had come to save them from the darkness and the error of their ways. Surely then, the Christians must be a higher form of being, carved in the image of their God of Mercy? Not that her Christian brethren generally behaved any better, or with more enlightenment, than the rest of humanity, in her opinion.

She had been curious to meet this young farang captain who had been well regarded by her late husband. Martim Rozells had thought him a fine man, unlike the other stiff and prejudiced Company officers, less venal than Scott, whom her husband had liked but always viewed with a healthy measure of mistrust. Yet Kapitan Light lived here in squalor. It puzzled her. Did he not consider his reputation? Did he not wish to save face? How would his business acquaintances and the sultan's court regard a man who did not seek to impress with an outward show of wealth and prosperity? They were strange people, these farangs. And they smelt.

A young Malay houseboy ran out to greet them. He was friendly but displayed little notion of courtesy or respect. '*Selamat datang!* What you want?'

Lady Thong Di waited in a cluttered room that seemed to serve both as living and dining quarters. An open door revealed an unmade sleeping cot in a tiny annexe, to the right of which was the kitchen, set on the back veranda. She could smell onions and spices frying and hear the sizzle of hot oil as pungent tamarind was thrown into a *kuali*. She considered sitting, but every chair was occupied with papers, items of clothing and other random objects. So, she decided to stand. The boy had disappeared through the only other door, which he had closed firmly behind him. That must be Kapitan Light's private chamber. Was he still abed?

'*Selamat pagi, nona.*' The door opened smartly and out strode a youngish European man, followed closely by the little boy, whose bright eyes and importunate grin brought her own son Felipe to mind. 'Beg pardon, ma'am ...' And he gathered up a handful of clothing on a chair, indicating that she should sit down. '*Silakan, duduk.*'

Thong Di bowed her head graciously but refused his offer. She was relieved that he spoke Malay. One of her own men had claimed some English, which she suspected was very little, so it was a relief to find that she could conduct the conversation herself. 'Thank you but no, Kapitan Light. I prefer to stand. My apologies for disturbing you in the morning without an appointment. I come with news of an interesting proposition. I would be most honoured if you would take the time to hear me out.'

Captain Light's expression was amiable but intrigued. An embassy from a foreign state led by a woman, whilst unusual in these parts, was not entirely unheard of either. Mature women of good family, particularly in Jangsylan or Malacca, played an active role in trade. Polite convention made it less easy to insult them during negotiations. They were also thought to be more gullible, a convenient fiction, and thus underestimated. European women, so Lady Thong Di had heard, had much less freedom, spent their lives at home in trivial pursuits, and were uninvolved in public life. Only the poor were allowed to work. Thus, she expected that her presence would completely take the English captain by surprise.

Notwithstanding, Captain Light recovered his composure quickly, offering her a polite smile. 'Please, continue, dear lady. How may I be of assistance?'

'I am sent as an emissary of His Royal Highness, Paduka Sri Sultan Muhammed Jiwa Zainal Adilin Mu'aadzam Shah II ibni al-Marhum Sultan Ahmad Tajuddin Halim Shah I ...' Lady Thong Di paused, casting her eyes slightly to the right, where her advisor stood, nodding his head in approval. She had feared to make an error in the lengthy official title that protocol demanded.

Light's demeanour changed perceptibly, his forehead furrowed at her introduction. 'The Sultan of Queddah sends word to me in the form of an official embassy? I am most honoured, my lady. But may I have the even greater honour of making your acquaintance? You appear to have the benefit of my name whilst I am at loss to address you by your correct title.'

It was smartly done. He had turned his surprise into a reminder that her etiquette was lacking. 'My apologies, sir. I am Nona Thong Di Rozells. You may remember my late husband, Martim. He always spoke well of you.'

'Ah, so you are dear Martim's wife!' Light's puzzlement changed to understanding. She was quite taken how his features so honestly reflected his thoughts. 'Dear Madam, I was heartsore at the news of poor Martim's passing. He was a fine man and a good friend. Please, accept my sincere condolences.' He pronounced the last word in English but he had said enough for her to construe his meaning. Since Martim's death, she had heard every manner of polite comfort. Such comments were always kindly meant yet only served to twist the knife deeper into her heart. She raised her hands both as a gesture of gratitude but also to indicate that his words on the matter would suffice.

'My husband had great respect for you, sir. Which in part explains my presence here today. May I also introduce Syed Harun ibni Ahmad? He is an advisor to the sultan and has accompanied me as my aide.' Her introduction was cursory. Light bowed at the Arab gentleman, resplendent in heavy brocade and elegant silk turban, a diamond brooch gathering its central folds. The minister reciprocated the greeting with a solemn obeisance of his own. Syed Harun's eyes then fixed upon Light and the lady in an icy stare that exuded a strong note of disapproval.

Baiting him in the guise of politeness, Light offered Syed Harun a chair, but was rebuffed with an imperious gesture. The advisor seemed content to stay in the background with the guards and female attendants. The tiny cluttered room was overwhelmed with bodies. Instructing Soliman to open wide the doors and windows and to wave a palm frond in the general direction of Nona Rozells, Light endeavoured to bring in some fresh air. But the atmosphere remained stifling and, with the shutters open, the putrid odours of the port were also given unwanted access. Syed Harun's lip curled in distaste, his long nose twitching at the smell.

'I insist that if we are to have discussions then we should at least sit down, Nona Rozells. Soliman, clear a chair and tidy my desk! Tell Ali to supply refreshments!' he barked the last in English.

There was an uncomfortable silence as the young boy scrabbled together a heap of objects from the table top: glasses, crockery, papers, books and various other implements. He then scuttled away while Light held out a chair for the lady. She sat down, her back straight and her head held high; he steered her seat neatly in place. The proximity of the man unnerved her. It also offended Syed Harun, who cleared his throat and pulled a face, but refrained from intervening. Anger was simmering on his neatly bearded face, his eyes glittering with cold disdain.

Taking his seat at the other side of the desk, Light glanced over at the Arab advisor, as if to taunt him further. It was unwise behaviour but Light could never resist. He doubted the man would ever look kindly upon him anyway. By now Soliman was back with a pot of ginger tea and two chipped porcelain cups, alongside a plate of *kueh,* sticky coconut rice cakes wrapped in leaves. A few ants already crawled across their surface; within moments an entire army was marching up the table leg to swarm over the tasty bites. Lady Thong Di shook her head at the proffered dainties, but accepted a cup of tea, which she refrained from drinking.

Setting down the cup, she began: 'Kapitan Light, I believe you are also a close acquaintance of my sister, Lady Chan?' Light near choked on his sip of tea at this unexpected statement of intent. Nona Rozells was revealing her mettle at the outset. It would be well not to underestimate her. For her part, the lady scrutinised his response. A flicker of uncertainty in his eyes and a bloom on his cheeks betrayed his embarrassment, where she had supposed she might find arrogance and bravado.

Light cleared his throat, adjusted his posture, and ran his hands nervously down his thighs. She had unsettled him mightily. 'That is correct, nona. Your sister is a remarkable woman. I have done much business with her.' At this ambiguous comment, he winced. Thong Di suppressed a desire to giggle. His boyish discomfort was charmingly refreshing. It caused her to appraise the man himself in more detail.

Captain Light was a well-favoured man, tall and lean, clean shaven, and with thick, wavy hair the colour of palm sugar, tied neatly in a bow. But it was his eyes that held her attention most: they were a strange light shade, neither blue nor green but somewhere in between, lit with a tawny glow. She had never before met any European who hadn't repulsed her.

'I have heard many good things about you from both my late

husband and my older sister. So, you come well recommended. The sultan also thinks highly of you. Thus, he thought it fitting to send me as his emissary because, although we had never met, our families have already formed bonds of mutual acquaintance.'

Light nodded gravely, sensing she was allowing him a gracious escape from his earlier discomfiture. 'You are too kind, nona. But, I must admit, I am curious as to the purpose of your embassy. Please, feel free to speak plainly.'

She nodded her head. 'The past few years in Queddah have been stormy, as I am sure you are aware. There was an uprising at court in which the sultan and his family barely escaped with their lives. Their palace was ransacked and set on fire. For many months, the sultan was forced to retreat to the old palace in Perlis in the north from where he has struggled to reclaim his throne.'

'We had heard that the rebellion had been vanquished and that Sultan Muhammed had been reinstated,' Light replied.

'Just so. But dangers loom everywhere. It is difficult to know who is with him and who secretly harbours dissent. The sultan is an old man, Kapitan. He knows his years are numbered. It is of the utmost urgency that he secures the throne for his favourite son, Prince Abdullah ...'

'... who would have helped his own cause greatly had he not spurned his Bugis bride,' Light added wryly. The famous marriage alliance between the kingdoms of Malay Queddah and Bugis Selangor that had offered the illusion of a settled peace in the Peninsula had collapsed in a matter of months, followed by a divorce and a discarded wife returned to her father in shame. The Bugis king of Selangor would never forgive Queddah for the insult.

Lady Thong Di did not rise to his bait. 'Unfortunately, the royal couple did not find each other to their individual tastes,' was her diplomatic reply.

Light raised his eyebrows. 'And so, the Bugis seized Jangsylan then gave support to a palace coup in Queddah. I sense the divorce was less mutually amicable than you imply, dear lady. Yes, I am aware that Sultan Muhammed Jiwa is now in a precarious position. Added to his problems with his own court and the Bugis, he also fears the encroachment of Siam and Burma. One might say he finds himself almost surrounded by hostile powers. It is not an enviable position, I agree.'

The lady acknowledged his observations with a dainty tilt of her head. Nona Rozells was dressed Nyonya-style for this embassy: silk sarong and a fine muslin kebaya blouse fastened with pearl *kerongsang* jewellery to reflect her status as a widow. Her hair was swept up in a tight bun pinned with ornate brooches. She wore no head covering. Whilst not strictly necessary for a Christian Siamese, her garb was somewhat improper for an emissary of a Muslim potentate. But the sultan himself had suggested that she dress thus – and remain uncovered. Thong Di suspected his motives. Was she truly an ambassador or a mere sweetmeat to catch a prey?

'The king also has an ally in the sultan of Trengganu,' she added.

'Trengganu?' Light scoffed. 'I doubt that Trengganu alone will be enough to scare his enemies off as I'm sure the sultan well knows. Am I to understand that you are here to seek assistance from Britain? Are you visiting in my capacity as representative of the Madras Association and thus the East India Company itself?

For if that is the case then I fear the sultan may have overestimated my importance. I am a mere spoke in the wheel, I'm afraid. I cannot sanction any involvement in local politics, nona.'

She drew herself up, squaring her neat and tiny frame. 'The sultan is fully aware of your position, sir. He is also aware that only a few months ago, you took part in a military expedition to Barus in Tapanuli, storming the fort and seizing it from the Dutch on behalf of the Sultan of Aceh. He has been reliably informed that your involvement was without the knowledge of your agency or the Company. Would that not be an example of "involvement in local politics"?' She held his gaze. Light smiled in admiration at her counter.

'For which act, I have been soundly disciplined by my employers and snubbed by the sultan. Hence my less than salubrious circumstances of late ...' He indicated the quarters surrounding him.

'But, you still have your head, sir,' came her sharp rejoinder.

'Indeed, nona, I still have my head. There is a saying in my country "a fate worse than death". My Company prefers to dole out said manner of punishment. It lasts longer and brings about a slow and wretched end,' he added sardonically.

Thong Di's lips quivered in what he knew was a smile, quickly repressed. This woman had spirit as well as intelligence. 'Captain Light, please do not reject my suit out of hand. First, let me set out the terms that the sultan wishes to offer you. I think you may find yourself persuaded by the proposal, especially as your current circumstances as you say ...' she looked about her in amusement, '... are somewhat straightened. Can you afford to turn down an excellent business proposition without even hearing it? I had thought you were a more enterprising merchant than that!'

'Checkmate, Nona Rozells,' Light said, in English. Thong Di did not know the word, but gleaned its sense, a satisfied expression on her face.

'The sultan fully understands that the English are unwilling to send their troops into local conflicts. He proposes that soldiers be sent merely as a show of force. An English fort at Kuala Queddah would be sufficient to quieten internal rumblings. The Bugis are loath to come into conflict with other Europeans for they are deep in a power struggle with the Dutch, whom they know are your enemies. They wish to court the English, not make war upon them! Siam and Burma would also avoid Queddah if they suspected the sultan was backed by a European force. Thus, without a shot being fired, the war would be won.'

'And what does the sultan offer the Company in return?' Light inquired, his mind alive with possibilities. Sultan Muhammed Jiwa was a very different ruler from the irresolute Sultan Alaudin. He had already correctly judged the response of his enemies to a putative English alliance. It was highly unlikely any adversary would move against Queddah if they thought they might find themselves embroiled with Company ships and men.

'He offers you sole licence to trade in the port of Queddah. The Dutch own Melaka. The Company wishes for their own base on the Straits. He promises that all trade in Kuala Queddah would pass through English hands, save the share of the profits that would be allocated for the sultan himself.'

'How much would his share be?' Light broke in. 'Beg pardon, nona, but what proportion of the revenue would the sultan expect to recoup?'

Lady Thong Di shrugged. 'That is a matter for your negotiations, Kapitan Light. Sultan Muhammed has instructed me only to extend to you an invitation. The details are not in my hands. But he offers you a monopoly, the right to build a fort and establish an English settlement at Kuala Queddah. He believes that is what the English Company seeks in the Straits and it is what the Sultan of Aceh will never offer. As I am sure you already know.'

Light breathed slowly, weighing up her words. What did he have to lose? His career was in the doldrums. Whatever prospective fortune he had already amassed had been trickling through his fingers these past few months. On the other hand, he doubted that the sultan's demands were quite as simple as the lady had suggested, but that did not signify. He was being offered an opportunity that he could not afford to ignore. Perchance a common ground could be found? Imagine if the Company agreed? He would be the cynosure of the Indies!

Should the offer be sufficiently promising, the Company might make an exception to their prohibitions. Furthermore, there were ways the two parties could be manipulated, given the impediment of distance in communications. He might make promises now to the sultan that would never be fulfilled in future, or exaggerate the potential benefits to his agency only to later claim he had been misled by the devious sultan. No one could dispute that Sultan Muhammed Jiwa was a ruler they could deal with and that Queddah was a prime location for the much-needed British establishment. He would write to Madras immediately.

'I am not at liberty to act without the explicit sanction of my employers. But I promise you I shall communicate your proposal to the Association forthwith.'

'That would take many months, Kapitan Light. The sultan would prefer that you attend him much sooner. He extends to you a personal invitation. Whilst you await word from India, you may thus present yourself at court and begin your negotiation, so that once permission is granted, we can move without delay. And in the meantime, the sultan will make it worth your while in advantageous trade concessions.'

She was right. If he wrote now, the earliest he could expect an answer would be April or even May. Even then the response might be hesitant, requiring further back and forth missives, drawing out the months into years. Should they fail to act expeditiously, they might lose their window of opportunity. The sultan might look to other powers detrimental to Britain's fortunes in the region.

Light's mind was made up. 'Return to the sultan and inform him that Captain Francis Light accepts his courteous invitation. Tell him that it will be a great honour to serve both my country and his kingdom in the pursuit of a mutually beneficial accord. However, I must forewarn that any contract is wholly contingent upon the decision of the Bengal Council. I will endeavour to do my best to present a favourable case to them.'

Lady Thong Di smiled and bowed her head, her hands joined in a very Siamese wai. Light was both charmed and amused by the many cultural nuances their conversation had encompassed. What a quagmire of protocol and custom they were stepping into!

'This is good news, Kapitan Light. Your arrival will be much anticipated. I can also promise you a more congenial living arrangement in Queddah than your current abode. I thank you for your precious time and bid you a fond farewell. And a safe crossing to Queddah in the near future.'

She leaned forward slightly and lowered her voice, suddenly lapsing into Siamese where before they had conversed entirely in Malay. Then, turning to Syed Harun, she offered a translation: 'Safe journey. It is a Siamese saying.' The advisor frowned. He was not happy that she had spoken in a language he did not understand, but then little about the events of the day had pleased him. Four short words could not be significant. He shrugged away her apparent lapse with a terse nod.

The party declined to stay for lunch, taking a leave that consisted of much bowing and touching of the heart, before repairing to the litter and making for the harbour. Light doubted they would linger in Acheen; they would wish to leave before Sultan Alaudin learned of their visit. He watched them go, his hand raised in farewell. What a fascinating woman! Would their paths cross again in Queddah? He suspected that they might. Her parting words had indicated where her true loyalties lay, and also revealed her naivety in the world of diplomacy. Lady Thong Di had given him a warning. 'Take everything with a pinch of salt,' was the nearest approximation of what she had whispered across the table. He had hardly required such a caution. For who in these forthcoming talks would be talking truth?

18

One More Bite of the Apple

The Governor's Residence, Madras. December 17th, 1771

On a cool and blustery Monday morning, Deputy-Governor Hastings stared out from the balcony of the Council chamber at the commanding view of the harbour of Fort St George, a strong breeze stirring his wispy brown hair. The ships at anchor pitched roughly about, buffeted by a cyclone far out to sea even now gathering strength. A storm was heading landwards. It was the nearest they would see to festive weather this Christmastide.

But Hastings' mind scarcely registered either the scene or the impending tempest. He was lost in thought, playing out the different strategies he might employ during the forthcoming meeting. He faced a challenge but was determined to provoke the Council into forward motion. Time was of the essence. He would assume his new position in January and did not intend to waste a moment. The Madras Council enjoyed nothing better than procrastination, it being their very *modus operandi.* Committing to any policy increased one's chances of making a mistake. God knew how they had managed to hold India as long as they had!

'Sir? The gentlemen are waiting to start, if you please …' muttered a nondescript lackey who had sidled up to him. Hastings nodded and took his place around the mahogany table, while a waiter offered tea. He shook his head, and demanded coffee.

The secretary of the Council embarked upon a tedious accounting of matters arising from the minutes to the previous meeting, followed by a report on other matters pertaining to it. From there he turned his attention to this morning's gathering, unnecessarily calling out a register, when he might just as easily have relied on observation, as there were only eight men present. Madras Council meetings adhered most particularly to the formalities, which usually occupied most of the proceedings. Hastings was determined another meeting would not pass with little real advancement, and urgent issues adjourned to some 'future' occasion.

Once the apologies for non-attendance were read out and a motion taken to admit into record the previous minutes, the chair finally passed to Governor Josiah du Pré to announce today's agenda. Hastings drummed his fingers on the table top, his face impassive, his body electric with nervous energy.

'The first matter, concerns the annual Christmas festivities ...'

'If I may, sir?' Hastings interrupted, rising from his seat, a sheaf of documents in his hand. 'Perhaps we might make an exception to the order of the day with the introduction of a matter of the utmost exigency? Once the more onerous duties of the day are complete, then we may move to the more enjoyable issue of our forthcoming celebrations.'

Josiah du Pré eyed him across the table. 'If an item is not on the agenda, sir, it shall have to wait until we reach the addenda. If there remains sufficient time, of course.' Du Pré could not abide his punctilious deputy. With any luck, considering his recent promotion, which also stuck in his craw, today's meeting might be the last time he would have to tolerate Hastings' bothersome presence.

'My apologies, sirs. The issue would have been on the agenda had I been consulted in advance. Having only just returned from Calcutta, it appears the secretary must have "overlooked" my contribution. Furthermore, I am sure the honourable members would not take issue with a slight change in protocol in what may likely be my final meeting? I beg your forbearance on this matter. I would so hate to hand over my responsibilities to my successor with important matters unresolved. If I may continue?'

Du Pré had been outmanoeuvred once again, as on many other occasions. He could hardly deny such a request to the future Governor of Calcutta, now soon-to-be his senior in rank. It would not look good in the report. Thus, he acquiesced. After all, he would be rid of the cavilling fellow soon enough. Let him have his way and get his business done. 'The floor is yours, sir!' he replied with a touch of mockery.

A similar undertow of disapproval pervaded the entire gathering, unspoken but unmistakeable. The other honourable members shared the governor's disdain for Warren Hastings. He was a boat rocker. They preferred stability. It did not deter the deputy governor. Popularity had never been his concern.

'Gentlemen, I shall get straight to the point. As you all well know, I have been appointed Governor of Calcutta, effective from the first of January. As you are also well aware, this is a position of great importance, the senior Presidency of India. I intend to sweep a broom through the closets and see no reason why this process needs to wait until the onset of my term. One of my immediate concerns is the pressing urgency to establish a forward base in Eastern waters, an issue that has been under discussion for some time. Yet little has been achieved, despite the financing of several missions at some great cost, each returning little by way of success. Conditions in the Straits are very favourable at this current time. The Dutch are heavily committed in Sumatra and elsewhere, the Siamese are in disarray, and the internal kingdoms are in their usual turmoil. Thus, we must strike while the iron is hot.'

'We have a factory in Acheen that already shows promise,' Francis Jourdan intervened. His agency, the Madras Association, had invested greatly there. He was unwilling to see Hastings steal the contract from under his nose.

'I am well aware of your sterling work in Sumatra, sir. If I may ... ? As you know, the captain charged with the Acheen trade, one Francis Light, has been in Queddah of late at the personal invitation of Sultan Muhammed. It seems he has built up a close relationship with the king, who is currently beset with many problems and offers us his thriving port at Kuala Queddah, together with a monopoly on the trade therein. There have been numerous communications between the good captain and the Council, as well as back and forth to his agency ... Mr Jourdan? Would you like to summarise his findings thus far?'

Francis Jourdan's displeasure at being put on the spot was evident. 'Captain Light writes in fulsome terms of the advantages of Queddah as a trading post. The sultan himself has also written. He is a desperate man and is offering concessions that are most interesting: the port itself, the major share of all its trade and, just recently, he has in addition promised the entire southern coastline from the port down to the offshore island of Pulau Pinang.'

'Including the island itself?' Hastings interjected

'Not as yet, Hastings. It's mostly uninhabited but well positioned. Mr DeSouza believes it has great potential as a magazine. We may be able to prevail on the sultan for the island as well. It's thick with pirates, no doubt, so it would serve us well to clear it out at the same time,' Jourdan replied brusquely. Hastings was remarkably well informed. Light had no doubt gone behind his back and given him the same report. Or how else would he have known so much?

Hastings nodded, reflectively. 'I believe Captain Light is concerned that interest has also been shown by the Dutch and the Danish, both of whom have sent emissaries to the king, offering support against his enemies in return for similar concessions. How much longer can we afford to sit around mulling this over? The sultan will not wait on our decision forever. His situation is precarious.' Hastings added, 'Although we must never become embroiled in local skirmishes, if we were granted these concessions, any hostile intent by another power would then become a threat to *our* interests. Therefore, we should be willing to agree to "defensive" support on behalf of the sultan, although he must understand that any "offensive" action is quite out of the question … Wouldn't you agree, sirs?'

There was nothing with which to disagree. Hastings was advocating long-standing Company policy, even if the regulations had not always been upheld. Jourdan would raise some opposition, concerned as he might be at his own agency's position, but it was up to him to fight that particular corner. Otherwise, Hastings was correct. Everyone wanted a stronger presence in the Straits. This proposition appeared to be ideal.

Only Governor du Pré remained unconvinced, predominantly

because of his antipathy to anything proposed by Hastings 'But how do the local nawabs feel about it? The court of Queddah is a viper's nest. The sultan is still in exile, isn't he? Does he even have the wherewithal to make good on all these promises? What guarantees do we have that we might not find ourselves in the midst of a full-scale war the very minute we set foot there?' If he made a rash decision, there might be an almighty scandal. He was only a year away from the end of his term. Du Pré preferred to concentrate the interim period on enhancing the fortifications, that least controversial of undertakings. He was always the most reluctant of men if there was a whiff of trouble in the air.

Hastings made a flamboyant show of consulting his notes. 'Light assures that he has "*stood his ground*" against the meddlers at court. He reports that "*The King is ready to grant him anything he desires*" ... I quote his own words.'

Jourdan harrumphed. 'That does not signify that the king is willing to grant the Company everything *we* desire, sir! Light has a reputation of being somewhat of a loose cannon. What *he* desires may be wholly different than what best serves the Council!'

'A rather disparaging observation of your own man, sir, if I may say so. Surely, you yourself sanctioned his presence in Acheen and then again in Queddah? So far, he has had much success in winning the trust of several indigenous rulers, none of them known for their particular allegiance to the British. I would have thought his achievements thus far would have recommended him to you, and yet you seem to question his integrity?' Hastings was intrigued. Jourdan knew the man better than he. Perhaps he had been hoodwinked? Or did bad blood exist between the two?

Hastings' probing put the older man in a bind. If Light's

mission succeeded, it would be of incalculable benefit to the Madras Association, yet he could not help but suspect that Light was playing both sides. 'Light is a very competent master and has proved himself able in winning the support of the locals. But in that very fact lies his weakness. He is much too free with the natives. He is also very ambitious. His reports on the wondrous trading potential of Queddah are highly exaggerated. I feel we must take his words with a sizeable pinch of salt.'

'All salient points, sir. I have considered much the same myself. For that very reason, I took the liberty of presenting Light's reports to Governor Cartier in Calcutta during my recent discussions with him. By chance, a number of London Directors were present, who were mightily interested in what Captain Light had to report. They immediately directed me to call upon this Council to proceed with negotiations both in respect of Acheen and Queddah. They regard this matter as of great urgency, given that other European powers are operating in these same waters.'

An audible gasp emanated from the shocked Council members at the *fait accompli* presented to them. Hastings had approached both Calcutta and London without their prior knowledge! He had completely circumvented their authority, no doubt a taste of things to come. Not that anyone was surprised. This was typical of the underhand style of Warren Hastings, who had shown on numerous occasions that he would have his own way or be damned.

Hastings gave the assembled gentlemen the benefit of a cold and haughty smile as he set down copies of a document he had already prepared. Turning to the clerk, he indicated they should be distributed. 'I have drawn up a schedule for the dispatch of two missions in the forthcoming months: one to Acheen to finalise the establishment of our factory there and a second to Queddah, where we might take charge of the negotiations with the venerable Sultan Muhammed. Perhaps you might propose a few suitable representatives to lead these delegations? I am sure there are some fine fellows twiddling their thumbs here in Fort St George who need more challenging responsibilities? I would very much like the matter undertaken before I leave for Calcutta to embark upon my new role. And now, if you would excuse me, I must return to my own office. There are many matters requiring my attention ... Please carry on, gentlemen ... I am sure you are eager to look over the vital arrangements for the upcoming festivities.' With that, he bowed a neat bow and tripped from the room with a bounce to his step that only served to emphasise his sense of victory. It was the final affront.

***

Nine months on in Queddah and Francis Light was chomping at the bit. It had been a most frustrating time. Not that the sultan had been anything but gracious – the very opposite. From his arrival, he had been accorded a place of great respect at court, now temporarily removed to the old palace at Kota Sena at Kangar in the north. Everything had been provided for him in Kuala Queddah, including a residence at the old fort at Kuala Bahang at the very entrance to the estuary, earmarked for the site of the future British military post when negotiations came to fruition. He had also been accorded the privileged status of senior merchant, with many concessions usually only open to members of the royal family and their closest associates.

Of course, it had transpired that the demands of the sultan were much more byzantine than the Nyonya lady had initially suggested. Sultan Muhammed's real purpose was for the British to supply him with a military force, completely unacceptable to his own masters in Madras. The sultan also expected a vast supply of weapons and the use of British troops to resolve several of his personal grudges.

One of those concerned a large haul of cannons and several vessels loaded with cargo belonging to Indian Chulia merchants based in Queddah, the very group most opposed to the British. When the Bugis had originally sacked his palace, during the recent uprising, they had shown their true colours, raiding the port and seizing the cargos and cannon. The storming of the sultan's capital revealed that the Bugis involvement had been nothing more than an opportunity to recoup their losses following the divorce of Raja Muda Abdullah and his Bugis bride, and to punish Sultan Muhammad for the insult. Now reinstated to the throne, the sultan wished to recover the goods, as much to appease the Chulias as to punish the Bugis. Light saw some advantage in this; the good opinion of the Chulias would be necessary in the event of their future plans in Queddah.

The sultan's demands could never be accepted, but by the same token the Company had not been informed of them. In his detailed reports, Light told them only as much as they needed to know and little else, praising the excellent depth of the Queddah river even at half flood, when in truth it was very shallow in parts. He waxed lyrical over the price that chests of opium might fetch, quoting an amount more than double the actual value, and likewise overvalued the bulk of annual trade that passed through the port. If Queddah was so rich, the Company asked, why then would the sultan wish to hand over such bounty to a foreign power? For the simple reason, Light had replied, that Sultan Muhammed was old and infirm, and his heir was mightily unpopular. If the king wished to retain his grip on power, he had no choice.

The Company did not understand the situation on the ground as he did, nor did they care to. Company officials disdained local potentates as child-like petty chieftains, whereas Light knew that Sultan Muhammed could outmanoeuvre every man jack of them, despite his advanced years. Whatever the sultan asked for, even he knew it was unlikely that all would come his way. That was the nature of treaty talks, as any wise negotiator knew. On the other hand, it hardly signified what the sultan wanted. Once the Company was established in Queddah, the British did not have to comply with what they had signed up for; loopholes could always be found to excuse them from their promises. What then might a beleaguered sultan do?

In any case, their very presence in a fort with well-armed sepoys, would probably be enough to keep the sultan's local enemies at bay. The Bugis would not wish to cross the British. Even the Siamese would think twice. Thus, the Company would have its establishment, and Light would corner the local trade, and would no doubt win an official role in the new administration. Should future conflict arise, it would be easy enough to present it as a viable threat to British interests, thus staying within the confines of the terms of a defensive alliance. It was simply a matter of the careful wording of the details. Each side would read it in their own way. If, at some later time, the agreement was found to be contradictory, blame would fall either on the sultan for being devious or the Company for its equivocation. Either way, Light would emerge as the mediator, the bringer of reconciliation, the master-diplomat. Or that was Francis Light's intention.

But nine months on, here he was in Queddah, still writing fruitless and increasingly more grovelling letters to both the Madras Association, and behind its back to Warren Hastings and the Council. Light deemed Hastings the most approachable, for he was a pragmatist and modern thinker, the sort of man who could see beyond the stagnant practices and the rank corruption to take the most viable course of action. Yet so far, apart from vague and bland replies, there had been no signs of active interest from either his agency or the Company. And Muhammed Jiwa's patience was running out.

Light took a trip to Jangsylan in late December to spend Christmastide with Scott and his family. They enjoyed an unexpectedly warm and eccentric version of a traditional Scottish celebration, with Scott's two 'bairns' dressed in nativity costumes underneath a paper star, performing muddled versions of 'The Holly and The Ivy' and 'Hark! The Herald Angels Sing', conducted by their proud father. The children spoke no English and had learned the words verbatim, with hilarious results. But their Malay mother Ina grinned, the children giggled, Light howled with laughter, and Scott threw the little ones over his shoulder in delight. They dined on a mishmash of local dishes and a large roasted pig, washed down by copious amounts of alcohol, despite the largely Malay complement of guests.

Light conversed well into the dark hours of the night with his friend, pouring out his frustration at the lack of progress with

Madras. 'I shall find myself back where I started soon enough with a whole year wasted on this fruitless venture, at the loss of all my good credit with the sultan! Much like the time I spent in Acheen. What's wrong with these fools in India? How did they win anything if they cannot see an opportunity that is presented to them on a damned silver platter, dressed up with an apple in its mouth?'

Scott was amused. 'I hate to say it, laddie, but I have been telling you so for many a year. Sultan Muhammed's opinion of you is worth a hundred times more than any fellow in Madras. Cut your losses and offer him your own services in a private capacity. Hire some mercenaries and call it your own army. Then become governor of your own Englishtown in Queddah. Why, you could always call it Kuala Suffolk, or some such name!'

Light scoffed at the suggestion. 'You're drunker than I thought, you mad fool!'

'Why not? What about your Bugis' chum, Daeng Theyan? He's no friend to Selangor – the sultan broke with Riau long ago – and Theyan's ensconced just a few miles away in Tharua port as we speak. Who would have imagined your pirate chief would end up governor of Jangsylan? What a strange world we live in, eh? Theyan trusts you, however, which is why he tolerates my presence here, of that I have no doubt. Furthermore, he has boatloads of mercenaries at his disposal. Pay him a visit while you're in town and do some hiring. Or what about that gang of renegades at the mouth of the Selangor river? White men all, if you discount the tattoos, armed to the bloody hilt.'

'Sultan Salehuddin of Selangor pays them 5 réals a month each to patrol the entrance to the estuary.'

'Then double it. You think they care who pays them? To the highest bidder is their only loyalty, my friend. And my bet is they would prefer to serve a British captain any day.'

'You'll get me hung, Scott.'

'You'll get yourself krissed one dark night. Take the advantage, man. You're in a position of strength for just so long and then the moment passes, after which every side will place the failure at your door.'

Light did not respond, slumping further into his cups, and deeper into his morose thoughts. The two men stayed like that for a time, on the brink of calling it a night.

Then Light suddenly opened up: 'I don't want territory or to be some self-appointed chief. I'm not a landgrabber. That's the problem, Jamie. All I desire is to be accepted at the table. If I acted as you suggest, they would cast me out forever, I would be the ultimate pariah … I would be entirely finished in England.'

'Like me, you mean? The degenerate Scotsman with his sarong and *janggut*? You think I don't know what they call me in Madras?' Scott grinned. 'You see, Francis, I don't give a fuck. I'm not interested in sitting at their table. I can make my own table, thank you very much. When you are sitting upon a fortune, then they come with begging bowls for the crumbs that fall from your plate. Now, that interests me. We're different men, you and I. We always have been. Take care you don't break yourself on their wheel trying to be something that you're not. You will never be the epitome of an English gentleman merchant. By God, Francis! You're worth so much more than that!'

Raking his hands through his now unruly locks, Francis gave Scott a prolonged stare. 'Was that a compliment, Mr Scott, in your rather topsy-turvy fashion? Yet, I fear you may be right. I'm no better than I ought to be, James, but I'm true to my word. No man can say otherwise. I think people sense that about me, whatever race or religion they espouse. It is why I am accepted where many others of my nation cannot go. I will give it one more attempt. I'm thinking of leading a delegation to Calcutta, perhaps even with an official retinue from Queddah, and presenting my proposition directly to the governor there. They cannot ignore me to my face. If they turn me down, then so be it. Do I have your support?'

Scott jumped up and grasped his friend's hand. 'Always, man. One more bite of the apple, I concur. Furthermore, I will return with you to Queddah. I could do with taking advantage of all your concessions to make a tidy profit for myself. I will stand by you – but not in Calcutta. The last thing you want is the degenerate Scott in your camp. I canna' imagine that would do anything for your reputation!'

The next day aboard his ship in the Tharua roads, Light threw himself into physical labour with his men to work off the sluggish torpor of the past few days' indulgences. Early afternoon, a local lighter pulled by, delivering an unexpected message. It was from Lady Chan. She intended to visit the next morning. Light was grateful for the notice. It was several days since he had shaved or bathed; Scott was careless of such matters, especially when in drink. Thus, it was a very different version of Francis Light that met the lady early the next morning, under a sky so blue that even the foul odours drifting from the nearby port could not detract from its tranquil perfection.

Shaved, brushed, drenched in cologne and wearing a white

frilled shirt over smart breeches, now the very picture of an English gentleman at leisure, Light helped Lady Chan aboard. She was accompanied by several silk-clad ladies, who tittered as his crew men leered. Taking her hand, Light kissed it lightly, aware but unconcerned that this was a breach of local custom. Out here they were far from prying eyes; her ladies knew better than to tell tales. Lady Chan's reaction was to be expected. She took his flamboyant welcome in her inimitable stride, returning Light her impassive face, with only her eyes betraying amusement.

'You are too forward, Kapitan. But it is your charm.'

Light led her to an area on the foredeck where his men had rigged a canopy; there they sat on cushions and drank tea. She kept her girls within sight, but out of earshot. The maids held up tiny parasols to shade their skin from the sun and flirted at a distance with the sailors. Soliman sat apart, a sullen expression on his face. He disapproved of Lady Chan, although he could not help but gawk at the pretty young servants, some not much older than he himself.

'This is an honour, Lady Chan. I had not expected to meet you this visit. I was unsure how much freedom the new governor allows you ...' Light began.

She waved away his concern with one toss of her heavily jewelled hand. 'I have complete freedom. Young Theyan is quite the character, don't you think? He and I have an understanding.'

Which could mean anything. It was entirely possible that Lady Chan had welcomed the arrival of the Bugis, when they had chased the Malays out during the recent turmoil in Queddah. Ever the opportunist, Lady Chan may even have invited them in herself. Furthermore, the 'understanding' might well refer to an intimate relationship. Theyan was a handsome devil, even if a complete rogue. Was Chan informing Light she now had a new amatory interest? If so, it came as some relief. Light had no wishes to venture there again. It was enough to retain her goodwill.

'I am very pleased to hear that. Daeng Merewah Theyan is a personal acquaintance. He is a clever fellow, if somewhat unpredictable. It is better to have him as a friend than an enemy, I believe.'

'Just so, Kapitan, just so.'

There was a pause when she beckoned to a maid to fill her cup; Lady Chan sipped her tea elegantly, dabbing neatly at her mouth after each drop. Light took the opportunity to observe her at some length. She was still a very striking woman although age was beginning to catch her up. He had heard she had given birth to yet another child, perhaps two in the intervening years. She was not as slender as before. Yet her constitution must be sound for a woman of her years. He guessed she was at least forty.

'May I extend greetings to your husband and family?' To fill in the silence, Light fell back upon the usual platitudes of social discourse.

'Unfortunately, my husband still resides in Phattalung province as its governor. He is not able to visit the island at present, for his position would be compromised should he be seen consorting with the Bugis.'

Light feigned concern. 'Indeed, that must be a great trial to you, my lady.'

'Most definitely. It is a great sadness for all of us,' Chan replied with no hint of irony. She was the mistress of the masquerade.

The niceties achieved, Light continued with the aimless

chatter, in no doubt that Lady Chan had not made the journey solely to drink tea and share pleasantries with a former lover. In her own good time, she would ease their conversation into the direction that she wished to go, her words as ever cloaked in a veil of intricate politeness.

'I am told you received an embassy from the Sultan of Queddah when you were in Acheen?' she ventured.

'Indeed, my lady. Led by your honourable sister, I believe?'

'So, you finally met Lady Thong Di! My dear sister and I have been apart these past years and I feel her loss greatly. She is a lady of honour and renown both in Thalang and Queddah. I am told you received her with great kindness, for which she was most grateful.' Lady Chan's eyelids had narrowed; she was assessing his response with sharp attention.

'Your sister is indeed a very adept and charming ambassador. It was impossible to refuse her offer, so sweetly was it couched in terms both advantageous – and tempting.' Lady Chan could make of that what she wished, Light mused.

'The sultan was most wise in his choice of envoy.'

'He was indeed, my lady.'

They carried on back and forth in this amiable fashion for some time. It was the Siamese way of conducting business. And then, with a strike worthy of a cobra, Lady Chan made her gambit. 'My mother is from Queddah, you know? She is a royal princess, a distant relative of the king himself. I am told Sultan Muhammed Jiwa has raised my sister to a position at court, according her the status of minor royal herself.'

Francis chose his words carefully, aware that they had now reached the crux of the matter. 'Then it makes perfect sense that

Sultan Muhammed should use her as his emissary. He places great trust in the lady.'

Lady Chan gave a stately nod, and introduced another lightning bolt. 'You heard the sad news of her husband's passing, of course? I believe you knew Khun Martim?'

'Martim was a friend. I admired him. I grieved at his death.'

Her gesture was dismissive. 'It has been several years now. Lady Thong Di is alone in Queddah. She has two children, you know? A girl and a boy. Very handsome, the girl most fair-skinned. Have you come across them?'

Light shook his head. 'I am based at the fort in Kuala Bahang, far from the old palace in Perlis where the court now resides. But I travel there from time to time to meet with his Royal Highness. I shall ask after them when next I visit.' The juxtaposition of her comments was telling. It was not difficult to read her intent.

Lady Chan's lips parted in a tight smile, her eyes gleaming. In these convoluted pleasantries, Light believed she was proposing a match between Light and her own sister, even assuring her fertility by mentioning her comely offspring. It was an idea to relish. He was thirty years of age and without a wife. Marriage with a member of the distinguished royal house of Queddah was something to consider, especially in view of a possible future establishment. Lady Thong Di was a beautiful and refined woman; he was honoured to be suggested as a suitor, although he doubted that his suitability as a spouse was the foremost reason in Lady Chan's mind. She was spinning her own web, with some unknown future strategy in play. How might the sultan view such a union? No doubt he would approve. Lady Thong Di was not a Mohammedan, so that would not be a problem, and she was under the sultan's protection. If this treaty was favourably resolved, what better than to seal it with a marriage alliance?

But was that what he really wanted? How would such a marriage enhance his reputation with the Company? It was a matter to which he must give deep thought. For now, it remained another intriguing proposition from this most perplexing of women.

Lady Chan had already signalled to her maids, rising from her cushion to take her leave, her business achieved. She had no doubts that her meaning had been crystal clear. 'I fear I must now return home. It has been a pleasant morning, Kapitan Light. I am most happy that we have met again after all this time. We must do more business together in future. I will send my agent to your ship tomorrow. Thank you for your generous hospitality.'

With that she was gone, leaving behind only the heady scent of her perfume, which lingered on the cushions for some time after her departure, despite the sea breeze. Her proposition, however, stayed with him even longer, playing on his mind for days. He envisaged his future as governor of a thriving new Straits Presidency, closely allied to both the local Sultan of Queddah and the richest family in nearby Jangsylan, thus dominating the trade of the northern Straits. He would become the foremost Company officer in the East Indies. His final bite of the apple may be the one he had sought for so long.

19
The Delegation

The Old Fort, Kuala Bahang, Queddah. 10th April 1772

No embassy to Calcutta was needed. In late February, Light received news that a delegation from Madras would arrive to finalise the treaty with the Sultan of Queddah. The juggernaut had finally moved. At the same time, another mission was despatched to Acheen, although the Council had concluded that Queddah was the preferred site as being more advantageous for the China trade. The terms of the letter contained one bitter note. 'We have instructed our officers to endeavour to establish *for the Company* a contract trade.' Any previous arrangements between private traders, namely the Madras Association, at either Acheen or Queddah, were to be set aside to ensure against malpractice and corruption. All current independent business operations in these territories were to be wound down.

Ill news indeed for Jourdan, Sullivan and DeSouza. A slap in the face for Francis Light. The air was blue when Light received the letters. He held no personal brief for his agency; it was typical of the Company to clamber over the private enterprise of country traders, just as it was common practice for the same merchants to abuse their Company ties. Yet, he himself had been almost the sole actor in both Acheen and Queddah! But for his endeavour, none of these missions would even have been possible. And for this contribution, he was to be relegated to a bystander with his merchant privileges denied.

'The sultan won't give them the time of day without your presence, Francis,' Scott reminded him. 'You must have known they would send their toadies to supplant you at the final hurdle. What did you expect? That they would give you carte blanche? Nevertheless, these Company fools will be wholly reliant on you throughout the coming talks. It is in your hands to play the cards to your advantage. This is the best chance you'll get, Light.'

Scott's optimism, however, proved unfounded. The British vessel *Triton* arrived in early April bringing a contingent of officials and soldiers who swarmed over the fort, expressed disdain for its ramshackle facilities, and informed Light that he would have to relocate somewhere else. The fort was now the British residence.

On the following evening, Light presented himself at his erstwhile lodgings with an official invitation to dine. The Honourable Edward Monckton and his party had spent the day on their vessel offshore whilst their quarters at the fort were prepared, and had still not arrived. Instructed to take a seat in the hallway to wait like an errand boy, Light was completely overlooked when the assemblage of gentlemen finally swept in. Whether it was by ignorance or intent, he could not tell.

The arriving party were loudly critical of the poor state of the building, braying out their dissatisfaction and fault-finding. It struck Light how long it had been since he had been immersed in British accents, for their clipped and strident tones irritated him, although he knew they resembled his own. Something in their rigid superiority caused him discomfort, an unwelcome reminder of past humiliations.

At last he was called forward into the inner room, where the other gentlemen were already toasting their safe arrival in schooners of sherry. A young man of ungainly figure, narrow of shoulder and bulky of hip, came forward in formal greeting. 'Ah, Captain Light at last, please come join us. Bring a glass for the captain, if you will! The Honourable Edward Monckton, head of mission. Very pleased to meet you, sir. Sterling work, man. Governor Hastings has spoken most highly of you.' Monckton extended his hand; it was white and damp, much like Monckton himself.

'Delighted, sir,' Light replied, resisting the urge to wipe his palm against his thigh. Monckton's skin was so pale that it had a bluish cast, his narrow, bony features so prominent that they seem exaggerated, and his eyes small and over-bright, like a startled rabbit. Light had been too long dipped in the deep, dark softness of the East. European features appeared sinister and pointed, long-nosed and sour, like creatures from a child's nightmare. He shook the peculiar imaginings from him.

'If I may introduce my colleagues? Mr Samuel Lucas, my deputy, Captain Herbert Waterhouse, Lieutenant Richard Roche, artillery, the Reverend Gideon Beezley, Mr William Fairlie, Company writer, Mr Thomas De Mello, interpreter, and an old schoolfriend of yours, I believe, Mr Charles Hythe, my good friend and advisor.'

Until that moment, Light had paid little attention to the other men milling about the room. His erstwhile tutor Hythe had kept his back turned, no doubt savouring the moment when he could reveal himself. It was impossible to keep the shock from registering on Light's face; he paled at the sight of his old adversary. Hythe, of course, had the advantage.

Recovering sufficiently to mutter a general greeting, Light made his way around the group to shake their hands. Hythe hung back until the last. When they came face to face, he grasped Light's hand too fiercely, under the guise of friendship, drawing him closer to his body than Light wished to go. 'Surprise, surprise, Francis!' he whispered into Light's ear. 'I've been charting your unorthodox progress for years, my old friend, and felt certain our paths would eventually cross. How satisfying to finally meet, and in such circumstances, too ...' The meanspirited youth had matured into an equally unpleasant man. Light recalled the harsh curl of the lip and the resentful expression, even though Hythe now had a prosperous swell to his belly and was dressed in a fine suit of clothes, bearing all the marks of a merchant of standing. Yet neither had improved his repellent appearance.

'Hythe. Who would have imagined it, eh?' Light found his voice, raising it so the audience might hear. 'I thought you were destined for a career in the church, *old friend*?' He refused to let the loathsome man assume the upper hand, nor could he resist poking around in the old wound, fully aware that Reverend Ray's influence had ruined Hythe's chances of a scholarly degree. 'Wasn't Cambridge once in your future?'

A tremor of annoyance flickered on Hythe's cheek, a tic that threatened to expose him. Somehow, he stilled it. 'As you well know, life has a peculiar way of taking us on different paths, sir. Who would have credited that the handsome naval officer would one day find himself stranded on this godforsaken shore? I'm sure no one, least of all yourself, expected that turn of events for the esteemed Lieutenant Light.' His sense of victory restored, Hythe reeked in self-satisfaction, no doubt having rehearsed his ripostes all crossing long in anticipation of such a moment. Charles Hythe would never have had the wit to cut *ex tempore*.

Light accepted a glass of sherry and made to position himself at the table, well away from his nemesis, but Hythe blustered forward, prevailing on Reverend Beezley to move along so that 'I might take the seat across from my old schoolfriend.' An uncomfortable dinner ensued during which Hythe gloated and Light endeavoured to avoid his gaze, but was nevertheless inhibited throughout.

The talk was on the general topics: the crossing, Hastings' new appointment, Company rumours, society chit chat, most of which excluded Light, for these days he was outside of the current India scene. It came as a surprise to him that Warren Hastings was so exceedingly unpopular amongst his officials, but Light soon realised that their dislike was solely grounded in his qualities as a reformer. The Company merchants all feared, without any sense of irony, that the new governor would curtail their opportunities for personal enrichment. Light had been too long out of the beating heart of the administration. Given this opportunity, it was essential he listen and learn.

At what seemed to him an appropriate juncture Light raised the issue of the imminent negotiations with the sultan, suggesting several approaches that would be favourable when they received a summons to the palace.

'When we receive a summons?' Monckton was amused, inviting the others to similarly share the joke. 'I, for one, do not intend to wait on the pleasure of some tin-pot native headman, Captain Light. I shall despatch a message tomorrow informing the king of our imminent arrival and that we expect full honours, as befits the appointed representatives of His Majesty King George III. Mr De Mello will frame it in their heathen tongue, isn't that so, sir?'

De Mello assented with a polite nod, his first contribution of the evening, although Light observed his wince at the pejorative references to the sultan and his language. He did not, however, offer an alternative opinion. It was left to Light to venture on alone.

'If I might say so, it may be preferable to follow their customary practices in these matters rather than bluster in and make a poor show before them, sir. The Malays are a very courteous people with a complex etiquette of behaviour, particularly in regards to their sovereign. They are very sensitive to the proprieties, and easily offended.'

'Etiquette? Proprieties? What the dickens do they know of decorum, sir, when they walk around with bare feet and clad in skirts?' There was a general burst of laughter round the table.

Light cleared his throat to hide both his embarrassment and his annoyance. 'I rather think their attire is a matter of culture not refinement. The kingdom of Queddah is of very ancient lineage, older even than most royal houses in Europe. It is important to respect their court and its traditions should we wish to have fruitful intercourse.'

Hythe took this opportunity to twist his knife. 'It would seem, Francis, that you have rather fallen under the spell of these natives, no doubt the result of having residing too long in their uncivilised company. Why, you will be telling us next that you have become a Mohammedan yourself!'

Titters and guffaws rang out across the table. 'I must chide Mr Hythe for his churlish observation. Only an old school pal could take such liberty, sir!' chortled Monckton, raising his glass to Hythe, who did the same to Light, as if to mark some invisible score. 'I must disagree with you, Captain Light, if I may. We gave the matter some thought on our journey over concluding that, considering the vulnerable position in which the king currently finds himself, the advantage is all ours. We must seize the high ground, to borrow a military term. Grind them down with a show of British force and superiority!'

Light opened his mouth to reply but Monckton raised a hand to silence him. 'Let us not spoil this pleasant gathering with petty quibbles, Captain Light. I know you have experience with these people but your instincts are those of the private trader who must bow and scrape to secure business in these waters. The Honourable Company does not lower itself to the level of indigenous people. You shall soon see how the sultan will flatter and fawn upon us, mark my words. We'll have this treaty wrapped up in a few days.'

There was no possible arguing with such blind and foolish ignorance. The Company, in its infinite wisdom, had seen fit to send a delegation of nodding sycophants, led by a posturing imbecile. A chasm suddenly yawned between British interests and those of Sultan Muhammed Jiwa, where Light had thought there might be open ground.

***

At three o' clock in the dark of night three days later, the mission departed from Kuala Bahang in two perahus and a longboat. Ten leagues north, skirting the coast that led to Kuala Perlis, they entered the estuary and took a long, slow wind to the palace at Kangar, situated some six miles upriver on a small hill overlooking the settlement. It was late afternoon when they dropped anchor and took row boats to the jetty, a rickety, wooden jumble of fishing boats and brightly decorated native vessels. Watching the arrival, the local crews slouched in brooding silence, their hooded eyes fixed on the gentlemen with an unsettling, almost menacing, fascination.

'Good God, are they pirates?' gasped Samuel Lucas, a bookish man who suffered greatly in the heat, his face a permanent lobster red. He mopped at his bald pate and clutched his bag closer to his chest. Light supposed he was the legal advisor, there to temper any youthful exuberance that Monckton might show.

'They're all damn pirates in these parts,' muttered Captain Waterhouse. 'The Malays fish and trade one day, and then raid the next. I wouldn't turn my back on any one of 'em.'

James Scott shot a glance over; he had already taken a dislike to Waterhouse, a burly East Indiaman captain with a brash and conceited style. 'This is their kingdom, man. I suspect they are thinking much the same of us.'

But their initial concerns were soon dispelled at the appearance of a procession of guards bearing spears, who cleared a passage through the loitering crowd. A young lord rode to the head, accompanied by an older man, the first to address them. He spoke in Malay, De Mello translated.

'Welcome, gentlemen of England! My name is Dato' Sri Paduka Raja Laksamana Kamal bin Mahmud. I am honoured to present Putera Ziyauddin, Raja Muda of Perlis.' The younger man, little more than sixteen, inclined his head in acknowledgement, placing his right hand against his chest, before turning his lively mount and leading the way to the palace.

Monckton addressed De Mello. 'At least they've sent a decent escort. Who's the fellow anyway? It would seem the further one goes from civilisation, the more grandiose the titles they bestow upon themselves!'

The Eurasian interpreter replied in a deferential tone, required for one whose origins were considered only partially acceptable in decent company, given that his Portuguese blood had long ago been diluted. 'The younger man is the son of the sultan. He bears the title of Crown Prince, sir.'

'The heir to old Muhammed? By God, we be may dealing with that same green boy any day now! Surely the old fellow isn't long for this world?' Monckton retorted, well pleased with the news.

Light leaned in. 'He's the younger son, Ziyauddin, recently raised to the title of Raja Muda, not of Queddah, but of the northern territory of Perlis, thus second-in-line to the throne. The actual heir is his half-brother, Prince Abdullah, who is married to the daughter of Laksamana Kamal himself. Amongst the Malays, Laksamana is an office akin to admiral, although it also bestows a senior administrative role at court. Dato' Sri Kamal is a man of great influence, sir. And I must warn you, he is opposed to the British presence. We must win his approval.'

'Oh, must we? I rather think it is the sultan who needs to stay on our right side if he wishes to keep his throne,' Monckton replied, dismissively. He surveyed the scene, now with disapproval on his face, suddenly underwhelmed by the welcome party. 'The younger son and a court minion, and not a cannon fired to announce our arrival? I'll put that right, soon enough. Bring up the artillery, Roche. We'll make our own show.'

***

Monckton proved true to his promise early the next morning at the public audience held in the square before the palace steps. The English party had passed a comfortable night in their allocated accommodations, a series of wooden pavilions furnished in velvet cushions and silk hangings, with lofty roof spaces and shady balconies that rendered the interiors dark and cool. The quarters did somewhat to assuage the party's criticisms, although the food was not to their taste. Despite their familiarity with Indian spices, the sweet and sour combinations of Malay cuisine, rich in coconut, tamarind and the ubiquitous *belacan*, did not find favour, except for those accustomed to it, like Light and Scott who polished off the exceptional array of dishes with gusto.

The Company men were ranged under a canopy on one side of the *medan,* seated on backless teakwood saddle stools that forced them uncomfortably upright. The delegation was flanked by an imposing guard of Indian sepoys and a small company of artillerymen. All wore full ceremonial uniform, or formal attire with wigs, which greatly added to their discomfort. Even at this early hour, the heat was a torment.

Facing them, under a similar shade, sat the dignitaries of Queddah, brilliantly clad in bright hues, seemingly unconcerned by either the heat or the long wait. The two sides weighed each other up. They made a curious contrast: one bedecked in colourful checks and patterns, the other monochrome and dour. Little commonalty existed between the two; Light hoped it was not an indication of things to come.

In the centre ground between them stood a low table, beautifully inlaid with tortoiseshell, its legs intricately carved in floral motif. On it was placed a similarly ornate wooden bookstand. By the side of the table was a large jar, crowned with a golden diadem.

'Where the devil is the sultan?' complained Monckton. 'Will he keep us out here until we melt?'

Scott, sitting in the back row alongside Light, piped up in response. 'It is the prerogative of a ruler to keep his audience waiting, sir. In Malay society, it is implicit that lesser men show their deference by waiting on the pleasure of their betters.'

'Betters? Pah!' Captain Waterhouse complained loudly, his fellows agreeing. Scott and Light exchanged nervous glances. They hoped De Mello would be euphemistic in his translations; it was unlikely Monckton would hold his words.

A series of drumbeats heralded the opening of the doors of the palace; officials indicated that all must rise and bow their heads. The royal party processed along a yellow carpet to take their places on the silk-draped thrones set at the top of the stairway, a perch significantly higher than the rest. Slaves held golden parasols above the heads of the sultan and his sons. Once they were seated, Monckton also made to sit, but was urged to continue standing. 'Prayers first then oathtaking,' muttered Light. 'It will take some time.'

He did not exaggerate. First an imam came forward to place a Quran of extraordinary beauty open on the stand. He called them all to pray. Hands raised skywards, the nobles attended to the chant, responding with their own supplications. The English party shuffled about, hands by their sides, sweating profusely. Reverend Beezley seemed particularly uncomfortable, as if his presence at this religious ritual was close to abomination. It was to be hoped that the royal party did not observe his thunderous expression.

Once the prayers were complete, several court officials processed in, bearing a series of ceremonial items, including weapons and symbols of office. They dipped each item into the jar, which apparently contained water, and then arrayed them on the table beside the Quran. De Mello seemed unsure what was taking place. He turned to Light for some explanation.

'These ceremonial goods are part of the *nobat* of the sultan, his regalia. This ceremony is carried out when oaths of great importance are to be taken. Naturally, our deliberations will culminate in a treaty, to which all parties will give their seal. This ritual ensures that all sides will conduct themselves fairly, for it contains sacred and religious vows.'

Monckton shook his head. 'Stuff and nonsense! Ritual magic, indeed. Christian gentlemen should not have to suffer such balderdash.'

'Quite right, sir, nor will their incantations bind those who do not subscribe to their pagan beliefs,' whispered Reverend Beezley. It was a singularly unrighteous response from a man of God. He was acknowledging that it was acceptable to break one's word to men of a different faith.

'They are not pagans, sir. They are Mohammedans. They believe in the same God as do we. It is but the practice that differs ...' Light replied. Scott nudged him mouthing, 'shut your damned mouth, Francis!'

Light ignored the warning, ever intractable in the face of ignorance. 'The purpose of this ceremony is to show us respect. That is all. The sultan knows we do not share his beliefs. As for binding us to the treaty, he expects our promises to be those of gentlemen, just as we do.' No one replied. Light caught Charles Hythe looking down the row at him, sniggering. He turned away in disgust.

At that juncture, an unctuous master of ceremonies spoke to De Mello, who relayed to Edward Monckton that it was time for the official opening of the negotiations. Monckton and Lucas stepped forward with De Mello in the rear. Light moved as if to join them, but Lieutenant Roche placed a hand upon his arm. 'Your services are not required, sir. This is Company business. I thank you to return to your place.'

As Light retraced his steps, seething with anger at the insult to his dignity, he heard the muttered words of Hythe. 'That put you in your place, you smug bastard!'

Light paused, leaning over him, muttering. 'One dark night, Hythe ... one dark night ...'

Meantime the ceremony was proceeding. Monckton presented a letter from Governor Hastings, which he read out in English. It was then translated into Malay by De Mello, with much nodding of heads and mutterings of approval. Hastings' words had pleased the sultan. The next formality was the crucial presentation of the gifts. The sultan's servants carried forth tray after tray of items: red *songket* cloth of wondrous design; a keris of gold, its sheath embedded with gems; a belt with a centrepiece of highly embossed silver; and a huge ceramic jar of blue and white porcelain, a fearsome dragon motif curled around its body, reaching for an elusive winged pearl. The Englishmen received the treasures with polite thanks; the sepoys carried them back to their pavilion.

It was the turn of the Company to present their gifts. Monckton summoned his soldiers forward and at the same time Roche approached the artillery. To the combined shock of all those assembled, with the exception of the British, a volley of rifle fire into the air accompanied the first of the offerings. For a second, confusion reigned. The Malay dignitaries cowered as if they were under attack. The sultan's guards ran forward, swords and muskets drawn; the artillery men adjusted their weapons to point directly at them.

But the old sultan raised his hand, laughing heartily, thankfully recognising that they were not in danger. '*Jangan takut, Jangan takut! Adat-adat Inggeris sahaja. Tong yang kosonglah yang selalu berkocak, nah?*'

The crowd broke into guffaws. The guards retreated. Roche indicated for his artillery to stand at ease. 'What did he say, Light?' young William Fairlie asked. 'For a moment there I thought we were in trouble.'

'That we were, sir. Firing a weapon without warning in the presence of a sultan is a dangerous practice. Fortunately, the sultan has both a sense of humour and an understanding of British ways. Perhaps more so than we have of his. He told them not to be afraid, that it was only a British custom.' Light judiciously left out the part that said: 'empty vessels make the most sounds.'

'The old bird never lets you down, eh?' Scott whispered in his ear.

With each gift that was carried in, another volley sounded, now received by the crowd with much amusement. Monckton beamed in satisfaction. He was sure his gifts would be highly valued by this local king, who undoubtedly would never have seen their like before. First, there was a book, bound in fine red leather, its cover tooled in letters of gold.

'Is that a Bible?' Light inquired in astonishment.

'It most certainly is,' Reverend Beezley replied. 'From the Bishop of Madras himself. It is time we bring God's grace to these heathens.' Light kept his thoughts to himself this time.

Next came a dinner service bearing the coat-of-arms of his Majesty George III, a set of crystal glasses engraved with his initials, and a silver cutlery of knives and forks. Finally, a basket-hilted cavalry sabre, its hilt hung with the royal colours. Sultan Muhammed reached out to take hold of the sword, and was finally impressed. As for the other gifts, he praised them with the formal courtesy of his people, but barely offered them a glance. Monckton was well satisfied.

The gathering ended with another volley as the royal party took its leave, and again when the British withdrew. There was to be a private audience that evening in the palace where discussions would begin. Monckton required the presence of Lucas, Fairlie, Mr De Mello and Lieutenant Roche, along with sepoy guards. The services of Captains Light and Scott were surplus to requirements. The latter retired to their quarters and spent the evening alone, venting their resentment at the Company's discourteous treatment of them.

'It's no accident, Francis,' Scott observed. 'They are reminding us we're mere lackeys. It seems, for all your work, that you were never going to be considered for your local expertise. I was wrong to think they might value it.'

'It's that bloody Hythe! He's set them all against me. I'll warrant he wormed his way onto the mission merely to stab me in the back.'

Scott was intrigued. 'So, what lies between you? From the moment you laid eyes on him, your face was thunder, while he smirked like a cat with cream. I take it you were not exactly friends back in your schooldays?'

Light laughed bitterly. 'Friends? I'll say not. Hythe was an older boy who tormented us young lads. I decided that he needed bringing down a peg or two … in fact, my plan worked even better than I had hoped. I completely knocked him off the ladder!' He could not help but recall the elation of that long-ago triumph. 'Oh, but it was a sweet victory, Jamie!' He recounted the tale of the scratchings on the window and the subsequent downfall of Charles Hythe. Despite his amusement Scott warned that Hythe would still be seeking vengeance.

'Was it worth it? What if this spineless creature should destroy your career now, all because you ruined his long ago?'

Francis barely considered his response. 'Worth every minute of it, Jamie. Then and now. I destroyed him once, and will do so again. He's a witless fool. You see if I don't …'

Just then, a messenger arrived from the palace, summoning Light and Scott to attend the sultan after *fajar* prayers on the morrow, suggesting that the evening's private audience had not gone well. The pendulum of opportunity may have swung back in their favour.

Not long after dawn the next morning, the sky still silvery and damp mists rising from the forest, Light and Scott made their way to the royal apartments. There, they were led into a private room, with only the sultan and his laksamana present. A most informal meeting ensued, very different from the night before no doubt, a proof of the high regard the sultan felt for these two men. The party broke fast with the king propped up on cushions around a table laid with fruit and little packets containing heaps of oily, coconut rice, each crowned with a spoonful of fiery sambal, and wrapped in banana leaves.

'So, my son,' the sultan began. 'What is happening? Why did you not attend the meeting last night?' His tone was guileless, although it was unlikely he had not made his own conclusions.

'We were not required, Tuanku. Mr Monckton wishes for my agency to step aside now that the Company is here to take charge. I have been instructed to close down my business in Kuala Bahang.'

'What madness is this?' the old man spat out, spraying them with rice and bits of half-chewed vegetables. He indicated his man should wipe them down. 'Who is this Mr Monckton? Has the Company no one else more suitable than a stuttering boy! It is obvious to me that they are not treating my offer with due respect. I asked for you, Kapitan Lait and Kapitan Sakat, not these fools. I cannot work with ignorant, uncouth men. Did you see the gifts? A Christian holy book, as if they expect me to renounce Allah for their Isa? And a mountain of useless plate, cup and forks! Do they not know we eat with our hands and that we do not drink wine? Ayaaaaiii! I tell you, Kapitan, I cannot do business with these people. I will chase them back to India on the end of my keris!'

The two men did their best to pour oil on the troubled waters of the negotiations. Light had spent the past year delicately easing through the forest of miscommunications that lay between the two parties; Monckton had demolished his work in just one day.

'He is young and arrogant, I agree, your Majesty, but he can be moulded. I assure you, sir, I will bring him to a better understanding. But first, may I know on what grounds you were unable to find agreement?'

'On everything!' the Sultan replied, commanding Laksamana Kamal to give an account of the evening's discussions.

'The main obstacle, Kapitan, concerned two matters. First, Mr Monckton refused any military support against Selangor to recover the guns and vessels belonging to our Chulia merchants. Their representatives were enraged at his outright insult, as if he regarded the Chulias of no importance, even implying that they would be lucky to be allowed to trade in Queddah under the British, so they should be thankful merely for that. He also would not accept the sultan's wish to exclude opium and elephants from the British monopoly. But they are royal prerogatives! It meant nothing to them. When the sultan objected, Mr Monckton threatened him. It is unthinkable! He asked whether the sultan had any idea how powerful was his Company? That they had no need of him for they had many offers from elsewhere. If he did not accept their terms, they would take their services to the Bugis at Ujung Salang, Selangor and Riau. It was the greatest of insults!'

It was even worse than they had imagined. Yet word in the English quarters the night before had suggested nothing of this impasse. Monckton and his friends had been toasting (in wine that they should not have brought into the palace grounds out of respect to local custom) that the talks had gone exactly as planned. The sultan had agreed to their conditions and, as long as they could keep the Chulias out of it, there should be a treaty with little delay. The Company officials had completely misread the other side. They did not understand that Malays do not shout and bluster, but couch their terms in soft and temperate language, appearing to concede on all matters, nodding their heads and smiling broadly. Their demands lay in their initial requests, still on the table, no matter how many times they bowed and smiled. No agreement had been reached at all.

'The English do not understand the protocol, my sultan. Business is conducted very differently in my homeland. But that does not mean that compromise cannot be found. *Garam di laut, asam di darat, di dalam kuali bertemu jua*,' Light reminded him. It was an old Malay proverb: 'Salt from the sea and tamarind from the land combine together in the cooking pot'. 'We will find a way forward, I give you my word. But there is one favour I ask of you. Inform Monckton that you insist Captains Light and Scott be mediators and should be present at all subsequent gatherings. They do not like us because we are trusted by you. They believe it brings our loyalty into question.'

'You are Englishmen! How could they imagine you would work against your own king?' the sultan shouted in disbelief.

'Well, that's the thing, your Highness,' grinned James Scott. 'I am a Scotsman which to the English is much like being a Bugis is to you. And Captain Light comes from a humble background. It isn't so different in our world than yours. These prejudices are the same amongst Malays as they are amongst Christian gentlemen. *Di mana bumi dipijak, di situ langit dijunjung*. Wherever the earth is walked upon, the same sky still remains above. So, we must find a middle way, just as you have done in the past with so many of those who would do you ill.'

The sultan nodded his head in agreement. Now he understood. It was the same the world over. Men always judged by status rather than worth. It was ever thus.

20

Of Opium and Elephants

Kota Sena Palace, Kangar, Perlis. 16th April 1772

Young William Fairlie mopped his brow and replaced the straw hat that he was wearing against the fierce rays of the sun. On open ground near their quarters, he was supervising the packing of the gifts presented to the delegation by the sultan. They were to be sent ahead to Kuala Bahang. Uncertainty about reaching terms with Sultan Muhammed now cast the success of their mission in doubt. Monckton was damned if they were going to be chased out without their prizes.

Whilst a large crate was stuffed with *kapok* fibre, Fairlie examined the blue and white ceramic vase. It was a fine piece, reaching almost shoulder height, with the aesthetic perfection of a Roman amphora, narrow neck flaring out to wider shoulders and then swelling to a smooth round centre that tapered to a narrow-footed base. There was something of the female form in its voluptuous simplicity, like the shapely, undulating back of a naked woman. William Fairlie had a keen eye for art, and an even keener eye for women. The restraint of the decorative motifs of this vase also appealed to him: a huge, finely-wrought dragon circumnavigated the entire body, brutal claws stretching for an elusive object, a winged sphere. He thought this piece a refreshing departure from the florid, cherub-laden styles popular in British circles. In his mind's eye, Fairlie saw his future, now returned to Scotland as a wealthy nabob with a fine estate in his native Ayrshire built from the profits of his many years out East. He imagined a conservatory full of tropical blooms and fruit, with Chinese vases such as this as centre pieces.

'It's impressive, isn't it?' Francis Light had been sitting on the veranda of his quarters, observing young Fairlie's fascination for the priceless vase.

Fairlie's head shot up, embarrassed to be caught out in his yearnings. He was a young man with ambition who generally kept his head down, preferring to listen rather than reveal himself until he was sure he knew the ropes. But there seemed no harm discussing something as insignificant as a piece of pottery. 'Yes, sir. Quite lovely. I have always had a taste for Chinoiserie.'

Light came over to inspect the vase himself, crouching down to gain a better look. 'The Chinese are masters of the porcelain craft. Nowhere else can be found the delicacy of their firing and the luminosity of their glaze.'

Light was well-informed. Unlike others in the mission, Fairlie appreciated the benefits of listening to merchants of real knowledge and experience. It was little more than a year since he had arrived in Madras; the Indies was still mysterious to him. Captain Light seemed exactly the sort of man who would treat his curiosity with respect rather than derision. 'May I ask, sir, why did the sultan present a Chinese vase?'

Light sat back on his haunches, tracing the outline of the dragon in motion. 'These vases have a place of great importance in the local culture of the Straits. Yet their origin is very humble. They began life as mere storage pots carried on Chinese junks, little different from our wooden barrels. But the native people in the Indies are fascinated by them, for in their belief, these pots contain powerful magic. Even now, when the Malays are Mohammedans and have forsaken their ancient ways, they still value these jars and use them in their mosques to cleanse themselves before prayer. What was once a simple earthenware pot, is now made of the finest blue and white porcelain. For the Chinese have an instinct for trade that is second to none. Demand and supply is one thing, but it is even better when one creates the demand in the first place.'

'How so?' Fairlie asked.

Light chuckled. 'Come let's sit in the shade awhile. It's too hot out here. These humble pots once fetched only a meagre barter. It would be so much better if the commodity came with a higher price, surely? So, the traders commissioned similar-shaped pots of finest porcelain, decorated with great beasts of Chinese legend. And the price thus rose. More people desired these highly prized objects because they now contained even greater magic, since they were adorned with dragons and the like. Thus, the price rose some more, and so it goes.'

Fairlie was impressed. 'But, surely the Malays disapprove of figurative art? I was told they disdain human and animal forms as being offensive to their god? Isn't a dragon from Chinese legend forbidden to them?'

'An excellent observation, Fairlie. I see you have taken the time to familiarise yourself with Muslim beliefs. You are correct in your assumption. But, in the ancient lore of these islands, a great serpent figure, somewhat akin to a dragon, has always had a central place. Even now, there is respect for the spirit of the *naga*. It is not always possible to entirely remove the pagan from a people. I believe the Yule log is a tradition that long predates the birth of Christ, yet where would Christmas be without it?'

Fairlie smiled in understanding. 'Thank you, sir, for your explanation. It has been most illuminating. One more question, if I may? What is the dragon pursuing? It seems to be reaching out for a fiery sphere?'

'That is the pearl, often portrayed with an attendant motif somewhat like a flame. Great significance is attached to the dragon and pearl that is immediately intelligible to people of the East. For they have a very different philosophy than the world in which we originate. Here, the earth must remain in balance or it will not survive. The universe is like a great weighing scales with opposing forces continually at war. Harmony can only be achieved if the forces remain equal. The dragon is the fiery male, and the pearl is the serene female. Man and woman, night and day, sun and moon. Opposing forces must both exist, or the world is doomed. It is a very odd notion to us. But it is important to understand how these people think or we will never reach understanding with them.'

'So, the dragon never quite catches the pearl, but always chases her across the skies.'

'Exactly. Just like men and women, eh? Once you catch the girl, the fun of the chase is gone!'

The two men laughed. They shared a pot of tea. A friendship was forged that day that was to last a lifetime. Such is the strange serendipity of chance meetings.

***

The compromise that Light and Scott had promised was hard won. For one, Monckton was convinced that he had already achieved his aim; it took another audience with Sultan Muhammed, during which Light walked on broken glass between the sensibilities of both sides, to reveal the distance between them. After that, there were several days of ranting in the British quarters, when the Honourable Edward Monckton dug in his heels, despite cautionary advice from Samuel Lucas, and arguments of reason from Light and Scott. By the end of each day their deliberations seemed to have brought him round, only to find their work must begin again the following morning, the stubborn Monckton having reverted to his earlier entrenchment. No doubt those bosom friends, the sinister Hythe and the malleable Monckton, had mulled the proceedings over a bottle of brandy during the evening, and all their careful work had been undone.

'If I may ask, sir,' Light began again the next morning. 'What exactly remains the sticking point? Let us consider where we might bend a little. Surely there is some matter upon which we might compromise?' He had said much the same each day for nigh on a week.

Monckton threw himself back in his rattan chair, thoroughly exasperated. His limited imagination and rigidity of opinion a near insurmountable obstacle to finding the middle way. 'Goddammit, man! We have been over this a hundred times! We will not solve this conundrum simply by endlessly returning to old ground. The Company will never agree to providing a force for the purpose of attacking Selangor, least of all on behalf of those wretched Chulias. Nor will we hand over the lucrative trade in opium and elephants. Thus, there is no possible solution.'

'Perhaps,' Light replied thoughtfully, rubbing at his stubble. 'Sultan Muhammed is a clever man. He knows that your hands are tied in certain ways.'

'Sultan Muhammed is a senile old fool who listens only to the last person who had his ear, which for the most part is that oily Siak minister of his and those scheming Chulias,' Monckton spat back. His patience was wearing thin. He was very close to taking the sultan's advice and retiring to Kuala Bahang to lick his wounds.

'Perhaps some home truths are in order, Light?' Scott suggested, raising an eyebrow to his friend. They, too, had spoken of stratagems late into the night, hence the swarthy, ungroomed appearance of both men this morning. 'When an Englishman does business, he states his intentions and one is invited to take or leave them. It is understood by both parties that there may be some ground for negotiation – but only to a point. For the advantage always lies with the party who wields the most power or, in the case of merchant trade, the one who has the most desirable cargo. The peoples of the East, however, do not conduct business in this fashion. It is essential for them that the transaction favours both sides equally. Or rather, that a negotiation should be seen to favour both sides equally. Therein lies the genius of their approach. No one party must "lose face". Each side must be seen to make some loss. Only then can all parties leave the table satisfied.'

'Madness!' Lucas chirped up. 'How can everyone win all the time? It is an impossibility! Someone must always take the upper hand! Furthermore, the Company will never accept deferring to a native king.'

Scott's observation suddenly reminded Light his conversation with Fairlie a few days before. An idea came to him, like a sudden clap of thunder on a cloudless day. 'But there's the thing! It isn't necessary for actual concessions to be made, only that they "seem" to be made. Once the appearance of face-saving is achieved, there are many ways of manipulating the agreement to one's own advantage. Here, try this. On the matter of opium and elephants. If you had to concede one of these items, which would it be? Surely we can say to the sultan ... we agree to surrender this cargo if you allow us that one?'

Monckton frowned, unwilling to forfeit anything to the bothersome sultan. Yet, of the two suggested commodities, one was significantly more valuable than the other. It would indeed be possible to surrender the less lucrative. 'Elephants, I suppose. These rajahs love to ride their elephants, don't they? He would jump at that one. It would show that we were ready to make a compromise. Perhaps we could offer him the elephants and insist on our monopoly of opium. I suppose we could all agree on that? I suspect the Company would not see that as too great a concession to make. Lucas, your feelings?'

Lucas gave his tight, obsequious lawyer's smile. 'An excellent decision, sir.'

Light held up his hand. 'But, what if we did the opposite?'

'The opposite?' Charles Hythe could not restrain from commenting from the other end of the table. 'Are you completely insane, man? It's the opium we're here for, you fool!'

Instead of bridling at the insult, Light turned his most pacific expression towards Hythe. 'Exactly. No one would expect us to forego our monopoly of opium. Such a suggestion would confound the sultan. He would believe he had forced a major concession; he had been treated with great respect and generosity as benefitted his position as potentate. From then on, it would be only a matter of judicious wording concerning defensive support. After all, should we be in a position of strength in Queddah, then it could be argued that any future hostile activity would be an attack upon us, thus our response could only be deemed defensive. Each side would be happy. Faces would be saved. The treaty would be secured.' He paused, his hands raised in mimicry of a balanced scale, and waited on the gentlemen's response.

From his lowly place as recorder of the meeting, William Fairlie raised his head and poised his pen, in admiration for the acuity of Light's argument. He caught Light's eye and mouthed: 'The dragon and the pearl, sir!' to which Light responded with a slight bow.

Lucas also showed consideration for the argument. 'It's a clever ploy, Light, I'll grant you that, and you may well be right to point out that the differences between defensive and offensive support are merely matters of technicality. But the Company will never ratify an agreement in which the trade in opium is taken from our hands.' At least he had weighed both sides equally and not dismissed the suggestion. This alone was a breakthrough; Lucas was a cautious man who rarely volunteered his own opinion until he had heard what his superiors had to say.

Hythe and Monckton, both disagreed, although more derisive than Lucas of Light's proposal, shaking their heads at what they regarded as his imprudence. 'If I didn't know that you were a loyal Englishman, Light, I would be inclined to think you were working on behalf of the sultan himself!' Monckton replied. 'I hope you don't imagine that you might finagle your way into being his opium agent? Is that your real objective, perchance?' It was a serious accusation, one which an official of more experience – or sense – would have resisted in public. The offhand remark was tantamount to accusing Light of treason, or at the very least criminal breach of trust. But Light chose to ignore the accusation, fully aware that it was steeped in the machinations of Hythe. Who knew what vile poison Hythe had been dropping into Monckton's ears when they were sequestered together in their evening drinking sessions?

'Please, gentlemen, do not jump to hasty conclusions! I have not yet finished. Of course, we must not renounce our rights to the opium trade. Good God, the Company owns all the opium in the Straits! We ship it in its entirety from India! Of course, we must retain the monopoly! But it is all a matter of interpretation. When we are in full control of the entire coast of Queddah, every single chest of opium in these waters must go only through our hands. Do you think his Highness has a single notion of the quantity we intend to sell? Or the price which we will demand once the monopoly is ours? The Company is already prepared to offer Sultan Muhammed a third share. So, give him his third, but tell him it is the entire amount! It will be such a fortune as to convince the king that he has retained his traditional rights, for it will render far more than he earns now, to be sure. Thus, he will be content. And we will have conceded nothing. It is just a matter of how the final clauses are worded.'

Monckton sat up straight, mockery fading from his pale skin to be replaced with a blush. He sensed an ingenious solution had presented itself, one he could wholly claim for himself. His career would be made. 'Are you saying we could circumvent this impasse merely by implying one thing and actually meaning nothing of the sort? But what if the sultan got wind of this by and by? What if he waved the treaty in our face at some later time and demanded the full sum?'

Light chuckled, his eyes dancing, for he already knew Monckton had bitten. 'Pray tell me what exactly the sultan might do once we were established here in Queddah with a fort full of armed men? That intimidation aside, according to the very terms of his own treaty, if the sultan tried to raise arms against us, I believe that would be considered as a threat to Company interests, thus we would be obliged to defend ourselves ... after all, isn't that the purpose of the sepoys?'

'My God, you're a genius, Light!' Monckton exclaimed, clapping his hands in pleasure. 'This is quite like one of those military strategies where Caesar tricked the Gauls into believing the legions were retreating only to surround them in a trap as they chased blindly after them! Lucas and Fairlie, get to work! I want this treaty ready for presentation to the sultan before the old fellow thinks of any other demands! Is it too early for a celebratory drink, sirs? I think we may have cracked this particular egg at last!'

While the other men were slapping each other on the back, Light flashed Hythe a knowing glance, wallowing in his victory. His adversary, for his part, kept his tongue, unwilling to oppose openly what the rest of the men were lauding. But the twitch in his cheek had reappeared. Light winked at him. Hythe's face flushed purple. Scott surveyed the two enemies, perturbed. This puerile gameplay between two grown men would ruin things for them all if he did not rein in his friend. Hythe would not let this matter rest here.

The inevitable wait began. Once the treaty had been drawn up, translated into the Malay tongue, rendered in *Jawi* script, inspected by interpreters to ensure there had been no 'misunderstandings', it was then presented to the sultan and another elaborate signing ceremony was held. Nor was that the end of it. It was now to be despatched to Calcutta for ratification, another long delay. Hythe and Lucas were duly ordered to carry the important document – and the array of official gifts – on the *Triton*, while Monckton returned to Kuala Bahang to wait out the response at the fort he disparagingly referred to as 'a few ruined walls built on a bog'.

***

Light had little wish to sit out the intervening weeks in close proximity to Monckton; the less he saw of that posturing fool the better. He had another plan. Since his perplexing meeting with Lady Chan in Jangsylan months before, he had been pondering the suggestion she had made so obliquely. It was time to visit Lady Thong Di and explore the nature of their relationship. After the death of her husband, she had settled at the estates of her Malay mother in the small hamlet of Merbok.

A letter was duly sent, written by Soliman in elegant Jawi learnt in his studies at the local mosque during their extended sojourn. Light knew that it was time for the boy to become familiar with both his own religion and traditions. It also served as a boon in his communications with Sultan Muhammed, for the young boy's proficiency meant Light no longer need rely on translators, whose discretion was not to be trusted. An answer arrived back promptly, written this time in Siamese, from Lady Thong Di herself. Circumspection was the watchword of the current times.

Light took the *Emily*, a speedy little sloop that could navigate the sluggish Merbok river better than his larger ships. It also had the advantage of concealing his absence, for it was usually sailed by one of his captains. Light preferred that his current business was known to as few as possible. With a small crew, ably assisted by Soliman, and Scott primed that Light was on a hunting expedition in the interior, he slipped away early morning.

To be out of Kuala Bahang, and away from the strictures of the past months, was a breath of fresh air. The journey was an easy sail south, skirting the very mangrove coastline that had been offered to the Company in the treaty. Soon these would be British waters, with warships patrolling against pirates, and merchant ships galore. Life in the Straits was on the brink of a great change, and Light could not but feel optimistic that, at last, he had set himself at the heart of things. For who but he was better placed to take charge of the new reality?

He spent the day on deck, deep in thought with another pivotal decision about his future in the balance. It was indeed time to take a wife. A home and family would bring respectability, an important aspect of his future position. He had no desire to import a suitable girl from England, nor to scour the salons of Calcutta for Company daughters looking to catch a man of the moment. But how might an alliance with a Christian woman of native birth be received in India? Light was already regarded as something of an oddity, too familiar with local ways to be entirely trusted. And yet, if the woman had connections to the royal family of Queddah, would that not bring a measure of desirability in view of this future alliance?

The wide estuary of the Merbok river welcomed them in the early afternoon when most of the riverine settlements were quiet, activity stilled by the oppressive heat. It was the hour of rest, an excellent time for passing through with little comment. Once the heart of trade in the region, the Merbok had long since been supplanted by the northern centres, but there was still a thriving local ingenuity driving its waterway traffic.

At this time of year, with the rainy season still some months away, the lower channel was deep enough but the waters of the upper reaches were low, and the river was heavily silted in parts. Sterling work with oars and paddles was required. At several points, sailors were forced to jump into the red-brown water to wade along, dragging and pushing the craft, searching for the deeper cuts. Light and Soliman remained on board with several others, scanning the water for the fast-moving ripples that might conceal a crocodile. There had been sightings of these mighty estuarine reptiles basking here and there along the riverbanks; the creatures had eyed them as balefully as did the odd local they had encountered.

The journey took far longer than anticipated. It was late in the afternoon as the heat of day waned that they finally reached their destination, a miserable little river port, all rotting wooden poles and rickety structures, swarming in clouds of mosquitoes under the watchful gaze of the river folk. Too late by then to trek the two leagues across the forest to the remote hamlet at the foothills of Mount Jerai where the Rozells family lived. Surrounded overnight by potentially hostile locals was a worrisome prospect, however, quite as menacing as the crocodiles. A small trading vessel marooned so far upstream was sure to attract the most unwelcome of opportunist raiders.

But their fears were soon dispelled when a small skiff pulled up alongside. 'Kapitan Lait? The Nyonya sent me to welcome you! I am Malik, her agent. We have been waiting for you long time. Too dark soon to travel. You spend the night on the perahu? More comfortable than this dirty town. We set out at morning time. Can or not?'

'I am grateful for your presence, Encik Malik. But, is this a safe mooring? I fear we may attract unwanted attention.'

The amiable Malik grinned widely. 'Do not worry, Kapitan. Everybody only very nosy. Want to see the English kapitan that friend the sultan! No one will harm you. But they will look and look. Very curious. Nyonya lady very important here. They not disturb her friends. I come back tomorrow, *ialah*?'

So much for arriving incognito. His identity was already known to all and sundry. Light laughed wryly and thanked the agent once again, mighty relieved that the only threat to their night's sleep would be mosquitoes.

***

The following morning's trek proved less burdensome than he had anticipated. Although the path was crude, it was firmly trodden down, with undergrowth well cut back. Soon enough the forest thinned out into cultivated coconut plantation and then opened out into a wide expanse of *padi*. The rice fields stretched out lush green, thronging with birdlife. In the distance the rolling landscape gave way to the verdant slopes of Gunung Jerai, the imposing mountain, the beacon that all sailors searched for as they crossed the Andaman Sea. Lady Thong Di's home was an unexpected rural idyll.

Nestled in the valley, in a copse of radiant flame of the forest trees, rose before them a striking stilted house with double-tiered roof of red Singgora tiles and delicate eaves carved like the finest lace. The house was built of silver-grey *cengal* wood, with panels of intricate leaf and floral whorls and shuttered windows framed in fretwork. It was quite the prettiest house Light had ever seen.

By the side of the structure stood a smaller version of the main building, a charming little cottage, to which Light and Soliman were led. The other members of the party were quartered with the servants. 'What a pretty little lodge!' Light exclaimed as they climbed the steps to the small veranda. Soliman clapped his hands in glee, equally charmed by this perfect miniature replica.

Malik was well pleased with their reaction. 'My mistress is very clever lady. Instead of rice barn, she make baby house for guests! It is *gajah menyusu*! Please enjoy your stay!' His comment confused Light. What did a baby elephant suckling from its mother have to do with it? Soliman recognised his puzzled expression and chortled. He always loved it when Francis misunderstood something that seemed obvious to him.

'Baby elephant in the shade of his mother, just like tiny house in the shade of big house! We call rice barn like that, but this time is baby house!' Soliman answered in English. While he mightily enjoyed teasing his benefactor, he would never allow anyone else to laugh at the captain. After the tense and difficult weeks in the north, this trip already felt like a rest cure. Imagine having this beautiful place for a rural retreat? The prospect of a future alliance seemed even more alluring now that they were here.

It was evening before he met the beautiful Lady Thong Di Rozells, when they attended dinner with the family. In an elegant alcove to the left of the entrance hall, settled on cushions, they were served simple but tasty food. The shutters stood open, wafting in a cool breeze, with the scent of orange jasmine. It was a relaxed, informal gathering: Lady Thong Di, her mother Tunku Mahsia, Martinha, a strikingly lovely young girl of fifteen or so, and the younger son, Felipe. Light introduced Soliman as his adopted son, at which description the boy beamed with pride. Not only was he treated to dinner with a noble family, but for the first time he had been openly acknowledged as Captain Francis' boy.

After dinner, the children withdrew to a nearby low table where they played *congkak* while their elders chatted. Lady Thong Di and Mahsia were eager to hear news of the negotiations, especially considering her role in bringing Light to Queddah in the first place. For the first time in months, Light felt he could talk freely. He regaled the ladies with amusing anecdotes about the wooden-headed British and the devious machinations of the sultan. The story of the cannon fire delighted them, as did Monckton's discomfort at having to chew a betel quid at the final ceremony. The ladies laughed until tears streamed down their faces.

As the pleasant evening slipped into balmy night, a sense that this might one day become his home dawned on Light – and he found the idea filled him with an unexpected pleasure. Until that moment he had rarely considered his loneliness, or how much Soliman needed friends of his own age. Of course, he had his women scattered about the region, but they meant little to him other than bed-mates for earthly pleasures. Perhaps it was time to establish some more lasting roots and have a family. Both he and Soliman would benefit from the civilising influence of women in their lives.

With an elaborate show of feeling sleepy and shepherding the children off to bed, old Tunku Mahsia eventually made her excuses, thanking Light for honouring them with his presence and hoping he would stay a few more days. They were somewhat isolated from polite company and his conversation had been a treat for them all. Taking his cue, Light rose to bid goodnight to the family, calling Soliman to say his farewells to his new friends.

'You are leaving so soon, Kapitan Light?' Lady Thong Di asked him. 'Please, I was hoping we could have a glass of wine together before you go. This is my mother's home so I do not serve alcohol in her presence but now that she has retired, I see no reason that we shouldn't share a glass ...'

He was taken somewhat by surprise by her offer, highly unusual in any company, particularly in the East. 'I do not wish to compromise you, my Lady,' he replied formally.

But Thong Di was unconcerned by propriety. 'Soliman here can be your chaperone. I am a respectable widow, Kapitan Light. I run this estate. In Siam I would be a business woman and this meeting would not be unusual. Do not worry about my reputation. No one here would suspect your intentions. And I rather like the occasional glass of wine, a habit I acquired from my late husband.'

A maid poured out two glasses, setting them on a table on the veranda, under a wine-dark sky speckled with a thousand stars.

A silver moon hung low in the heavens, cool and serene. Leaving Soliman inside to play with the *congkak* board, Light nursed his glass and felt a shiver of apprehension. Was this the moment to make an approach?

'A beautiful night, madam. Your home is quite enchanting,' he began, falling back on pleasantries for want of a better opening gambit.

'You are too kind. We rebuilt the old house that had long been neglected and had fallen into disrepair after my grandfather died and my mother lived in Ujung Salang. The farm lands had been worked of a fashion by our villagers but there was much to do to restore its potential. We are very proud of our achievements in but a few years.'

'I'm astonished at this place! It is so remote and yet a thriving agricultural community!' he replied.

'This area was once at the heart of the wealth of this region. Even now it is well connected by both river and inland routes. It did not take much to revive its fortunes. Mother may be old but she is wise. The inland ways connect with Pattani on the east coast; there have always been Siamese in these parts. We needed more workers to clear and plant land, so she let it be known that Siamese were welcome to farm here, and many came down to settle.'

'Do the local Malays not object?' Light queried, wondering whether this was simply small talk or if she was setting out what she had to offer. A rich heiress with land and loyal tenants?

Thong Di shook her head. 'The migrants are Samsams, Captain, Muslim Siamese. They left because they were fearful of what may happen to them under Siam or Burma in the future.

The local Malays welcome them for they bring more prosperity and they are happy to shelter fellow Muslims who are in danger of persecution. It is a happy, safe place. Far enough away from the sea to keep us free from raiders. We export good quantities of rice already and the lowlands of Gunung Jerai provide excellent crops of fruit and vegetables.' She breathed out gently on the night air, a long sigh of contentment. 'For the first time in years, I feel truly safe. Free from most of the worries of these dangerous times in which we live.'

'The treaty with the British will be good for Queddah,' Light opined.

Lady Thong Di paused, a pursing of her lips suggesting disagreement. 'Perhaps. If I may say so, sir, I am wary of any foreigners who come with promises of friendship and cooperation. In my limited experience, there is little evidence of beneficial results from such relationships.'

Light acknowledged her opinion by raising his glass in salute. 'You are wise, dear lady. Wherever men see profit, trust and honesty soon fly out of the window.' Now that the conversation had turned once more to the turbulent political climate, he saw his chance. 'This is a good place indeed, but do you ever feel the lack of a protector? Two women and two children are a temptation for the unscrupulous.'

At that Thong Di turned to face him head on. She too was ready to address the subject. 'My daughter and son are no longer children, Kapitan Light. Martinha is almost sixteen and Felipe is only a year younger. They are both receiving an education. My daughter will be married soon ...'

'Which might one day find you lodgers in your own home.

Malay law would regard the husband as the rightful owner.'

'It would rather depend on the husband, surely? My daughter is not a Muslim, you will recall. She is a Christian. I wish for her to marry a man of her religion. The estate belongs to Felipe. He is my mother's heir. I myself am not concerned about the ownership of the land. We will always have a home here. But I am concerned about my daughter ...'

It was an unexpected shift in the conversation. Where Light had been leading towards an amorous declaration, he suddenly found himself somewhat adrift in a different line of thought. Why were they now speaking of the child? 'Perhaps you could send her away to school? There are excellent Christian schools in Calcutta ... and she would meet gentleman from good families there.'

Thong Di looked shocked. 'Send my daughter away? Let her be paraded on the marriage market to catch some aging English gentleman? That would be worse than what might lie in store for her here! No, Kapitan Light, I would never do that. Yet, if she remains here, I fear that soon the sultan will arrange a marriage for her to some Queddah noble, condemned to *purdah* for the rest of her life. My daughter would shrivel up and die in such a world! No, I shall not allow it to happen. That is why I have so much wanted to talk to you in private ever since we met in Aceh!'

Light set down his glass, the light dawning on him at last. Lady Chan had suggested that he marry into her sister's family and he had jumped to the conclusion that Lady Thong Di was his intended bride. That was not at all what either women had meant.

'I'm not sure what you mean, Lady Thong Di. How might I be of assistance in this matter?' He pretended ignorance although he already knew the answer.

'Kapitan Light, I would like to offer you my daughter's hand in marriage. You are a man of prospects, a Christian gentleman, and a friend of my late husband's. You are well respected by both the sultan and my family in Ujang Salang. You have standing amongst the British. Only you can keep Martinha safe. She is a beautiful girl. Any man would desire her. She will be a good wife to you, and give you handsome children.'

'But she is a child of half my age, nona! I cannot marry a girl of fifteen!' Light exclaimed.

Lady Thong Di waved away his objection. 'You are a young man yet. It is the perfect age difference. Martim was older when I married him. Do you think the sultan will find her a dashing young lord? It will be a toothless old pervert. Please, sir. I beg you to consider my proposal!'

Light fell silent, walking away a distance to rest his hands on the rail, staring out at the night. 'Lady Thọng Di ... You must understand something ... I came here tonight because I believed I had a chance, not with your daughter, but ...' his voice tailed off, but she still grasped his meaning.

'... with me? You thought to ask me to marry you? But I am a widow with children grown! No man wants a woman past her prime!' Lady Thong Di gasped, her hand fluttering to her heart. Her surprise was genuine, as was the break in her voice. He had not been wrong. There had been a spark between them from the very start. She had felt it, too.

Light turned around to gaze at this proud and courageous woman, smiling sadly. 'You are the same age as I. A woman in her prime. What do I want with an innocent girl when I could have a wise and beautiful grown woman as my partner?'

Thong Di's eyes were moist with tears; two spots of blush coloured her cheeks. 'And that is why it must be you, sir. My sister knew you would be the perfect choice. Martinha will be safe with you. Think on it, please, I beg you. We will talk further tomorrow.'

21
Retribution

The Council House, Calcutta. June 1772

It had not taken the gossipmongers long to leap upon the scandal of the moment. Calcutta thrived on rumour and innuendo at the best of times but a nugget of such gargantuan proportions concerning the already notorious Warren Hastings, a German baron and his charming but faithless wife, was in an entirely different league. It was even reported that Baroness von Imhoff herself was ensconced at Belvedere House, Hastings' personal residence, since her husband had left for England.

Into this cauldron of whispers came the delegates from Queddah, small fry indeed in the political vortex that radiated from Government House. But if they anticipated that Hastings would be distracted by his personal affairs, Samuel Lucas and Charles Hythe were mistaken. Summoned into his presence, they found him as business-like as ever, clad in unpretentious brown silk, his wispy greying hair severely brushed back from his receding forehead. Governor Hastings sat perched at his desk, one hand resting on his brow and the other holding documents, which he was carefully perusing. It was the treaty proposal and a letter penned by the Honourable Frederick Monckton.

Glancing up as they were ushered in, Hastings fixed them in his pale grey gaze, both men squirming under the piercing scrutiny. Lucas betrayed his unease by an outbreak of profuse sweating, Hythe by obsequious deference. Hastings cut them both short.

'Sit down, gentleman. I have read through the proposal. Is this the best that could be done?'

Straight to business.

'It was a very difficult negotiation, sir. The sultan was intractable on many issues, no doubt egged on by the meddlesome Chulias at his court. This was the only possible compromise that could be reached given the great gulf that exists between our instructions and the sultan's ever-increasing demands,' Lucas began, stumbling through his nebulous defence, mopping his face and neck throughout.

'Do you require a glass of water, Mr Lucas? On the side table, if you will …' Hastings was irritated. Lucas gratefully accepted the opportunity for a respite from interrogation, scuttling off to pour himself a glass and take slow, measured sips.

'I have also read through Mr Monckton's letter. He seems to regard this treaty as a triumph of diplomacy. If he is to be believed, it is only through his genius that a path could be forged through the forest of … let me find his exact words … "*dissimulation and dishonesty in which the Malay court delights*" … So, this settlement is entirely Monckton's work, in your opinion? Please be candid, gentlemen. This is not a court of law but a private meeting between gentlemen. Your personal thoughts would be most constructive when I submit my report to the Council.'

Aware that Lucas would continue to equivocate until he had ascertained Hastings' inclination, and then fall completely in line, Hythe saw his chance. 'Mr Monckton is a very capable negotiator, to be sure, but he is unfamiliar with the region, sir. Although the terms set before you appear to him to be the most conducive, we believe that he has been wholly misled by his guileless trust in Captain Francis Light. Whilst the captain is a very experienced and well-qualified fellow, ideal for offering advice on matters pertaining to the Straits people and its trade, his unusually close relationship with the sultan has rendered him somewhat partial in these deliberations.'

Hastings leaned forward in his chair, every sinew now tensed, uncannily resembling a predator stalking prey. 'Are you implying that his loyalties are in question, Mr Hythe? I have received several missives over the past year from the captain. He has always shown himself to be supportive in the matter of a British settlement in the East Indies and has submitted several interesting proposals, each thoroughly corroborated with local knowledge and connections. But I have never personally met the man. Your observations as to his character are very pertinent,' Hastings added. He had caught the whiff of controversy and it had piqued his interest, where before he had seemed disparaging of their opinions. It encouraged Hythe to open up further.

'I have known Light since boyhood, sir. We were at school together ...' he began with an oily smile. 'He was always a clever boy, but not at all what one would call a decent fellow. His origins are unknown. He is of no particular family. But for the generosity of a local squire, Light would have been a river rat at best, his mother a lowly widow of dubious character. There was also some uncertainty regarding her relationship with the squire.'

The reference to rumour and scandal was ill-judged. Hastings immediately bridled. 'Get to it, Mr Hythe. I fail to see what part ancient gossip has to do with anything. Keep to the matter in hand! So, you and Light were not fond of each other at school, I take it?' The scornful tone reappeared. Hythe gathered himself together, intent now on a careful examination of each word. Hastings was rapier sharp and would not be easily bluffed.

'As you so rightly assume, sir, we were not friends. Light was not the right sort of gentleman. He was nothing but a rough lout. Expelled for destruction of property, I believe. In my judgement, he is trying to worm his way into decent society by portraying himself as a skilful merchant factor and expert linguist, when in actual fact he has mostly been living rough with the local sea folk, peddling in any commodity he can get his hands on. I have heard he has spent time with Buggee pirates and, even when entrusted with an official role for his agency in Acheen, he took it upon himself to attack a Dutch fort using Company sepoys on behalf of the sultan! He's a renegade, sir. Little more than a buccaneer himself, Mr Hastings.'

Hastings held up his hand curtly. 'I have heard tell of these incidents. Don't forget I was deputy governor of Madras and I know Francis Jourdan well. Which is why I despatched Mr Monckton and you fellows to conduct the negotiations. Captain Light was merely to be the man on hand to make the initial approaches on account of his established relationship with Sultan Muhammed Jiwa. Beyond that, he has little official authority other than his presence as a general advisor.'

Hastings' answer was clipped and impatient. Hythe's clumsy attempts to smear Light's reputation irritated the governor, who was not in the least interested in the snobbery and vindictive resentments that were common order in the Company, especially directed towards men of humble birth – or those of outstanding abilities. In Hastings' opinion, Francis Light was a man of both these qualities, although he was shrewd enough to believe Light was as capable of dissemination and self-serving as every other Company man. 'Lucas ... what say you? Is Light to be trusted?'

Lucas had heard out Hythe's comments tight-lipped. He disliked his spiteful companion, but he had his own reservations about Captain Light. 'Light's a charming and very able fellow but there's no doubt he has gone native. His best friend is that dissolute James Scott of Jangsylan, who favours Malay garb and consorts openly with any number of local harlots. Light and Scott are thick as thieves, sir, and Scott is no lover of the English or the Honourable Company, as you know. His loathsome values must have influenced Light somewhat. But to be fair, Captain Light is very well acquainted with the politics and culture of the Straits and he has a remarkable grasp of their languages. He gave us sterling support and provided invaluable information.' Lucas was more complimentary than was usual in a man of his cautious nature, a fact that Hastings noted. The man respected Light and held no brief for Hythe nor his malice.

'In respect of that, would you say that Mr Monckton reached the only possible compromise with the sultan? That the terms of this treaty could not have been influenced negatively by any unethical intention from other parties?' Hastings would not allow Lucas to prevaricate. He wanted direct answers.

'Well ...' Lucas began, before tailing off nervously. Hythe looked across at him with contempt. Lucas was loath to corroborate Hythe's opinion yet could not deny his own suspicions.

'Well, Mr Lucas?' Hastings reiterated tetchily.

The older man sighed, his forehead again trickling with sweat, his eyes darting around as if seeking a place to hide. 'While accepting most of the clauses as advantageous to our intentions in Queddah, I must admit to some concerns over the more controversial items upon which Captain Light's persuasive influence may have swayed the day. Although I applaud his ingenuity, I do not believe that there is sufficient clarity in certain articles ...'

Hastings grunted in frustration. 'Is it impossible that a lawyer might answer a question with yea or nay, and be done with it for once? I also have great concerns over several salient clauses, not the least that we seem to be offering to hand over the opium trade entire to the sultan. Furthermore, the vague ramblings about allowing our warships to patrol in the Selangor river but without active participation unless attacked, seem to me tantamount to provocative action by another name. How would you interpret these particular issues?'

Lucas swallowed. 'Captain Light believes that if we set the clauses down in this manner, the entire treaty will be acceptable to the sultan. In reality, however, it would never be enforceable. We will not be surrendering the opium monopoly in any *de facto* sense, as we control its import wholly, nor shall we ever engage in military action save that which we would deem justifiable if our interests were threatened.'

'At last, some clarity! So, the devious Captain Light managed to talk you out of the strict exclusions that we set down by means of his chicanery. Is that the sense of it, or have I mistaken your meaning?' Hastings' response was deceptively mild but neither man was fooled by his tone. The governor was circling for a kill.

'Yes, sir. That is the gist of it, sir.' Lucas added lamely: 'Light said it was "how things are done in the East Indies", I believe.'

'I'm sure he did, sir,' Hastings snapped back. 'Hythe? Have you anything to add? This is your chance to add some of your particular poison to the glass.'

Hythe flushed with embarrassment at his failure to hoodwink his superior. 'I believe that Light is hoping that the sultan will give him the rights to operate the opium contract, in which case he will be perfectly positioned to defraud us all. That would be typical of the underhand methods of Francis Light. In my humble opinion. Sir.' Hythe added.

'Indeed. Which would make Light much the same as every other Company official since the East India Company first opened its doors,' Hastings observed wryly. 'Yet, I had hoped for more from Captain Light. It seems I should have learned my lesson by now. The employees of the East India Company seem incapable of principled behaviour.' It was a slur on his audience as much as Light. Hastings had a low opinion of everyone, saving himself.

'Monckton writes that the sultan believes the mere presence of a British force in Queddah would cause the Bugis to withdraw, thus we need have no concerns that our forces might be drawn into unwelcome conflict. I deem this assertion to be woefully ill-judged, given that the Bugis have shown no compunction in attacking the Dutch. Where did this notion come from? The sultan's own mouth?'

Lucas and Hythe exchanged glances. 'We were not present at the private interviews, although Captain Light was there on the insistence of the sultan,' Lucas admitted. 'But I did hear Light repeat this assertion as fact, attributing it to the sultan ...' It was to be the final word from them. Hastings had heard enough.

'Thank you, gentleman. I will refer the document to the Council tomorrow morning together with my findings. Please expect a decision by the beginning of next week. Thank you for your endeavours. A safe journey back to the Peninsula. Good day, sirs.'

Their dismissal was summary, providing no insight into how the Council might decide. Lucas thought the treaty would be ratified, but with clear stipulation as to Company rights to appoint the opium agents. It would also require a reworking of the clause pertaining to Selangor. How the sultan might respond was uncertain. It could mean a return to stalemate. They might be in for a long haul before any agreement was possible.

Hythe was of a very different opinion. Hastings might be an arrogant troublemaker, but the governor was fervently against any hint of corruption or private deal-making amongst Company officials. He would never tolerate any settlement that deviated from his original proposal. Light was finished.

***

Following his visit to Merbok, Light spent several weeks at sea, determined to be as far from Monckton as he could during the interminable wait for a decision from Calcutta. He also needed time to think, untrammelled by any other hindrances, while he pondered Lady Thong Di's offer. He had asked her for time to consider his decision, at least until the Company affair had been resolved. She had urged him not to delay, for the sultan might turn his attention towards Martinha at any time.

In his heart, Light knew he was prevaricating. He had no wish to offend the lady but nor could he consent to marrying the girl. Scott offered little help, shrugging away any honourable considerations. The Rozells family was rich and influential. Such a marriage would give him the virtual keys to Queddah. Francis could carve a little kingdom for himself in the Straits and every Tom, Dick and Harry would want to deal with him, rather than the Dutch, the Company or the Bugis.

'But she's a child, James! And I have no romantic feelings for her!' Light exclaimed.

'Good God, man! She's marriageable age both here and in England, what's the matter with you? You say she's a little beauty. Feelings? What in God's name do feelings have to do with it? You sound like a starry-eyed maiden. Marry the girl and be done with it! If the treaty is agreed, the sultan will give you anything. If the treaty fails, he will need you more than ever. And that's before we speak of Ujung Salang. Lady Chan would be your Aunt. You'd be one of the family, lad!' Scott had rubbed his hands together in glee at that prospect.

Light's dilemma would receive no sympathy from his friend. Thus, he fled to sea in the vain hope of finding clarity in the tranquillity of open water. A month passed, in which he ventured in and out of every port on the Straits, sailing league after league, until he could think of no further excuse to stay away. It was already July. Calcutta must have sent their decision by now. His mind was made up. There was indeed only one honest course of action open to him. Whatever the cost, he could not marry this child.

As the *Speedwell* entered the Queddah estuary, they moored

offshore near the *Triton*. A reply had been received. Light noticed signs of feverish activity in the old fort, although he was unsure what that indicated. Had they begun to reinforce the dilapidated building for settlement, or were they making preparation to leave? With pounding heart, Light headed for Scott's house, bursting through the door to find his friend was absent. But a letter was waiting for him, propped up on a table, its envelope embellished in an elegant hand, bearing the Company crest. A personal letter from the governor's office? What did that mean?

Light tore at the seal and pulled out the letter, all fingers and thumbs, roughly shaking the delicate paper open. With bated breath he scanned its contents, his heart sinking as his eye was drawn particularly to one section at the end.

> *We find that the promise of Queddah has been vastly exaggerated and its liabilities intentionally disregarded. A Privilege as local representatives was extended, perhaps unwisely, to certain merchant captains whose intentions have proved wholly partial. They have abused our Trust for their own Profit, in a fashion that has been destructive to the future Prosperity and Security of their employers. While the Honourable Mr. Monckton may have demonstrated his inexperience, the Council holds you, Captain Francis Light, entirely responsible for the failure of this Mission...*

It was a shattering assault on his good name. The stigma for the abject failure was to be placed entirely on his shoulders.

Sometime later, after downing the best part of a bottle of

brandy, Light stormed out in the direction of the British fort, Soliman trailing in his wake, already alarmed at the captain's intentions. At the door, Light managed to persuade the sepoys that he was a dinner guest and gained entry. Soliman was left outside, pacing nervously about. Meanwhile Light pushed aside the servants and burst into the dining room. At his unexpected appearance, the gentlemen had the good grace to put on sombre faces and to offer their sympathies, but Light was not to be placated. The fact that they were fully aware of the extent of his humiliation only fired his anger more.

'You miserable cowards! Without me you would have been chased out of Queddah long ago! I gave you the settlement on a platter, and this is the thanks I get!' he raged, with little thought to how his outburst would be viewed. His rational judgement had deserted him.

'Control yourself, Captain Light! Let us discuss this as gentlemen,' Monckton countered, rising from his seat, his expression thunderous.

'Gentlemen? You think you have behaved like gentlemen? You stab a man in the back and expect him to say thank you very much for it? How dare you lay the blame for your inadequacy at my door! You are a rank, incompetent, damned Irish bogtrotter,' Light retorted, in a flagrant assault on Monckton's Anglo-Irish origins.

Before they could digest that blatant insult, Light turned his attention to the man sitting next to Monckton, who was observing the disintegration of Captain Light's composure with scarce-concealed amusement. 'This is your doing, you filthy little rat! You have scuppered an entire treaty merely to get your own back on a schoolboy who bested you twenty years ago. You have all let this venomous toad lead you by the nose with his obsession for petty revenge!' Light lunged for Hythe, dragging him from his seat and throwing him roughly against the wall. The other men sprang up to restrain him but Light was too fast.

'I should have done this years ago … !' he spat out, and punched Hythe square in the face, knocking his head back against the wall and loosening a few teeth into the bargain. Hythe slumped to his knees, clutching his bloody nose and whimpering; Light dragged him up again and drew back his arm for a second blow. With difficulty, William Fairlie hauled Light off, struggling all the while, cursing and screaming threats at his enemy. The captain had completely lost his wits.

'Please, sir, calm down,' William Fairlie begged. 'This will do you no good. Think of your reputation!

'Fuck my reputation, you loathsome dogs … It's already destroyed anyway. I might as well earn it,' Light mumbled, but the heat of his blind rage was slowly subsiding. He shook off Fairlie but made no further attempts at violence.

'Get him out of here,' Monckton shouted to the sepoys who had charged in at the sounds of angry voices. 'Throw him into the gutter where he belongs, the drunken wretch. Captain Light, if you think this display will bring you any sympathy, then think again. You have finally revealed your true colours, which we suspected all along. You are nothing but a brutal ruffian. Get out of my sight!' Monckton flung himself back in the chair and poured himself a brandy, while the others helped Hythe to a seat and called for a doctor.

Light was dragged out unceremoniously and dumped in the

street, but not before the soldiers levelled a few free punches and kicks at him. He fell face down in the dirt, observed by a curious crowd, who were laughing and pointing at the sight. Englishmen fighting each other! What could be better?

Moments later Soliman returned to the scene with Scott panting in his wake. The boy had known disaster was at hand and had managed to locate Scott, dragging him off some harbour moll. 'Sweet Jesus, what have we here! Francis, what have you done, man?' Between the two, they hauled Light to his feet; he threw them off, staggering slightly, but fortunately none the worse for his experience.

'I broke his fucking nose, though!' Light hissed, before bursting out in manic laughter. 'And knocked out his buck teeth ... Hythe was an ugly bugger to start with ... but you should see him now ... !' Hysteria had set in. Light was even drunker than Soliman had at first thought.

Scott groaned. 'You bloody fool, Francis! How does that solve anything? The treaty is already dead in the water, man. It serves no purpose proving you're the low born wretch they already think you to be.'

'Serves no purpose? Who gives a damn? It felt bloody good! It might not change a goddamn thing but sometimes a man has to give full rein to his inclination. And today I was inclined to punch that scoundrel in his bastard face!' Light noticed Soliman, dancing back and forth around the two older men. The boy was anxious but also proud. Captain Francis was a real man. He would take no insult from his enemies. Light ruffled up his hair. 'What say you, Sol? Was I wrong to punch the bastard?'

Soliman grinned. 'I would punch them all, those stupid *orang putih!* They lucky no one kriss them already!'

'There's still time, boy!' Light replied. 'The sultan will be furious. They'd better watch their backs now. Come, let's go home. I need to clean myself up. And think on what next to do with my life. For I fear that I have burnt my boats with the Company good and proper. I may be in dire need of a new employer come the morrow ...'

22
Dewa Raja

Kota Sena palace, Kangar. July 1772

After his initial fiery reaction on the failure of the mission, Light was remarkably sanguine. Whilst still angry and bitter, the disappointing outcome focussed his mind, now that the reality of his position was plain. Scott had warned him time and time again of the impossibility of ever finding acceptance in the halls of the high and mighty. He had tried to steer his course through turbulent waters, but had finally been broken on the rocks. So be it. But all was not lost. He would continue to forge his own path in the Straits, ply his lucrative trade, exploit his network of contacts, and in doing so, acquire himself a great fortune. It would provide ample opportunity to compensate for the loss of his good name and offer the tempting prospect of appropriating as much trade as possible from Company hands.

His first port of call was the court at Perlis, where he found Sultan Muhammed Jiwa himself almost apoplectic with rage, so much so that his doctors hovered, on hand to attend the old ruler should he have a seizure. Soliman had the right of it. Had Monckton and his associates been at hand, they would have found themselves on the wrong end of a blade.

'They dare to refuse my demands? I am the Sultan! Queddah is mine! It is I who refuse to deal any further with these faithless infidels! I have already despatched a letter warning them to get back to India or face the consequences! If they wish to remain, they take their chances as private traders, but I have warned them that no one who wishes to remain in my friendship will ever do business with them! They are finished in these waters! Finished!' The sultan stopped merely because he had run out of breath. His manservant, Agus, stroked his brow with a cloth soaked in flower water and held out a spouted jar for the king to drink water.

Light and Scott had remained in a position of subservience throughout this tirade, heads lowered. They had not been entirely sure of their reception at the palace, but it was already evident that the sultan did not hold them responsible. 'Kapitan Lait! Kapitan Sakat! I am not angry with you! Through all this sorry mess, you have been the only ones who have had the interests of Queddah at heart!'

Light shrugged. 'Unfortunately, your Highness, that may have been the problem. The Company has laid the blame at my feet. It seems they think I have betrayed my own country by my friendship with the court.'

The old man flared up again. 'Blame you? The only ones to blame are the stupid and ignorant men they sent to Queddah. Does your King George know how they insult and demean a fellow ruler? Does he know how they belittle the traditions and religion of another nation? These little men with their ugly, sweaty faces have dared to trample over our rights and privileges, yet they blame you for the disaster? Kapitan Lait, the only honourable Englishman in that entire country, it would seem, for you tell me Kapitan Sakat comes from Sakatland, which is a different state entirely.'

Light struggled to repress a smile at the sultan's acute grasp of his world, set against the woeful ignorance of his own people, wallowing as usual in their blind superiority. 'I am afraid your Majesty is correct. They still believe that they can bully your Highness into the settlement that they want. It is futile. They will not bend.'

Sultan Muhammed nodded his head and slumped back against his chair. 'But … what are we to do about our enemies? We are back where we began with the same intractable problems!'

'Perhaps. Perhaps not,' replied Light. 'Scott and I have given some thought to "alternative" strategies that may be of interest to you, your Majesty. That is, of course, if you are still prepared to listen to the ramblings of Christian gentlemen …' he added playfully.

The sultan brightened up. 'Speak! You fellows have agile minds and always have our best interests at heart. I would be very curious to hear what you have to say. Bring cushions for Lait and Sakat. Serve refreshments! I think we may have a long discussion before us!'

***

In the early mists of morning several days later, two merchant ships were spotted at the entrance to the Selangor river, just out of range of the hundred or so cannons positioned on either bank. They continued to hold that position for several hours, ignoring the craft that came and went, much to the puzzlement of the garrison of men encamped further up the hill. When curiosity finally got the better of them, an armed group sailed out, and from a distance shouted a warning.

'Bugger off, or we'll fire!'

'Come aboard, gentlemen, please,' shouted back Captain Light. 'We have a proposition for you.'

The apparent leader of the motley bunch, a burly Dutchman from his fair hair and guttural English, threw back an aggressive retort. 'We warn you. Fuck off or we fire the cannon.' He indicated the cannons on his boat, small but deadly at close range.

Light shook his head. 'No, you won't. Not when you hear my proposition. Or do you not like money? Boys, have you ever heard of mercenaries who don't like money?' His men, none of whom could actually understand English, burst into mocking laughter, whipped up by little Soliman. It confused their assailants further.

'You think a cannon ball in your belly funny?' the Dutchman threw back.

'Come aboard and talk, lads,' Scott joined the conversation from his vessel. 'We're not here to fight. Stand your men down. We're here to offer you employment, for we have been told that you are soldiers for hire. And we have a need of good men.'

The Dutchman looked around at the expectant faces of his companions, their interest clearly piqued. 'We got a job already. We don't need your offer,' he added, but it was clear he wanted to hear more.

'Maybe you don't remember me, Dutchie,' Light stood forward into the sunlight. 'Any of you others remember me? I was here a while back. Brought a cargo of pistols for Sultan Salehuddin. Name of Light.'

There was a murmur of recognition from the other men, all bare-chested and burnt red-brown, their torsos heavily tattooed.

They wore Malay headcloths but their clothes were a mishmash of various articles of European dress. This band of mercenaries, a feral bunch of deserters and renegades from all over Europe, were the human flotsam and jetsam of the Straits. Light had first come across them in Riau; they had later joined forces with the enigmatic Raja Haji, the younger brother of Sultan Salehuddin of Selangor and the leader of the Bugis forces who had tried to oust Sultan Muhammed Jiwa the previous year. It seemed Salehuddin had continued to employ them to guard the Selangor estuary with the haul of cannons seized from Queddah. Light had come to do what he did best: negotiate a deal.

'Okay, so you been here before. So, what you bring? More pistols? We got enough already,' the Dutchman taunted, waving around his own piece.

'No guns today. We want men. I have been reliably informed that Sultan Salehuddin pays you 5 réals a month for your service. I can offer ten. Ten réals a month each man to serve the Sultan of Queddah instead. They tell me there's at least forty men living here. That's over fifty silver dollars a month. Double what you're paid now.'

A buzz of interest arose from the boat as the men discussed the proposal amongst themselves. They liked what they had heard. The spokesman took note of the consensus, and then turned back to Light. 'Where would we be based? Not another shithole like this ...'

'At Kuala Bahang. In the fort. Bring your cannon. You can keep some for your guard duty, but the rest goes back to the rightful owners. And the sultan will allow you to trade at Kuala Queddah. No questions asked as long as you take nothing from his state or any of the ships that visit his ports. But he would be most accommodating to hear that you were raiding Dutch or Bugis ships in the channel. Consider yourself given a carte blanche to his enemies. Any problems with that, Dutchie? I thought not. In fact, he has a few other propositions that would suit you down to the ground. You're not averse to slaving, I presume?'

The mercenaries shrugged. 'We cannot afford to be choosy,' the Dutchman responded meekly. 'What if the Bugismen don't like all this?'

'You fight them. And the sultan promises to double your pay in the event of military action. That seems a fair exchange to me, good fellows. Just remember, when in Queddah, you behave. No killing, raping, or stealing from the merchants. The rest of the Straits ... help yourselves!'

There was cheering from the mercenaries. They were more than willing to take the deal.

'Good, then come aboard, lads, and we'll talk business. Just leave your weapons and we'll lower ours. We wouldn't want any unfortunate accidents, now that we are partners, would we?'

***

The securing of a company of European mercenaries to defend the coast of Queddah had been a considerable coup for Sultan Muhammed Jiwa, the final piece in restoring his authority, so damaged by the rebellion and the Bugis destruction of his royal palace. Reports arrived at much the same time that the new Siamese king Tak Sin was advancing south towards Ujung Salang with the intention of driving out the Bugis interlopers there. It was welcome news indeed. Governor Daeng Merewah Theyan had not lingered at the news. It was said the Bugis had already fled back to Riau rather than face the wrath of the Siamese. The rebuilding of the palace at Anak Bukit was almost complete. The court would soon return. With the characteristic seesaw politics of the region, the pendulum of power had suddenly swung back in favour of Sultan Muhammed.

And central to the new security stood Francis Light, with the more circumspect James Scott by his side. At a ceremony held at the old palace in Perlis, the sultan rewarded both men with gifts and honours, saving the highest accolade for Captain Light himself. He was bestowed as *Dewa Raja*, the lofty titled 'God-king', more hyperbole than fact. It marked him out as a person of distinction, but carried little other significance. The sultan hoped that Light would now settle at Kuala Queddah to set up a private trading company, but Light had respectfully declined. His plan was to join Scott in Ujung Salang where they would establish a joint enterprise, with Queddah as its closest partner. In many ways this was even more valuable to the sultan. An ally in Ujung Salang would be invaluable; Light would be his eyes and ears on the Siamese restoration.

'If not a trading establishment, then I must offer you something else to demonstrate the deep regard in which I hold you, Dewa Raja!' the old king exclaimed. 'You have no wife. This is not good. A man should have a wife. In fact, he should have several wives so that no single wife becomes too proud. I will give you one of my *gundiks*! Let me assemble an array of the youngest and most beautiful for you to choose.'

After years as a bachelor, Light suddenly found himself

assailed on all quarters with offers of suitable wives, it would seem.

'You are too generous, your Majesty. It is not necessary to offer one of your own precious ladies,' he answered, desperately searching for an avenue of escape without offending the sultan. In his heart of hearts, he had not entirely abandoned hope of one day regaining some measure of status with the British administration in India. With a former concubine as his wife, he doubted that would ever be possible.

The sultan waved away his objection. 'I have too many women and am too old for pleasure. The girl would be delighted to have such a lusty young fellow as yourself! Take your pick, my kapitan!'

Backed into this corner, there was really only one option left. It was the devil or the deep blue sea. But his decision would at least have the added benefit of bringing comfort to a friend. He was planning to make a fresh start in Ujung Salang. His commitments in Queddah should be concluded, with no ends left untied. Furthermore, the cultivation of the best possible climate for trade in his new endeavour was imperative. Sometimes a man must put his obligations before his preferences.

'Your Majesty, with the greatest respect, I must admit that there is someone I was already hoping to marry. In fact, I had intended to make my request to you today, since you have always taken interest in her family and its welfare, and she is under your beneficent protection. As her father is no longer with us, I deemed that I should seek your permission for her hand. Do not be offended that I dare make this bid. It comes from my deepest admiration ...'

'Enough of this nonsense! Tell me, who is the girl that has stolen your heart, and be done with it!' the Sultan grinned.

Light bowed. 'Her name is Martinha, the daughter of Lady Thong Di and my good friend, Martim Rozells, may God have mercy on his soul!'

Scott snorted, disguising it as a cough. Light blushed beneath his tan. The sultan beamed. 'An excellent suggestion! I should have thought of it myself. The girl is ripe for marriage to a Christian gentleman. I gladly give my permission. Furthermore, I shall hold the wedding here at court. It will be a fitting resolution to our collaboration, my dear Francees.'

'Well, well, well,' Scott whispered, 'So you *are* going to marry the little girl after all!'

'What else can I do?' Light muttered under his breath, as they backed out of the royal presence. 'It was either that or an odalisque. At least I keep the family safe from some local lord who wants to get his greedy hands on their property.'

'It's a stroke of genius, another sign that you are the most fortunate of bastards!'

'Most fortunate of bastards? Discharged from my agency, slighted by the Company, and my bridges burned with the Bugis? That is hardly luck in my estimation, Scott.'

'You have the opportunity to rise from the ashes with a beautiful young bride, the best of trading partners, and with Ujung Salang and Queddah at your very feet. Most of all, you're still alive. That alone is a feat after the many adventures you have had. Be grateful for that, man.'

Light shrugged away the response, but the gleam in his eye suggested he was not insensible to the truth of Scott's words. As one door closes, another opens. Who knows where destiny will lead?

'Furthermore, dear Francis, whilst you bathe in the golden glow of the favour of the sultan and the marital bliss of your newly wedded state, I hope you'll continue to work your charm on old Muhammed Jiwa. Why not hint at a little bit of a land grant as a wedding gift? He would deny you nothing at the moment.'

'I'm not interested in farming, Jamie,' Light retorted, although he was listening. Scott was right. This was the best chance he would ever have to gain territory of his own on the Peninsula.

'Who's talking about farming? Ujung Salang has its undoubted advantages, but a man must always have a second strategy tucked in his back pocket, for one never knows what the future might hold.'

'What's in your head, you conniving old devil?'

Scott tapped his nose playfully. 'Come on, man! You know I've always had a hankering for Pulau Pinang. It's a little jewel. It would make for a most amenable magazine, owned and operated entirely by our agency, as a complement to our interests in Siam.'

His suggestion was greeted with a burst of laughter. 'A deserted island fit only for pirates? It would take years and a fortune to turn it even into a trading post!'

'Everywhere was deserted land once upon a time. Pinang's ideally placed, with no natural predators – of the human variety, that is. No one to contest us for it. Just a thought, my boy. Just in case. Young Martinha's the descendant of Malay royalty. Surely an uninhabited isle would be a small gift to bestow on her on the occasion of this inestimable wedding, eh?'

They strode through the grounds to the palace gate where

their transport awaited to return them to the jetty. Scott did not push Francis further. It was enough to plant the seed, or so he had often found. It would worm its way into his friend's head until ready to germinate. It was ever thus. Francis had to make an idea his own before he warmed to it. The silence alone told him Francis was considering the notion.

Scott might have been surprised had he access to the contents of his friend's head, which had already stowed away the suggestion, considering it an interesting but impractical notion, and returned to the contemplation of where he actually stood. Francis must now set aside his past failures and mistakes and look forward to a different – but no less successful future – one he would carve out entirely for himself, in the face of every possible hurdle that his station in life had thrown against him.

For he was Francis Light, Captain, Dewa Raja of the court of Queddah, partner in a prosperous trading company and soon to be member of the leading family in Ujung Salang. Quite an achievement for a nobody from Suffolk, not deemed good enough even to gain a navy commission. What would that boy think of where his life had taken him thus far? It might not be the advancement that he had been working for, but he had indeed found his own place at last. What if the only ones who valued him were strangers from the other side of the world? He would build his kingdom here and turn his back on those who spurned him. It would be their loss.

But somewhere, in the deepest recesses of his mind, perhaps provoked by Scott's needling, a voice still lingered, calling him to keep his eyes still fixed on the ultimate prize. For the dragon cannot be contained. He must always strive for the elusive pearl, no matter if it edges from his claws. Light smiled across at Scott as they rode forward into the sunlight. For now, it would be enough. For now.

Terima Kasih

To my editor and publisher Philip Tatham of Monsoon Books, whose support and advice has made the process from manuscript to printed page such a fascinating and enjoyable collaboration. Without the friendship and encouragement of Marianne Khor, Nisha Dobberstein, Maganjeet Kaur, Karen Loh, Judith Kveton and Joaquina Testa, my dogged and sharp-eyed readers, this novel would have been so much poorer – to you all, my eternal thanks. To Ro King for her unfailing support, advice and optimism, and Mariana Isa for her generous assistance with the Malay language. And, as ever, to my husband and children who have sustained me throughout the years of research and writing with such good humour and patience. They always believed even when I did not!

Rose Gan, Kuala Lumpur

Pearl

(Penang Chronicles, Vol. II)

Francis Light, the enigmatic Martinha, and the island of Penang

The eponymous pearl, Martinha Rozells, embodies the rich and diverse heritage of the Straits in the 18th century. Her husband, Captain Light, is the dragon in search of his elusive pearl: a British settlement on the Straits of Malacca. Through their eyes we experience the rich culture of the region and its tumultuous politics. From the courts of Siam and Kedah, to capture by the French and Dutch, from the salons of Calcutta through gun-running in the Straits, *Pearl* takes the reader on an astonishing journey culminating in Captain Light questioning where his allegiances lie if he is to outmanoeuvre the Sultan of Kedah and raise the British flag on Penang.

Emporium

(Penang Chronicles, Vol. III)

A possession must be held: the struggle for Penang

A paradise on earth. Penang – the Pearl of the Orient – has fulfilled its promise, becoming the most vibrant port in the Indies in a few short years. But paradise comes at a price for Francis Light and his family. Penang's meteoric rise from deserted island to thriving port attracts unwanted attention from both the Dutch and the French, while the Sultan of Kedah rages at the treachery of the British. As the 18th century draws to a close, Penang must fortify and prepare for war, and Light's partner, Martinha Rozells, learns to negotiate the murky waters of colonial prejudice and corruption for the sake of her family.